THE LOOSE THREAD

LIZ HARRIS

HEYWOOD PRESS

1

London, February 1938

Rose Hammond stood outside the first of her family's three haberdashery shops in Queen's Crescent, where their shops, one near each end of the Crescent and one in the middle, were known by everyone in Kentish Town as 'Upper Hams', 'Mid Hams' and 'Lower Hams'. She looked at her watch.

The hands had hardly moved since she'd last checked the time. It was still too soon to return home, she thought in frustration, so she wandered into the shop.

The three girls behind the horseshoe-shaped counter promptly straightened up. She smiled at them, indicated by a brief flick of her wrist that they should continue working, and strolled along the gangway, taking care not to obstruct the shoppers.

Every so often, she paused to survey the orderly array of colourful cotton reels, zippers, buttons, needles, pins, safety pins and scissors displayed beneath the glass-topped counter, then carried on without making a comment.

On any other day, she would have found something to remark upon, something that might be praiseworthy, something that might not. But that day her mind was on what was happening at home, not what was going on in the shop. And when she reached the end of the counter, she gave the salesgirls a quick smile and went back out into Queen's Crescent.

Had she allowed enough time for Tom to have asked her father, she wondered. Her watch showed that she had been out for just over an hour.

Yes, she had, she decided.

Walking more briskly, she passed Mid Hams without stopping, reached Allcroft Road and turned left. With the noise of traffic and shoppers receding, she hurried along.

The road was lined on both sides by terraced three-storeyed brick houses, fronted by small gardens bordered by a low brick wall or a shrubbery. The houses were narrow, with two sash windows on both floors, and each was topped by a steeply pitched slate roof. In sharp contrast with the yellow brick walls, white stucco moulding arched above the white-painted windows and the front door.

Reaching her house, she ran up the short path and the four steps leading up to the bright blue front door. Her heart beating fast, she let herself in.

At the sight of her two younger sisters in the entrance hall, she stopped abruptly.

Violet, her middle sister, was sitting halfway down the staircase, while Iris, the youngest of the three, was standing at the foot of the stairs, facing the front room door, her back against the wall.

Hearing Rose return, each instantly tore her gaze from

the door that had been closed against them, and turned it towards her.

'Well?' Rose asked, kicking the front door shut behind her.

'Father's furious,' Iris said. 'You should have heard him yell at Tom. Didn't he, Violet?'

Violet nodded. 'That's an understatement. But that won't surprise you, Rose. You know he wants you to continue supervising the shops and to help him with the expansion. He's said that often enough. He was so angry at Tom that he called for Mother to go in.'

'There's nothing I'd be doing for the shops that both of you couldn't do,' Rose said sharply. 'You took over my job when Tom got here, Violet, so you can carry on.'

'I've no intention of doing so!' Violet snapped. 'I'll soon be eighteen and old enough to register for teacher training. And that's what I'm going to do. It's why I didn't leave school at fourteen. Father knows I'm going to be a teacher and he's pleased about it. You're the oldest so the shops are *your* job.'

'No, they're not! Right, if Violet doesn't want to take over from me, Iris, then you can. After all, you're sixteen so you're old enough. You already help in the shops so you could easily step up and take my place, if you wanted.'

Iris scowled at her. 'Well, I don't want. Whatever I do, it won't be that.'

'We'll see. But since Mother helps in the shops a lot less these days, both of you might have to think again,' Rose said, and she pulled off her green felt cloche and hung it on the wooden hallstand.

She shook her long dark hair loose, then swept it behind her ears, undid the belt on her mid-calf green wool coat, tucked her gloves into her coat pockets, and hung the coat next to her hat. Smoothing down the skirt of her plaid woollen dress, she turned to face the door to the front room.

'I've no intention of changing my plans,' Violet hissed at her angrily.

'Nor me,' said Iris. 'I may not know what I want to do at this very moment, but I certainly know what I *don't* want to do.'

'I'm marrying Tom,' Rose said steadily, 'and I'm going to be a farmer's wife. At twenty-three, I don't need Father's permission to marry, so by the end of March, I'll be Mrs Benest and I'll be on my way to Jersey. And that's the way it is.'

'Good luck with living on a farm,' Violet said. 'You don't know one end of a cow from the other.' She glanced at Iris, and both broke into a fit of giggles.

With Iris and Violet's laughter ringing in her ears, Rose took a deep breath, opened the door and went into the room. As she closed the door behind her, she saw her father's face. She hesitated.

John Hammond was standing with his back to the green-tiled fireplace, facing Tom. Her father's face was red with anger. Her mother was hovering at his side, visibly upset.

Tom had his back to her. His hands were gripped tightly behind him. His knuckles were white, she noticed.

She went straight up to Tom and stood at his side. He gave her a fleeting smile, before looking back at her father. Sensing Tom's relief at her presence, she inched closer to him.

Her father took a step forward and angled himself to look at Tom, rather than at her. 'I can't tell you how disappointed I am in you, Tom,' he said stiffly. 'And I know how upset your parents will be when they learn how you've betrayed my hospitality.'

'Falling in love with Rose can hardly be described as betraying your hospitality, sir,' Tom said, a note of incredulity in his voice. Shaking his head in disbelief, he unlocked his hands, and ran his fingers though his fair hair.

'I disagree!' her father said. 'You were here expressly to find a wholesaler for your mother's shop and then to visit the people who'd known your parents years ago. You wanted to get to know us, or so I believed. You weren't here to encourage my daughter to leave her family and move far away. I expected better than this from William's son.'

'I'm sorry you see it that way, sir. I didn't expect to fall in love with Rose, but that's what happened.'

'So you say. I'd like you to go to your room now as I wish to talk in private with my daughter,' John said, unsmiling. 'We'll call you when Mabel's ready to serve the dinner.'

'Of course, sir.' Tom turned to Rose. 'I hope that when I come down later on, you'll still be keen on marrying me,' he said.

Hearing the anxiety in his voice, she squeezed his arm. 'I will be,' she assured him. 'There's nothing I want more than that.'

His shoulders relaxed. 'Good.' He nodded towards her mother. 'Mrs Hammond,' he said, and he left the room.

'Come and sit down, John,' Mabel Hammond said, going to the armchair he favoured and plumping up the cushion. 'You look tired.'

He nodded. 'I am a little.'

His limp more pronounced than usual, he grasped Mabel's hand, took a few steps back, sank heavily into the armchair and closed his eyes. Her mother rested her hand on his shoulder for a moment or two, then crossed to the armchair on the other side of the fireplace.

Rose went and sat on the deep green velvet sofa facing the fireplace. Her feet together, she clasped her hands around her knees.

The clock on the oak mantelpiece sounded loud in the still of the room.

'Now what's this all about, Rose?' her father asked at last, opening his eyes. 'You hardly know Tom. He's not been in England five minutes. That's no basis for a marriage.'

'He's been here for almost three months, and that's long enough for me to know that he's definitely the right person for me. And if you're fair, Father, you'll admit you like him enormously. At least you did until this afternoon.'

'Tell her you agree with me, Mabel,' John appealed in despair. 'Tell her she should put this lunatic idea in the dustbin, where it belongs.' He turned back to Rose. 'You've got a position of responsibility, Rose—you manage the shops. That's no small task. And you're ambitious like me and want to see us opening new shops. At least you used to. Your future's here with us, doing something you're good at. Not on some island miles away with someone you don't really know.'

'Your father's right,' her mother said. 'Three months is no time at all to get to know someone. And you've only seen him here in England, when he's more or less been on holiday. You haven't seen him in his working life.'

'It's more than enough time,' Rose said stubbornly. 'And he's the same Tom, whether he's here or working in Jersey.'

'But that's not really true, is it, Rose? A person holidaying, which in effect is what Tom's been doing, can be very different from a person at work.' Mabel leaned forward. 'The thing is,' she said gently. 'I know you, and I don't believe you truly love Tom. You've convinced yourself that you do, but I think you're mistaken. And I don't believe you'd be happy with him, or that you'd enjoy the life you'd have if you married him.'

'Of course I would!' Rose laughed. 'If you think I wouldn't, then you certainly *don't* know me.' She shifted her position to look more squarely at her mother. 'Tell me then, if I don't love Tom, why do I want to marry him?'

Her mother gave her a wry smile. 'You like him. And why not? He's a handsome man, and very personable. But you've spent a lot of time listening to him tell you about Jersey, and how beautiful it is with the deep blue sky and the sun on the sea, and it's made you think that everything here is very drab and very ordinary. As a result, you want to escape Kentish Town and go to a lovely place. And although I don't think you realise it, you've come to see that marrying Tom is a way of doing that.'

Rose made an exclamation of disbelief.

'You never showed any inclination to live somewhere else or do anything different until Tom arrived,' Mabel continued. 'Before that, you were happy in your work, and you were excited about the kind of future that Hammond's could have. You're a town-bred girl, Rose. I honestly don't think you'd enjoy being a farmer's wife, or being confined to a small island. But him being here has unsettled you and you aren't seeing things clearly.'

'I'm bound to be unsettled, as you put it. I fell in love with Tom. Being in love would unsettle anyone.'

'As I say, I think it's the idea of going to Jersey that you love. We're a respectable family so you could hardly live there on your own, and that's where Tom comes in. But marrying someone in order to live somewhere else is a high price to pay.'

'I'm marrying Tom because I love him, and for no other reason,' Rose insisted.

'Have you given any thought to what happens if I'm correct about you not enjoying life on a farm?' her mother asked.

'I shall love being on the farm, and I shall love being in Jersey because I'll be with Tom.'

Clearing his throat, John leaned forward in his chair. 'Believe me, Rose,' he said, 'I've nothing against Tom. On the contrary, his father was a good friend to me, and I feel a warmth towards Tom because of that. If William hadn't gone into partnership with me all those years ago, Hammond's wouldn't be what it is today. I'll admit that Tom appears to be a chip off the old block, but it's too soon to know that for certain. Give it a while longer is all I ask.'

Rose made as if to speak.

John held up his hand to stop her. 'He needs to go back to Jersey for the ploughing now, I know. I understand that. But let him go back alone. He could return to us after the harvest. That would give you time to see how you felt about each other after a few months apart. And if you still felt the same, you'd marry him with my blessing.'

'Your father couldn't say fairer than that, Rose,' Mabel said, and smiled approvingly at John.

Rose folded her arms in front of her. 'I love him and I want to marry him now.'

'You'd be leaving at an exciting time for the business,' her father said, a note of desperation entering his voice. 'Prices are lower now than they've been for some time, while people are earning more. We need to do everything we can to take advantage of that. If you waited, you could be part of our future expansion, while giving yourself time to know your mind.'

Her mouth set in a determined line. 'I know it now. I'm marrying Tom and going to Jersey with him, and that's that.'

Her father glanced helplessly at her mother. Mabel shrugged her shoulders.

'Well, I don't like it,' John said after a few moments, 'but at the age you are, I can't stop you. Nor would I want to be at odds with a daughter who's always been such a help to me.' He wiped his eyes. 'So, with great reluctance, I'll give you my blessing.'

Tears sprang to Rose's eyes. She jumped up, ran across to her father and hugged him tightly.

'Thank you, Father,' she said, her voice breaking. 'That means a lot to me and it will to Tom, too. But you mustn't be upset. I'll come back and see you as often as I can.'

'All I can say is, he's a lucky man,' John said gruffly.

Releasing her father, she turned as her mother came towards her, her arms outstretched. Drawing Rose close, her mother embraced her, and then held her at arm's length, and looked into her face.

'We very much hope that you'll be happy, love,' she said. 'But if things don't turn out as you think they will, know that you'll always have a home with us. And we'd never reproach you.'

She hugged Rose again, then turned to John. 'The girls might as well come in now, don't you think? I'm sure they've been listening at the keyhole anyway, and their ears and knees must be quite sore. I suggest you pour us all a sherry to toast the occasion, and I'll call Tom down to join us.'

'I'll call him,' Rose said. Laughing joyfully, she ran to the door. As she started to open it, she looked back at her parents, her eyes shining with excitement. 'Tom and I are going to be extremely happy. You'll see.'

2

That evening

ROSE AND IRIS sat on the sitting room sofa, one at each end, their knees curled up under them, pieces of paper on each of their laps. Sprawled out on the floor in front of them, Violet lay on her stomach on the rug that lay between the sofa and fire, trying to read her book by the glow thrown out by the dying embers.

'Are you excited, Rose?' Iris asked.

Rose laughed. 'About what exactly?'

Iris shrugged. 'I don't know. About getting married, I suppose. About having a home of your own. Maybe having children.' She giggled.

Rose altered her position. 'Of course I am, silly.'

Violet glanced up at them over her shoulder. 'Relieved is probably a better word than excited, Iris. It's more accurate.' She returned her attention to her book.

Rose uncurled herself, jumped down from the sofa and grabbed Violet's book from the floor. Clutching the book to her chest, she sat down on the sofa again.

Violet sat up angrily. Crossing her legs, she faced Rose. 'Give me back my book! You know my history teacher said it could be useful.'

'She's not your teacher any longer, even if your group of would-be teachers does meet up with her every week. You can have it back when you've told me what you mean.'

Violet scowled. 'I would've thought it pretty obvious. Assuming you know what "relieved" means.'

'Don't try to be clever, or an unfortunate accident will befall this book,' Rose said loftily, and she stared pointedly at the fireplace. She waited a moment. 'Well?' she prompted.

'All I meant was that at your age, you must be relieved that someone's asked you to marry them. I bet Mother and Father are, though they're sorry you're going away. They must have worried you'd end up a desiccated old spinster, a fossilising pillar of Hammond's, living with them here for eternity, or in digs with a narrow-minded landlady, or in a tiny flat with a shared bathroom and kitchen. I bet that's why Dad gave in so easily, and Mum, too, even though they're right. You can't possibly know Tom from the short amount of time you've spent with him.'

Rose sniffed. 'It's quality, not quantity, Professor Violet. Tom and I have had the chance to talk a great deal since he got here. Thanks to Father letting me leave the shops in your reluctant hands while Tom was here, and not insisting that Mother come out with us every time, I know him better than you think.'

'That's good, then,' Violet said, her voice laden with disbelief. 'But if you're just saying it, remember you're going to have to live with your decision for a very long time. For twenty-four hours every day. Seven days a week. Fifty-two weeks every year. For the rest of your life.'

Iris straightened up. 'You're wrong about that last bit, Violet. The law's changed and it's now much easier for women to get a divorce. You can still divorce your husband if he's been unfaithful, but you can also do so now if he's mad or has an unpleasant disease, or if he's been cruel to you or deserted you for three years. Ivy in Mid Hams told me that. She's delighted the law's changed as she hates her husband, who's a pig, and she's met someone else who's much nicer.'

'It'll still cost far too much for the likes of us,' Violet said firmly. 'You'd be wise to be absolutely sure of what you're doing, Rose.'

'I *am* sure, so the subject's closed.' She glanced at Iris. 'When Violet goes to her teacher training college, *you'll* have to start supervising the shops, and do all the other things I did. If you can stop flirting with the customers for long enough, that is.'

Iris gave a forced laugh. 'Very funny, I don't think. And it's even funnier if you really believe I'm going to work in Dad's shops. D'you honestly think my lifetime ambition is to supervise salesgirls mopping a shop floor at closing time, keeping an eye on them as they squeeze filthy water into a galvanised bucket? D'you realise it takes forty minutes each day to get the shop floor clean? I can find a better use for those forty minutes.'

'And that's not the end of it,' Violet said with mock seriousness. 'Just as they've finished the floor, someone arrives in urgent need of a needle or zip. We let them in, of course, and have to smile brightly while their every footstep turns the gleaming floor into a mixture of bleach and footprints. And—'

'And after their profuse thanks and goodbyes, the whole ghastly mopping process has to begin again,' Iris finished.

She and Violet burst out laughing.

'So what work do you plan to do, Iris, if mopping floors is beneath you?' Rose asked.

'Mopping floors must surely be beneath me. The floor's down there and I'm up here,' Iris said in feigned reproof. She looked down at Violet and again they both laughed.

Rose smiled. 'Very funny. So what *are* you going to do if it's not work in the shops?'

'I'd rather not do anything, but if I have to, I'd like to work in D.H. Evans. I'm old enough now. It's the tallest and quite the nicest of the shops in Oxford Street, and because they've got so many floors, they sell everything. You should see the different sales' areas—each is like a small shop with a canopy over it, and it's got special lighting. If I sold jewellery or perfume, I'd make heaps of commission.'

'They'd never put you in either of those departments,' Rose countered. 'They'll be the ones everyone wants.'

'But haberdashery won't!' Iris said in triumph. 'With what I know about the subject, I'm sure I could get into haberdashery. I could advise customers about dressmaking patterns and needle sizes, for example. Not everyone could do that.'

'So you won't help Father with his haberdashery shops, but you'd be happy enough to sell haberdashery in D.H. Evans, making money for whoever it is who owns that store!' Rose said, contempt in her voice.

'Honestly, Rose. You've got it all wrong! I don't really want to be in haberdashery, silly. But I'd be mad not to take advantage of what I know. It'd be a stepping stone to a better department, like jewellery or perfume.'

'What's the real reason, Iris?' Violet asked. 'I don't

believe you're any more keen on selling jewellery and perfume than you are on selling buttons.'

Iris giggled. 'You're wrong about that. But you're right, too. I'm not madly enthusiastic about selling anything—it's more about the person I'd be selling the product to. They're the sort of items a man would buy for his wife or girlfriend. It means I'd be meeting a steady stream of men.' She giggled again.

'Of men who're already attached to someone,' Rose said. 'Not men who're searching for a wife. If you're looking for a husband, you'd do better in one of the Hammond shops. A man who comes in for cotton and needles doesn't have anyone at home to do the sewing for him.'

Iris waved her hand dismissively. 'Such a man wouldn't interest me. The sort of person I want would get his maid to do his sewing. We see the maids of men like that in our shops, but not the men who pay them. As for a man who's already got a girlfriend, he can dump her if he meets someone else.'

'With a selfish attitude like that, I can see you being the one who ends up an old maid,' Rose said, with a trace of a sneer.

'Talking of selfish,' Iris said, straightening up. 'You should look in the mirror. What's Father meant to do if you stop helping him? You know Violet's going to be a teacher, and you know I'm not cut out for the shops.'

'Take on more girls,' Rose retorted. 'Like he's done in the past.'

Iris shrugged. 'But they wouldn't *run* the shops. That's for family to do. Father taught you everything you need to know, so you're the only one able to do it.' She paused. 'I suppose Mummy could do more than she's been doing. She'll have time on her hands with you miles away, knee-deep in manure, me in D.H. Evans, and Violet in her college before too long.'

'It's years since she's run the shops,' Rose said dismissively.

'But it's the sort of thing you'd never forget,' Iris countered. 'In the war, she ran everything by herself when Father was away fighting. Yes, she had girls to help, but she was in charge overall. She was cashier and saleslady, and she ordered supplies from the wholesaler's. It can't have been easy, but she managed. If she could do it then, when things were more difficult, she could certainly do it now.'

'Not necessarily,' Rose said. 'She's older now.'

'Not that old! She could if she wanted,' Iris said airily. 'The only difference is there're three shops now, not one. But there isn't a war and I bet there won't ever be one again. Whatever's going on with those other countries will all be sorted out. And running three shops today can't be as hard as running one during a war. But if you're so worried about Mother,' she added, 'perhaps you and Tom should live here, and not in Jersey.'

'Hm. That's not a bad idea, Iris,' Violet said. She put her finger to her chin to indicate deep thought. 'After all, who would want to live in a place known for lovely sandy beaches, beautiful wooded valleys and a perfect climate? No one would. Not when they could live here, with the hustle, bustle and dirt of the market on their doorstep, and grey skies day after day, not to mention the constant rain. Good thinking, Iris.'

Rose glared at her. 'You're not being helpful, Violet. But just in case there was an element of seriousness in your ludicrous comment, Iris, Tom loves working on the farm, which he'll take over from his father one day. He's really missed it while he's been here. And he also misses his sister,

Kathleen. She isn't much older than I am, and they sound as
if they're quite close. I hope she and I will be, too. I'd never
ask him to live here.'

'Perhaps you should try it just to see what he says,' Iris
said, a challenge in her voice. 'You could tell him you'd like
to visit Jersey, but you want to live in England, and you'd like
both of you to work in the Hammonds' shops.' She threw a
sly smile at Violet. 'What do you think he'd say?'

Rose went red.

Iris raised her eyebrows. 'I assume you're not answering
because you don't want to admit that Tom would go back to
Jersey without you. But that's the truth, isn't it? You don't
believe he loves you enough to place your wishes above his,
or to compromise. How very romantic.'

Violet glanced up at Rose's flushed face.

'There's a body of water that separates England from
Jersey, Iris,' Violet said quickly. 'It's called the Channel. They
can't really compromise, can they? Or are you suggesting
they make their home on a boat in the middle of the sea?
There was never a suggestion of Tom staying here. He's
needed in Jersey and Rose knew that when she met him. If
he chose to return to Jersey despite Rose asking him to stay
here, it wouldn't mean that he didn't love her. He'd just be
doing what he had to.'

'That's right, Violet,' Rose said, and smiled at her in
gratitude.

Iris shrugged. 'Well, if you're happy to spend the rest of
your life on a tiny island, seeing the same boring people day
after day, I'm pleased for you. I wouldn't like it, though.'

Violet pulled her knees up to her chin and locked her
fingers together in front of her knees. 'I suggest we change
the subject. Tell us about your wedding plans, Rose. Are we
going to be bridesmaids?'

Rose beamed. 'I'm hoping so. We'd like to get married in six weeks' time in St Silas' Church. If we can, it means getting the first of the banns read on Sunday. It'll only be a small wedding. After the church, we'd like to go to the Malden Arms, but if someone's already booked their function room, we'll have to think again.'

'D'you think Tom's family will come over?' Violet asked. 'It would be lovely to meet his father. Dad's often mentioned him over the years and it'd be nice to put a face to the name.'

Rose shook her head. 'Tom telephoned them this afternoon, and they said it'd be impossible to leave the farm at such a time. For a start, it'll be exactly when they must harvest the potatoes. But we knew they'd say that. It can't be helped.'

'That's a pity,' Violet said. 'But it's understandable as they're farmers. I bet his sister's disappointed as she could've been a bridesmaid, too.'

Rose nodded. 'I wouldn't know. But it's not really the most important thing.'

Iris sniffed. 'If you ask me, the fact that they're not bothering to turn up means they're less than pleased that Tom's marrying you.'

Rose rounded on her. 'You're wrong about that. Tom said his father sounded surprised at first, then really pleased. He knows Mum and Dad, and he thinks it's brilliant news. Anyone who knows anything about farming would understand why they can't come.'

'Then why don't you hold off marrying until the potatoes are done?' Iris suggested.

'Because they'll be busy till the end of autumn, and they need Tom's help long before that. It's why he booked to return at this time. He's going to get a ticket for me, too.

We'll be sailing on a steam turbine ship, whatever that is. So you're wrong about what his parents think, Iris.'

Iris tossed her head. 'If you say so.'

'I do,' Rose said. 'And what's more, they're giving us the cottage his grandparents used to live in. It's sort of next door to the main farmhouse, Tom said. They're going to make the inside of the house more up-to-date for us.'

'You *are* lucky, Rose,' Violet said wistfully. 'It's not what I'd like, but it's the ideal start for most people getting married.'

Rose smiled broadly. 'Thanks, Violet; it really is. Tom said I'd love his family's farmhouse. It's got thick granite walls and a view of the sea. Our little cottage will have the same view. Apparently, there are lots of stone houses in Jersey. Some are grey, and a lot of them are white. As I'll see when I get there. And as both of you will see when you come to visit,' she added, laughing happily.

3

London, April 1938

Beneath a leaden grey sky, Rose and her father walked along Queen's Crescent, trying to avoid getting caught up among the people ambling down the centre of the market, or clustering in front of stalls groaning beneath the weight of goods.

Occasionally, John would pause in front of one of the many trestle tables that lined the road, and study the items for sale with interest. After a few minutes, he would move on, passing stalls protected by canvas canopies, stalls that were open to the mercy of the weather and stalls which had three canvas walls enclosing railings from which cheap clothes were hanging.

As they neared the area where wagons of fruit and vegetables were interspersed with covered carts from which white-coated traders sold meat, dairy produce and fish, John nodded in greeting to the traders, who acknowledged him with smiles.

When they reached the point where Mid Hams was visible in the gap between two stalls, John halted and stared at his shop. Rose moved to stand at his side.

'Times have changed, Rose,' he mused, his eyes riveted on the shop.

She looked at him questioningly. 'In what respects, Father?'

'In all respects,' he said. He smiled at her before looking back at Mid Hams. 'Long before the war, when I was a mere lad, we lived closer to Camden Town. That was where your grandfather started out. One table in the market was all he had at first. It was quite a while before he got a second one.'

'I know that,' she said, trying to hide her impatience to get back to the house and to the preparations for her wedding, and fervently hoping that her father wouldn't embark on one of his lengthy reminiscences about the past.

'Money was tight,' he went on. Her heart sank. 'There was no such thing as pocket money. Youngsters were expected to make their own way, so I got a job in a nearby shop. A bit like that one,' he remarked, turning to indicate a shop on the road behind him.

She followed his gaze. 'I didn't know that,' she said, surprise replacing impatience. 'I thought you'd always worked for your father. You never told us that you worked for someone else before Grandfather.'

'Maybe I didn't want to put ideas into your head,' he said drily.

She laughed and started to walk again. But realising that he hadn't moved, she went back to him.

'I had to be in the shop by eight sharp to take down the shutters and store them inside,' he told her, still staring at the shop on the other side of the road. 'Then I had to wash the windows. I was so little that I needed to stand on wooden steps to do that. After that, I cleaned the door fittings with Brasso and brushed the pavement. I had to sweep the shop floor and polish the glass display cabinets. I had to do all that before the doors opened at nine.'

'That's a lot for a young boy to have to do,' she said. 'When did you start to work for Grandfather, then?'

'Not till I was ten. By then, he'd got a second table and was taking in more money, so it was more useful to have me working for him than for someone else.'

'You make me realise how lucky the three of us are,' she said quietly. 'We've had it so much easier than you,'

'That's right; you have. But that's as it should be. Each generation should have a better life than the generation before.'

'All I can say is, I'm very relieved to have been born when I was and not earlier,' she said, with feeling.

'There was a good side to it, too, though, Rose. Yes, people worked very hard, but on the whole they were closer to each other than they are today, and they helped each other in times of trouble.'

'You mean in the war?'

'Not only then. For example, if the bailiffs threw a family out of their home because they'd got behind with the rent, neighbours would take the children in for the night and they'd find a tarpaulin tent for the parents. Someone would give the parents a cup of cocoa and maybe some broth. The family would be helped by all their neighbours for as long as it took to get them on their feet again.'

'I'm not surprised. I've always thought the people round here very kind.'

Her father nodded, and they resumed walking.

'And that's another thing that's different,' he said a moment or two later as they skirted a group of children who ran across their path. 'You see far fewer children in the streets these days. Whenever you went out, you always used to see fifty or sixty of them. In groups, they'd be jumping puddles or dodging the horses. Large shire horses they were, their fetlocks covered with long fringes of hair. If a horse fell on the shiny cobblestones and broke its legs, it had to be destroyed. They'd shoot the horse in the street, you know. With no screen around it. The children would stand and watch in silence. That was the way it was.'

'That's awful,' she said. 'Was your father ever tempted to move to a market somewhere else?'

John shook his head. 'Never. He loved the area, just as I do. He was very popular in the neighbourhood. Not surprisingly—he was a kind man and good to the girls who worked for him. As you know, your grandmother was one of those girls.'

'I wish they'd both still been alive when we were born.'

He shrugged. 'I do, too, but people didn't live as long in those days.'

'So you and Grandfather both married someone who worked for you, didn't you?'

He nodded. 'That's so,' he said. He glanced at her in amusement. 'It must be a hazard for traders. It's what Tom's father William did, too.'

'I can't wait to meet him,' she said, smiling broadly.

'He's a good person. I owe him a lot. It's thanks to him I was able to get the first of the shops.'

He stopped and looked back down the street at the jumble of hats, scarves and flat caps bobbing up and down, of canvas fringes flapping in the breeze, of wooden struts that supported the stalls.

'Yes,' he said, almost as if to himself. 'He was the best of friends.'

THEY HAD MET SOON after William had started working at Ferguson's, the wholesaler where John bought most of his goods. They'd hit it off at once, and before long, William was helping him out in the market on Saturdays, running one table, while he ran the other.

As the weeks had passed, an idea had gradually taken shape in his mind. And one day he'd blurted out to William that if William were to put fifty pounds into the business, he would do the same. If they were in partnership together, they would be able to rent a depot.

In his enthusiasm, his words were a jumble as he'd explained that if they had a suitable space in which to store the merchandise that was stacked at that time in the corners of the rented rooms in which he lived, they'd be able to buy in bulk, and so pay a lower price for the goods. The profit would, therefore, be higher.

And as they would be able to store a greater volume of goods, he had added, they would be able to think about getting a shop. If they had a haberdashery shop, they could sell throughout the week, not just on Thursdays and Saturdays, the market days.

What did William think, he'd asked.

And he'd held his breath, hoping against hope that he hadn't misread the signs of ambition in William.

He hadn't.

He had been thinking for some time about leaving Ferguson's, William told him. Working the till and keeping the books had been an interesting experience, and they had given him an appetite for trying his hand at something on his own—he hadn't known what, though. He just knew that he wanted it to be something that would give him a different experience from farming.

His indecision, he had gone on to explain, was partly because his choices were limited.

He had no intention of spending the rest of his life in England, he'd told John. He would definitely be returning to Jersey at some point, where he would help to run the family farm, and he would be happy to do so.

There was no urgency about when he went home as his father had plenty of help from the farm workers he hired, but it had to be borne in mind.

However, he did have a small sum of money that he'd brought from Jersey, which he had set aside, and to which he had added some savings he'd made while working at Ferguson's. While it wasn't sufficient for him to start out on his own, it would enable him to buy into a going concern.

So John's suggestion, he'd said in mounting enthusiasm, could be the answer to his prayers. He would be working in a thriving business in which he had a stake, and there could be no better partner to have than John.

John had felt a tremendous surge of excitement. With William's head for figures, and his for business, such a partnership was bound to be extremely fruitful.

But there was one difficulty, William had added quickly, and this had been one of his constraints.

If his money was tied up, and he had to return to Jersey at short notice, it could cause a problem. But if John would consider him an equal partner for the time he was in England, with an equal share in the profits, and if he agreed that when William returned to Jersey, however short the notice, he could have his fifty pounds back, they had a deal.

John had readily agreed, and he had held out his hand to William, who had taken it.

Both of them smiling broadly, they'd shaken on it.

Would William mind if the shop was called Hammond's, John asked, trying not to sound too anxious. Only, he was already known in the area as the person to go to for sewing necessities.

William hadn't. As he'd eventually be going back to Jersey, he had said, it made sense for the business to be in John's name.

So he owed a lot to William, whom he'd liked very much. He'd never had as good a friend before, or since. So while he was fearful that Rose would find that her hasty marriage had been a mistake, he was sure that William's family would do what they could to help her.

'WHAT ARE YOU THINKING ABOUT, FATHER?' Rose asked, breaking into his thoughts. 'You're very quiet.'

'Just about the past,' he said. He turned to smile at her. 'About William and Annie and the first shop we bought. I already had my eye on your mother, who was working for us at the time Annie joined the team. The day Annie started behind the counter, William took one look at her and fell for her at once.'

'How romantic,' Rose said, beaming.

'I suppose it was. But it wasn't surprising. Like your mother, Annie's a fine-looking woman. At least, she used to be. They made a striking couple, she and William, both with that very blond hair and those deep blue eyes.'

'Like Tom,' Rose said with a broad smile. 'He's older than I am so they must have married before you married Mother.'

He nodded. 'That's right. Tom came soon after they'd wed,' he added with a wry smile. 'He was a scrap of a thing with a mop of fair hair.'

She laughed.

'From the outset, the business was a great success, but a few years later, William's father was taken ill, so I gave him back the money he'd put into the business and the family left for Jersey. Tom can't have been more than three.'

'Was William upset about going back?'

'I don't think so. I believe he was ready to go home, as that's what Jersey had always been to him. Annie would have liked them to have stayed here—I don't think she was very keen on being a farmer's wife—but she knew he'd always intended to be a farmer, so there was nothing she could say, and off they went.'

'Does she like it there?'

'I don't really know. She'll tell you herself, I'm sure. But as it turned out, it's just as well that they went back when they did, as later that year, war broke out. A few months after that, Kathleen was born. Annie will have been pleased —she'd always wanted a daughter. By the time the war had ended, both of William's parents had died so at least he'd got to spend time with them first.'

'That was lucky,' she said.

'I married your mother as soon as war broke out, and then went off to fight. I was lucky to end up with nothing worse than shrapnel in my leg. Some of the injuries I saw still give me nightmares.'

'Mother told us how frightening it was, waiting for news. Every time there was a knock at the door, they thought it meant the worst.'

John shook his head. 'She's a strong woman, your

mother. On her own, she kept everything going throughout the war. Not many women could do that.'

'Would Annie have been able to do it, too?'

'I should think so. She must've been interested in the business or she wouldn't have got herself a small haberdashery shop in Jersey.'

'I'm so glad she did! If she hadn't, Tom wouldn't have come looking for a wholesale supplier in England to add to the one they've got in France.' She hesitated. 'To be honest,' she went on, 'I'm a bit nervous about meeting Tom's parents.'

John nodded reassuringly. 'That's only natural.'

'But I'm worried they might think as you do, that we haven't known each other for long enough. Tom said they were fine about it, but maybe he wanted to spare me the truth.' She looked at him anxiously. 'From what you remember of Annie, d'you think she'll like me?'

He smiled warmly at her. 'I'm sure she will, love. She's a very pleasant woman. She had plenty of spirit, and you do, too. I think she'll like you for it.'

'I do hope you're right. Just think, in two days' time I'll be married. And this time next week, I'll be in Jersey.'

'It's not something I want to think about,' he said, his voice cracking. 'I'm going to miss you, Rose.'

As he turned again to look back at the market, she stared at his profile. His dark hair was greying, she realised with a shock.

'Look at all this.' He pointed towards the market.

A lump in her throat, she followed his gaze.

'I suggested our walk today to impress on you before you move away that this is where you were born and raised,' he continued, his voice trembling. 'The market will always be in your blood, Rose. You're one of their own. And just as in the past, people here looked after each other,' he said, turning to her, 'if at any time you feel you've made a mistake, you'll always be welcome back.'

'Thank you, Father,' she said, her voice breaking. She flung her arms around him and hugged him. 'I'm going to miss you all so much. I intend to come home as often as I can.'

4

The evening before the wedding

THEY SAT side by side on high-backed wooden chairs they'd dragged out on to the landing, with Rose's dark head resting lightly against Tom's shoulder. From the sitting room below them, they could hear the muffled sounds of her parents and sisters talking.

'Your mother looked a little disapproving, I thought, when she saw me on the doorstep just now,' Tom said, breaking the companionable silence. 'She'd probably imagined I'd be spending the evening in the room I've taken for tonight. But I couldn't resist a final few minutes with the unmarried you.'

She nestled closer to him. 'I'm so glad you did come over. After all, it's only on the day itself that you mustn't see me before the church. And as most of our things are already in the car that'll be taking us from The Malden Arms to

Waterloo Station tomorrow, there's not much left for me to do this evening.'

'That's what I hoped. But when I saw your mother's expression, I did feel a weeny bit guilty. She probably hoped to spend this last evening with you. But because I wanted to see you so badly, I refused to put myself in her shoes, and I stood on the doorstep, a smile on my face.'

She giggled. 'I'll have breakfast with her tomorrow. Violet and Iris are sure to still be in bed when I get up, so Mother and I will have some time together then. To be honest, I was overjoyed to get out of any more wedding talk this evening. It's beginning to drive me mad. Even though it's my wedding,' she added with a laugh.

He stiffened slightly and turned to her. 'You're not having any regrets, are you, Rose?' he asked, anxiety clouding his eyes. 'Your parents have made it clear that they think us marrying now is a mistake. You're not starting to think like them, are you?'

'Of course I'm not,' she said, gazing into eyes of the deepest blue. Raising her hand, she traced the planes of his face. Then she let her hand fall into her lap. 'I love you, Tom. I've loved you from the moment I saw you standing next to Father at the foot of the stairs, clutching your suitcase, looking bewildered. I was rushing down the stairs two at a time, late for the cinema, and you looked up at me. My heart stopped. In that moment, my world changed. I loved you, and that was that.'

'Your hair was hanging loose, long, dark and shining,' he said. 'Then you looked down at me with those lovely deep brown eyes. You stood still, and pushed your hair back from your face. I thought I'd never seen anyone as beautiful. And I fell in love.'

For a long moment their lips almost touched, then, smiling at each other, they settled back against their chairs.

'Yes,' she said with a loud sigh. 'I forgot all about the film and my friends. I just wanted to stay with you. And it's all I want now. If this was just about me going to Jersey, I'm sure I could have come up with a less extreme way of arranging that.' She turned her head again to look at him. 'I'm marrying you because I love you, Tom, and that's the only reason.'

'And I feel the same way, Rose.' He leaned over to kiss the top of her head.

She felt a flutter low in her stomach. Sliding her hand behind his head, she pulled him closer to her. 'Oh, Tom,' she whispered. 'Not long now.'

Their lips met. Lightly at first, and then more strongly. And stronger still as a wave of heat engulfed them.

Then he drew back sharply, breathing heavily.

'We'd better stop,' he said with a groan, and straightened up in his seat. 'You don't know what you're doing to me. This time tomorrow, we'll be married and on our way to Weymouth. I can't wait for you to be my wife,' he added, his voice thick with emotion.

'Nor can I,' she said, sliding her hand across his chest, and leaning against his shoulder. 'You mean everything to me, Tom.'

'And so do you to me,' he said with warmth. 'I just wish I could give you a better honeymoon than a night in Weymouth. Later in the year, when the harvest's done, I'll give you the honeymoon you deserve.'

'I don't care about a honeymoon. Being with you is all I want. Plus for the sea to be calm,' she added with a laugh.

'I'll echo that,' he said, putting his arm around her shoulders. 'But we've got an early crossing after a big day, so unless the waves are really bad, or the boat creaks especially loudly, we might be able to find somewhere to stretch out and sleep until we reach Guernsey.'

'Is that the first stop?'

He nodded. 'That's right. St Helier's after that. My father said that he and Mum will be on the quay when we dock, and my sister, too.'

She bit her lip. 'I do hope Kathleen likes me. I'm so used to having sisters around, and even though Violet and Iris are younger than I am, I think I might have missed them enormously if you hadn't had a sister. I'm really looking forward to meeting her. And to being the younger sister after being the oldest all my life,' she laughed. 'Even if there's only about a year between us.'

'She'll be as keen to meet you, I'm sure. It's important the two of you get on well as I want you to be happy, Rose. I worry that you won't be.'

Hearing the anxiety in his voice, she glanced up at him. He was looking at her with real concern.

She slid upright.

'Why wouldn't I be?' she asked, her heart beating fast.

'Because I'll be taking you away from London, which is full of places you can go to when you're not working, like the Hammersmith Palais, theatres and cinemas, tea dances and cafés. And you can get fish and chips! I've never even seen them in Jersey. I'll be taking you to a small island, with hardly anything to do. You might hate it. And then you might start to hate me.'

'You're wrong, Tom!' she insisted. 'I feel as if I already know Jersey. You've told me so much about it that I can see it clearly in my mind. It sounds a really beautiful place to live. Unlike Kentish Town, which isn't exactly lovely to look at. So there's no need to worry.' She beamed at him.

'But I *do* worry,' he said. 'Yes, it's beautiful, but beauty will only take you so far. No matter how much I describe it to you, you can't possibly know what it's like to live in somewhere that tiny. You probably can't even imagine how small it is. We do have a cinema in St Helier, and a theatre group, and there're dances in Sion Hall and locally. But Jersey people are nothing like Londoners. The island's mainly rural, and people tend to stay in the place where they were born. They hardly ever move out of their parish, and as communities rarely mix, people's whole lives are often lived within just a few miles.'

'But that's true of some parts of England.'

He nodded. 'But not the part you live in. Admittedly, things are changing slightly in Jersey. We're getting more newcomers—retired army colonels and civil servants, for example, who like the warmer climate—but they tend to stick with their own kind. And of course, there're tourists from all over, especially from France as we're really close to the French coast. But we don't mix with them.'

'None of that matters, Tom,' she said, putting her hand against his cheek. 'The most important thing is who you're with, not where you are. And I'll be with you.'

He hugged her tightly to him. 'I'm glad you think that. I do feel better for warning you, though, that people there can be insular,' he said. 'I probably should have told you that sooner.'

'It wouldn't have made any difference.'

'Thank you,' he said in audible relief.

'I'm pleased we'll be living with your family for a while,' she said as they drew apart. 'It means I'll get to know them better than I would've done if we'd been in a different house right from the start.'

He smiled broadly. 'That's a good way of looking at it.

And it means you'll have company if I'm away overnight. It wouldn't happen often, but if I went to Guernsey, for example.'

'D'you often go to there?'

He shook his head. 'Not really—it's almost thirty miles from us. But I've got some fisherman friends, and if they have to go there, I've been known to go along. We always have a good time, both in our group and with their friends in Guernsey. There's a kind of harmless rivalry between the islands. The people in Guernsey refer to Jersey as "the other island", and they call us *crapauds*, which means toads.'

She wrinkled her nose. 'Why toads?'

'Because we've got toads, and Guernsey hasn't. The toad's become a sort of Jersey mascot.'

'So if you're toads,' she said in amusement, 'what d'you call the people in Guernsey?'

He laughed. '*Les ânes*. It means the donkeys. It's because they can be stubborn.'

She nestled up to him. 'Well, I'm very glad that this *crapaud* came over to stay with us.'

He kissed the top of her head. 'And I think you'll be even more glad when you see what a lovely island he's taking you to. Just as you can't appreciate its smallness until you live there, you can't imagine how lovely it is till you've seen it for yourself. No matter how much I describe the forested hills and valleys, and tell you what it's like to walk through heathland that's blazing with yellow gorse, and how exciting it is to clamber down cliffs into bays that few people know about, you can't appreciate it till you've been there.'

'Well, I'll be there very soon,' she said in excitement. 'Oh, Tom. I can't wait for tomorrow!'

'Nor me,' he said. He put a finger under her chin and

raised her face so she could look into his eyes. 'Nor me,' he repeated, and bent his head to kiss her.

They heard the door to the sitting room open.

'Why don't you come down and have a whisky with me, Tom?' her father called from the foot of the stairs. 'Mabel's about to go up and help Rose with her clothes for tomorrow, and you and I will be in the way. After our whisky, I'll walk round to your room with you. I could do with stretching my legs.'

'I'll be right down, sir,' Tom called.

They stood up. Each stared hard at the other and smiled.

'I'll see you at St Silas's tomorrow,' Tom said. 'Make sure you turn up.'

Feeling very emotional, she nodded, unable to speak.

short while later

HAVING POURED a tumbler of whisky for each of them, John returned the bottle to the wooden tray on the oak cabinet, and took his seat in the faded armchair opposite Tom.

'Well, Tom,' he said, holding up his glass. 'Who'd have thought three months ago that I'd be sitting here today about to toast your future happiness with Rose.' He raised his glass higher. 'Cheers!'

Tom lifted his glass, and they sipped their drinks.

'Thank you, sir,' Tom said, putting his glass back on the occasional table next to him. 'I appreciate your good wishes. All the more so as I know you think we're rather rushing into things.'

John waved his hand vaguely. 'That's as may be. What matters is what's about to happen, not what Mabel and I would have preferred.' He paused. 'I hope you don't hold our concerns against us.'

'I don't, sir. In fact,' Tom added with a rueful smile, 'you weren't the only ones with reservations. I haven't told Rose, but my parents said much the same thing.'

'Did they indeed!'

'They were anxious about Rose being uprooted from everything and everyone after knowing me for such a short time.'

John nodded. 'I'm not surprised. Three months from meeting to marrying is hardly any time at all.'

'I've loved her from the moment I saw her,' Tom said. 'And I'm going to do all I can to make her happy. We'll be getting off to a good start as we're going to have a lovely home. She'll have told you that we're starting out in the family's farmhouse, which is fairly impressive. Our ancestors built it in the eighteenth century. They were leaders in their parish assembly and they wanted a house to suit their status. Benests have lived there and farmed the land ever since. And when it's ready, Rose and I will move into our own house, almost next door.'

'She's a lucky girl.'

'I'm the lucky one, having Rose at my side. You can be sure, sir, that my family and I will do all we can to help Rose settle.'

'I know you will, lad. William won't have forgotten what it's like to return from a large town to a small island, and nor will Annie, who'll have had to adapt in the same sort of way as Rose will. Knowing they'll be able to anticipate any difficulties Rose might face is a big relief to Mabel and me, I can tell you.' He paused. 'There *is* something else, though.' He cleared his throat.

'What is it, sir?'

John picked up his glass. 'I'm not a man who does a lot of reading,' he said, swirling the dregs of his whisky in the depths of his tumbler, 'but I do keep an eye on what's going on in the country, as any businessman must. And I'm also aware of what's happening in countries like France and Germany. Particularly Germany. But France, too. Jersey's quite close to France, I believe.'

'That's right, sir. We're fifteen miles from Normandy. We're the closest Channel Island to France.'

John nodded. 'So I understand. I read this week that Hitler has forced Austria to let Germany participate in governing it. Now that's clearly wrong to any right-thinking person.'

'It definitely is.'

'I know it's not something that need concern us unduly,' John continued. 'But what happened not so many years ago, which was supposedly the war to end all wars, shows how easy it is to get caught up in trouble elsewhere. It's all to do with the treaties we've signed in the past with other countries.'

'I can see where this is going, sir. You're worried that Germany and France might cause problems for Jersey, and you're obviously concerned as Rose will be living there.'

'That's right, lad. Jersey's much closer to them than it is to us. Rose will be a long way from us.'

Tom smiled. 'I understand. But it might put your mind at ease, sir, to know that the British have a garrison in the Channel Islands, and also that we've once again got our own Militia, which includes a rifle company and a machine gun company.'

'That is a relief, I will admit,' John said.

'Father may have told you that when the Militia mobilised at the start of the last war,' Tom went on, 'he volunteered. At the same time as he was running the farm, he took turns at standing on guard over the coast and key installations. That Militia was disbanded just before the end of the war, but they've got another unit now.'

John nodded. 'In one of her letters to Mabel back then, Annie told her what William was doing. If I remember rightly, Annie was panicking about a run on the shops and banks in Jersey that would have been economically disastrous, and she was wondering whether to suggest to William that they return to England.'

'Yes, she told me about that. But, as I'm sure she wrote to you, the worst didn't happen, thanks to the firm measures taken in Jersey, and what turned out to be a significant Allied victory in France,' Tom said. 'You've no need to worry about Rose, sir. Jersey's too remote to be of interest to anyone. But not so remote that she won't be able to visit you,' he added with a smile. 'And I hope you'll come and stay with us.'

'Thanks, lad. I'm sure we will. I'm going to miss my Rose. Of the three girls, she's the only one who's ever shown any interest in the shops, and I had high hopes she'd help with our plans for the future. I'd have made her responsible for extending our range of threads, for example, especially for crochet and embroidery, and for increasing the variety of textiles we stock. But instead, she's going to be a farmer's wife. Not that there's anything wrong with that,' he added quickly.

'Rose will obviously help on the farm. But there's no reason why, if she's not needed for farm work, she couldn't do a few hours in Mother's shop. It's in St Helier. It's on the other side of the bay, but she could easily cycle there. I'm sure Mother would be glad of her help.'

John nodded. 'That's good to hear.'

'Until now, Kathleen's been helping Mother during her busy periods, and occasionally Kathleen's closest friend, Emily, too. But Rose knows much more about haberdashery than those two put together. Like Kathleen, Emily comes from a farming family. Her parents own a farm not far from ours. We grow more potatoes than they do, and they grow more wheat and oats than us. We only grow a small quantity for cattle fodder and for making bread. Both of us keep cows for milking, and make a bit of butter, and both of us keep a few pigs and chickens. But Mother's the only true haber-dasher among us.'

'I was so pleased when I heard that she'd kept up her links with haberdashery,' John said with a smile. 'That's how your father met her, of course. And I'm glad to hear that Rose won't have to abandon something she's good at, some-thing I know she enjoys.'

Tom picked up his glass. 'I'll do everything I can to make Rose happy, sir,' he said. 'You can count on that.' He finished his drink and stood up. 'And now I think I'd better get off. It's a busy day tomorrow. There's no need for you to walk round with me, sir.'

'Then I think I'll stay put,' John said, 'and save my energy for tomorrow. And I need to have a last look at my speech.' Rising to his feet, he faced Tom. 'Whatever happens in the future, Tom, I'm trusting you to do well by my Rose.'

'I will, sir.'

John held out his hand, and Tom shook it.

6

Jersey, April 1938

Escorted by gulls that were streaking the deep blue sky with white and pale grey, the St Julien glided over the sparkling water towards the distant grey stone walls that jutted out into the sea, creating the harbour of St Helier.

Her arm tucked in Tom's, Rose leaned against the ship's railing and stared in delight across the bay to the villas and small white houses that traced the sweeping wide curve of yellow sand that defined the edge of the water.

'It's all beautiful, Tom,' she breathed. 'And it's lovely and warm. But very windy,' she added with a laugh. Raising both arms, she tightened the knot in the scarf holding her hair back from her face. 'How different from London where it was quite cold for April.'

'Chilly or not, yesterday was the best day of my life,' he said, turning to look at her. 'And to see your head on the

pillow next to mine when I woke up this morning was something I'll never forget. I love you so much, Rose.'

'And I love you, too,' she said, gazing up into his face.

He put his arm around her and pulled her gently to him.

She moved as close into him as she could, slid her arm
across his chest, and feeling the rapid beat of his heart next
to hers, she hugged him tightly.

Then they drew apart, smiled at each other and turned
back to the view, his arm still around her shoulders, her arm
around his waist.

'I can't believe I'm going to be living somewhere like
this,' she said, shaking her head.

'Well, you are,' he said in satisfaction. 'And not that far
from here, in fact. This is St Aubin's Bay. Our farm's at the
top of a slope that looks out over the bay. We're lucky—we
can easily get to St Aubin and St Helier, as well as to everywhere else inland.' He looked towards the harbour. 'As you'll
soon find out. We're almost there, Rose.' His voice rose in
excitement.

She followed his gaze, and felt a sharp pang of nervousness. His parents might already be on the quay, waiting.

Suddenly it all felt very real.

Suppose they didn't like her? Or she didn't like them?

She moved closer to Tom, and felt his arm tighten
around her.

Reassured by his nearness, she tried to dismiss her fears
as silliness. Her father had very much liked William and
Annie, and they him. And although that was long time ago,
there wasn't a single reason why they wouldn't also like her,
and why they wouldn't get on really well.

It was just that she was so used to the way her family did
things. Now she was about to meet Tom's parents, who were
sure to do things very differently.

Until that moment, they had been no more than names. But now, owing to their nearness, the dream-like bubble she'd been in for the past few weeks had burst, and the reality of her situation hit her for the first time. She was many miles from her family, about to start living with people she didn't know, who'd have their own way of doing everything. The strangeness of it all could prove difficult to get used to.

And then there was Kathleen.

Kathleen wouldn't have expected Tom to present her with a sister-in-law on his return. Would she be pleased to have another woman in the house, whose needs in future would have to be considered as well as hers, she wondered..

And what did a farmer's wife actually *do* all day? She really should have asked Tom when they were still in London, so she'd be better prepared.

Vigorously pushing some stray strands of hair back under her headscarf, she tried to quell her rapidly growing nervousness.

'My parents are going to love you,' Tom said, as if he had read her mind. 'I can't wait to see them again, and for you to meet them.' He glanced sideways at her in amusement. 'And I can't wait for our first night together in a comfortable bed.'

She laughed. 'It *was* a bit lumpy,' she said.

'You can say that again! And in trying to avoid the largest of the lumps, I nearly did myself a serious injury.'

'And one to me, too!' she exclaimed.

As they smiled happily at each other, she felt some of her anxiety fade.

Leaning back against the railing, he faced her. 'Tonight will be different, Rose,' he said, his voice suddenly serious. 'And every day and every night hereafter. I love you so much, and I'll always do my best to make sure that everything's perfect for you.'

'If you're with me, it will be.' She reached up and kissed his cheek. She lingered a moment, her face against his, then she turned back to the view.

'What's that?' she asked, pointing to a castle that stood on a rocky outcrop a little way out from the shore. 'It looks quite dramatic.'

Strong waves were slapping unevenly against its stony base, then rolling back, leaving rings of creamy pock-marked froth on the shiny wet granite slabs. Moments later, the sea surged forward again, and a fresh influx of powerful waves rolled over each other, smashed against the rocks in a mass of seething white foam, and drew back, leaving new collars of foam encircling the outcrop.

'That's Elizabeth Castle,' he said. 'It was built when Elizabeth I was queen, hence its name. Twice a day, when the tide's high, it becomes an island. At low tide, though, you can walk to it across a causeway.' He smiled at her. 'We'll do that one day. But right now, I think we'd better return to our suitcases and get ready to disembark. We'll be there very soon.'

He held out his hand to her, and she took it.

Wobbling slightly with the movement of the boat, she tucked her scarf into her pocket. Then she pushed the tortoiseshell clip more firmly into the hair she'd coiled on top of her head, put her cloche hat back on, picked up her suitcase with one hand, and holding the railing with the other, hurried down the gangplank after Tom.

He had already reached dry ground and was waiting for her at the foot of the gangplank. As soon as she neared him, he reached out, put his hand under her elbow and helped her on to the quay.

Seeing the crowd of people scanning the arrivals from behind a barrier, she looked at Tom. 'Do I look all right?' she asked, her voice shaking.

'You look beautiful, Rose,' he said. 'You could never look anything but. Come on, let's find the family. They'll be dying to meet you, and I can't wait to show you off.'

He picked up her suitcase as well as his and headed for the barrier.

'Tom!' she heard a voice shout.

Beyond the barrier, a plump blonde woman had broken away from the crowd and was pushing forward, frantically waving.

'Mum!' he cried.

He hastened round the barrier, let the suitcases fall to the ground and opened his arms for his mother to run into them.

Rose followed him, keeping a little way back.

Seconds later, she saw a tall, well-built man shake Tom's hand, and then pull him to his chest and hug him hard.

Then they turned towards her.

Three sets of piercing blue eyes stared at her, two sets with interest, one with pride.

She swallowed hard.

'Hello,' she said, moving slightly forward, but coming to a stop a little way back from them. 'I'm Rose.'

'And I'm Tom's mother,' the woman said, disentangling herself from her husband and son and hurrying up to Rose. 'We're so pleased to meet you, Rose,' she said and embraced her warmly. 'Welcome to Jersey, and to the family.' Then she held her at arms' length and looked at her face. 'Tom said you were lovely,' she added with a smile, 'and you certainly are.'

'It's very kind of you to say so, Mrs Benest, even though I must look a windswept mess,' Rose said.

'You'll soon get used to the wind,' Tom's father remarked coming up to them. 'The nearer the sea you are, the stronger the wind. And as we're a small island, there's wind just about everywhere. It's seldom as breezy as it was on the boat, though.'

'Now that there are two Mrs Benests,' Tom's mother said, 'it could get confusing, so I think we should decide right now what we're going to call each other. You'll obviously be Rose, and I'd like it if you called me Annie. Unless you have a preference for something else, that is.'

Rose shook her head. 'I don't. In fact, I already think of you as Annie because whenever Father mentions you, he says Annie.'

Annie beamed. 'It's good to know he still thinks of us at times.'

'Oh, he does! And so does Mother, too. You and Mr Benest definitely haven't been forgotten,' Rose said.

William stepped forward and held out his hand to Rose. 'I'm delighted to meet you, Rose. As Annie suggests, let's use first names. I'm William.'

'And I'm hungry,' Tom said with a grin. 'It seems a long time since we ate.'

William laughed. 'So you've still got hollow legs, have you? Clearly the dismal food in England didn't manage to kill your appetite. It's just as well that lunch is waiting for us at the farm. Here, I'll take the suitcases.' He picked them up and turned towards the town.

Tom swiftly scanned the people nearby. 'Where's Kathleen, Dad?' he asked, frowning slightly. 'Didn't she come with you?'

'Unfortunately she couldn't, Tom,' Annie said hastily. 'She was going to, but at the last moment, Emily asked for her help with something to do with their farm. Emily Gorin is Kathleen's best friend, Rose. Our families are very close. Kathleen's going to stay at Emily's tonight so you won't meet her till dinner tomorrow evening.'

'I'm afraid I don't know anything about farming,' Rose volunteered, quashing her disappointment at having to wait so long to meet her sister-in-law.

Annie smiled reassuringly. 'Nor did I when I first got here. But when you're living on a farm, you soon learn. Well then,' she said, her smile embracing them all. 'If we're ready, shall we go home?'

ANNIE LED ROSE into their large kitchen, followed by Tom.

'You'll be more rested tomorrow, Rose, so we'll leave showing you the rest of the house and outbuildings till then. And tomorrow we'll take you to what will be your house and Tom's. It's almost next door. We always refer to this as the farmhouse and to the house that'll be yours as the cottage.'

'A cottage sounds so heavenly,' Rose said, and she beamed.

'The room we're in now is one of the most important rooms. In the daytime, if we're not in the fields or working in any of the barns, we tend to gather in here. You'll find there's nearly always a pot of coffee on the range.'

'I can see why you like it in here,' Rose said, looking around the high-ceilinged room. 'It's lovely and airy, and very welcoming. And look, you can see the sea!' she added in excitement, pointing to the window.

Annie smiled. 'Indeed we can. As you can see, the cooking area is on the other side of the kitchen, and the window at the back looks out on to the yard and outbuildings. In the evenings, we often take our coffee into the small sitting room, which is next to the front room. The sitting room's where we had our cup of tea when we got back.'

'I love what I've seen of the house,' Rose said happily. 'Our house in London is much narrower. It's got fewer rooms and is poky by comparison. And our kitchen is nothing at all like this,' she added. 'I've never seen such a wonderful kitchen. I love the open fireplace. What's that?' she asked, staring at a metal door in the wall near the fireplace. 'It's not a bread oven, is it?'

'Well guessed. But I can't say it's used as such very much,' Annie said with a laugh. 'And the rack hanging from the ceiling is meant for bread and home-cured bacon, but we don't use that much, either. We leave both of them there, though, as we like their rustic look, and they're part of the history of the house.'

'I think it's a lovely room.'

Annie smiled at her. 'Thank you. But I expect you're now impatient to see where you and Tom will be staying till your house is ready. We've set aside two bedrooms so that you can use one as a sitting room. One of the rooms is your bedroom, Tom, but we've put in a new bed,' Annie told him.

Both she and Rose blushed.

'We redecorated it at the same time,' Annie went on quickly. 'And the bedroom opposite that will be your sitting room. It looks out across the yard to the barn with the *pressoir*. That's where our cider is made, Rose. Now the *pressoir* is something we *do* use,' she said with a laugh.

Tom moved to Rose's side and took her hand. 'Thanks, Mum. That sounds perfect.'

'We've made you a sitting room because we thought you might not always want to sit with us in the evenings. But you're more than welcome to join us whenever you want,' Annie explained. 'Now I suggest that you take Rose upstairs, Tom, while I deal with the meal. It'll be in about an hour. William's already taken your bags up.'

'Is there anything I can do to help?' Rose asked.

'Not a thing, thank you, but it's kind of you to offer.' She went across to a wooden clothes rack hanging on the wall and unhooked a floral pinafore apron.

'I suggest you show Rose the bedroom and bathroom, Tom, then let her unpack,' she said slipping into the apron. 'You could leave your unpacking till later, and go and find your father. I know he's dying to show you what they've done on the farm in the past three months. You can fill me in tomorrow about the wholesaler you've found.'

'Right, let's go, then,' Tom said to Rose. 'I'll save the carrying you over the threshold bit for the day we move into the cottage,' he added with a broad grin. 'After breakfast tomorrow, I'll take you to see the cottage and the rest of the farmhouse. But for now, when I've shown you upstairs, I'll go and find Father.'

And together they went out into the hall and up the wooden staircase to the right of the hall.

'THANK you so much for making our rooms so pleasant, Annie,' Rose said as she came into the kitchen almost an hour later. 'I hadn't expected to have so much space and as many cupboards.'

'I'm glad you like it,' Annie said, looking pleased. 'But

don't think you have to sit up there by yourselves every
evening. Come down here whenever you want.'

'Thank you.'

Annie picked up a large tureen. 'Your timing couldn't
have been better. The meal's ready. Come and sit down.'
And she led the way to a rectangular heavy scrubbed-wood
table in front of the window that looked out towards
the sea.

'I sit here,' she said, 'closest to the cooking area, and
William sits at the other end. Sit on whichever side you
want. I'll call the men. And when we've eaten, I want to hear
all about your family, starting with your father.'

FEELING TOM'S gaze on her back as she leaned on the sill of
their bedroom window, watching the night sky deepen from
an intense indigo-blue to a star-filled mantle of black, Rose
turned to look at him.

He was lying on the bed, his hands behind his head,
watching her. A lock of hair had fallen across his forehead,
and shone gold in the light thrown out by the bedside lamp.
His unbuttoned pyjama top had fallen open and his bare
chest gleamed.

Her breath came fast, and she shivered in her thin cotton
nightdress.

'Come to bed, wife,' he said, tapping the place next to
him. 'You look cold.'

She ran across and lay down next to him. He turned on
his side to face her, enveloping her with his warmth. Her
every nerve tingling, she pulled him closer to her. Feeling
his body hard against hers, she shivered again.

'Oh, Rose,' he breathed, her name a long low sigh of
love.

'I love you, Tom,' she whispered. her voice filled with longing.

He leaned across her and extinguished the light of the lamp.

SHE LAY ON HER BACK, staring at the ceiling. Then she turned towards Tom. He was lying on his stomach, his face to the wall, his back slightly rising and falling with his breathing.

This was the man she loved, the man with whom she'd be spending the rest of her life.

Now that they were back in his world, what did he do when he wasn't working on the farm, she wondered as she stared at the head on the pillow next to her. She had no idea at all. They had got to know each other so quickly, and it had been in her house, not his, so she didn't yet know what he did in his own home in the evenings.

She was going to enjoy finding out, she thought, and she looked back up at the ceiling.

And how would she spend *her* day?

Ideally, she'd find farm work interesting, and in the evenings, she and Tom would find things they enjoyed doing together. Going for walks, perhaps, unless the weather was too bad. Or dancing. Assuming he genuinely liked dancing, of course. But he certainly seemed to in London. Or maybe even something to do with haberdashery.

He was obviously interested in haberdashery or his mother wouldn't have entrusted him with finding a wholesaler in England, so that would be an interest they shared. Her father had been right about her enjoying supervising the shops. She had liked the work and had loved the challenge it had given her.

But if it was something else, not that, it wouldn't really matter. The most important thing was that they would have things to talk about that weren't to do with work. She'd hate him to find her boring and begin to regret marrying her.

Especially as she was now on her own, with her family much too far away to help her if anything were to go wrong.

She closed her eyes and tried to blot out her sudden overwhelming sense of the enormity of what she'd done.

7

T

he following day

STANDING NEXT TO EACH OTHER, their backs to the sea, Rose and Tom faced the two houses on the other side of the wide sandy track from where they stood, the farmhouse on their right and the smaller stone house next to it, which was to be their house.

An iron gate separated the cottage from the main farmhouse, preventing any animals from straying outside the large back yard that was jointly shared by the two houses.

On the other side of the farmhouse, a granite wall extended along the front of the yard to the point where it met a garage. There were two arched openings in the granite wall, which were closed off by wooden doors that had been painted green: a large opening for farm vehicles and a smaller one for people.

'The houses look so attractive,' Rose said happily.

'Let's look inside our house then, shall we?' Tom said, taking her hand.

She was thrilled to see that their sitting room was on the first floor, giving them a clear view of the sea. A balcony with metal railings led off from the sitting room, just big enough to take a small table and a couple of chairs. It meant that they'd be able to see the sea, she realised, whether inside or out.

After they'd had a look around, they went outside through the back door that led from the kitchen. A large fenced vegetable garden was clearly visible at the back of the yard.

She fervently hoped that the vegetable garden would be one of Annie's jobs, she thought as they walked diagonally across the yard to the outbuildings that lay behind the farmhouse. She had never done anything in the garden at Allcroft Road except play in it with her sisters, and she wouldn't know where to begin.

But before she could ask Tom about the garden, he was leading the way into the first of the barns. They had a barn for the pigs, though they were often out in the field where they had individual metal sties, he told her as they moved into the next of the barns.

When he had taken her through the barn for the cows, the milking barn, the potato barn, and the barns used for storage and for the *pressoir* and butter churn, and had shown her where the chickens were kept, they went round to the fields behind the outbuildings.

On the way to the fields, they passed a number of glass frames which, Tom told her, were where they brought on the young plants. When they came to a large field in which cows were grazing, Tom stopped and leaned on the wooden fence. She did the same.

'Don't they look beautiful?' he said, his gaze on the cows that were light tan and cream in colour.

'I'll see if I can find make-up that will achieve a similar effect,' she murmured.

He glanced at her in amusement, then looked back at the cows.

'Are they fierce?' she asked.

'Not the cows. But at times, the bulls can be aggressive. Jersey cows tend to be curious and friendly rather than fierce. And they can be stubborn and spirited. They're cows with a personality, you could say.'

'And what's in those fields?' she asked, looking to her left.

'Wheat. We plant winter wheat in the autumn and harvest it mid-May. And we also plant wheat in the spring and harvest it in the autumn. Unlike our friends the Gorins, though, we don't grow much wheat. We grow just enough for our own use and for cattle fodder. When we look at the vegetable garden, you'll see we've got root vegetables, but again they're for our own use.'

'I see,' she said.

'Our main crop is potatoes,' Tom went on. 'And as you can see, we've got a lot of cows, pigs and chickens. We deliver the cows' milk to the dairy, and we make a modest amount of butter. The butter's for our own use, but we also supply some of the local shops. And we supply them with eggs, too.'

'It sounds a lot of work,' she said as they started walking along the path that ran alongside the field with cows. She glanced ahead and exclaimed. 'Don't tell me! In addition to the potato plants on the slope going down to the sea, those are potato plants, too,' she said, pointing to the plant-covered undulating hills ahead of them.

Tom laughed and put his arm around her.

'I've never seen so many potatoes,' she said when they finally returned to the yard.

'And you'll see more tonight at dinner,' he said with a smile.

HAVING HAD a bath and changed into a cornflower blue dress that she knew was one of Tom's favourites, Rose went down for the evening meal a little early, keen to meet Kathleen, and hoping to do so before they sat down for dinner.

It had been a brilliant day, and she was very much looking forward to the evening, but to her disappointment, although the table was set, there was no one in the kitchen.

She went out into the hall and crossed over to the front room.

That, too, was empty. So, too, was the sitting room. Feeling at a loose end, she went across to the sitting room window and stared towards the line of stone outbuildings. From deep within one of the buildings, she could hear the lowing of cows, and between the house and barns there were a number of chickens pecking at the ground, but there was no human being to be seen.

Tom must still be out in the fields with William, or inside one of the barns, she decided. She started to turn away but a sound from the yard stopped her. It came from her right. Pressing her face against the glass and peering to her right, she glimpsed Annie unpegging the washing from a line outside the kitchen.

Well that's one of them accounted for, she thought, straightening up. There was still no sign of Kathleen or any of the men, though. And apart from the cows, and some clucking from the chickens, there was nothing to be heard.

It was a bit different from the continuous hum of the traffic on Queen's Crescent, but pleasantly so.

Smiling to herself, she returned to the kitchen.

Earlier that day, when she'd mentioned that she enjoyed cooking, Annie had pointed to cookery books on the top shelf of the large dresser just inside the kitchen door, so she thought she'd take a look at them while she waited for Annie to come in.

She wandered over to the dresser and reached up to the nearest book. As she was pulling it down, she heard footsteps in the hall. Clutching the book, she turned to face the door as a girl with long blonde hair came into the kitchen.

The girl saw her and stopped abruptly.

Rose's face broke out into a broad smile. 'Are you Kathleen?' she asked.

Unsmiling, the girl nodded. 'That's right. And I take it you're Tom's wife.'

'Yes. I'm Rose.'

She wondered whether she should offer to shake hands. Or if it would be more friendly to hug her.

But Kathleen walked straight past her, and sat at the kitchen table. 'He's on his way in,' she said tersely.

Rose hesitated a moment, her brow creasing in surprise. Then she put the book back on the shelf and sat down opposite Kathleen.

'That's Tom's seat,' Kathleen snapped.

Taken aback by Kathleen's unfriendliness, and lost as to why that should be, Rose repressed her instinct to tell Kathleen what she thought of her rudeness, and moved to the next chair without comment.

Silence hung heavily in the air.

'You'll hate living here,' Kathleen volunteered, her tone

icy. 'Nothing ever happens. You'll be running back home in no time at all.'

'No, I won't,' Rose retorted. 'This is my home now. My home will always be where Tom is.'

'Prettily said, but we'll see,' Kathleen said with a sneer. She picked up the stone jug in the centre of the table and poured herself a glass of water.

'Ah, you've met,' Annie said, coming in from the yard through a door at the back of the kitchen, carrying a basket of washing. She put the basket on the floor at the back of the kitchen and busied herself by the range.

Her voice sounded strained, Rose thought, which suggested that Annie had known that Kathleen would be unwelcoming, and probably knew the reason why.

So what could it be, she wondered.

She glanced over her shoulder towards Annie, but Annie still had her back to her.

Since Tom had only just returned to Jersey and had been with William for most of the time since he'd got back, apart from when he had shown her around the house and the farm, and since then she had either been with Annie or had been relaxing by herself, this must relate to something that had happened before Tom left for England.

If so, would Kathleen be rude to him, too?

She glanced surreptitiously at Kathleen, who was concentrating on the piece of bread she'd put on her side plate.

With an inward sigh of relief, she heard Tom and William come into the kitchen, talking to each other. Tom came straight to the table and sat down next to her. William took the seat at the end of the table.

Tom smiled broadly at her, then looked across at Kathleen.

'Hello, little sister,' he said cheerfully. 'Long time, no see.'

Kathleen stared hard at him, then looked back at her plate.

His smile faded. He turned to Rose and raised his eyebrows.

She shrugged her shoulders.

'So, what d'you think of the farm, Rose?' William asked, helping himself to a piece of bread. 'Tom said he'd shown you round it today.'

'It's really lovely,' she said. 'It's so attractive. And so is our house. Or should I say the cottage? It's really kind of you and Annie to let us have it.'

He nodded. 'It's a good solid house. You wouldn't believe it, but the walls are actually three feet thick. It's the same here, too.'

'So Tom said. That's remarkable.'

'Our front room here's a little musty, as you probably noticed,' William added. 'But that's because we don't use it much. Just for big family things and special occasions. Like the front room in Allcroft Road, I imagine,' he added. 'It should make you feel at home.'

'How kind of you to have made your front room feel musty and unused for my benefit,' she said with a laugh.

He laughed with her.

'Did you go for a walk this afternoon?' Tom asked her.

'I was going to, but I was quite tired after lunch—it's been a busy few days—and Annie insisted I sit outside so I did, and I feel better for it. The view over to the sea, with St Aubin's harbour on the right, is really lovely.'

'It is, isn't it? And I see that at some point you and Kathleen met.' He glanced again at his sister, and his smile embraced them both.

Kathleen's gaze remained on her plate.

Tom was obviously as much in the dark as she was, Rose realised.

'We met just now,' she said, to fill a momentary awkwardness, and she fell silent.

Annie came across to the table and set down a large casserole. 'It's a rabbit casserole,' she said. She brought over two tureens, one full of boiled parsnips and carrots, and one heaped high with small brown potatoes. Then she sat down.

'You're all very quiet,' she said, ladling a portion of casserole on to the plate on top of the pile of plates next to her and handing it to Rose. 'Help yourself to vegetables, Rose.'

'The potatoes are home-grown,' William said. 'They're particularly delicious because they're fertilised with what we call *vraic*. It's Jersey seaweed that's harvested from the island's beaches. We either pile it directly on to the soil, or burn it and sprinkle the ash. Or we can dry it and use it as fuel. There's no better fertiliser. And there's so much available. Jersey has some of the strongest tidal flows anywhere in the world, and the sea very kindly regularly deposits loads of *vraic* on the shore. Jersey farmers have been using it since the twelfth century.'

'Goodness! That's a long time,' Rose said, as she put a spoonful of potatoes on to her plate.

Stony-faced, Kathleen helped herself to carrots.

When they had all served themselves, they picked up their knives and forks.

'The potatoes are really delicious!' Rose exclaimed.

'Nothing beats home-grown potatoes,' Annie said with a smile. 'The smell of freshly dug potatoes in the morning is heavenly.'

'So now that you've seen everything we've done in your

absence, Tom, what did you think of the farm?' William asked.

'It looks very good, Dad. Mind you, three months wasn't quite long enough for you to manage to kill off the cows and strangle the vegetables,' he laughed. 'Not even with Kathleen doing her worst.'

He smiled across at his sister. Her face sullen, she was moving her food from one side of her plate to the other, and gave no sign of having heard him.

He frowned. 'What's up with you, Kathleen?' he asked. 'Normally, we can't shut you up. But not tonight. You've not even said hello, welcome back. And what's with the sour expression?'

'Nothing,' she said, and she speared a carrot with her fork.

'Well, there's clearly something!' He stared at her in annoyance.

'Eat up now, Tom,' William said, gesturing to Tom's plate before attacking the piece of rabbit in front of him.

A hush descended again.

Minutes later, Tom dropped his knife and fork on the plate, pushed his plate away and glared at Kathleen. 'Are you going to sit here throughout the meal without saying a word, creating an atmosphere that's obviously getting to everyone? You're ruining Rose's first proper family meal with us. She'll think we're always like this, and we're not. So what is it?'

Kathleen picked up another carrot.

'Tom's right, Kathleen,' William said. 'You might as well say whatever it is you're dying to say, and then perhaps we can enjoy the meal your mother's prepared.'

Kathleen glared at him.

'Well?' he prompted, his voice a shade louder.

Kathleen glanced from William to Annie. 'You both know what this is about, so why pretend you don't? You know how I feel about Tom marrying *her*—' she indicated Rose, '—when he'd as good as promised to marry Emily.' She stared accusingly at Tom. 'Emily was devastated when she heard you were marrying someone else. Everyone was so surprised. They all thought that you and Emily would marry. And you did, too,' she rounded on her parents.

So that was it, Rose thought with a mental thud. She glanced questioningly at her husband, who was gazing at Kathleen in bewilderment.

'I haven't a clue what you're talking about!' he exclaimed. 'I'd never given a minute's thought to marrying anyone till I met Rose. And I've certainly never given Emily any reason to think I was interested in her in a romantic way. She's a pleasant girl, but that's all. I don't know how you and Emily could think I intended to marry her. I wasn't even walking out with her.'

'You always used to dance with her at the local dances, and you'd sit and talk with her whenever our families visited each other,' Kathleen said accusingly.

Tom made a helpless gesture. 'I was being polite and welcoming because she was a family friend. As for the dances, I've never particularly enjoyed them, which you well know. I went because everyone did—it was expected of you —and I danced with Emily because she was a familiar face and I didn't have to make any effort. It was no more than that.'

'The trouble is,' William said quietly. 'I can see now, how on a small island, dancing with the same girl at every dance might give rise to an expectation on the girl's part.'

'I danced with other people as well,' Tom retorted. 'I

danced a few times with Madeleine Le Feu. Are you saying that you or she expected me to marry her?'

'It was a little more than that with Emily, wasn't it?' William said. 'Every time we've gone to the Gorins, or they've come to us, you've always chatted to her. Your mother and I even wondered about it. So I suppose it isn't unreasonable for her family to have thought there was something more to this than mere politeness.'

'Of course they would. Poor Emily's so upset,' Kathleen said, glaring at her brother. 'And so are her parents.'

'That explains why they've not called us or commented on Tom's engagement,' William said slowly. 'I must admit, I was bit surprised at that, but everything happened so quickly that I didn't give it another thought.'

'Well, perhaps you should've done,' Kathleen said rudely. 'Tom's behaved really badly to Emily. Apart from anything else, she's ever so embarrassed about what people will be saying behind her back.'

'That will do, Kathleen,' William said heatedly. 'I think we've heard enough from you. I realise you're upset, but Rose is with us now, and we're delighted that she is. I can't imagine what she must think of us. The whole thing's an unfortunate misunderstanding, and Tom will go over to the Gorins tomorrow and have a word with them. Won't you, Tom?'

Tom nodded. 'Of course.'

'I'm sorry about this, Rose,' William said. 'This isn't the best introduction to Jersey that you could've had, or to us as a family. I hope this won't colour your feelings about having come to live here.'

Feeling close to tears, Rose opened her mouth to answer him.

'Here comes the little speech about wherever Tom is,' Kathleen said, her tone sneering.

'The matter's closed, Kathleen,' Annie said sharply. 'Or don't you agree?'

Kathleen scowled. 'No, I don't. *You're* not the ones who've been made to look fools.'

'And nor have you,' Annie retorted. She glanced along the table at William. 'I think it might be a good time to have a change of subject, William. Why don't you open a bottle of our special cider?' She turned to Rose. 'We'd like to welcome you into our home, Rose,' she told her with a strained smile. 'We thought we'd do it with cider from our *pressoir.*'

Kathleen got up and went out, slamming the kitchen door behind her.

8

M*inutes later*

HER BLONDE HAIR flying loose in her wake, her eyes brimming with tears, Kathleen strode across the yard to the narrow rutted track that ran along the side of the field of cows closest to the house.

Once again, Tom had got away with it.

He had never been able to do any wrong. And she'd never been able to get anything right.

No matter how hard she'd tried.

She always did her best to be helpful on the farm, despite not really enjoying the work, but no one ever seemed to appreciate the efforts she made. She tirelessly helped her mother in the house and the shop, but her help was taken for granted. It was never commented upon or applauded.

Whereas everything Tom did was invariably noticed and praised, endlessly.

She didn't put it down to not being loved. It wasn't that. She was certain her parents loved her.

No, it was because it was Tom who'd be running the farm after they'd gone.

It was Tom who was the one who was important. It was he who had to be bolstered up and encouraged in everything he did. Not her. She would get married and move somewhere else. Quite simply, Tom held the future of their farm in his hands, and the means of keeping alive the name of Benest. She didn't.

She wiped her face with the back of her hands.

They probably didn't even realise that they treated Tom any differently from her, but she had felt the difference all her life. It was a situation she would have to put up with, she had long since realised, until the day she married and moved away.

But if Emily had married Tom and moved into the house, everything would have been so much more endurable. She would have had Emily's company, and Emily's help with the chores, and her life until she left the farm as a married woman would have been so much more pleasant.

She and Emily got on extremely well, having known each other since they were in nappies. Unlike her, Emily loved all aspects of farm work, and she would have willingly lightened her load. She would have been the ideal sister-in-law.

Only Tom hadn't married Emily.

Rose had supplanted her.

And to make matters worse, after initial reservations

about how little Rose and Tom could possibly know about each other, her mother had been noisily enthusiastic at the idea of there being another woman on the farm who not only had a real interest in haberdashery, but who knew something about running such a business.

What she, Kathleen, knew about haberdashery her mother had taught her. What Rose knew about haberdashery came from Rose's father, who owned several shops, and who knew so much more about it than her mother. Increasingly, her mother would turn to Rose for help and advice, not to her own daughter, and in no time at all, Rose was bound to usurp her place in the shop.

So, like farmer Tom, haberdasher Rose would become a valued member of the family, and would be appreciated by them in a way that she, Kathleen, never would.

If only Tom had married Emily, she thought in despair.

A sudden thought hit her, and she stopped in her tracks.

It was true that Tom had married someone else, but he didn't have to *stay* married to her. Everyone said divorce was easier than it used to be. It was still possible, therefore, that he and Emily could marry one day.

All that was needed was a little intervention on her part to make Rose yearn to return to England. But she'd have to do it sooner rather than later, before children arrived to complicate the matter.

Failing that, Rose could be encouraged to find someone in Jersey she preferred to Tom. After all, she hardly knew Tom, and the more she got to know him, the more likely it was she'd discover that they weren't at all suited.

Rose was a town girl, from somewhere much larger than St Helier, the largest town on Jersey. She knew nothing at all about farming. She might have romantic notions about it from children's stories, but when she was introduced to the actual work, which was arduous, back-breaking and very repetitive, she would hate it.

A complaining Rose would, of course, look to Tom for support, but in that she'd be disappointed.

When her parents had spoken about their concern that Rose and Tom didn't yet know each other well enough to marry, they'd been right. Rose had no idea how wedded to the farm Tom was. And she wouldn't have realised that he had no real interest in haberdashery.

He had used the fact that his mother wanted a wholesaler in Weymouth as an excuse to visit the place where his parents used to live and to meet the people he had heard a lot about. But never once in his letters home had he so much as hinted that he wished he could stay in England. His letters had always talked about things to do with the farm.

And unless Tom had changed in the months he'd been away, and there was no indication that he had, he would be up early every morning, have a quick breakfast, and go out to the barns and the fields for the day. He wouldn't come back to the house for anything other than lunch and tea until the sky was darkening and it was time to come in for dinner.

Rose didn't yet know this.

And when she started to understand the structure of Tom's life, she was sure to be very upset at the long hours he worked, and at how little she saw of him. Tom should have warned her how it would be, she might start to think, and resentment could creep in.

She'd be even more upset, and quite possibly horrified, to learn that not only did the farmer have to work on the farm, but so, too, did his wife. And the work was quite heavy. Jersey women weren't treated as delicate flowers who shouldn't be asked to do anything too onerous. They were expected to go out into the fields when the potatoes were ready, for example, and to dig them up alongside the men.

Yes, she'd be able to escape to the haberdashery shop on occasions, but the needs of the farm would always take priority. And as potatoes, their most important crop, required year-round labour, there wouldn't be that many chances to get away.

Her ideas rapidly taking shape, she started walking again.

The first stage was for Rose to start to feel very alone. And she could help with that, she thought with an inward smile. She'd make it look like the jilting of Emily was a thing of the past, and that she, Kathleen, was befriending Rose, as any good sister-in-law would do.

But the opposite would be true.

When people were around, she would speak pleasantly to Rose. But when they weren't, she'd ignore her. And if they were given a joint task which required them to talk, she would say only what was absolutely necessary.

Rose would inevitably look towards Tom for some warmth during the day. But in that she would be unlucky. Busy in the fields all day, he wouldn't have any time, patience or inclination when he came home to fuss over her. Nor would her parents, whose days were filled with tasks of their own.

Very soon, therefore, Rose, who was used to having her family around her, and to working with people with whom she could chat, would start to feel isolated. When she did, she'd look either to England, or to any friendly neighbour.

Should any of their female neighbours pick up on Rose's loneliness, and decide to befriend her, she'd casually drop an unpleasant titbit about Rose into her next conversation with them, whether or not it was true, and they would be sure to change their minds.

If any male neighbour looked at Rose with romantic interest, Kathleen would do everything she could to help him into Rose's bed. And then make sure that Tom knew.

Increasingly, Rose would either miss the warm embrace of her London home, or start to enjoy the warm embrace of someone other than Tom.

From what she'd seen of Rose, and what she knew about Tom, the two of them could be trusted to take over at that point and do the rest by themselves. In this, they were sure to reach an outcome that had been inevitable from the start.

Only someone born into a farming life would be able to understand the depth of Tom's feelings for the farm, and not be jealous of the amount of time he spent in the fields.

Someone like Emily.

Emily might not be as striking as Rose, but she was still very pretty. And as a farmer's daughter, she loved living on a farm, understood the requirements of farming and knew what was expected of a farmer's wife.

When Emily and Tom used to talk to each other, a large part of what they enjoyed discussing was what was happening on their respective farms. And with Rose growing increasingly miserable, and disgruntled about the tasks she was expected to undertake, feelings which, with her background of managing three shops, she would be unlikely to hide, Tom would start to think back to how much he'd always enjoyed talking to Emily.

The more Rose walked around looking morose, the

more Emily, who took farm work in her stride with skill, enjoyment and a cheerful smile, would shine in Tom's eyes.

Her steps speeding up, Kathleen turned along the wide track leading to Emily's farm. She couldn't wait to tell Emily her thoughts about Rose, and that she could see a day in the not-too-distant future when Emily might, after all, become her sister-in-law.

9

M *ay, three weeks later*

JOHN PUSHED his empty dinner plate away, wiped his mouth with his napkin, and regarded Mabel, Iris and Violet.

'It seems strange, doesn't it, not having Rose with us for our Sunday meal?' he remarked. 'I'm still not used to her being gone. She was always so lively, and she always had something of interest to say about the shops or the customers. We're really going to miss her at meals.'

'Thank you for that vote of confidence in your other two daughters, Father,' Violet said. She looked at Iris and they both giggled.

'Your father didn't mean it to sound as it did,' Mabel said, with an amused smile. 'As you well know.'

'Of course I didn't,' John said quickly. 'But you must admit, Rose is the only one who's ever shown any interest in the shops.'

'Maybe so,' Violet said. 'But there are other things people should know and talk about, and I've never heard Rose show any interest in those. We might be interested in them, though, and this could lead to a pleasant discussion at the table, even without Rose.'

'Such as?' John asked.

'Such as the things our history teacher tells us in our discussion group,' Violet replied. 'She always explains the situation in the outside world and we talk about it. It's so that when we start at the college, we'll know what's happening in other countries. There *is* a world beyond our shops, you know.'

'I do know,' John said with a smile. 'And Tom will vouch for me. We touched on it the evening before the wedding.'

'What has your teacher been telling you, Violet love?' Mabel asked as she leaned across to remove Violet's empty plate.

'That Adolf Hitler's ambition could threaten the stability of Europe,' Violet said. 'And that could be very serious.'

John smiled reassuringly. 'I think that's a bit of an exaggeration, don't you?'

'No, I don't. My teacher doesn't think so. She said that Hitler's broken loads of the terms in the Versailles Treaty, and that he's definitely rearming Germany. No one builds up a supply of arms unless they intend to use them.'

'I think we'll leave it at that, Violet,' John said firmly. 'There's no need to cause unnecessary alarm. Your teacher's entitled to say what she wants, but I'd rather you kept her opinions to yourself, and limited your comments to things that will help us to enjoy our meals together.'

'Do you mean things like a discussion about your shops, Daddy?' Iris asked brightly. 'Would that be more to your taste? I'm afraid such a subject is miles away from Violet's field of interest, but I can help.'

He looked at her in amusement. 'I'm sure you can, Iris. After all, you've been an employee of D.H. Evans for all of one week. There can't now be anything about shops that you don't know.' He leaned back in his chair, smiled across the table at Mabel, and then looked back at Iris. 'So, what can you tell us?'

'That you could learn from what they've done. The way they've designed the store is brilliant. It makes people want to spend their money there. You're stuck in a rut, and so was Rose. To both of you, shops are just trestle tables with a slate roof and a sheet of glass above a wooden counter.'

'I think that's a little hard on your father, Iris,' Mabel said. 'His shops have given us a comfortable life.'

'I know that,' Iris said impatiently. 'But that doesn't mean you can't ever do anything different. There are loads of new ideas about shop design, and there's a mass of infor-mation out there about what persuades people to buy things. You and Daddy ought to take a good look at the shops in Oxford Street and Regent Street, and apply what you see to the design of your new shops.'

John turned slightly towards her. 'Exactly what are you talking about, Iris?'

'The appearance of the shop, Daddy. It's really impor-tant. In D.H. Evans, the glamorous finish they use makes the people who go there feel glamorous, too. The walls and pillars are a sort of creamy pink marble, and they seem to glow. And they've got polished cork on the floors. And there's a satin sheen on all the metal displays. They use a lot of glass. They've hundreds of display cabinets made of glass. The shop feels luxurious, and the people who shop there want to be part of that world.'

'All that costs money.'

'Not as much as you might think, provided you're careful. And in the end, it would pay for itself as you'd have much more money coming in because sales would go up.'

John shook his head. 'In Oxford Street maybe, but not here in Kentish Town. Our clientele here is very different.'

'Our clientele is now starting to get on the underground and go to Oxford Street,' she retorted. 'Like everyone else, they want to feel special, but our shops don't make them feel that way.'

'With all due respect, Iris, we sell haberdashery,' Mabel said, smiling at John. 'We sell what people need. Buying a zipper won't make you feel special, and it's not something you buy on impulse.'

Iris turned to her mother. 'My point is, they could be persuaded to do so. If you displayed a finished dress, for example, in a glass cabinet, a swishy dress of the kind you might buy in D.H. Evans, and you added a display of everything used in its making, including the pattern, people might buy the items and pattern, even if they hadn't come in to get such a thing.'

John sat upright. 'D'you really think that could happen?' he asked.

'Yes, I do! And, of course, you'd sell the material that was used to make the dress. Lots of people still prefer to make their own clothes as it's cheaper, but their imaginations are limited. We'd be putting in front of them something elegant or glamorous that they'd never have seen before as they didn't go into the shops that sold that sort of dress. It would open their eyes as to how they could look, and they might buy what it takes to make the dress.'

John sat back and stared at Iris. 'Well, you do surprise me, Iris. You've just talked a deal of sense, and you've given

me something to think about. I might well be asking for
your advice.' He shook his head in wonder. 'Who would
have thought it?'

'What were you saying a few minutes ago about Rose,
Father?' Violet asked.

She and Iris exchanged an amused smile.

OVERJOYED THAT IT WAS SUNDAY, and that she'd hadn't been
given any instructions about the vegetable garden that day,
nor asked to grade any newly harvested potatoes, Rose
stood in the yard and stared up at the farmhouse, her focus
on the several small stone ledges that stood out around the
chimney stack. What were they there for, she wondered.

'So that's where you are!' Annie exclaimed, coming
through the doorway from the kitchen, wiping her hands on
her apron. She stood next to Rose and looked up at the roof,
following the direction of Rose's gaze.

'You're looking at the ledges, I see,' Annie said. 'Years
ago, that's where they used to fix the thatch. They'd tuck the
thatch under the ledges, which protected it from any water
that ran down the sides of the chimney stack. But they use
slates these days, not thatch, and slate's not as thick as
thatch. So the ledges are very visible. People call them
witches' perches.'

'Why witches' perches and not gulls' perches, for example?' Rose asked. 'There're lots of gulls around.'

'More exciting, I suppose! In folklore, witches would rest
on the perches on the way to their gatherings. Householders
were keen to make sure that the witches had somewhere to
sit as they didn't want to incur their ill favour,' Annie
explained with mock gravity, 'so it's become something of a
tradition to build houses with ledges like this, even though

there're few thatched roofs these days. If you look, you'll see that you and Tom have witches' seats on your house, so you'll be safe from any curses, too!'

'I see,' Rose said. 'Thank you. That's interesting.' She gave Annie a smile, and headed for the kitchen door.

'Wait, Rose!' Annie called, going up to her. 'I've been wanting to speak to you,' she said. 'I'm not blind—I can tell you're unhappy, and I want to know how I can help.'

Rose shrugged her shoulders. 'I'm fine, thank you,' she said.

'But you're not, are you?' Annie said gently.

Rose's eyes filled with tears.

'What is it, Rose?' Annie asked.

'I never see Tom,' she said, and she burst into tears.

Annie put her arm around her shoulders. 'Let's have a cup of tea, shall we? In the front room, I suggest. No one will expect us to be there, so we'll be left in peace.'

A SHORT TIME LATER, Rose and Annie were sitting in upholstered wooden-framed chairs in the front room, an occasional table between them, on which there were two cups of tea and a plate of cakes.

'Help yourself,' Annie said, indicating the cakes, 'and tell me what's worrying you.'

Rose took a breath. 'Since the first couple of days, when Tom took me around the farm and showed me this house and ours, I've hardly seen him. I know he's at the table for meals, but he's either too tired to talk, or he and William are going on about something to do with the farm, and he doesn't really notice me. And at night, he's too exhausted to want to sit and talk in our sitting room. It's Sunday today, Annie, and he's *still* working. I didn't think it'd be like this.' She dug in the pocket of her skirt for a handkerchief.

'Have you said anything to Tom?' Annie asked gently.

'I've tried to, but when I tell him I'd like to see him when he isn't always so tired, and that I'm finding it hard to get used to the work,' she went on, her voice catching in a sob, 'he doesn't seem to understand. And the other day, he even got annoyed that I wasn't as excited as everyone else that we'll be having the first new potatoes of the year later this month. It's a May tradition, he told me like an angry teacher. But how could I know that?'

'Perhaps "tradition" is a little strong,' Annie said, 'but the harvesting does tend to start in April, and the first new potatoes of the year do feel special to us—the early batch is exceptionally delicious.'

Rose wiped her face with her hands. 'Maybe so, but that's another thing—I feel as if I'm drowning in potatoes. I seem to be forever peering into a barrel of loose dirt, pulling out a handful of potatoes, grading them and filling bag after bag with them, ready for them to go wherever they have to.'

'When you were in London, didn't you ask him about what we did on the farm?' Annie asked.

Rose shook her head. 'Not really, no. He talked a lot about Jersey as he obviously missed it, and he was always mentioning the farm and the cows and the fields. He did say you grew Jersey Royals, but he didn't describe the work involved. I assumed I'd do some shopping and cooking and cleaning—the sort of things you do in London when you're married. But *you* do that, and you don't seem to need any help.'

'And you'll do that, too, when you're in your own house.'

Rose nodded. 'I realise that. But from what I understand, I'll still have to do the potatoes, and the vegetable garden, too. And help with the chickens. I didn't expect my life would revolve around household chores and potatoes, and that at the end of every day I'd be so tired that even if Tom wanted to talk, I'd be too exhausted to do so.'

'Believe me, Rose, I do understand. Listening to you reminds me how hard I found it when I first came to Jersey. I was lucky that I had Tom to occupy me, and Kathleen arrived not long after we got here. But it was difficult all the same. I fear we've rather thrown you in at the deep end, and we've failed to recognise that it wouldn't be easy for you.' She paused. 'What about Kathleen? Chores are more enjoyable when you're doing them with a friend.'

'Kathleen's dead set against being friends with me. If anyone's around, she speaks to me. If they're not, she doesn't. She's obviously not forgiven me for marrying Tom. But how was I to know that people thought he'd marry Emily? Kathleen's blaming me for something that wasn't my fault.'

'I see,' Annie said. 'I didn't realise quite how badly she was behaving. It's most unfair of her, and I'll speak to her about it.'

Rose shook her head. 'There's no point. It's obvious that she's never going to like me.'

'I'm sure you're wrong,' Annie said with a reassuring smile. 'From what I've seen of you, Rose, you're very likeable. I can easily see why Tom fell in love with you. Just give Kathleen time. As for Tom. I imagine that he's worried about you. After all, you've been looking more and more miserable as the weeks have gone by. I think that as soon as possible you should tell him what you've just told me.'

'If he *is* worried, he hasn't said anything.'

'It could be that he suspects what the problem is, but doesn't know what to say. All the men and women on a farm have to pull their weight, so Tom can't really tell you not to do your share of the work. But you can't carry on feeling like this. Tom and I will have to find a way of making you happier.'

'It's very kind of you, Annie, but it's really up to me to do that for myself,' Rose said gloomily. 'I feel guilty at how I must seem to you. When I heard myself just now, I thought how lazy I sounded. But I'm not lazy—I worked very long hours for my father, and really enjoyed it. I didn't feel nearly as drained at the end of the day, though, as I've been feeling since I got here.'

'You poor thing.'

'But you're right, Annie—I can't continue like this. I'm going to take myself in hand and find a way of coming to terms with the work.'

Annie leaned forward in her chair. 'I've a suggestion. I have to go to the shop tomorrow, so I'll be cycling into St Helier, leaving here at around ten in the morning. I'd always intended to ask if you'd do a stint in the shop sometime. With your knowledge of haberdashery, I know you'd be a great help. I was going to wait until you'd settled into the life of the farm, but why don't we make a start tomorrow?'

'Oh, I'd love that!' Rose exclaimed. A broad smile broke out on her face.

'That's decided, then. We've a bicycle you can have. I take it you've ridden before.'

Rose nodded. 'Yes, but not for a long time. The roads are quite busy at home, and as I can walk to Father's shops from the house, that's what I did.'

'Fortunately, once you've learned to ride, you never forget how. We'll cycle down to the esplanade that joins St Aubin to St Helier, and ride along to St Helier. It's a pleasant journey, which takes you past Elizabeth Castle. How does that sound?'

'Perfect,' Rose said tremulously. 'Thank you very much, Annie. I'm really keen to see the shop.'

Annie waggled her finger at her. 'Just leave that smile where it is. It's a joy to see, Rose. Let's hope it'll still be there when we have lunch in about half an hour.'

Rose beamed. 'It will be.'

10

T *he following day*

THE FIRST THINGS Rose saw when she left the farmhouse the following morning were two bicycles propped up against the stone wall.

She looked around, but there was no sign of Annie, so she went up to the bicycle which had a front basket only and dropped her bag into the basket. Then she moved the bicycle slightly forward and squeezed the brakes. Satisfied that they would work if she needed them, she balanced the bicycle back against the wall. Straightening up, she glanced towards the front door. Still no Annie.

While waiting, she strolled over the track in front of the farmhouse and across the stretch of grass between the track and the steep slope leading down to the road below.

Standing at the top of the slope, she stared down the hill,

which Annie had told her was called a *côtil*. Neat rows of lush green potato plants striated the slope. Some way to her left, there was a large patch of brown earth where, with her help, the early potatoes had been harvested, and near it, a pile of wooden crates was waiting to be filled with potatoes.

That means more grading, she thought. But not by her. Not that day.

That day she would be in St Helier with Annie, getting to know Annie's haberdashery shop.

Smiling to herself, she stared down the green-carpeted slope to the low stone wall that separated the bottom of the slope from the esplanade. On the other side of the esplanade, beyond a line of trees lay a broad strip of yellow sand, and then the deep blue sea. Across the wide bay, a cluster of roofs on shops and houses gleamed in the morning light.

St Helier. Her destination for the day.

On the expanse of sea between her side of the bay and the far shore on which stood St Helier, the crests of the waves glistened beneath the morning sun, and the pristine white sails of the small yachts crossing the bay caught the light and dazzled against the cloudless blue sky.

She turned to look to her right. The little boats moored in St Aubin's harbour were bobbing up and down on the water.

At the sight of the lush green potato plants at her feet, the broad ribbon of golden sand, the sparkling sea and the numerous small boats, a wave of happiness washed over her. It couldn't be more different from Kentish Town, she thought in delight. And that's what she'd wanted.

Her spirits soared. It was going to be all right, she thought. It might take a little effort, but she'd get used to the work, and she'd find a way to pace herself that left her with some energy for the evening.

She would start by allowing herself to think only about what she liked about her new life, and she would ban any thoughts about what she didn't.

Also, she'd have a word with Tom and ask him to find a way of balancing his day so that he had some time in the evening with her when he wasn't too tired to talk. They couldn't carry on as if they were still single. Now that they were sharing their lives, each needed to make time for the other.

She turned to go back to the farmhouse. As she did so, she caught sight of a narrow sandy path to her right further along on the *côtil*. Pausing, she followed it with her eyes as it wound down the slope to the esplanade. She looked back to the top of the path and saw that it started a little way past the front door of the cottage.

It was perfectly placed, she thought happily. Once they'd moved into their house, if it all became too much for her, as it had done a few times recently, and she felt the need to escape the farm, she'd be able to slip off without everyone seeing her. It would be better to do that than hide away somewhere, wallowing in self-pity, and shedding tears that she wouldn't want Tom or his family to see.

Feeling more cheerful than she had felt for some time, she went back across the track to the bicycles. At the same moment, Annie came out of the farmhouse. Seeing Rose approach, she stood still and smiled broadly.

'I'm so glad you're here!' she exclaimed in obvious pleasure. 'I was worried you might have changed your mind. And what's more, you're still smiling. I'm more pleased than I can say.'

'From now on, Annie, I'm focusing only on what I like. I

like living on an attractive farm owned by lovely people, with beautiful scenery outside the front door, and fresh eggs every day. I like being about to go to a haberdashery shop, which I very much want to see. And I like being able to ride a bicycle alongside the sea. You can't do that in London!'

Annie laughed. 'No, you can't.'

'I guessed that one was yours,' Rose said, pointing to the bicycle which had two wicker baskets, one fixed to the handlebars and one behind the saddle, 'so I took the other.'

'You guessed right,' Annie said. and she put her handbag into the front basket and a carrier bag into the one at the back. She glanced at the light cardigan Rose was wearing over her green cotton dress. 'I know it's a lovely morning, but when we cycle near the water, the wind can be fairly sharp. Should you wear something warmer, d'you think?'

'I'm sure I'll be fine, thanks,' Rose said.

'We'll go slowly,' Annie said, wheeling her bicycle to the track. 'There's no rush. Kathleen went in early and opened up for me. I had a quick word with her last night,' she added, 'and she admitted she wasn't being fair to you. I think you'll find her a different person today. Right, let's go, shall we?'

'IT'S LOVELY, ANNIE,' Rose said as she moved from one glass cabinet to the next, a touch of surprise in her voice. 'When Tom said you had a little shop, I was thinking it would be really small, with very little room for display. But I couldn't have been more wrong. This is amazing.'

She gave Annie a wry smile. 'To be honest, I feel quite envious of you,' she went on. 'There's a lot of shop, and it's laid out in such an attractive way. I love the mahogany everywhere, and the drawers of haberdashery items under the glass counters, and all those bales of textiles on the wall shelves. And it's such a good idea to have one or two chairs where people can sit. And I love the idea of the clothes rail. Are they second-hand?' she asked, fingering a lilac silk dress hanging from the wooden rail in the centre of the shop.

Annie nodded. 'All of them are. I don't make a big thing of it, but it's got around that if someone has clothes in an excellent condition that aren't needed any longer, I'll sell them and share the takings with the person whose clothes they were.'

'That's such a good idea,' Rose said.

'It certainly means that there's plenty going on in the shop, and Kathleen's help is invaluable.' Annie smiled at Kathleen, who was wiping the counter with a cloth.

'What's upstairs?' Rose asked, looking up at the floor above, which was reached by a mahogany staircase at the side of the shop.

'More textiles,' Annie said. 'I'd like to do more with the upstairs area, but for that Kathleen and I would need extra help. The hours we can spend in the shop are limited as we also have to work on the farm. As you're finding out,' she added with a dry smile. 'Emily has helped on occasions when we were very busy, but she doesn't really know anything about haberdashery.'

'I hope you'll let me help,' Rose said quickly. 'Had I stayed in England, I would have carried on managing Father's shops. He's got three now, but is planning to open at least two more.'

Annie smiled. 'So Tom said. That's kind of you, Rose; thank you. I was hoping you'd offer.' She glanced at her watch. 'Oh, dear. Time's moving on, and I'll be late for my bank appointment if I don't go now. I won't be long. Carry on looking around while I'm gone, and ask Kathleen anything you want to know. I'm sure she'll be happy to answer any questions you have.'

With a nod at them both, she went out.

For a long moment, neither Rose nor Kathleen moved.

Then Rose went across to the wooden railing and started looking again at the dresses. At the same time, Kathleen stepped out from behind the counter and went across to a door under the staircase.

She hesitated a moment. 'I'm going to make myself a coffee. Mother and I usually have a cup at around this time. You can have one, too, if you want,' she muttered ungraciously. 'It doesn't take long to make. We grind the beans at home and bring them with us.'

Rose looked up from the dress she was holding. 'Thank you,' she said, in pleased surprise. 'I'd like that.'

'Put a second chair behind the counter then,' Kathleen said, and she opened the door and disappeared.

Not long afterwards, she returned with two cups of coffee. 'I've put milk in yours as I noticed you take it like that,' she said handing a cup to Rose, who was sitting on one of the chairs behind the counter.

Rose nodded. 'So do you, I believe.' She took a sip of her drink. 'That's nice. You make a good cup of coffee.' She put her clean handkerchief on the counter and stood her cup on top of it. 'Obviously, you like haberdashery. D'you sew as well?'

'We don't have to make small talk, you know,' Kathleen snapped. 'I'm sure you haven't the slightest interest in my hobbies.'

Rose raised her eyebrows. 'You're right about that. And if I'd had any interest before, I'd have even less now. But we've got to be seen to be talking about something when your mother returns, and that seemed as good a subject as any.'

'To you, maybe, but not to me. I've a far better subject in mind. And it's a pretty obvious one. Since you got here, you've gone about the place with a face like a wet weekend. So when're you going back to England?'

Rose glared at her. 'I'm not. And if that's what you were hoping for by being so unfriendly, you're in for a big disappointment.'

Kathleen laughed scornfully. 'You're the one in for the disappointment. Tom will have seen the expression on your face, too, and if you think he'll put up with your attitude towards the farm for long, you're mistaken. And don't think he'll let you escape farm work by coming to the shop, because he won't. The farm always comes first with him and Dad. The shop's a long way behind.'

'I know that. But I love Tom and I'll get on top of what I have to do. You'll see.'

She finished her coffee without speaking, then went to the other end of the counter, where she started looking at the contents in the different drawers.

Kathleen picked up the coffee cups and took them back to the room beneath the stairs.

So Kathleen's unfriendliness was a ploy to make her go back to England, was it, Rose thought. Well, she was going to fail. And in a strange way, knowing what lay behind Kathleen's open hostility was going to help her.

It was true that she'd had moments recently when she'd wondered if she could be strong enough to leave Tom and return to her life in England, despite loving him deeply. But every time, she'd known that a day filled with work she didn't enjoy was still infinitely better than life without Tom.

But after what Kathleen had just said, she must put all thoughts of England behind her. It was an indulgence, and it was making her sad. Life in England lay in the past; her life in Jersey with Tom was her future.

She'd make sure that she had a smile on her face at all times, no matter what she might be feeling underneath. She could do it. It was just another challenge in a life during which she'd already encountered several difficult challenges.

Trying to keep her mother's attention for herself had been her first challenge.

She'd been born a few months after her father had gone to fight, but because of the war, he hadn't come home until she was almost four. For her first four years, therefore, it had been just her and her mother.

It had been strange and unpleasant suddenly to have a father in her life. She'd been angry with him that she wasn't allowed to sleep in her mother's bed any longer, which she'd got into the habit of doing as the wartime noises at night had been frightening.

And she had resented having to share her mother's attention, especially as he seemed to have the larger part of it. It had only been much later that she'd come to understand that he was often in a lot of pain with his wounded leg and needed her mother's help.

She had also resented not being allowed to go to the haberdashery shop anymore. While her father was away fighting, her mother would take her to the shop with her. As her mother was running everything by herself, she'd find something for Rose to do, even if it was just copying the picture on a dress pattern.

But when her father returned, he said that the shop was no place for young children, and he forbad her mother to take her there. Instead, he paid one of the neighbours to look after her in the daytime until she started school. She very much missed the hours they used to spend together, just her and her mother.

Her second challenge had been to draw her father's attention away from her two younger sisters, and to focus it on her.

By the time that Violet and Iris were born, the family had moved into Allcroft Road, close to her father's shops. Unlike when she was born, her father was able to watch them grow up from the start. He clearly adored them, and the contrast between the way he was with her sisters and the way he had been with her was huge.

When she'd been little, he had always been working, even when the shop was closed. He had never had any time to stop and play with her. But it was different with Violet and Iris: he was never too busy to wrestle with them in the garden or join in their water fights.

She had seen the way he was with her sisters and had grown increasingly determined to make him like her as much as he liked them. And when she saw how pleased he was whenever she asked anything about the shop, she realised that the shop would be the way to win his affection. From then on, she frequently offered to help in the shop, and she started to learn all she could about the business.

Not a natural needlewoman, she hadn't been keen on haberdashery at first, but the more she had learnt about it, the more caught up in the business she had become.

Her father had been so pleased at the interest she showed, and that she seemed to have a flair for haberdashery, unlike Violet and Iris, that he started to notice her, and to want to sit in the evenings with her and talk about the shop.

That challenge, she'd won.

The challenge of not letting Kathleen get to her was

going to be easy by comparison. And in addition, if a suitable occasion presented itself, she wouldn't hesitate to get her own back on Kathleen for being so unwelcoming and so unpleasant.

It was just a shame that convincing Tom and his parents that she was happy doing farm work would necessitate smiling daily in the face of mountains of potatoes, she thought ruefully. But if every time she saw a crate of potatoes waiting for her to grade them, she thought of Kathleen, it wouldn't be hard to look cheerful as she reached for the nearest Jersey Royal.

Feeling Kathleen's dislike of her weighting the air, she started to hum a little tune.

11

L *ater that evening*

HEARING the sitting room door open, Rose looked up from her knitting as Annie came in. Annie closed the door behind her, and hesitated.

'May I join you?' Annie asked.

Rose smiled. 'Of course,' she said, and lowered her knitting needles as Annie sat in the armchair opposite her.

'You prefer being down here rather than in your sitting room upstairs, do you?' Annie asked.

'If Tom was with me, I'd want to sit up there with him. But when I'm on my own, it feels less lonely to be down here.'

Annie nodded. 'I can understand that.'

'But I'm surprised to see you in here,' Rose remarked. 'I thought you'd gone upstairs.'

'No, not yet. With William and Tom out in the barn,

seeing how many potatoes still need planting, and Kathleen up in her room, I thought we could have a little chat.'

Rose pulled a face. 'That sounds ominous.' She put her knitting wool and needles on the table next to her.

Annie smiled. 'It isn't meant to be. What're you knitting?'

'Just a tea cosy. It's for the teapot when we're in our house.'

'What a good idea.' Annie settled more comfortably. 'No, it's just that although you and Kathleen were making a good show of getting on with each other when I got back to the shop this morning, and also at the table this evening, I know Kathleen well enough to know that that's all it was—a show. I'd hoped that by leaving you girls alone this morning, you might start talking to each other, and that if you did, you'd find things you had in common. But I seem to have been wrong.'

'I was ready to be friends, but Kathleen wasn't.'

'Well, I'm afraid you're both going to have to find a way to get on,' Annie said bluntly. 'It looks as if the cottage will be ready for you to move into next week, but even then, you'll still be part of the farm and we'll all be working together, often under pressure. No one can afford to be at loggerheads with anyone.'

'And I don't want to be. It's Kathleen who won't be friends, not me. She's ignored what you said to her before we went to the shop. I'd been looking forward to having a sister here, with Violet and Iris miles away, and I'm really disappointed that she's so hostile. It's because she wants me to go back to England, presumably to leave the way clear for Emily.'

'I do apologise for her. I can see how unfair she's being.'

'Perhaps she'll mellow when Tom and I are next door.

After all, she won't be forced to see me every time she has a meal.'

Annie nodded. 'I hope so. In the meantime, I'll have another word with her about her attitude. Things must improve. But talking of meals, the reason I actually came in here was to ask you if you'd mind if we invited the Gorins to lunch on Sunday. We used to see them a lot, but have hardly done so since Tom got back. Apart from Kathleen, that is. She's up at their farm whenever she doesn't have any chores to do here. And often when she does,' she added with a wry smile. 'They must be getting fed up with seeing her.'

Rose laughed.

'And Emily hasn't been here at all since Tom's return,' Annie continued. 'If we leave it much longer, things could start to feel quite awkward.'

'Of course I don't mind,' Rose said. 'I'm actually looking forward to meeting Emily.'

'And it's time you did. She's a sweet girl and I'm sure you'll like her. She's not the sort to dwell on any disappointment she might've felt. If Kathleen sees the two of you getting on, it might soften her towards you. Anyway,' Annie said, standing up. 'That's all I came to say. I'll have a word with Kathleen tomorrow.'

'And I'll do all I can to make her feel more friendly towards me,' Rose said with a bright smile.

'Many thanks, Rose,' Annie said, and she left the room.

As the door closed behind Annie, Rose's smile faded.

'To what do I owe this unwelcome visit?' Kathleen asked icily as she opened her bedroom door and saw Rose standing there.

'Blame your mother,' Rose said, walking past Kathleen

and into her room. She sat down on the stool in front of Kathleen's dressing table, her back to the mirror. 'She spoke to me a few minutes ago, and told me that our performance today hadn't fooled her. She's determined we've got to get on.'

Kathleen closed the door and perched on the end of her bed. 'So what did you tell her?'

'That I understand the importance of harmony on the farm and that I'll do my best. But as both of us have got to want this, and you don't, it's unlikely to happen. I miss my sisters and I would have loved you to be a sort of sister to me, but you obviously don't want that.'

'If we'd grown up together, like Emily and I did, it would've been different. We'd have swapped clothes and told each other girlie secrets, and so on. But we didn't, and now it's too late for all that. Emily's like a sister to me, and I don't need anyone else. Certainly not someone who's made such a mess of their life.'

'You might not like me being here, but that doesn't make my life a mess.'

Kathleen inched herself back and leaned against the wall. 'That's a matter of opinion. The future will show which of us is right. You're doing the reverse of what my dad and Tom did. But it's one thing to live somewhere else for several months, quite another for a lifetime. You think you'll get used to living here, and start to enjoy the life, but you won't.'

'I'll see that I do.'

Kathleen gave a scornful laugh. 'It's not something you can *will*! So far, you've seen only the tip of the iceberg.'

'I won't have to make that many adjustments. We'll be in our own house, so we'll do some things my way, and some yours.'

'The reality is, you'll be only minutes away and you'll be

over here for most of the day, every day. That's because, apart from the vegetable garden, which you'll be expected to look after, and a few chickens, too, this is where the work is.'

'You've forgotten the shop,' Rose cut in. 'Your mother said she could use my help. I expect I'll often go into St Helier.'

'I doubt you will. You'll only go if you're not needed here, and that won't happen a lot. Your routine, like ours, will be built around the needs of the farm.' She paused. 'Believe me, Rose,' she said, her voice slightly softer. 'I genuinely think you'll always be unhappy here.'

'And this is nothing to do with the fact that you've had Tom's attention all your life,' Rose countered, 'but you've got to share it now, and you don't like that?'

Kathleen's voice hardened once more. 'I'd have willingly shared it with Emily. Emily's right for him, and you're not.'

'And I suspect you're worried that your mother might want me in the shop, rather than you,' Rose went on. 'Tom said you didn't like farm work, so you'd obviously prefer to be in the town.'

'You can be sure that Mother will give me my share. She's *my* mother, not yours.'

'So that's it, is it? You're determined to continue as you were, despite upsetting your mother and everyone else in the family?'

Kathleen shrugged. 'That's it in a nutshell. I'll avoid you as much as I can. If we meet, I'll be polite, but don't expect any more than that. And don't think that once you've moved out, you can slope off when you should be working. If you don't pull your weight I'll make sure that everyone knows it. And you can count on Tom being really mad at you.'

Rose stood up. 'I'll settle for politeness. I'm no keener on spending time with you, than you are with me.'

And she walked out, leaving the door wide open.

Had she looked back, she would have seen that Kathleen was watching her go, a satisfied smile on her face.

SITTING ON HER BED, Kathleen pulled her knees up to her chin. It had been an inspired idea to remark to her mother earlier that day, while feigning an anxious look, that she felt bad that they hadn't invited the Gorins for a while, given that she went over there so frequently. She'd added that she'd decided to make them a cake and take it over the following day.

Her mother had instantly taken the bait.

Kathleen was right, she'd said. It had been remiss not to have invited them to lunch soon after Tom's return. And as far as she knew, Tom had been there only once since he'd come back, and she and William were in the same position. They had popped in the day after Tom.

It wasn't good enough, her mother had said. They must try to get things back to the way they were before Tom went to England. She'd give Kathleen a letter to take to the Gorins the next day, inviting them to lunch on Sunday. And then she'd hurried off to the walk-in pantry to check what she needed to buy.

Kathleen stretched out on her back, locked her hands behind her head and stared up at the ceiling.

It was time for Tom to be reminded what lively company Emily could be, how pretty she was, and how much she knew about the work on a farm. The farm would be the main topic of conversation, she'd make sure. She'd only have to introduce the subject once, and Tom and her father, and Emily's father, too, would do the rest. Emily could easily hold her own in any conversation about farming.

Rose would have nothing to contribute.

It was impossible that Tom, besotted though he seemed to be, would fail to notice the difference between Rose and Emily, and he must surely wonder if he'd been rash to have married at such haste.

That's all it would take—one little seed of doubt, planted by her, which could be watered and made to grow.

And Emily would do the watering.

She'd invite Emily to come back the day after the lunch, at the time Tom often came in for a coffee. It would ostensibly be for a proper catch-up, but in reality it'd be to build on the positive impression she'd have made the day before.

It was an infallible plan, Kathleen thought, and she smiled up at the ceiling.

12

T*he following Sunday*

SEEING Annie starting to clear away the pudding plates, Rose picked up the glass serving bowl in the centre of the table and stood up.

'There seem to be a couple of spoons of trifle left,' she said with a smile. 'Can I tempt anyone?'

George Gorin leaned back and patted his stomach. 'I'd love to volunteer, but I just couldn't eat another thing,' he said. 'According to Annie, you made the trifle, Rose. Lucky you, Tom.' He smiled at Tom. 'Your wife's an excellent cook.'

'Yes, she is,' Tom said, beaming at Rose.

Rose laughed. 'Hm. I'm not so sure about that. It would be difficult to wreck a trifle—you just throw in everything you've got. More complicated dishes require skills that I'm sorely lacking, as Tom will find out all too soon, I fear.'

She smiled down at him.

'As I could do with losing a little weight,' he said, grinning up at her, 'that's fine by me.'

'How long is it since you moved into your house, Tom?' Martha Gorin asked as Rose took the bowl over to the sink.

'Just two days,' he told her. 'Mum and Dad have been amazingly generous with their help. When everything's straightened out, the three of you must come and visit. We'd like that, wouldn't we, Rose?' He smiled at her as she returned to the table with a small bowl of sugar and a jug of milk.

Rose nodded. 'Definitely.'

Martha smiled. 'We'd love to.'

'My house-moving gift to Rose was a new pair of gardening gloves,' Kathleen said, with a little laugh. 'I thought the old ones must've worn thin as she seemed reluctant to pull up any potatoes.'

She threw a sly smile at Emily.

'It's hard work, growing potatoes,' George said, shifting slightly to face Rose. 'And very different from what you're used to, I imagine. Kathleen's been telling us how difficult you're finding everything, and how miserable the work's been making you.'

'Miserable!' Tom exclaimed. He turned anxiously to Rose. 'I didn't know that, Rose. That's awful. You should've told me. I feel really bad that I didn't realise it.'

'Kathleen's mistaken, Tom,' Rose said quickly. 'I'm fine.'

'There'd be no reason to be ashamed if things were getting on top of you,' George said reassuringly. 'It takes a while to get used to our sort of life, and you've been here no time at all. You used to work in your father's haberdashery stores, I believe. Indeed, you helped to run them, William said. Farm work's a far cry from that.'

Swallowing her anger with Kathleen, and forcing a

warm smile to her face, Rose said, 'It's very kind of Kathleen to be so anxious about me, and she's right that I'm finding the farm work tiring, as I'm sure anyone new to it would. I'm used to working hard and for long hours, but not as long as these, and the work I did wasn't so back-breaking. But being tired is very different from being miserable.'

Martha cut in. 'We realised that, dear, but after hearing what Kathleen was saying, we'd like to suggest that Emily comes over every day this week to help you harvest the potatoes. We've fewer potatoes, so we can easily spare her. We benefit enough from Kathleen's help, so it's the least we can do.'

'What!' Emily exclaimed.

'It's very kind of you, Mrs Gorin,' Rose began.

Martha leaned forward. 'Please do call us Martha and George, dear. And I think you're old enough now, Tom, to do that too, don't you?'

'Thank you,' Rose said. 'That's very kind of you.' She continued as if she hadn't heard Emily, nor seen the look of horror she'd thrown at Kathleen. 'But such kindness isn't really necessary,' she said. 'The work is certainly different from what I'm used to, but how could I be miserable, living among such a lovely family, with Tom for a husband, in a beautiful house on a gorgeous island?'

She beamed around the table. 'I couldn't be further from unhappiness. I'm finding the work easier all the time, and I can truthfully say that I'm starting to enjoy it.'

'That *is* good to hear, Rose,' William said heartily.

She felt the warmth of Tom's smile and turned to him, took the hand he stretched out to her, and squeezed it.

'I think I might have reached this stage earlier if I'd known how delicious the finished product was,' she added with a laugh. 'I've never had potatoes as wonderful as the ones Annie serves. It makes all the hard work worthwhile. But—' She directed a wide smile at Emily and Martha, 'if you're still happy to send Emily for at least a day or so, I should love to get to know her.'

Surreptitiously, Rose glanced at Kathleen. Kathleen was scowling down at her plate.

Her smile became even wider.

'Of course, Emily can still come over here, even if it isn't the mission of mercy we thought it would be,' Martha said. 'If she'd like to, that is.'

Rose saw Kathleen frown warningly at Emily.

'I'd have loved to,' Emily said quickly. 'But it's not the best week. I've several things on that I can't change.'

Kathleen smiled at Emily in quiet satisfaction.

'To go back to the subject of potatoes, Rose,' George said. 'William will have told you, I'm sure, that we have a secret ingredient, the Jersey seaweed called *vraic*.' And he explained to her what William had already told her.

Rose nodded. 'Yes, he did. It's hard to think of seaweed in such a positive way. I always think of the seaweed we used to find on the beaches when we were little. Long green strands of slime that stuck to your legs when you went in the water. We used to squeal in horror.' She wrinkled her nose in disgust.

He laughed.

'I'm sorry to have taken so long with the coffee,' Annie said, coming to the table carrying a tray with a large pot of coffee and cups and saucers. She put everything on the table, returned the tray to the kitchen area, came back and sat down.

She picked up the coffee pot. 'When I've poured the coffee, will you pass the cups along, Kathleen, please?' she said. 'And from now on,' she added firmly, 'any mention of potatoes or *vraic* is banned. Poor Rose will think that's all we ever talk about. Perhaps one of you, Kathleen or Emily, could start the ball rolling by telling us if there are any dances coming up in Sion Hall. Are there?'

LEAVING ROSE, Annie and Martha to clear the table, Tom, William and George headed for the glass frames to see how the new plants were doing.

Kathleen and Emily slipped into the hall and went quietly out through the back door into the yard and across to the fields behind the barns. Leaning against the wooden fence, they contemplated the cows grazing, their fawn coats shining in the sun.

'I'm glad my dad's followed the example of yours and gone over to mechanical milking,' Kathleen said. 'It's so much easier than having to hand-milk them in the barn or the fields twice a day.'

'That's true. But I do miss the feeling of their warm breath on me when I was sitting close to them, perched on my little three-legged stool, and I miss the low mooing they made, and the way the milk swished as I squirted it into the bucket.'

Kathleen nodded. 'But I bet you don't miss the early rising.'

'No, I certainly don't,' Emily said fervently, and they both looked back at the cows.

'Well?' Kathleen asked after a few minutes' companionable silence. 'What did you think of dear Rose?'

Emily shrugged. 'Well, I wasn't going to like her, was I, seeing that she's got Tom? But if it hadn't been for that, I might've liked her. She seems to feel quite settled, which was a surprise after what you've said, so that's that.'

'It doesn't have to be a case of that's that, though, does it? Everything I said about her still holds true. You didn't believe what she said today, did you? She was trying to make me look silly. The truth is, she loathes farm work. You should see her expression when she doesn't think anyone's looking! She won't be able to keep the act up indefinitely, and you and Tom could still get married.'

Emily turned round. She leaned back against the fence and looked at Kathleen. 'Unfortunately, I don't think that'll ever happen,' she said steadily. 'You made me think so at first by what you said, but now I've met her, I know I was wrong. Even if she hates it here, no one would know it from what she does or says. My parents think she's telling the truth. And what's more, I can tell they like her. My father was still a bit against her when we set off, but she's clearly won him over.'

'That's an exaggeration, don't you think?'

'No, it isn't. Usually, he never says much, but today he went on and on about potatoes and *vraic*. He only does that with people he likes.'

Kathleen giggled. "It sounds more like a punishment for those he *doesn't* like.'

Emily laughed, then became more serious. 'It's obvious that Rose isn't stupid. Your mother likes her, and if Rose dislikes farming as much as you think she does, she'll manipulate your mother into letting her work in the shop as often as possible. And why not? She knows far more about haberdashery than we do. So Rose will end up doing the work she enjoys, and she won't be going anywhere.'

'Suppose you're mistaken?'

Emily shook her head. 'I don't think I am. And there's Tom, too. I hate to say it, but he's nuts about her. And she'd have left long ago if she wasn't genuinely keen on him. She's here to stay, Kathleen, and we just have to accept it.'

'I think it's too soon to give in,' Kathleen said stubbornly.

'I don't. And I don't want to live my life trying to bring about something I think very unlikely to happen. It would be madness. And it would stop me from finding someone for myself.' She paused. 'I suppose I'll have to accept Paul's invitation to take me to the next dance at Sion Hall,' she said with a slight sigh.

Kathleen straightened up. 'Paul Mauger!' she exclaimed.

'Yes, that Paul. He's not Tom, but he's all right. His brother's very nice, too. You used to be quite keen on Josh. And he's even better looking than he used to be. From comments he's made, I think he really likes you and wishes you were still together. I'm sure he'd ask you to a dance if you weren't so cool towards him.'

Kathleen pulled a face. 'Joshua's keen on anyone in a skirt. He's got to be one of the biggest flirts on the island. I'd be a fool to take him seriously again. He wasn't interested in settling down before, and I'm sure he's not changed that much.'

Emily shrugged. 'What's the alternative? If we want to get married, and I certainly do, they're the best of the ones we've met.'

THE GORINS HAD LONG GONE and the afternoon light was starting to fade when Rose knocked on Kathleen's bedroom door.

'Oh, it's you,' Kathleen said, scowling when she opened the door. 'I thought it was Mum.'

'Tom and I are about to go back to the cottage and I wanted a quick word first.'

'That's more like twenty words. So now you're done, you can go.'

Rose went into the room and closed the door behind her.

'I know what you were trying to do today,' she said, 'and I can tell by how sullen you were for the rest of the day that you know you failed. That was really nasty of you. You're determined not to like me. And I'm sure it won't surprise you that I could never like anyone as mean-spirited as you. It's a shame, but you'll never feel like a sister to me.'

Kathleen glared at her. 'I'm glad you've got the message at last.'

'You can be sure that I have,' she said coldly. 'Now that Tom and I are next door, you and I will only need to meet when it comes to work on the farm or in the shop, and perhaps the occasional meal with your parents. When we do, I'll be friendly towards you, rather than upset the others, and I hope you'll be pleasant to me for the same reason. But it'll be on the surface only.'

She turned and went out, closing the door firmly behind her.

Well, that was one challenge won, she thought in triumph as she ran lightly down the stairs. Kathleen's face had been a picture when she'd realised that both sets of parents and Tom believed that she was actually enjoying her work on the farm.

Her next challenge now was to make good her words and actually try to enjoy the work.

But she could forget all that for what was left of the day, and for the following day. Before Tom had gone back to the cottage, he'd told her that they were going to have the next day off and would be spending it together.

They were going to take a picnic with them, he'd said,

which Annie was going to prepare, and go first to La Corbière Lighthouse, then to St Ouen's Bay. They would eat their picnic in the dunes that ran alongside the sea, a favourite place of his.

It would be just the two of them. She couldn't wait!

13

T *he following day*

THEY PUSHED their bicycles up the side of the hill until they finally reached the top.

Panting heavily, they left their bicycles lying on the grass, the wheels spinning, and went close to the edge of the steep slope that led down to the sea. With their arms around each other, they stared across a line of rocks to the concrete lighthouse.

A lonely shape that gleamed creamy white in the morning sun, the lighthouse topped a cluster of jagged rocks that soared up from the intensely blue sea, lashed on all sides by a fury of waves that surged relentlessly forward in a frenzy of effervescent white foam.

Looking down at the foot of the stony slope on which they were standing, they watched the sea pound with violence against the shining wet rocks, sending up spray after misty spray, each one higher than the one before.

Instinctively, they took a step back.

'So that's La Corbière lighthouse,' Rose said. 'It's stunning.'

Tom nodded. 'It's certainly dramatic.'

'What does Corbière mean?' she asked.

'The haunt of the crow, which is a bird of ill omen. It's not hard to see where the name came from. Ships used to founder on the rocks here, so there'll always be a sense of danger associated with the place.'

'When did they build the lighthouse?'

'In 1870. Large numbers of steam-packets had started coming this way from the south of England as it's a much shorter route to France. To stop them from being wrecked, they built the lighthouse. It's safer for ships now, but not necessarily for people.'

'What d'you mean?'

'If the tide's out, you can walk across the causeway to the lighthouse. But the tide comes in swiftly and silently, and people have been caught out.'

'That's a scary thought,' she said with a shudder. 'But it does look lovely.'

'And so does our next destination, but in a different way. We're going over there.' He turned slightly and pointed to the right. She followed the direction of his gaze to see a huge expanse of sea and sand that stretched as far as eye could see.

'That's St Ouen's Bay,' he said. 'You'll find the cycling easier as we'll obviously be going downhill to get there.'

'I like the sound of that,' she said laughing. 'And I'm looking forward to seeing another bay.'

'You'll find it very different from St Aubin's Bay. Windswept and desolate are the words I think of when I think of St Ouen's Bay. It's very long and quite spectacular. But the water's treacherous and no one should swim there unless they're familiar with the undercurrents and are strong swimmers. I'd never swim there. Too risky.'

'Are we eating on the beach?'

He shook his head. 'No, among the sand dunes, I thought.'

'Good thinking. The dunes will shelter us from the wind.'

Tom nodded. 'That's right. We'll easily find a good spot as there're miles of sand dunes covered by clumps of grass and sedge. I love it there. In the right season, you'll see birds and butterflies, dandelions and buttercups and masses of wildflowers, but you'll hardly ever see another person. I've not been back since I returned, but in the past, if I needed a few hours away from the cows or potatoes, that's where I would go.'

'I'm looking forward to seeing it up close,' she said. 'And I can't wait to find out what Annie's made for our lunch. I'm quite hungry now.'

He grinned at her. 'That makes two of us! Let's go, then.' He held out his hand. She took it, and swinging their entwined hands, they returned to their bicycles.

'I'M FULL,' she said happily, inhaling the salty tang of the sea that melded with the coconut scent thrown out by the patches of gorse that grew on the dunes. 'I shouldn't have had a second piece of ginger cake. But I couldn't resist—it was delicious.'

Smiling, she leaned forward, clasped her hands round her knees and stared out at the miles of sea that swept away from the sand until it became one with the sky.

'I love it here, Tom. It feels so remote, but it isn't really—it's not that far from where we live. And it feels private, as if it's just you and me alone in the world.'

Lying on his side, he propped himself up on his elbow and looked at her. 'I know just what you mean, Rose. We should have more time alone together like this, and I intend to make sure that we do in the future. But to come back to the present, you mentioned privacy,' he said, his voice taking on a note of amusement. 'Indeed, it's so private that there's nothing to stop us from doing whatever we want. And when I look at you, I know what I want very much to do.'

She turned towards him. Her gaze took in the fair hair falling across his forehead, the crinkles at the corners of smiling blue eyes, the skin that was bronzed from hours spent in sun-drenched fields, the ripples of muscle in the hard chest showing through the open neck of his shirt, and she felt a yearning ache deep in her stomach.

'D'you think we dare?' she whispered, lying down next to him.

'Oh, yes, I do,' he said, his voice thick with emotion.

Laughing, she pulled her lightweight blue jumper up over her head, tossed it across to the nearest dune, and slid her white cotton shorts down her hips.

THEY LAY BACK on the sand, gazing up at the cerulean sky, their bodies close to each other, his arm around her shoulders, her hand lightly against his chest.

'There's not a single cloud,' she murmured. 'I know it's

only late May, but it feels like midsummer. It was such a great idea to come here. Thank you so much for thinking of it, Tom. I've loved every minute of today.'

'It's actually Kathleen you should thank,' he said wryly. 'It wasn't till I heard what she said to the Gorins that I realised I'd been neglecting you.'

She turned her head to look at him. 'No, you hadn't,' she said. 'You were doing what you had to do, which was looking after the farm. Kathleen was mistaken.'

'Was she, though?' Tom asked.

Two blue eyes pierced her, and she looked quickly back at the sky.

'It was different in London,' he said, his eyes tracing her profile. 'I didn't have any actual work to do. And as your dad let you take me around, we spent most of the time I was in London together, day and evening, and we weren't tired from hours of work.'

She smiled at him. 'I know,' she said. 'And it was wonderful. Like today's been.'

'But now I'm home,' he continued, tightening his hold on her, 'it's different. I've got things I must do every day. For example, the cows have to be milked early in the morning, when it's still dark, and again in the evening. Animals don't know the difference between a weekday or the weekend, so I don't get the weekend off. I forgot you wouldn't have known this.'

'If I'd given it any thought, I would have realised it. It was silly of me. Not that it would have altered anything,' she added hastily. 'I would've still wanted to marry you. I just would have been more prepared.'

'There's no reason why it should've occurred to you. Your father spends his evenings with you all, and Sundays, too, so you'll have expected us to do the same here. But we can't. I knew that, and I should have eased back into farm life more slowly, making sure I had time in the day to spend with you.'

'You mustn't think like that, Tom,' she said, nestling closer to him. 'Whatever I found when I got here, it was always going to be all right in the end—it's just that it's taken a little more adjusting than we'd assumed it would. But if you love someone as much as I love you, you know you'll be able to make it work. And I do love you, Tom.'

He pulled her to him and hugged her hard, before looking into her face. 'And then there's Kathleen.'

Her brow wrinkled. 'What about her?'

'Well, when we got here, I know you were looking forward to the two of you being good friends. I'm sure you've done your best to get on with her, but even a blind person can see that you're miles apart. And that's Kathleen's fault.'

'"Fault" is a bit strong. You like someone or you don't. And she doesn't like me. I'm afraid it must have shown. Whenever there're people around, we've been trying to look as if we get on with each other. But if you've picked up that we don't, then obviously we've failed.'

'I'm not sure you have. You've done a great job of hiding it and I don't know that I would have guessed if Kathleen hadn't made those comments at lunch yesterday. If she'd been genuinely concerned about you, she would have come to me, or she'd have gone to Mum and Dad. That she didn't spoke volumes. She was clearly out to cause trouble. So after that, I watched you more closely when you were together. I've seen you with your sisters, and it was soon clear to me that the two of you were playing a part.'

'I hope that'll change with time,' Rose said. 'But even if it doesn't, it won't affect the way I feel about your parents, who are lovely, or about you, who are absolutely everything I could ever want.'

'I don't know what someone as wonderful as you can see in me,' he said, and he buried his face in her hair.

'Then let me help.' Her voice carried a smile. 'I love the way you feel about your home, your family and your work. They all mean a lot to you. Not everyone can say that. We're the lucky ones—you, because you love your work, and me, because I'm married to someone with such a good heart and attitude, someone I love more than I can say.' She kissed his cheek.

'Nevertheless,' he said after a moment or two, 'I've been spending too little time with you in the week and that's going to change. And I'm going to ask Mum to give you more time in the shop and less on the farm. We'll manage. If necessary we'll take on a girl for a few hours each week on the farm—the extra money you take in the shop would help with that. It would be a better balance of work for you and it would be good for Mum to have someone else in the shop who knows what they're doing.'

'You don't have to alter anything,' she told him. 'As I said, I'm finding it easier now.'

'But I want to,' he insisted.

He raised himself on his elbow and looked down into her face. 'I love you, Rose, and I want you to feel that love every minute of every day. Actually,' he said, breaking into a smile, 'we could make a start on you feeling my love right now. If you felt up to it again, that is.'

She giggled. 'It's funny you should say that,' she said, and she rolled on to her back, stretched her arms out wide and gazed up at him.

Laughing, he positioned himself above her. She put a hand on either side of his head and inched his face slowly down to hers. When his mouth was about to meet her lips, she paused, and held his head still.

'I must get the recipe for your mother's ginger cake if this is the effect it has,' she murmured.

And she slid her hands behind his head and brought his face down to hers.

14

London, September 1939

'Well, our customers seemed cheerful today, despite what's been happening these past weeks, and even though we still don't know the outcome of the ultimatum to Hitler,' John told Violet and Iris as he entered the sitting room, followed by Mabel.

He sat down in his armchair and smiled broadly at the two girls.

'Yes, the shops are thriving,' he continued. 'Yesterday's takings made it one of our best days for a long time. Now that Chamberlain seems to have avoided a war, and everyone's confident that Hitler will do as he's been asked, the mood has lifted. And that's despite the fact that they've introduced a blackout.'

'The mood most definitely has,' Mabel said, sitting down opposite John. 'I'm hoping we'll hear that Hitler's agreed to the ultimatum before we have our Sunday lunch.'

John nodded. 'Me, too. When we do, it might be time to give a bit of thought to the future. I know the depot's full, but I'm wondering whether I shouldn't get in more stock.'

'But where would you store it?' Mabel asked.

'In Rose's room. Just as a temporary measure.'

'That could be a little premature, Father,' Violet said, looking up from her book. 'Nobody knows if Hitler will agree to withdraw from Poland.'

'But most people seem to think he *will*,' John said, with a reassuring smile. 'That's what we sensed this morning.'

Violet raised her eyebrows. 'Really? Well, I for one don't think he will. It said on the Home Service that Germans were bombing Poland and that thousands of their troops had marched in there. And the Government doesn't think he'll withdraw his soldiers, either.'

'You'll alarm your sister for no reason, Violet,' Mabel said. 'You don't know that.'

'I strongly suspect that they aren't fitting anti-gas doors on the Houses of Parliament for fun, or heaping sandbags against the basement windows for the sake of it. And I doubt we've been told to cover our windows with blackout material and criss-cross the windows with tape that'll stop glass from being blown in, just so that we won't be bored.'

'You're so gloomy, Violet,' Iris said with an exaggerated sigh.

'So are the parents of the children who've been evacuated!' Violet retorted. 'I went past the railway station on my way back from the library yesterday. The children standing in groups looked so small, each with their little gas-mask box and a suitcase or pillowcase for their clothes. I felt so sorry for them. People are moving to the coast or into the country as they think they'll be safer there. The situation's more serious than anyone in this room seems to think.'

'Not everyone thinks it's serious,' Iris countered. 'Crowds of people were at the opening games of the football season yesterday. They wouldn't have gone if they'd thought they might be bombed at any minute.'

'I didn't know you were interested in football, Iris,' Mabel remarked in surprise.

Iris giggled. 'I'm not. But the brother of a girl I work with is, and he's rather good-looking. Whenever he meets Doreen from the shop, he always mentions football.'

Mabel exchanged a glance with John. 'On the subject of D.H. Evans,' she began. 'Your father and I think you should hand in your notice and work full time for the shops.'

Iris straightened up. 'Absolutely not! I like going to the West End. It's one thing to help out with a few design ideas and to do a bit of selling in one of the Hams when I'm not in D.H. Evans, but it'd be quite another to be stuck there all of the time.'

'Rose didn't find it too unpleasant,' John said mildly. 'And we aren't exactly in prison here. We can get to Hampstead Heath easily enough, and have a stroll around the lower ponds, or go to Primrose Hill Gardens, like your mother and I have just done.'

'And where is Rose now?' Iris asked. She put her finger to her chin and pretended to think. 'Oh, yes, miles away in Jersey. With beaches and sun. And having a wonderful time.'

'I'm not so sure she is,' Violet said.

Iris groaned. 'The voice of doom speaks again. Honestly, Violet, you never try to see the bright side of things. What makes you think she isn't having a brilliant time? I would if I were there.'

Violet shrugged. 'I think she was really unhappy at first.

While I don't think she is any longer, I don't think she's still completely happy. If that makes sense.'

'It doesn't,' Iris said bluntly.

'Well, in her last letter she said it had been raining a lot. She said that when she washed her hair, she leaned out of the bedroom window and dried it in the sun and the wind. She said she helped Annie plant wallflowers in the garden and she cycled to St Helier with Tom and William to have a look at a couple of local markets.'

'What of it?' Iris asked.

'Yes, what's wrong with that?' John echoed.

Mabel nodded. 'It's who she *doesn't* mention, Violet, isn't it?'

'That's right, Mother. She didn't mention Kathleen and she never does. I know that she and Tom are in their own house now, but they're still on the farm so she must see Kathleen around. You'd think they'd do things together. It's a bit strange that she doesn't write about them.'

'I think you're reading much too much into something she didn't say,' Iris said dismissively. 'If I wrote a letter, I probably wouldn't mention you.'

Violet frowned. 'You might be right. But I'm inclined to think they don't get on and that it's upsetting her.'

'If you're right about her being upset, it could be for a different reason,' John said thoughtfully. 'There's been a lot of war alarmism in the newspapers and on the wireless—'

'And from Violet!' Iris exclaimed.

Violet glared at her.

'And if you recall, back in June, Rose wrote that they were discussing what would happen in the Channel Islands in the event of war,' John went on, ignoring the interruptions. 'She stressed that such discussions weren't common knowledge as they didn't want to worry people, but

William's a good friend of the Bailiff of Jersey, and he was party to some of the conversations.'

Mabel gave a dismissive snort. 'I know what Rose said, but Jersey's such a small, out of the way place that no one would even notice it. What's more, as Tom told us, there're British soldiers on the island,' Mabel said. 'So they're protected.'

John nodded. 'Yes, that's true.'

Violet sat upright. 'It's not all that out of the way. It's very close to France. So close that although English is the main language, Rose said French is still widely spoken in the island. And also a Jersey language, which is a sort of French.'

'Surely it's Poland we're worried about, not France,' Iris said with a touch of impatience.

'You're right, Iris,' John said. 'And we're hopeful that Hitler will recall his troops. Of course, if he doesn't, it becomes a bit complicated.'

Mabel glanced towards the grandfather clock in the corner of the room. 'It's almost a quarter past eleven, John. Switch on the wireless, would you, dear? Let's hear if there's any news yet. Then I'll check the beef and make sure it's browning nicely.'

She went over to the kitchen door and waited there as John moved over to the cabinet next to the fireplace, turned the knob on the wireless and went back to his chair.

Listening in silence, they heard that there had been no response to the ultimatum issued to Hitler. Chamberlain, in weary tones, informed them the country was now at war with Germany.

For a moment, no one spoke.

Then John turned the volume down and looked around the sitting room.

His gaze took in the wooden table that stood between the sofa and armchairs, the fireplace with its dark-green tiled surround, the mantelpiece lined with family photographs, the bookcase to one side of the fireplace, which housed the black plastic telephone, and the oak cabinet on the other side, on which the wireless stood.

He raised his eyes to the wall above the fireplace, to the painting of Hampstead Heath that he and Mabel had bought on an impulse at a time when they'd not really been able to afford it. Then he looked at his wife, standing in the open doorway, her hand to her mouth.

'You look very serious, Daddy,' Iris said, with an anxious look at Violet.

'War *is* serious, Iris,' Violet said quietly.

John nodded. 'Yes, it is. If you want to know, I was wondering whether at the end of it we'll still have a home, or the shops. And more importantly, each other.' He stood up. 'I think a sherry would be in order. I'd like to propose a toast to the past, which has been good to us, and to the success of our country in the future.'

'Can I have one, too?' Iris asked.

'On this occasion, yes.'

John poured a sherry for each of them. Mabel came over and sat down. 'The beef can wait a moment,' she said as she picked up her glass.

The girls and John did the same.

'To our victory,' John said quietly, holding up his glass. They each took a sip of their sherry. 'May it be a short war,' he added, putting his glass back on the table next to him. 'And may we all survive it.'

A hush descended on the room. They sat there, none of them keen to go out of the room and leave the others.

Picking up indistinct words saying that there were to be

a number of announcements following the Prime Minister's speech, John quickly turned the volume up.

Theatres, cinemas, music halls and other places of entertainment were to be shut down at once, and there would be no football games. Iris cried out in misery at that. But before she could put her disappointment into words, there were further announcements.

Everyone would have to observe a blackout from dusk to dawn, listen regularly to the BBC news broadcasts, carry a gas mask everywhere, and make sure that they wore a metal disc at all times bearing their name and address.

'The Prime Minister's sounding really old,' Mabel said. 'His voice was trembling. And so it should. He could've prevented this if he'd tried harder. Now men will have to go off to fight, and they could be killed or taken prisoner. And we could be bombed.'

'There's nothing to be gained by that sort of talk,' John said hastily, seeing that the girls' faces had lost their colour. 'I'll see if I can get hold of a kit for one of those corrugated-iron Anderson shelters that people have been putting up in their gardens. In the meantime, we'd better find out where the nearest public shelter is. We'll go and have a look when we've eaten. And we must decide what to do about the shops. It might become difficult to get sufficient supplies to keep all three of them open.'

Mabel stood up. 'The meal must be about ready.' She paused. 'I feel awful saying this as I know I'm being selfish, but I'm glad I've got daughters, not sons. And I'm so relieved that your age and injury means you won't have to fight this time, John.'

An air-raid siren screamed outside.

For a moment, no one moved.

'It must be a warning!' John shouted. They all jumped

up in panic. 'To the doorways,' he yelled. 'Get in a doorway —it's the strongest part of a house.'

They ran to the nearest doors, opened them and crouched down, their hands protecting their heads. Breathing heavily, their hearts beating fast, no one moved until they heard what they assumed to be the All Clear.

'I'll get us a shelter tomorrow if I can,' John said, standing up. He bent over and rubbed his bad leg. 'And we must always carry our gas masks with us.'

'I wonder how Rose is feeling, knowing we're at war,' Violet said as she went into the kitchen with Mabel to help her serve up the dinner.

'She'll be relieved she's not here,' Iris said, hurrying after them. 'Who'd want to be here, where there's not going to be any fun to be had? Believe me, she'll be glad she's where she is.'

15

Jersey, September 1939

A sombre air hung over the sitting room where Rose and Tom sat with Annie, William and Kathleen, listening to the news from England.

'I think we've heard enough,' William said. He got up and switched off the wireless. Sitting down again, he saw how pale Rose was.

'I don't think you need to be too alarmed, Rose,' he said gently. 'I know you'll be worrying about your family, but your father's too old to fight, and even if he wasn't, the injury to his leg would rule him out. Your mother's already weathered one war, and she'll cope with this one, too. She's a strong woman, and she'll set an example to your sisters.'

'But what if they're bombed?' Her voice trembled.

'They've a pretty good air force, so the country will be well protected. Britain's an island: an invasion is just about impossible.'

She nodded. 'I'm sure you're right. And what about us? How will the war affect us here?'

'It'll probably be much as it was last time, or may even be a little easier. The last war took us by surprise, but this time, anyone who's been following the German advance through Europe will have realised that another war was likely. It means we'll be better prepared this time and shouldn't feel the impact as much.'

'What impact was there?' she asked. She heard the tremor in her voice. And Tom must have done so, too, she realised, as he took her hand in his. She smiled at him gratefully.

'Well, for a start,' William said, 'although we're an agricultural community and capable of feeding our population in wartime conditions, we're not entirely self-sufficient. We rely on imports of flour, meat and margarine, and also on coal for fuel. When the German submarine campaign in the Channel intensified last time, inevitably there were some shortages, and there was real concern that things could be difficult in the winter months. But as I say, we'll be better prepared this time.'

'What about Tom? Will he have to fight?' Rose gripped her husband's hand more tightly.

'It's highly unlikely,' Annie said. 'I hope not, anyway. If it's anything like before, we'll need all the farmers we have. Last time, we had to send more and more food to Britain. It wasn't easy, I can tell you. We were short of labour because so many French and British army reservists had left Jersey at the start of the war to rejoin their units, and we'd mobilised our Militia. So when they introduced conscription halfway through the war, they exempted farm-workers. I'm sure it'll be the same this time.' She smiled at her son. 'I don't think Tom will be going anywhere.'

'I do hope you're right,' Rose said fervently.

'And don't forget, Rose,' William cut in. 'We're our own boss, in effect. Jersey isn't part of the United Kingdom, although the United Kingdom's responsible for Jersey's defence. Islanders can't be called up. If they want, they can volunteer. But we're a self-governing British Crown Dependency, with our own financial, legal and judicial systems.'

'Tom explained it all,' Rose said, 'but it seems very strange. English is spoken everywhere. You use the pound, not the French franc. You drive on the left, like in Britain. You listen to British news on the wireless, and you like cricket. It feels as if we're part of Britain.'

'But we aren't,' Annie said with a smile. 'And I think you'll find that Jersey remains relatively untroubled for the duration of the war.'

FEELING the need for some fresh air, Rose excused herself, went out into the hall, threw on her jacket, took her headscarf from its pocket and went outside.

As she crossed the wide track in front of the farmhouse while tying her headscarf beneath her chin, she felt the sting of the salt-laden wind blowing in from the sea. Hugging her jacket more tightly around her, she went to the top of the slope and stood there, staring at the expanse of blue-green sea.

She could just about see the line of land on the far side of the bay. Crouching at the water's edge was the jumble of houses and shops that was St Helier. People would be in the town, going about their business, she thought. Just as with any other day.

But it wasn't any other day.

A movement above her head made her look up sharply.

A single bird was winging its way across the sky, its dark shape stark against a background of pale blue.

The lines of swifts and swallows that had daily fanned the sky a week or two earlier as they'd made their way south were no longer to be seen.

The only thing left appeared to be one solitary migrating bird, flying alone to join its family.

A part of her wished she could fly away, too. She wouldn't go south, though—she'd return to London.

In fact, from the moment she'd heard that England was at war, in her head she'd been in London with her family, sharing their worries about what was going to happen in the months, or years, that lay ahead.

She knew they'd be in Allcroft Road, making plans, and she'd like to have been able to contribute some suggestions.

Despite the fact that people would be leaving London in large numbers, fearing that the capital would be the target of enemy warfare, she was sure that her family wouldn't be among them.

People would need clothes, and they'd need to be able to mend their clothes, and just as her mother had stayed in London throughout the last war while her father had been away fighting, her family would remain in Kentish Town during the coming war. And if they couldn't keep their shops open, they'd take two or three stalls in the market instead.

That meant they'd be at risk. So she should be with them.

But how could she be?

She could never leave Tom—she wouldn't have a minute's peace of mind if she wasn't at his side.

He was her family now. And so were the Benests. As a Benest, too, she should be thinking of them and taking part in the discussions they were bound to be having, not anguishing about what might be going on in London.

Several times since she'd come to Jersey, she'd had to remind herself that London was her past, that her life in Jersey was her future. But so far, this had been mere words. It must now become a recognition she embraced whole-heartedly, and there was no time like the present.

She turned and went back to the sitting room.

'YOU HAVEN'T MISSED MUCH,' Annie told her when Rose had hung her scarf and jacket on a peg just inside the front door, and had joined the family again.

'I just felt like a couple of minutes outside,' Rose told them. 'My parents suddenly seemed a long way away.'

'You could always go back home to London. If you did, they wouldn't be so far away,' Kathleen said snidely.

Rose smiled at her with exaggerated sweetness. 'What's it they say, home is where the heart is? That means I'm already home, doesn't it, Kathleen?'

She beamed at Tom, and he looked back at her with love.

Kathleen wrinkled her nose in disgust. 'It's enough to make one sick!'

'Now, children,' Annie said in mild rebuke. She indicated the pot of coffee from the low table in the middle of the room the table. 'That's a fresh pot of coffee, Rose. Fill up your cup, then pass the pot to Tom in case he wants a top up.'

Rose picked up the pot. 'Many thanks,' she said. 'So what did I miss?'

'Nothing really. I was just saying that I think it'll be pretty much as it was in the last war,' Annie said. 'Tom will probably do the sort of Militia duties that William did last time, while still working on the farm. And William will be on the farm.'

'William will be doing what he did last time, Rose— Militia and farm,' William intervened. 'I'm in my early fifties, Annie, not in my dotage.'

Annie smiled. 'We'll see how it goes. At least we know what part we'll be playing. It's essential to keep the farm going as we won't receive any more food from countries that are now at war. We should consider increasing the amount of wheat we grow, William, don't you think?'

He nodded. 'I agree. And maybe add a few oats.'

'What about the shop?' Rose said. 'That could play a part, too.'

'You're right,' Annie said. 'If the war lasts for any length of time, clothes shops will run out of stock, and people will start repairing what they already have. We'll need to stay open to supply their needs. I think the three of us—that's you, me and Kathleen—ought to sit down tomorrow morning and make a list of what has to be done.'

'We'll need more stock, won't we?' Rose said.

'Definitely. We must contact Pierre,' Annie said. 'He's my main supplier, Rose. He's got a warehouse in Normandy. His parents died a few years ago and Pierre took over the wholesale business. He and his wife run it.'

'And you've also got the Weymouth contact, haven't you?' Rose said.

'That's right. so far, we've had one delivery from them. It was a trial rather than a full delivery, but it was satisfactory. We must send them another order at once.' She leaned over and poured herself another coffee.

'Of course, we don't know what situation they'll be in,' she continued. 'The British government's almost certain to start restricting movement between Britain and the islands, if they haven't already done so. So in addition to contacting the Weymouth supplier, we need to find out what Pierre can let us have. We must do that soon—we won't be the only ones looking for stock.'

'Is that a hint for me to get in touch with him, Mother?' Tom asked.

'Thank you,' she said laughing. 'I was hoping you'd offer. You and Pierre get on so well together that I'm sure he'd do for you what he wouldn't for anyone else. And your French is so much better than mine.'

Tom locked his hands behind his head and looked up at the ceiling. 'I'm thinking how much I'd enjoy some rock cakes,' he remarked.

Annie laughed again. 'If you do it, I'll make you the rock cakes you love.'

'It's a deal,' Tom said in satisfaction.

SITTING ON THE SOFA, Rose snuggled up to Tom. With his arm around her, and her head resting against his shoulder, they gazed at the view though their sitting room window.

The last rays of the dying sun had caught the sails of the boats far out on the water, rendering them into small triangles of gold that bobbed along on a glossy black sea.

'What are you thinking about?' she asked as the sun melted slowly into the horizon.

'Probably the same as you,' he said. 'Whatever Mother says about nothing much changing, we're bound to be affected by what's happening in England, even if it's just a constant worry about your family.' He hesitated. 'If you really wanted to go to them, I'm sure that'd be possible. Or d'you think they might agree to come here?'

'They'd never leave England,' she said.

She straightened up and turned to look at him. 'And I don't want to leave Jersey. I'm naturally concerned about my family, but I love you, Tom, and I couldn't get from one end of the day to the other if I wasn't with you. I thought I loved you when we got married, but that was nothing compared with what I feel now.'

'And it's the same for me, Rose. Although I loved you the moment I met you, I've grown to *really* love you. If that makes sense. Even if it doesn't, I don't know how to say it better. You're the person who puts the sun into my every day. Even when it's raining.' He grimaced. 'I think I kind of messed that up,' he said ruefully.

She shook her head, smiling. 'You didn't, Tom. I heard you loud and clear.'

For a long moment, each stared into the face of the other. Then Rose rested her head on his shoulder again, and he put his arm around her.

'No one's more important to me than you, Tom,' she said after a few moments of restful silence. 'And also, I care about your family, who've been very kind to me. So there's nowhere I'd rather be than here.'

Tom tightened his hold on her. 'You don't know how happy it makes me to hear you say that,' he said. 'I wanted you to know you could leave, but I would've hated every minute without you. You make my life complete, Rose, and I never want to feel incomplete again.' He glanced down at her in amusement. 'I got the right words that time, didn't I?'

'You definitely did,' she said, trailing her fingers across his chest. 'So much so, that there's no need to say anything else. Even though it's a bit early, I think it's time for bed.'

16

Jersey, May 1940

Rose propped her bicycle against the wall at the side of her front door and hurried into the cottage. As she'd expected, it was empty—Tom was somewhere on the farm with William, she knew.

He had told her the evening before that he and William might go out first thing in the day to check the fence around one of the fields where the cows grazed. They were concerned that the wooden posts in one corner of the field seemed to be unstable.

She was delighted to have a few moments of to herself before going next door to help with cleaning the still in the cider *pressoir*. It meant she could sit and read the letter from Violet that the postman had just given her.

She grabbed a glass of water and hurried upstairs to the sitting room. She put the water on the table by the sofa, sat down, curled her feet under her and tore open the envelope.

.   .   .

ALLCROFT ROAD,

Saturday, 27*th* April, 1940

Dear Rose,

I thought I'd write to you today as I'm sure you must be anxious about us and will want to know what's happening. As Father and Mother aren't the greatest letter writers, you'll have to make do with me. They talk about you often, though. We all do. We all wish you lived closer.

I'll start with the family news as you'll be wondering what we've been doing.

Mother regularly helps in the shops as Father goes to an office in Islington every day. He's working for the Government now. He doesn't like to talk about what he does, so that's all I can tell you.

Iris is pretty fed up that she no longer works in D.H. Evans. She had to leave as she's needed in Dad's shops. She consoles herself by flirting outrageously with all the single male customers who come in. Not when Mother and Father are around, of course, as they'd be very disapproving. She's denied it, but I'm not sure that she hasn't met up with one or two of them after work.

I work in the shops every weekend, but during the week, I help in one of the local schools. Although I'm registered for the two-year teachers' certificate, my teacher training college has moved to Huddersfield for the duration of the war. I wasn't keen to go with them as I wanted to stay and help Father, so when a local school asked for help, I volunteered to go there.

I'm still officially a student, but I'm now also a teacher. What do you think of that! For the moment, I'm replacing a teacher who's gone to Wales with a group of schoolchildren who've been evacuated. It's excellent experience, and it's proved that this is the job I really want to do.

A lot of the male teachers have gone to fight, so it's rather a *strange staffroom—most of the men who are left are too old or too unfit to fight, and at the other end of the age range, there are a few other young teachers like me.*

What about you, Rose?

We haven't heard from you for a bit. I know you wrote that when was war declared, Tom said you could visit us if you wanted to reassure yourself that we were all right, but you didn't want to leave him. We were pleased to read what you said as it meant you were happy. We hadn't always been sure that you were.

I expect you know that a month ago, the Government relaxed restrictions on travel between the UK and Jersey and the other Channel Islands. They're even encouraging people to go there on holiday. Unfortunately, because of our work, we're not able to do so. However, if the farm could manage without you for a short time, perhaps you might think again about coming to us.

We'd love to see you. So please do think about it.

As for the war, it all feels a bit strange here, and a bit of an anticlimax. We know we're at war, and we're ready and waiting, but nothing much has happened.

The 'ready' bit is that lots of signposts have been removed from roads so that the enemy will get lost if they invade, and there are sandbags in the streets. Car lights have to be dimmed, so we've had to mask the van's headlights.

There are heavy metal screens over the bus windows to protect passengers from flying glass or debris. All our windows have masking tape across them for the same reason, and we've got blackout curtains. Air-raid wardens come and tell you off if there's any light showing. The wardens actually look quite frightening in their tin hats, combat jackets and special extra-protective gas masks.

We've all got gas masks, too. We have to carry them wherever we go. They come in small, medium and large. When you put them on, there's a horrible smell of rubber. We've worn them at home a few times to get used to them, but I hope we never have to wear them in a real gas attack.

Fortunately, the shops are still well supplied. Stockpiling food is now a punishable offence, and every time you meet your friends, the main topic of conversation is the question of when the rationing will begin. We're sure that they'll start to ration some foodstuffs before too long.

So that's the ready bit.

The 'waiting' bit is that nothing much is happening. Before the declaration of war, Hitler caused crisis after crisis. He took over Austria, then bits of Czechoslovakia, and then attacked Poland, which started the war. I tried to tell the others what my tutor was saying, but none of them seemed interested. They all said I was an alarmist.

Well, I'd have been happy to be an alarmist, and for there to have been nothing too much to worry about. There is, though; it's just a matter of when. Although we've been at war for months now, we're still waiting for something terrible to happen. It's as if you invited people to dinner, set the table and cooked the food, but nobody turned up. At the same time, if what turned up was a fraction as ghastly as the last war sounds, you wouldn't want anyone to come.

It seems strange to say this in the circumstances, but life seems to be going on as usual, or perhaps it's more accurate to say, almost as usual. Everyone has to carry an identity card now, showing who they are and where they live. Even children must have a card.

Father's bought a new wireless to be sure of getting the news. The sound on the old one was really poor. It kept crackling, if you remember. It'll surprise you to know that Father's taken to reading the newspapers every day, and also 'Picture Post'.

You might not have heard of 'Picture Post' as it's fairly new, *and we never used to get it. It has lots of photos of events, as the title suggests, and it's campaigning against what's now happening to Jewish people in Germany.*

The ordinary newspapers are full of advertisements for long-handled shovels and scrapers that could be used to dispose of any incendiary bombs. At first it was quite frightening to see them, but as nothing's been happening, they no longer alarm us.

The only other thing we've bought is something that's not at all scary. We bought some new blankets. It was a strange thing to buy at this time, we thought, but Mother said you never know when they'll be useful. That's typical of Mother!

I must end now as I'm off to Mid Hams.

We can't stop thinking about you and wondering how you are. Please, do write soon, or better still, come. We're longing to hear from you or see you.

Give our love to Tom, William and Annie, will you? And to Kathleen, too, of course. I hope things are better with her. She must surely be used to you by now.

Love,

Violet

As ROSE WAS PUTTING the letter back into the envelope, she heard Tom coming up the stairs.

'I was just about to go over to the farmhouse,' she said as he came into the sitting room, 'but I got a letter from Violet, and I couldn't wait to find out what was happening in Kentish Town.'

'So what *is* happening?' he asked, sitting down next to her.

'Here.' She handed him the letter. 'There's nothing private in it so you can read it yourself.'

He quickly scanned it and handed it back to her. 'It's very friendly, and informative,' he said.

'I know.' She looked at him. 'About not wanting to go back to England,' she said, putting the letter into her apron pocket, 'it's a while since I've seen them, and I was wondering about going there for about a week. My parents aren't getting any younger. But don't look so worried,' she said, leaning forward to kiss him. 'I'll be back before you know I'm gone.'

'I'm afraid that's not such a good idea now,' he said gently. 'It's a month since Violet wrote the letter, and the war's not going quite so well. I'd worry about your safety if you were in London.'

She stared at him in alarm. 'Why, what's happened?'

'Hitler's forces are moving into northern France. The British troops are in retreat. They've been pushed back to the French coast.'

'In retreat?' she echoed. Her hand flew to her mouth. 'You mean we're losing the war?'

'I wouldn't go as far as that. Let's just say, things could be better. I won't be able to get to Pierre again for a while, that's for sure. But the war's unlikely to affect the island, so I hope you'll stay here. I couldn't bear it if I thought you were in danger of bombs and goodness knows what.'

'I'll keep my fingers crossed that my family will be safe,' she said, her face very white. 'But don't worry, Tom. I'm not going anywhere.'

17

Jersey, June 1940

'I thought I might find you in here, even though it's between meals,' William said as he walked into the kitchen and saw Annie, Tom and Rose standing around the table, staring down in horror at the *Jersey Evening Post.*

He sat down heavily in his seat. 'You've seen it, I see.'

Tom and Rose moved to their chairs, and Annie went to get the pot of coffee from the range. When she'd filled each of their cups, she returned the pot to the range and joined them at the table.

'Thanks, Annie,' William said. He took a drink of coffee and put his cup down.

'Is it true?' Tom asked, indicating the newspaper.

'I hate to say it, but yes,' William said wearily. 'I've just come from the Bailiff's office, and the British are, indeed, going to demilitarise Jersey. They're withdrawing their two thousand troops immediately. Added to that, the Jersey Militia has left *en masse* to join the Hampshire Regiment.'

A stunned silence greeted his words.

'We'd hoped the paper was wrong,' Annie said at last.

'And because the British troops are leaving,' William continued, 'the lieutenant-governors are being recalled. It means there won't be any official representatives of the Crown in Jersey for at least the duration of the war. Alexander Coutanche is taking their place. He's an excellent Bailiff so at least Jersey will be in good hands. But as you can imagine, the town's in chaos.'

'So we've been ditched by Britain, have we?' Annie said bitterly, a tremor in her voice. 'And after all Churchill said not so long ago about fighting on the beaches and not surrendering.'

William nodded towards the newspaper. 'I suppose you can't really blame them. Realistically, they've no choice but to remove their troops and redeploy them,' he said. 'Just think how many soldiers, anti-aircraft guns and fighter planes would be needed to defend Jersey and all the other Channel Islands. Having them here would leave the English coastline vulnerable to attack.'

'But what about us?' Annie countered. 'Don't we matter?'

'Of course we do. But they'll have weighed it up. With France defeated and the Germans in Paris, Britain's got its back against the wall. It needs all the soldiers it can get if it's going to defeat Hitler. They must've decided that as we aren't strategically important to Britain, or to Germany, for that matter, the Germans will very likely leave us alone.'

'But in the paper it says they're going to evacuate any women and children who want to leave Jersey, and also men of military age,' Tom said. 'So they're not certain they're right.'

William nodded. 'And that's why the town's overrun. A number of islanders are jittery, and apparently since early this morning, there's been a long queue to get into the Town Hall. No one's going to be allowed on a boat unless they've got the right paperwork.'

'*You* might not blame the British Government, William,' Annie said, raising her voice. 'But I do. The Germans can see Jersey from the Cherbourg peninsula, so why would anyone think that Hitler would stop at France when he could so easily get to us? When he finds out we've no protection, he'll be over here like a shot. And what a coup for him that would be, Germans on British soil!'

William frowned. 'So what're you saying, Annie? Some of our neighbours will probably leave, and we know that others have been quietly leaving in the past few weeks. While it's harder for farmers like us to go, it's not impossible. Are you saying you want to return to England?'

Annie shrugged helplessly. 'I don't know what I'm saying. It's certainly something we should think about. The idea of leaving our home and everything we love about it is so awful, but so's the alternative of staying put, not knowing what's going to happen, or if we're going to see jackboots on the streets of St Helier.' She glanced towards the door. 'Kathleen should be here, talking about this with us.'

'Is it a stupid question to ask where she is?' William asked.

'She's either at Emily's or in town,' Annie said. 'I don't know which. She went off to Emily's when she'd finished syringing the bees with water.'

'Why would she do that?' Rose asked in surprise.

'To incapacitate them. Bees are terrible swimmers and even a little water will stop them from leaving the farm. Germans or not, we need the bees to stay here and pollinate our plants. But I imagine she'll be back soon. The Gorins will want to discuss what to do, and they won't want Kathleen there.'

With a sudden exclamation, Tom sat up straight. 'I've just had a thought! I'm of military age, aren't I? If the Germans came here, they might expect me to fight for them. If they did, I'd absolutely refuse.'

'They wouldn't let you refuse, Tom. You'd be thrown into prison, or worse.' Annie stared across the table at William, her eyes fearful. 'Tom's right, William. They could insist he fight for Germany.' Her voice shook. 'The only answer is, he and Rose must go to England at once. We'll hire someone to take over their work.'

William held up his hands in protest. 'Hold on, Annie! You're moving too fast. We don't know that the Germans *will* come here. Indeed, they probably won't.'

'But if Tom wants to be evacuated, he's got to act now,' Annie said. 'He needs the necessary papers. The offer won't stay open for long.'

There was a sudden loud bang as the door to the kitchen burst open and hit the wall. Kathleen appeared, red in the face and breathless.

'I cycled back so quickly that I'm boiling hot,' she said, fanning her face with her hand as she went to the sink and poured herself a glass of water. She drank it, and joined the others at the table.

'Where've you been?' Tom asked.

'In St Helier with Emily. You've no idea what it's like, both in the town and at the harbour. We had to walk our bicycles on the pavement when we got to the town as you couldn't cycle on the street—the whole area around Gloucester Street was filled with cars.'

'Your father's been there, too,' Annie cut in. 'He said the same as you.'

'It was almost eerie, wasn't it, Dad?' Kathleen said, shaking her head in wonder. 'The people queueing around the Town Hall were ever so quiet. It was really strange. Someone in the queue said they'd been waiting for ten hours. That's such a long time. It was noisier around the banks, though. People were pushing and shoving each other, trying to get to a window to withdraw their savings.'

'They'll be remembering what happened last time,' Annie said.

'They can't take out much, though,' Kathleen told her. 'They've capped withdrawals at twenty-five pounds. And we heard that some of the bank staff were packing up all the negotiable bonds, whatever they are, and other documents. They're making a list of them and are going to send them to England on a mail-boat. '

William nodded. 'That's the right thing to do. We don't want our economy to collapse.'

'But the harbour was even worse,' Kathleen went on. 'Honestly, Mum, there were thousands of people waiting behind the barriers that were stopping them from going on to the piers. Whole families were sitting on the ground in the boiling sun, with all their bags and belongings piled up around them. And you could hear gunfire from France.'

'How frightening,' Annie said, going pale.

'It was. And on the way home, we could've helped ourselves to any number of bicycles and cars. People are just discarding them as they leave. You wouldn't believe it.' She leaned back in her chair. 'So what have I missed by being there and not here?'

'We've been discussing whether to stay or leave,' Annie said bluntly. 'I was saying that as Tom's of military age, he and Rose ought to consider going to England, and I was about to suggest they went for their papers now. But having heard what you and your father have been saying, I think we should wait for the queues to die down. Don't you agree, Tom?'

Tom turned to Rose. 'What do you think?' he asked. 'You said that you wanted to see your parents. This could be your chance. Shall we go?'

Rose thought for a moment. 'I'm not sure,' she said slowly. 'If you're in England, you might have to fight for the British. I know you'd be fighting on the right side, but if you stayed in Jersey, you wouldn't have to fight on any side, would you? Farming's a reserved occupation. And if the Germans were to come here, they'd have to eat like everyone else, so they'd leave the farmers alone. So for the sake of your potatoes,' she added with a laugh, 'I think we should stay.'

William beamed at her. 'You make an excellent point, Rose; thank you, And thank you for being willing to stay with us. Are you agreed, Tom?'

'I definitely am,' he said. 'Staying is actually the right thing to do. With so many leaving, Jersey could end up with too few people to look after the animals and crops. If we left, we'd be adding to the island's woes.'

'It's a good job you stocked up a while ago, Annie,' Rose said. 'Haberdashery items could soon be in great demand.'

'That's right,' Annie said. 'I hadn't thought that far ahead, but you're correct.'

'So we're staying, are we?' William looked round the table, and saw the nods of agreement. 'Then there are things we should do.'

He finished his cup of coffee.

'The evacuation offer has made everyone believe that

the Germans might really invade us. Personally, I think it's highly unlikely, but it might be wise to prepare for the worst. First of all, I suggest we make a place on the farm where Tom could hide, should he ever need to do so.'

Tom smiled broadly. 'That's a really good idea, Dad. I'd feel more comfortable if I knew that I had a concealed bolthole.'

'Then, that's something for William and Tom to do,' Annie said, picking up the cups closest to her. 'They can go out now and start looking for a suitable hiding place. Ideally, it should be near the kitchen. As for you, Kathleen, you could check that the bees are where they should be, and Rose, there are potatoes that need grading. Life goes on. I'll get the meal going.'

As they rose to their feet, they heard a car come along the track and stop outside the farmhouse.

While Annie hurriedly removed the last of the dirty cups from the table, Rose took the pot with the dregs of coffee to the sink. Kathleen rushed to the window and peered out.

'It's Emily and her father!' she exclaimed.

She dashed out into the hall, and returned a few moments later with George and Emily.

'I do apologise for turning up like this,' George said awkwardly. 'We really should have telephoned first, but so much has happened so quickly.'

'It's no problem at all, George. Do sit down,' Annie said. 'I'll make some fresh coffee. And you can give me your verdict on the orange cake I made yesterday,' she added as she went across to the coffee grinder. 'I prised the recipe from Madeleine Le Feu.'

'We've just been talking things through,' William said,

pulling up a chair for George. 'I imagine you've been doing the same.'

George nodded. 'Yes, we have.'

Tom and Rose sat back down again, and Kathleen dragged a chair over for Emily to sit next to her.

'Yes,' George went on. 'To stay or to leave, that's the question on everyone's lips, isn't it?'

'And what've you decided?' Kathleen asked.

Emily looked across the table at her father. 'We're leaving,' she said. She turned to Kathleen. 'Are you going, too?'

Kathleen shook her head. 'No, we're staying.'

'I thought you would,' Emily said.

William looked at George in surprise. 'But what about your farm, George?'

'Well, that's one of the reasons we're here. I was pretty sure you'd stay, and I'm hoping you'll take the cows—we don't have that many—and the few pigs and chickens we have. Joshua Mauger is going to look after the wheat and the oats and generally keep an eye on the farm while we're away. We're a bit of a distance from the Maugers' farm so Joshua will probably live at our place for some of the time.'

'D'you think he'll be able to cope?' William asked in surprise. 'He's not another Paul. As far as I know, he's never shown any interest in farming. I thought the town was always his destination, not the family's fields.'

George shrugged. 'With so many leaving, we've not really got any choice. If we aren't back here before the harvest, Josh knows he can hire any help he needs. But I was hoping that you and Annie might occasionally check the place to see that all's well. And in return, some of the harvested crops would be yours.'

'We'll do that with pleasure, George,' William said.

Annie came back with the coffee and two extra cups.

She went round the table filling everyone's cups, and sat down.

'We'll be sorry to see you and Martha go,' she said.

He smiled ruefully. 'Believe me, the feeling's mutual. I just hope it won't be too long before we're back.'

'As you'll obviously be leaving in a day or so, why don't I come over later and we'll go through everything?' William suggested.

'That would be very helpful. I'm grateful to you,' George said. 'And Martha will be, too. She's going to the Town Hall first thing tomorrow and she'll wait for as long as it takes to get the papers we need.'

'D'you mind me asking why you've decided to go?' Tom asked.

'To be honest, it's Martha,' George said apologetically. 'She's got herself into a bit of a state. It's all very well for the Bailiff to say we should keep calm, and that he and his wife have no intention of going anywhere, but Martha has family in England, and having a place to go has unsettled her. Also, I'm pretty sure she's not forgotten the propaganda during the last war, where the Hun was depicted as being a terrifying beast, bent on raping women and killing babies. That made a deep impression on her.'

'How do *you* feel about going?' William asked.

'Given there's a war over there, I'm not that enthusiastic. But Martha's family lives in a small village in the heart of England, so we should be safe enough. But how the British Government's going to transport all the people from Jersey, as well as from the other Channel Islands, I don't know. I'm not looking forward to being crammed in a dirty boat with thousands of other people. And as I don't think there'll be an escort, we'll be a sitting target.'

Kathleen pulled a face. 'That's scary.'

'And what about the thousands of islanders who'll be pouring into Weymouth or Southampton?' William said. 'You could be leaving one lot of chaos and going into another.'

George shrugged. 'That's their problem, not ours.'

William nodded. 'True. And our problem is how we'll be able to keep the day-to-day life of the island going if too many people leave.'

'They won't,' George said flatly. 'I'm pretty sure that quite a few of those who rushed to get their papers will change their minds when they've thought things through. Once you know you can go, you can relax and see clearly the disadvantages of leaving. Alas, I fear the exception will be Martha,' he added with a wry smile.

'What do you think, Emily?' Kathleen asked.

Emily looked down at her plate. 'I don't really know. Part of me doesn't want to leave. Paul seemed to be getting quite keen, and he'll probably have found someone else by the time we get back.' She looked up at Kathleen. 'And no matter what happened here, you and I would have had a laugh together. Now I might be stuck in a tiny village, on my own, dying of boredom.'

'What part of you wants to leave, then?' Kathleen asked, her tone accusing. 'You love the farm.'

Emily shrugged. 'I suppose it might be nice to meet some people I don't already know. It could be quite exciting, in fact. There might be someone really good-looking on one of the farms near where we'll be living,' she added. 'And before you say he'd be called up—no, he wouldn't, being a farmer.'

George stood up. 'We must be going,' he said. 'I'll see you later, William. We'll try to drop by before we leave, if possible. Come on, Emily.'

'I wish you were going to England, too,' Emily said as she and Kathleen followed the two men out of the house. Seeing George and William pause by the car and start talking, they wandered across the track and stood facing the glittering sea.

'So do I,' Kathleen said, nodding. 'I wouldn't have to look at that simpering Rose every day.'

'That feeling won't last for long,' Emily said with a touch of bitterness.

Kathleen glanced at Emily, her brow furrowing. 'What d'you mean?'

'With only Rose for company, you'll soon stop thinking she's awful,' Emily said. 'And by the time I get back, you'll have forgotten about me and you'll be best friends with her.'

'But if you have your way, you won't be back. It's pretty clear that you hope to marry a farmer and live on a farm that's miles away from here. So why does it matter who I'm friends with?'

'I still want us to be best friends. All I'm doing is making the most of the situation my parents are forcing me into,' Emily said hastily. 'If I had my way, I'd stay.'

Kathleen stared at Emily in mounting excitement. 'Then tell them you want to live with us! Mum and Dad would love to have you here. And obviously I would, too.'

Emily coloured slightly. 'I can't really do that,' she said awkwardly. 'Mother said she wouldn't go without me, and if we all stayed, and the Germans *did* come here, then I'd never hear the end of it.'

'I see,' Kathleen said, her face falling.. 'And what would have happened, I wonder, if Tom had never met Rose? If he hadn't, you would have been living next door, not Rose. And as he and Rose are staying here, you wouldn't have been going anywhere. But from what your father said, your mother would still be leaving as that's what she wants to do. So, really, there's no reason why your parents can't go on their own. If you made that argument, they'd probably let you stay.'

Emily shook her head. 'I think it's too late for that.'

'You'd better go, then,' Kathleen said. 'Your father's in the car. Heaven forbid that he leaves without you, and your poor mother has to leave you behind when she goes to England,' she added bitterly.

18

Jersey, 28th June 1940

Rose paused in the task of clearing her front path of weeds, straightened up and stretched herself. Then she strolled across to the edge of the *côtil*, her fork in her hand.

She stood a moment, tilting her face to the sun, then lowered her gaze to the bay.

From such a distance, St Helier was no more than a collection of small white houses and windows off which sunlight was bouncing. But on the beach down below her, people of every age were laughing and playing, splashing in the water, kicking a football on the sand, having fun.

She could hear their happiness and she smiled to herself at how normal it all was.

To the family's relief, the initial panic that had followed the evacuation had faded with the passing of each day.

Increasingly, the people they met on the paths or in the shops had started to say that the war looked as if it was going to pass them by, just as the worst of the last war had done.

And who wouldn't think that, when it was so peaceful there, and so lovely, she thought happily. It was no real surprise that George had been proved right—of the twenty-three thousand who'd registered to leave, only six and a half thousand had finally gone. But to Kathleen's misery, the Gorins had been among them.

She stood in the sun for a few more minutes, allowing herself to enjoy the scene that she'd grown to love, then turned to go back to the path, and to continue forking out the weeds.

A low hum in the sky made her stop and look up. Shielding her eyes against the sun, she made out a number of black flecks high above her.

Just more British planes on their way to drop their bombs somewhere, she mentally shrugged, or German reconnaissance planes.

If they were German planes, the people inside them would see only a patchwork of yellow and green fields dotted with houses and villages, and countless dark green wooded slopes. They would see an island bordered by rocky cliffs to the north, and wide sandy beaches to the west, south and east. And they might make out people playing and relaxing.

But they wouldn't see any anti-aircraft guns, or any naval vessels in the small harbour at St Aubin or in the larger harbour of St Helier, so they'd know that the island posed no threat to them.

Three of the planes broke away from the others and turned towards St Helier.

Her heart lurched. She dropped her fork and her hand flew to her mouth.

The planes were heading at speed for the town, their guns blazing.

From beneath their bodies, small black objects started to fall. Like flashes of silver, they fell. Small sticks that glinted in the light.

They're bombs or bullets, she thought in a panic.

Before she could move, a loud explosion sounded in the St Helier area, and a massive ball of fire enveloped the town. The island vibrated beneath her.

They were bombs, she realised.

Spinning round, she ran terrified into the cottage.

She paused in the hall, uncertain how best to protect herself.

Then in desperation she rushed into the kitchen and threw herself beneath the table.

Her breathing ragged, her heart beating wildly, she listened as the planes flew low overhead and bullets hit the track. Frantically praying that the rest of the family were somewhere safe, and dreading that Tom was out in the fields, a visible target, she curled into as small a ball as possible.

As she crouched there, trembling, her hands over her head, she heard the hum of the engines fading into the distance.

For a few moments, she remained where she was, too paralysed by fear to move. And then she heard someone come running into the kitchen.

'Are you there, Rose?' she heard Annie call.

'I'm under here,' she cried, clambering out from beneath the table.

They hugged each other in relief.

'That was a good place to go,' Annie told her. 'Kathleen and I dived into the cupboard under the stairs.'

'Where's Tom?' she asked.

'I'm sure he's safe. Kathleen's gone out to find him. It's William I'm worried about,' Annie said, her face ashen. 'He went into St Helier this morning. Let's go back to the farmhouse and wait for news, or better still, for William to get back.'

'I WOULDN'T WANT to have to do that too often,' Tom said, pulling the last pieces of straw from his hair and his shirt and piling them up on the kitchen worktop. 'It's lucky I was near the barns when I heard the planes. The moment I saw the bombs, all I could think of was being hit by glass from the frames if they broke, and I made for the nearest barn and scrambled inside the biggest haystack.'

'He looked just like a scarecrow when I found him,' Kathleen said with a laugh.

'You did the right thing, Tom,' Annie said. 'Clothes can be washed. I just hope that William found somewhere to hide.'

'He did,' they heard William say.

All three turned to the door as he came into the kitchen. A wave of relief swept through the room.

Annie ran to him and hugged him. 'I was so worried,' she said, her voice trembling. 'Come and sit down and tell us what happened. Kathleen, pour your father a cider.' She pulled William to his chair, and stood next to him, her arm around his shoulders.

'There's not much to say. I was driving along the esplanade on my way back to St Aubin when I saw the planes. But there hadn't been any air-raid warning, and

there'd been a lot of low-flying planes in recent days—
they'd been taking photos, so I'd been told—so I didn't
think anything of it. Not until they started dropping bombs.
As soon as they did, I left the car and ran for safety. There
weren't a lot of places to hide, so I threw myself into one of
the large tamarisk bushes at the side of the road, and hoped
for the best.'

'Well, as you aren't injured, you obviously chose a good
place,' Annie said, hugging him again.

'From where I was hiding, I saw the planes flying low
above the esplanade towards St Aubin. Patches of tarmac
were pinging along the road under the volleys of machine-
gun fire, and people were throwing themselves to the
ground on both sides of the road.'

'It's so lucky you weren't hurt,' Annie said, and she
kissed him on the top of his head.

'It certainly is! Anyway, as soon as the planes had gone,
I crawled out of the bush, dusted myself down and drove
back to the port to see if I could give any help.' He shook
his head. 'I saw some terrible injuries, I can tell you.
Heaven knows how many were killed. The area around the
harbour was devastated, and the sea was covered with
wrecked boats and yachts. Some of the nearby stores were
on fire—you couldn't see the sun for black smoke. And
both the Pomme d'Or and the Royal Yacht Hotel were
damaged.'

'When I think that I might've been there!' Kathleen
exclaimed, wide-eyed. 'I was thinking of going to St Helier
this morning, but with Emily gone, it's not so much fun, so I
didn't. I'm so glad I stayed at home with Mum.'

'In future, you'd be wise to avoid St Helier, Kathleen,'
William said, 'particularly the harbour. It's the obvious
place for them to attack. And so's the town itself. We'll have

to think about the shop, Annie. We don't know if there'll be another attack like this morning's.'

'Poor St Helier,' Annie said. 'It doesn't bear thinking about. It's lucky you were there to help.'

'Everything seemed under control, and there wasn't really anything for me to do, so I came back. It was a worrying journey home, I can tell you. A lot of the furze on the hillsides was on fire and I saw shattered windows and doors that had been blown off their hinges. I didn't know what I was going to find when I got home. Until I saw you all sitting there, and felt the relief, I hadn't realised how frightened I'd got.'

'You should've gone back to England while you had the chance, Rose,' Kathleen snapped. 'Now you're just one more person for Mum and Dad to worry about.'

'Shut up, Kathleen,' Tom said angrily. 'There's no need to be so bitchy.'

'Yes, that will do, Kathleen,' Annie said sharply. 'Another way of looking at it is that someone else will be sharing a workload that might've been yours alone.'

'I'm glad that I'm here, able to help you, and not across the Channel, worrying about you,' Rose said.

'That's a kind thought, Rose,' William said. 'We appreciate it.'

Kathleen glared at Rose, who gave her a slight smile into which she managed to inject a touch of triumph.

Tom looked around the table. 'Now that we've seen the reality of war in our little island, the question is, what comes next?'

ALONE IN THEIR sitting room at the end of the day, Tom and Rose sat together on their sofa, their arms around each other, staring towards their sitting room window. The window had been covered by a sheet of blackout material, and unremitting blackness stared back at them.

'I miss seeing those lovely sunsets,' Rose said with a sigh.

Tom nodded. 'Me, too.' He hesitated. 'I know what you told my family, Rose, but do you regret deep down that you didn't return to England when you had the chance? Tell me honestly. I wouldn't blame you.'

'Not for one minute,' she said, gazing deep into his eyes. 'I'm where I want to be, here with you, Tom, no matter what lies ahead. I love you so much that it hurts.'

She felt the tension in his muscles relax, and she slid her hand across his chest.

He looked down at her hand, and then back at her face.

Each smiled slowly at the other, then they turned towards the curtain of black that blocked out the world and sealed in their togetherness.

19

Jersey, July 1940

After a fitful Tuesday night's sleep, Rose sat on a chair in the yard behind the cottage on the Wednesday morning, watching the chickens pecking in the yard. What a long two days it had been! And what a frightening two days, she thought looking back.

ON THE MONDAY, they'd been terrified to see two parachutes fall from German aircraft near St Helier.

They'd thought at first that the Germans were dropping soldiers on to the island. But at about ten o'clock that morning, William had found out otherwise when Robert Le Feu telephoned from St Helier and told him that the parachutes had landed on the beach at low tide, each with a long cylinder attached to it, not a person.

Inside each cylinder was a batch of Nazi flags and official

messages for the Commander-in-Chief of Jersey, Robert told William. The messages had been passed to the Bailiff, who'd called an emergency meeting that morning.

William promptly cycled to St Helier and joined the crowds of people in the Royal Square—their faces drawn, their eyes full of apprehension.

Part of the Royal Square was cordoned off, and there were one or two workmen standing by with large paint brushes and pots of paint. Several people asked the workmen what they were doing, but they wouldn't say.

When the Bailiff came out of the States' Building, he looked very tense as he went across to the golden statue of George II, and stood at the foot of it, waiting until everyone had settled down.

They had no choice but to surrender, the Bailiff told them, and before the German troops arrived, every property on the island was to display a white flag as a token of no resistance. If this wasn't done by seven o'clock the following morning, there would be a heavy bombardment.

As he spoke, the workmen moved forward into the cordoned area and started painting a huge white cross in the centre of the Royal Square.

The crowd dispersed, and William pedalled quickly back to St Aubin to tell the family what they must do.

But when he got there, he found that they already knew. The Bailiff had ordered copies of the ultimatum to be rolled off the printing presses and plastered in prominent positions throughout the island, and by the time that William walked into the kitchen, Annie was in the act of fixing a threadbare white vest to a broom.

'I'm not using anything good,' she said. 'We'll hang this from one of the bedroom windows. You don't need to bother, Rose.'

But Rose wasn't going to take any chances, and back at the cottage, she found an old white blouse, affixed it to the handle of a broom as Annie had done, and hung it from their sitting room window.

Later that day, while she and Annie were preparing the dinner, having decided that they'd eat every meal together for as long as their island was occupied, and while Tom and William were in the fields dealing with the cows and Kathleen was feeding the pigs, they heard the roar of aircraft flying low over the farm.

Hurrying outside, they looked up at the sky. A formation of aircraft was flying west towards Jersey airport.

Rose turned to Annie. 'I bet that's the first lot of German soldiers,' she said.

AND SHE WAS RIGHT.

When Tuesday dawned, they heard that the night before, the soldiers who'd been dropped had commandeered a bus and been driven into St Helier.

People who saw the bus go by said that the soldiers seemed very young, and quite normal. They were friendly, and waved as they went by.

A troop-carrier bearing German officials arrived early afternoon in St Helier harbour, and a deputation led by the Bailiff, who had first driven to Fort Regent and personally lowered the Union Jack, went out in a boat to greet them.

Later, the Bailiff directed a States' official to find rooms for the Germans in local hotels, and they started billeting German soldiers throughout the town.

For the rest of the day, German planes came and went. Rumour had it that St Helier was filling up with German soldiers. The German navy, they learnt, had taken over the Pomme d'Or Hotel, and was using it as its headquarters.

That evening, William read aloud the front page of the *Jersey Evening Post*, which listed the orders imposed on them by the German Kommandant—orders which had to be obeyed or serious measures would be taken. The rest of the family listened, aghast.

The first order imposed a curfew. Everyone had to be in their home by eleven o'clock at night and must not leave it before five in the morning.

It was forbidden to listen to any broadcasts except those from German and German-controlled stations. They mustn't communicate with anyone outside Jersey, nor get any news from them at all. Communicating with people outside Jersey, the Kommandant made clear, would be viewed as a hostile act and as such could result in bombardment.

Anguish swept through Rose at learning that she could no longer contact her family, nor they her.

From eleven o'clock that evening, the island's clocks had to be moved forward by one hour to match Berlin time.

There was a brief amnesty for all forms of guns, daggers and other weapons, plus all ammunition, which had to be handed in to the town arsenal by noon the following day.

The use of boats was restricted, and it was forbidden to use cars for private purposes. The sale of motor spirit was prohibited, except for use by the essential services, such as for doctors' visits, the delivery of foodstuffs, and for sanitary purposes. A permit for these would be issued.

Blackout regulations were to remain in force, and banks and shops were to stay open as before. Price rises were strictly forbidden.

Rose and Tom held each other close in bed that night.

. . .

GLOOM WAS STILL PREVALENT when they'd woken on the Wednesday morning.

'The banks acted just in time, by the sound of it,' William told them at lunch, when he joined them after a series of telephone calls. 'They've been ordered to continue business as usual, and that's what they'll do. But fortunately, by now they've destroyed any codes, specimen signatures and mandates that might have been useful to the Germans.'

'That was quick thinking,' Tom said.

'Unfortunately, that's not all. Would you believe it, but German Reichsmarks are to be the currency of the island! No longer will we have pounds sterling.'

'Reichsmarks!' Annie exclaimed, looking up from the sock she was darning.

'I'm afraid so. And as the banks keep all their accounts in sterling, there's sure to be a constant battle with exchange rates.'

'But why would they change the currency?' Annie asked, frowning.

William shrugged. 'You can be sure it'll give them some financial benefit.'

'What a cheek!' she exclaimed. 'I bet they'll steal from us.'

'They probably will. But they won't care what we think. As far as they're concerned, the Occupation has gone without a hitch, and is another great victory for Hitler, even though we gave in without a fight.'

'I bet their soldiers are pleased to have ended up here,' Tom said resentfully. 'They've taken over an island with miles of beaches and coves, and cliffs covered in wildflowers, and with deep blue sea all around them! Not for them the lousy weather and difficulties in Russia, where other Germans have been sent. The Germans here are going to have a good life on our island, while we're forced to live like prisoners. It isn't fair.'

'What do you think they'll say about it in London?' Rose asked. 'After all, they left us defenceless.'

William hesitated. 'I'm guessing they'll be dismayed at the loss of the islands. We're not the only island occupied by Germans; the other islands have been, too. And the others are closer to England. I'd be surprised if Churchill wasn't now worried at the real prospect of the Germans landing in Britain.'

'I don't know about Churchill,' Annie said, 'but I'm worried about my shop. It's almost a week since I went there, and it's been closed all that time. I think I'll go there tomorrow morning, open up and check the stock. I'll also get some groceries while I'm in town.'

'I'll come, too,' Rose said.

'And so will I,' Kathleen said hastily. 'I want to see what the Germans look like.'

'You shouldn't go on your own,' Tom said anxiously. 'If Dad can spare me tomorrow, I'll go with you.'

'Definitely not! You must keep away from the towns unless you absolutely have to go there, Tom,' Annie said quickly. 'We don't want the Germans to see you. And anyway, I'm sure we'll be all right. But thank you for the thought.' She smiled gratefully.

William opened his mouth to speak.

'And before you step in, William, and say you'll come with us,' Annie said, 'that won't be necessary, either. We'll be just fine by ourselves. You must go to the Gorins' farm as you planned, and see how Josh is getting on. Then you need to work on the hiding place for Tom. It's now very important to get that done as soon as possible.'

'Have you decided where it'll be?' Rose asked William.

He nodded. 'Yes, but I'm not really satisfied with it. I'm hoping I'll come up with a better idea.'

'Where were you thinking?' she asked.

'In the large barn with the hay bales,' Annie told her. 'They're going to build a false wall at the back. There'll be a concealed door behind the big bale in the corner.'

'Paul Mauger's family has done the same thing,' Kathleen cut in.

'I know,' William replied. 'And that's my worry. I've an awful feeling that before too long, just about every farm in the area will have a false wall in at least one of their barns. The Germans only have to find one false wall to know to look for a similar hiding place on every suspect property. But until one of us comes up with a more original idea, we'll have to stick with that.'

'I'll try to think of a better hiding place,' Kathleen said.

Tom smiled at her. 'Thanks, Kathleen. And so will I.'

'There's one other thing,' Annie said. 'I think we should start making potato flour. I know it doesn't make good bread, cakes or biscuits, but it could be useful for puddings if we get too low in flour. I'll need to show you what to do, Rose. It means scraping potatoes, pulping them, washing the pulp, drying it, and then grinding it. It means we'll be scraping potatoes more than we'll be grading them from now on.'

Rose nodded. 'Just tell me what has to be done, and I'll do it.'

'To come back to tomorrow morning, girls,' William said. 'If you change your mind about me going with you, just tell me. I can always go to the Gorins' later in the day.'

'We will,' Annie promised. 'It's a shame we can't take the car as it means we won't be able to take much with us.' She looked around the table, and shook her head in bewilderment. 'I can't believe I'm actually dreading going into St Helier, where I've been more times than I can count. It's like a horrible dream. I keep thinking I'll wake up and everything will be normal again.'

William got up and went to her end of the table. He put his arms around her and held her tightly.

'One day it'll all be over, Annie,' he said. 'We just have to keep our heads down until then. We'll try to live as we've always done, but within the rules they've imposed on us. The most important thing is that we're all together.'

20

T *he following day*

WITH SO MANY white pillowcases still hanging from the windows, cycling to St Helier was like having a string of washing continually blowing in your face, Rose remarked to Annie when the two of them and Kathleen reached the weighbridge at the end of the esplanade, and stopped to take in the signs of devastation.

'I know what you mean,' Annie said, staring towards the piers. 'It's hard to believe that people were killed here.' She gazed around. 'It's just too tragic for words.'

They got back on their bicycles and cycled up to the shop. A quick look round showed that there hadn't been any bomb damage. Greatly relieved, they decided to leave their bicycles in the small back yard behind the shop, and before they opened up, go and buy the items on their list. Others would likely have the same idea, Annie remarked, so the earlier they did their shopping, the better.

'Also,' she added, 'as we're going to have to see the German invaders at some point, we might as well get it over with soon as possible.'

To their surprise, there were only a few Germans walking around the streets, and those there were, wore ready smiles and looked quite relaxed.

The same was true of the area around the Town Hall, where only one soldier was on guard. He was wearing a tin helmet and carrying a rifle. Nearby, two young soldiers were leaning out of a window, but they were chatting to each other while smoking their cigarettes.

'Everyone's been making a fuss over nothing,' Kathleen remarked after three young German soldiers stepped into the road to allow them to remain on the pavement. The soldiers grinned at them as they walked past, and Kathleen, trailing behind Rose and Annie, smiled back.

'They look all right to me,' Kathleen told her mother when she caught her up. 'And they're not bad looking, either.'

Annie glared at her. 'They're the enemy, Kathleen. Don't you forget that. You're to have nothing to do with them.' With her mouth set in a firm line, she led the way into the grocer's shop.

'It's fortunate that you came today, Mrs Benest, as I don't know for how much longer you'll be able to buy what you want,' Mr Le Conte told them as he filled their order. 'They're saying that the Germans will soon be introducing rationing. Mind you, you've got a farm so you'll be all right.'

Annie frowned in surprise. 'But why would they need any more rationing? They've been rationing some items for quite a while now, so food stocks are high, aren't they?'

'But they won't be for long. The Germans have commandeered a large proportion to feed their troops. There may not be many soldiers here at the moment, but you can be sure that there soon will be. And we're no longer getting any food from Britain.'

'What else d'you think they'll ration, then?' Rose asked.

'If I've been told correctly, butter, sugar, cooking fats and meat,' Mr Le Conte said as he weighed the coffee beans, wrapped them and put the packet next to the jar of Marmite and bag of sugar that had been on Annie's list. 'And shop-keepers will probably unofficially ration other items as their supplies get low.'

'Well, for all our sakes, I do hope you've been misinformed, Mr Le Conte,' Annie said as she paid for their provisions. 'Give my regards to Mrs Le Conte, will you?'

As soon as they'd left the shop, she turned to the two girls. 'We'll go straight to the shop, dust and tidy it,' she said. 'Then we'll take a full inventory. We need to know exactly what we've got in stock. We may have to consider limiting how many items people can buy at any one time. We won't be getting anything else from Weymouth for a while, and I'm not sure whether Pierre's still going to be able to supply us. We'll try him, though.'

'What are we going to do after that?' Kathleen asked. 'Only I was thinking of having a walk around town and seeing if there's anyone I know.'

'I'm afraid you'll have to leave that for another day, Kathleen. I need both of you in the shop. You can sell, while Rose and I do the inventory. Then I need you with me back at home. We must check our stock of food and essentials, and make a list of anything we need to get while we still can. We'll come back tomorrow and buy what's on the list.'

'Surely, it can wait a day,' Kathleen said sulkily. 'I haven't seen any of my friends for ages.'

'No, it can't,' Annie snapped. 'We won't be the only people who've been warned about possible rationing, and there could well be a run on the shops as early as tomorrow. I need your help, Kathleen, and that's that. You should check your cupboards, too, Rose, although you haven't been here long enough to have accumulated much in the way of reserves.'

IN THE SITTING room after dinner that evening, William told them all that he'd been informed that when they harvested their wheat, they would have to hand a proportion of it to the Germans, possibly as much as half of it.

'So much for Mr Le Conte thinking that everyone with a farm would be all right,' Annie remarked in despair.

'All right is certainly too strong,' William said. 'But we'll be in a better position than those who don't have a farm. I've a horrible feeling that things are going to become very difficult over the next few months.'

'You always see the worst side of things,' Kathleen said sullenly. 'Everyone said how ghastly the German soldiers were going to be, but down at the harbour, we saw some of them buying ice creams for the children. And several came into the shop today and were very polite, which people said they wouldn't be.'

Rose nodded. 'Kathleen's right. It was a pleasant surprise. They even held the door open when a customer came in.'

'Well, at least the Occupation's done one thing—it seems to have brought you two together,' Annie said cheerfully.

'They didn't threaten us at all,' Kathleen went on,

ignoring her mother's comment. 'It was the clothes on the railing they were interested in, and some of the textiles. They said they were sending things back to their families in Germany. And they didn't just help themselves to what they fancied and walk out. They clicked their heels, saluted and paid for the goods. And not that it matters, one or two were rather good-looking,' she added.

Sinking lower in the armchair, a smile hovered above her lips.

'Just as I don't want Tom to be more visible than he needs to be, the same goes for you, Kathleen,' Annie said sharply. 'There'll be no gadding about the town in the evenings. For as long as there's a war, you're not to go out after dinner. Is that clear?'

Kathleen glared at her mother. 'I'm not a baby, but you're treating me like one. Other people of my age will be going out.'

'But you won't. You're not other people, you're my daughter and I need to know that you're safe. You're to stay in all evening. Is that clear?' Annie repeated.

'I suppose so,' Kathleen said sulkily. 'But I think you're panicking for nothing. It seems to me that it's going to be fine.'

'Much as I hope your optimism's justified, Kathleen,' William said, 'we have to behave as if it isn't. You'll stay in after dinner, as your mother says. And she's right about filling any gaps on our shelves. So that you can carry more, I'll see that you and Rose have a bag on the back of your bicycles tomorrow, as well as your front basket. But we'll get only what we need. We won't be stockpiling goods.'

'And about the farm,' Tom said. 'Since we learnt how much we'll have to give the Germans, and that may only be for starters, Dad and I have decided to soundproof the pigs' sties. We don't want the Germans to know how many pigs we have as we think they might come after the animals as well as the crops at some point in the future.'

'It's only a precaution at this stage, but a necessary one, we think. And Tom had another idea, too. Tell them, Tom,' William prompted.

'We've already got the Gorins' chickens as well as ours, and Dad's going to take the wagon out tomorrow to see if he can get even more. We'll build some coops at the cottage end of the yard, so that we'll end up with the chickens we've always had in the barn, which are fairly well hidden, and also chickens behind the cottage, which will be more visible.'

'That's a very good idea, Tom,' Annie said with a smile. 'If anyone sees the coops outside the cottage, they'll assume they've discovered all our chickens, and won't look any further.'

'I'll look after the chickens, Tom,' Rose said. 'I'll do the ones in the coops as well as those in the barn.'

'What rules will they impose next, I wonder,' William said, his face drawn. 'Tomorrow, I'll see if there are more chickens to be had. When you get back from town tomorrow, you girls had better dig up all the potatoes that are sufficiently ready. Grade some, and keep some for the potato flour. Tom, you'll go for the necessary wire and wood, and start making the coops. Later on, you and I will do a stint in the fields. For the present, though, I think that's all we can do.'

STANDING in the dark of the bedroom, Rose stood at the window and inched the blackout blind away from the glass. She drew in a deep breath of the jasmine-scented night air.

No matter what miserable things were happening in the day, the night was really beautiful, she thought, and she felt herself relax as she gazed up at the full moon through the narrow gap she'd made. Oblivious to the depression that weighted the island, the moon shimmered bone-white above the bay, silvering a vast expanse of water beneath it.

Closing her eyes, she stayed as she was, motionless, feeling the day's anxieties drain away.

A slight sound coming from outside the window made her open her eyes.

She pulled the blind a little further towards her, leaned closer to the window frame and peered down towards the farmhouse.

Framed by the moonlight, her bicycle propped up against the wall, Kathleen was unlocking the front door, clearly doing her best to avoid being heard.

Rose bit her lip and looked over at Tom. He was lying in bed in the same position as he'd been in when she'd slipped from under the sheets and come across to the window. And if she'd had any doubts about his level of consciousness, his rhythmic breathing told her that he was fast asleep.

Should she disturb him, she wondered. Perhaps not. He'd done a lot of physical work that day, and had a lot more to do the following day. He needed his sleep.

She glanced outside again, but Kathleen and her bicycle had disappeared. So she pushed the blind back into position, returned to the bed and climbed in. As she did so, she glanced at her bedside clock. It was minutes before eleven o'clock.

At least Kathleen had kept to the curfew, she thought. But she'd expressly disobeyed her mother and father by going out.

At the same time, she wasn't a child, and being treated as

one, which in a way was how Annie was treating her, had clearly made her resentful, and could tempt her to do something stupid.

What should she do, she pondered as she stared up at the ceiling. Should she tell Tom, or Annie and William, or all of them? Or should she confront Kathleen? Or should she just keep what she'd seen to herself?

She was still trying to decide upon the best course of action when she fell asleep.

21

T *hree weeks later*

THE AFTERNOON SUN was high in the sky as Tom and Rose started cycling along the track towards the main road that led down into St Aubin, and beyond that to Noirmont and to St Brelade's Bay.

When they reached the road to St Aubin, they went straight across and continued along the track, catching occasional glimpses of St Aubin's harbour down below, where the small boats were lying at angles on the rippled wet sand as they waited for the incoming tide to stand them upright again.

When they reached the crossroads for which Tom had been aiming, they left the road and followed a narrow pathway beneath an arch of trees.

A short time later, they emerged from the woods and got down from their bicycles. Wheeling their bicycles between huge golden clumps of fragrant gorse and broom, they headed for the open heathland that was visible in the distance.

'When you see the view of St Brelade's Bay from the top of the cliff, it'll take your breath away,' Tom said warmly. 'It's a really beautiful bay, and it's one of my favourite places. You see all kinds of birds nesting in the crevices of the cliffs, especially shags and oystercatchers.'

'It was an excellent idea to come here,' she said happily.

As they neared the edge of the open heathland, Tom stopped abruptly with a loud exclamation of annoyance.

'There are soldiers there,' he said. 'It hadn't occurred to me that they'd be here. And from the concrete slabs, it looks as if they're planning to build some kind of fortification. It means they'll always be here from now on as they're unlikely to leave the place unprotected.'

He glanced regretfully at Rose. 'We'd better not go any further. If we do, we'll be out in the open and they'll see us. I'd so wanted a couple of hours before dinner with you, just the two of us, away from the farm, which is something we haven't had for a while. And while we were gazing down at the sea, I thought you might tell me what's bothering you.'

'Who said anything's bothering me?' Rose asked, avoiding looking directly into his eyes.

'I did,' he said. 'And as we're here now, probably the last time for a while, we might as well stay. We could sit over there in the gap between the bushes. We'd still be able to enjoy some of the view, but not see the Germans or be seen by them. And then you can tell me what's on your mind.'

He took a bottle of cider and two cups from his saddle-bag, pushed his bicycle into the bushes, and sat on a fallen trunk set back from the path. Grinning up at Rose, he patted the place next to him. She pushed her bicycle up to a tree, arranged a few branches over it and sat down where he'd suggested.

'Here,' he said, pouring a cup of cider and handing it to her before pouring one for himself. 'Well?' he asked, putting the bottle back in his bag.

'It's Kathleen,' she replied bluntly.

'I thought it might be. What's she done this time?'

Rose heaved a sigh. 'I'm torn about whether to say anything. It's really none of my business, but I'm worried about what might happen.'

'Why don't you should start at the beginning?' he suggested. 'What's she up to now?'

'All right, then.' And she explained how she had seen Kathleen return late at night three weeks earlier, even though she'd been told to stay in.

She hadn't said anything to Kathleen, she told him, or to anyone in the family, as Kathleen was old enough to know what she was doing. And if she was going against her mother's wishes, it was for her mother to speak out, not her sister-in-law.

But she'd kept an eye on her ever since then, and she had seen her return every night of the week, always just before the curfew. She was now getting anxious that one day Kathleen would bring a German soldier back to the house. Obviously not *into* the house, she said quickly. But perhaps into the yard. Having any German become familiar with their farm and its layout, which might happen, was cause for concern.

'It doesn't mean that she *will* bring a German back, though,' Tom said after a few moments. 'Going out might just be some small defiance against all the orders and prohibitions, and the restrictions on movement. It can't be much fun for her, especially as she's at an age to think of getting married. And now that Emily's no longer here for company.'

'Part of that's true. But she's defying her mother and father, not the Germans.'

'And of course the person she's interested in,' Tom continued, 'if she's interested in anyone, could be a Jersey boy. Joshua or Paul Mauger, for example. It doesn't have to be a German soldier.'

'That's true.' She frowned thoughtfully. 'Joshua's working at the Gorins' farm, after all, and he's an attractive man. And Kathleen goes there from time to time to check that everything's all right so she'll have seen him several times recently. We all have. Could it be him, d'you think?'

'It's possible,' he said, 'but no more than that. She used to go out with him a few years ago, and I think she was quite keen on him, but that ended. I don't really know why. After that, she started seeing an Arthur Costain, who worked in an insurance office. Compared with Josh, he was drab and colourless. She seemed to like him, though, and they got engaged. But just after they started planning their wedding, Arthur was unexpectedly transferred to his firm's branch office in Southampton. So that ended, too.'

'Didn't she want to go with him?' she asked in surprise.

'She'd have gone like a shot, but she didn't get the chance. Arthur said it'd be hard enough getting used to his new position, and a new town, without also having to get used to being married. And off he went. Poor Kathleen. But she could have now picked things up again with Josh, I suppose.'

Rose thought for a moment. 'I'd like to think you're right about Joshua, but I don't think you are. What's more, I'm sure I've seen the German she likes.'

Just recently, she had been cycling back from the Gorins'

farm after taking some eggs to Joshua, she told Tom, and she'd seen Kathleen ahead of her, leaning against a wooden fence that surrounded a field in which a group of Germans were involved in exercises.

She'd quickly dismounted, laid the bicycle flat on the ground, and crouched down behind a large bush from which she could see Kathleen and the soldiers, with little likelihood of them seeing her.

They were running, jumping and crawling about on the ground, and taking turns to leap over a low wall near the bottom of the field. All were engaged in the activities, apart from two soldiers, one of whom was shouting instructions to the men, while the other was standing a little way back, watching what was happening. The uniform of the man standing apart from the others suggested that he was an officer.

After a couple of minutes, the man she thought was an officer turned and went across to Kathleen, whose face lit up as he did so. When he reached her, he stood with his body very close to hers, separated only by the wooden bars of the fence. They exchanged a few words, and then he returned to his supervisory position.

He was standing at an angle from which he could glance frequently at Kathleen, Rose told Tom, so she got a good look at his face. He was a handsome man, and it wasn't hard to see why Kathleen had fallen for him, which she appeared to have done. Her worry was that it could be difficult to persuade Kathleen to refrain from spending time with someone to whom she was so obviously attracted.

But that someone was the enemy.

And the higher the rank, the more dangerous the enemy.

. . .

A FEW DAYS LATER, she continued after a brief pause in which they'd eaten the apple and cheese that Rose had brought with her, she'd been heading for the shop in St Helier when she'd seen Kathleen with the same officer. They'd been standing in front of the Caesarea pub in Cattle Street, close to some German soldiers and a group of Jersey girls who were dressed to the nines and flirting madly with the soldiers.

There hadn't been room to slide a rasher of bacon between Kathleen and the blond officer, she told Tom.

And that had got her really alarmed.

It could only be a matter of time before the German soldier accompanied Kathleen back to the farmhouse, she said. She was pretty sure that up to that point, he hadn't done so, but if a serious friendship developed between them, he was almost certain to see her home before too long.

Apart from the reputation Kathleen would get if she continued to carry on in such a way with a German, there were other risks.

Soldiers were now being billeted to houses where there were empty rooms, and the number of rooms needed was increasing as more German troops were arriving all the time. Unsurprisingly, the island was fast filling up.

The size of the farmhouse, and the extent of their outbuildings, could only be guessed at by anyone standing outside. But if Kathleen's officer came into the building, or even just into the yard, he'd know at once that several Germans could be billeted there.

And if Germans were lodged there, it wouldn't be long before they discovered how many pigs and chickens they had. And they might notice that William, like many of their farming friends, wasn't being entirely honest in recording how much wheat and oats they'd harvested, and how many eggs they'd had.

Kathleen's friendship with the German was a situation fraught with danger, she concluded, and she didn't know if she should tell William and Annie.

Rose finished her account and looked hopefully at Tom for advice.

'I'll have to talk to her,' he said at once. 'She must stop hanging around the German soldiers. It would be horrendous if they started dropping by. You're right about the risks to us. Apart from the fact that we could be given a harsh punishment, such as prison, for altering the produce figures, people might think we were keeping food back for our own use. But you know the opposite is true. We're giving food to neighbours who haven't got farms, now that rationing's really starting to bite. I'll definitely speak to Kathleen.'

'Thanks, Tom. You'll have to be really careful what you say, though,' she said, anxiously. 'I heard Mrs Le Feu tell your mother yesterday that the Germans had taken away several men of military age. If she was right, and if Kathleen was angry at you, you don't know how she'd react.'

Tom shook his head. 'I can't believe she'd ever turn me in.'

She put her arm around him. 'I hate saying it, Tom, as she's your sister, and I don't think she'd deliberately hurt you or your parents, but people say things without thinking when they're angry.'

He nodded. 'I know what you mean. Don't forget, though, farming's still a reserved occupation.'

'But the Germans are making the rules now, aren't they? They could argue that there's no shortage of workers. After all, several farms closed down when the farmers evacuated, leaving a number of farm-workers without a job. Some of those men could be sent to replace you.'

'I take your point. It's not going to be as easy as I thought at first,' he said slowly. 'I need to think about this.'

'I'm wondering if it mightn't be better if you stayed completely out of it, and I was the one who spoke to her,' Rose said. 'Kathleen already dislikes me, so it'll make no difference to me if she dislikes me a little more. It'd be safer to have me the butt of her anger, rather than you.'

'Well, if you don't mind doing it,' Tom said. 'That's really kind of you.'

He took her face in his hands, and stared into the depths of her eyes. 'Don't you take any chances, though. I'd much rather the Germans took me than that they inflicted any sort of punishment on you. I love you with all my heart, Rose.'

Then he bent his head and kissed her hard on the lips.

22

Night lay heavy outside. Shrouded in darkness, Rose sat in the farmhouse kitchen and waited.

A key turned in the lock.

Moments later, she heard a faint creak as the front door opened, and through the open doorway she saw Kathleen emerge from the blackness outside and creep into the shadows that filled the house. Trying to avoid making any noise, Kathleen closed the front door behind her, and turned to face the staircase.

Rose went silently across to the kitchen door. 'Hello, Kathleen,' she said quietly.

Kathleen gasped. She turned to look at Rose, and stood still.

'Come and sit down, will you?' Rose pointed to Kathleen's chair, then moved back to the table, switched on the lamp she'd put in the centre of the table, and sat down.

Kathleen hesitated a moment, then stepped inside, noiselessly shut the door, and went and sat down on William's chair. 'This had better be quick,' she said. 'I'm tired and I'm not in the mood for a heart to heart.'

Rose forced a smile. 'It will be short. It's just that I've seen you coming home late almost every night, and I'm pretty sure that Annie and William aren't aware that you've been going out after dinner. They'd be furious and alarmed if they knew.'

'So what?' Kathleen retorted.

'And I've seen you with the same German soldier more than once,' Rose continued. 'It's got me a little worried. I know it's none of my business—'

'You're right—it isn't,' Kathleen cut in. 'And if that's what this is about, I'll say goodnight now.' She started to stand.

'No, don't go! Hear me out, will you?'

With a theatrical sigh, Kathleen sat down again.

Keeping her voice as low as possible so as not to disturb Annie and William, Rose went straight to the point, explaining her concern about the risk posed if Germans started coming to the farm, either into the house itself or merely to the outbuildings.

'You're just jealous,' Kathleen said with a sneer. 'I'm having a good time, and you're not.'

'I'm not jealous—I'm just worried that you're putting us in danger.'

'I'm not stupid,' Kathleen snapped. 'I know all of that. You're so smug that you think you're the only one with the welfare of the family at heart, and that only you know the best way to keep everyone safe. Well, I know it, too. The best way to protect my parents and Tom is to have the Germans on our side. And that's more likely to happen if I'm the friend of a German officer who's got some clout.'

'And what happens when he meets some other girl who drools over him like you do? It's fairly obvious that lots of Jersey girls would like to be given nylons and chocolates, and taken for rides in a car and out to dinner or a dance. When he loses interest in you, he can take his pick.'

'Trust you to think he will,' Kathleen countered. 'Well, you'll find you're wrong. Klaus is not like that. But while we're about it, you could look to your own behaviour. For a start, stop watching for me at night. Don't think I haven't seen you in the crack between the blind and the window, because I have. You look absurd.'

'If he turned against you,' Rose said steadily, struggling to hold back her temper, 'it could be bad for the family. But you don't think of anyone but yourself, do you?'

'And *you* don't think at all,' Kathleen said. She leaned towards Rose. 'I know what this is about, Rose. Being married to Tom is a big disappointment. You never expected to find yourself knee deep in potatoes and chickens, and you're jealous of all the things I can do.'

'Don't be ridiculous,' Rose retorted.

'You're stuck in a rut that you dug for yourself,' Kathleen sneered, 'and you envy me being with a powerful man like Klaus. Well, if you decide you want a Klaus of your own to spice up your life, there's a dance every Thursday night. I suggest you try your luck at one of those. As for me, I'm off to bed now.'

As Rose watched her leave, she decided to tell Tom that she'd spoken to Kathleen, but leave it at that. There was no point in making him anxious about something they were helpless to alter.

And there was always a chance, however unlikely it seemed, that she might have made Kathleen think seriously about the risk she was putting them at, and if she did that, perhaps she would change her behaviour.

She switched off the lamp, and returned to the cottage and Tom.

.   .   .

LYING ON HER BED, Kathleen seethed at Rose telling her what to do, and in her own house, too! The cheek of her, she thought.

Unfortunately, the days of hoping that Rose would be so bored and despairing that she headed off back to England were long gone—the Occupation had brought that line of thinking to an end.

And the other idea she'd had soon after Rose's arrival, that Rose might meet a man who wasn't a farmer and to whom she felt better suited that she did to Tom, hadn't developed into anything, either.

Again, she had the war and the deprivations of the Occupation to thank for that.

It was true that her hope that Rose would, through her dislike of farm work or her actions, bring about the end of her marriage and leave the way clear for Emily, was now irrelevant as far as Emily was concerned.

But she still fervently hoped that Rose's marriage to Tom would come to an end. She'd come to hate Rose, her initial hostility towards Rose having been stoked by Rose's attempt to come between her and Klaus. And now, seeing Rose and Tom happy together was like having a knife plunged into her side, and she'd do anything to wipe that self-satisfaction from Rose's smug face.

Unfortunately, it wasn't that easy to see what she could do to facilitate the end of the marriage.

Had Rose been the flirtatious type, she might have hit it off with one of the German officers who stopped daily for a coffee at Forte's. But with so many girls hanging around the place, all of them trying like mad to catch the eye of a soldier, there was no need for the Germans to make any real effort with any of the women there, and they were certainly unlikely to do so with someone who wasn't attempting to be noticed by them.

And there was little chance of her attracting the attention of a random soldier passing in the street, because in common with most of the Jersey women who weren't on the lookout for a man, Rose kept her eyes down whenever she passed any Germans.

But maybe she shouldn't be too ready to abandon her hope of Rose finding another man, she mused. With a little thought, she might still come up with a possible candidate.

That candidate would clearly have to be a Jersey man, and he would have to do the running. With so many men gone, and with most of the remaining men tied up in farming, it wouldn't be easy to find a man for Rose, a man whose life didn't revolve around the readiness of wheat for harvesting, but there must be someone who'd fit the bill.

Moreover, it would have to be someone who wasn't so hungry that his thoughts turned continually to food rather than to the thrill of a dalliance.

It would have to be a man like Joshua Mauger.

She sat up in bed.

That was the answer, she thought in excitement.

Josh was looking after the Gorins' farm and initially had been making such a poor job of it that either her parents or Tom kept on having to go over to help him. Rose, too, had been there several times. In Rose's case, it had been to give Joshua his share of the eggs.

But *that* was a situation with possibilities.

She'd have a quiet word with her mother the following day, she decided. She'd point out that the shop needed more attention than her mother had been giving it during the past few weeks, and blaming that on her parents going across to the Gorins' so frequently.

She would then suggest that now that Joshua seemed to know what he was doing, Rose could take over some of the visits to the farm, going there on a regular basis. Her mother could then concentrate on the shop.

She could add that she wasn't volunteering to go to the Gorins' herself as it made her too miserable to be there when Emily wasn't.

So Rose and Josh would be thrown together.

In a situation like that, spending hours close to a very good-looking man, who had no real interest in farm work, but plenty of interest in attractive women, and who was extremely good company as she knew from her past experience, something might well develop between them.

And even if it didn't, it could be suggested that it had done so. A few words in Tom's ear might be all it would take.

She lay back in bed and laughed gleefully.

23

London, September 1940

The schoolchildren are amazing,' Violet told Iris as they sat in the sitting room after dinner, waiting for their father to return from visiting a wholesaler in the Guildford area. Their mother was in the kitchen, setting the table for breakfast the following day.

'Their shelters are nothing like the Anderson that Father's installed for us,' Violet continued. 'Mother's made ours as cosy as she can, but theirs are damp and quite dark, and they have to huddle for ages on uncomfortable benches along the sides of the shelter. But they don't seem to mind.'

'What happens when they want to go to the toilet?' Iris asked.

Violet pulled a face. 'There's a bucket behind a sacking screen. The less said about that the better!'

'Well, at least you get out of teaching,' Iris remarked. 'Sitting with a bunch of children, doing nothing and getting paid for it, isn't that bad, even if the surroundings are fairly awful.'

'We don't sit doing nothing, as you put it,' Violet retorted. 'We work really hard. Children get restless if they aren't occupied, and we have to distract them from what's going on outside. We chant the multiplication tables, sing songs, read them stories. Things like that. Believe me, it's not easy keeping children focused at a time like this, especially when they begin the day tired after a night of heavy bombing. You should try it.'

'No, thank you. I'm happy to leave it to you. I'm far too busy at the shop. A year ago, I'd have laughed at you if you'd told me that people would be clamouring today for cotton and everything needed to make clothes, and that they'd be buying any scraps of material they could find, not just to make clothes for their children, but also for themselves. But that's what's happening.'

'Well, it's hardly a surprise,' Violet said. 'There aren't enough ready-made clothes in the shops these days, and what clothes you find are very expensive. I'll be amazed if they don't start clothes' rationing soon. They're already doing food and petrol, so why not clothes?'

'I'm sure they will,' Iris said. 'It was a stroke of luck that we had a large amount of white linen in stock. We thought we'd sell it as interlining or for tablecloths, but because of the blackout, people want clothes that make them easy to see in the dark, so they're buying up all the linen. Also they're buying up that range of buttons which look normal in daylight, but lurid at night as they glow in the dark.'

'Keeping a sufficient stock must be a worry for Father.'

'It is. We've virtually no knitting wool to sell. Mother's actually taken to making balls of wool. You should see her when she gets going. There can't be anyone better at taking discarded woollens apart, then washing the wool, stretching and rewinding it.'

'It's not that difficult when you've done it a few times, Iris,' Mabel said, coming into the room and sitting down. 'And when there's as big a demand for wool as there is.'

'But it's the middle of summer!' Violet exclaimed in surprise.

'That's irrelevant. Those women in the Women's Voluntary Service have got everyone knitting in the air-raid shelters and in lots of other places, too. Knitting for Victory, they're calling it, and sewing circles are springing up everywhere. Thanks to the heavy bombing of the past few nights, they must have added a lot to the pile.'

Violet frowned questioningly. 'Piles of what? What're they making?'

Mabel shrugged her shoulders. 'Anything that'll help the war effort. Socks, for example, and balaclavas, pullovers, gloves and comfort items for our soldiers. Anyone can join a circle—even the Queen's got one in Buckingham Palace.'

'What about cotton reels and the like? Are they in demand, too?' Violet asked.

Mabel nodded vigorously. 'As Iris said, everyone wants sewing essentials. Now that the clothing factories are making uniforms and parachutes rather than frocks, people have to manage with the clothes they've got.'

'I take it that's why Father's gone down to Guildford today,' Violet said.

'That's right, love. We badly need more stock. We don't know how long the war will last, but from past experience, I think we can safely assume it'll last a lot longer than people think it will.'

'Lucky Rose to be out of all this, even if her life did seem to be focused on potatoes,' Iris mused.

'It can't be much fun to be occupied,' Mabel said sharply. 'While it's frightening for us not knowing what's going on, it must be worse for her. I won't relax till we get a letter telling us that she's all right.'

'It could be ages before there are any more communications between us and Jersey,' Violet said. 'But the day we're allowed to write again, I will.'

'At least she's surrounded by water, and can submerge herself,' Iris moaned. 'I wish I could have a bath that's more than five inches deep! It's ludicrous. Who can get clean in such a small amount of water?'

'Do stop complaining, Iris,' Violet snapped.

They heard the front door close, and all looked towards the sitting room door as John came into the room, looking tired.

Mabel rose to her feet. 'I'm relieved to see you back, John. I was starting to get worried. I'll get you a cup of tea, and would you like something to eat? I know you were going to get something out, but did you manage to do so?'

'I did, thank you, so I'm fine. A whisky would go down well, though, better than a cup of tea,' he said, sitting down. He sighed heavily. 'It's been a long day. And driving back, I made a decision.'

He looked apologetically towards Mabel, who was pouring him a whisky. 'I'm afraid we're going to have to stop selling from Upper and Lower Hams.'

'What!' Mabel exclaimed. She turned to him in amazement.

'I've been wondering for some time if we should do that, and I think it's become unavoidable. I'll keep Mid Hams open, and we'll have two stalls at the market for the duration of the war.'

His wife and daughters stared at him. 'I thought all the shops were doing well,' Iris said.

John nodded. 'They are at the moment, but they won't be for much longer. Two more girls told me yesterday that they were leaving to work in the munitions' factory. We can't compete with the pay, and it's becoming a real struggle to get staff. Also, it's getting much harder to keep all three shops fully supplied, now that we can't get goods from overseas. And from what I saw today, we're going to be limited in what we can get from our local suppliers. I can just about stock one shop and the stalls, but not three shops.'

'What did they say in Guildford?' Mabel asked, handing him the tumbler of whisky, then sitting down.

'It's not so much what they *said*, as what I saw. When Hitler announced in July that he was getting set to invade and that German troops would be landing on the south coast, we thought it was wishful thinking, something that would never happen. But when you get further south, you can feel the fear, and see that people are taking the risk of invasion very seriously.'

Violet frowned. 'But what can they do about it?'

'Build defences. I saw some of them. Basically, they're taking villages and towns at key points along the route inland from Kent and turning them into fortresses.'

'How?' Violet asked.

John shrugged. 'They've built gun pits, installed barbed wire and attached explosives to some of the wire. The idea is that there'll be unexpected obstacles in the path of the invading tanks, and while they're hesitating, they'll attack them.'

Violet nodded. 'I'm not surprised. My tutor was certain the Germans intended to overrun us.'

'And that's not all,' John continued. 'They expect the enemy to use the main roads, so they're creating a network of barriers and armed posts from the Bristol Channel up through Cambridgeshire and possibly further north than that. They're building lines of pointed stone blocks into the roads that will slow any enemy tanks that breach the coastal defences. So will the pillboxes they're erecting across the south.'

'Pillbox hats are quite popular now,' Iris said. 'We sold them in D.H. Evans.'

'They're armed posts, Iris,' John said, smiling. 'The walls and roof are built of concrete, not out of felt, and they're reinforced with any kind of metal available. Funnily enough, I didn't see any that had been reinforced with strips of velvet. And unlike hats, they've slits in the side for light machine guns and rifles to poke out.'

Violet frowned. 'D'you think Hitler's invaded the Channel Islands to have stepping stones from which to launch a full invasion?'

John nodded. 'It's quite likely. He'll have been thinking ahead, like they've been doing in the south. And like we should be doing. On the way home, I started questioning whether we, too, were fortifying ourselves against what might happen in the future. Hence my decision about the shops.'

'What will you do with Upper and Lower Hams?' Violet asked.

'Nothing. They'll go back to being shops after the war. Until then, they'll effectively be two extra depots. It makes sense to have our stock in more than one place. At present, everything is stored in the main depot and there's a limited amount of stock in each of the shops.'

Mabel nodded. 'You're right, John. If one of the buildings

were bombed, perish the thought, at least we'd have stock in the others.'

'That's the idea,' he said. He glanced at his watch. 'Now, if no one's anything to add, I suggest we switch the wireless on. It's almost time for the nine o'clock news. And I think it'll be *It's That Man Again* afterwards. A touch of Tommy Handley would be welcome—he'll cheer us up after the depressing decision that had to be made today.'

24

Jersey, October 1940

The early morning rain had ceased, but a strong gale was blowing as Kathleen cycled to the Gorins' farm, her head bowed against the wind.

When she reached the farm, she dismounted and walked the bicycle along the path. The grass on either side of the path looked a bit of a mess, she noticed. It was covered in twigs and fallen leaves and was badly in need of being cut before the winter descended.

Not that it was any surprise to see the place looking less than well cared for—Joshua had always been unlikely to give the farm the attention it needed. But at least he had successfully done the most important part, she thought, which had been getting in the grain.

Her parents had been anxious about the grain ever since bands of German inspectors started going from farm to farm, urging speed, and they had been greatly relieved when Rose had told them that Joshua had hired men to help with the autumn harvest.

He had taken on some of the men who had found themselves stranded in Jersey after coming over from England for the potato season, and with the hired men, had gathered in all of the wheat, corn and oats under the watchful eye of the inspectors.

The threshing machines had been working all day, and when the threshing was done, Joshua had been on hand when the Germans had measured the amount of grain produced, and then requisitioned a proportion for their own use, just as they did with the milk at her farm.

When he'd given the Germans what they'd ordered, he had told Rose that William could go to the Gorins' with his cart and collect his share of the produce. The rest he would store. When Rose had conveyed his message to Annie and William, they had been pleasantly surprised at the diligence shown by Josh.

With the demands on farmers increasingly stringent as supplies from the outside world dried up, many had learned to conceal a part of their crops and livestock. But if Joshua, less familiar with what you could get away with, had attempted to cheat the Germans, she would have been quite worried.

Much as she loved Klaus and thought him a good man, she was aware that the Germans expected to be obeyed, and would punish severely anyone who broke the rules.

But fortunately, Joshua knew that, and there was nothing to suggest that he was taking chances.

It was now about three months since Rose had started going to the Gorins' farm for two or three days a week, and it would be interesting to know if there was anything developing between her and Josh, especially as Tom had been quite irritated with Rose on a couple of occasions recently, which suggested that all might not be well between the two of them.

The first had been a couple of weeks earlier, when British planes had dropped leaflets headed 'News from England' during the night. There'd been a message from the King and Queen and a photo of the two of them in the bombed part of Buckingham Palace.

Rose had taken one look and burst into tears.

Tom had assumed that she was wishing she was back in England and had never come to Jersey. Rose assured him it was just worry about her family, exacerbated by the picture of the Royal Chapel in ruins. Although they had let the matter drop, they seemed a little less easy with each other in the days after that.

The second time was at the end of the first week in October, when Rose, who had come back early from the Gorins', had been left in charge of making jam, their stocks having been depleted by their failure from the outset of the Occupation to restrict how much jam each person spread on their bread.

Determined to make as much jam as they could, they had scoured the countryside, picking the few blackberries that hadn't already been picked, and had soaked them in two buckets.

Rose had been given some of their dwindling stock of sugar to use for the jam. Their sugar supply was precious: although they had started to grow sugar beet to use as a sweetener, it wouldn't be ready for a while.

Annie had a suitably large pan, but it was too heavy to take next door, so Rose had to make the jam in Annie's kitchen. She had just put the berries on to boil, sweetened by a little honey from their bees and by their treasured sugar, when Annie came back from St Helier, waving the *Jersey Evening Post*. She'd handed it to Rose and gone out to speak to William.

The paper had announced that people could send a message to relatives in England through the Red Cross. They were allowed up to twenty-five words. In great excitement, Rose had grabbed a piece of paper from the worktop, rushed to the kitchen table, and started to write to her family.

In her effort to tell them in twenty-five words that they were managing despite the straightened circumstances, while also asking how they were, she completely forgot the jam, and it had boiled over, creating a glutinous scarlet mess that slowly spread across the range and congealed there.

Tom had been furious that she'd prioritised writing to England, which could have been done later that day or on the following day, rather than keeping her focus on their precious jam.

Although he'd apologised later and told her that he understood her concern about her family in the light of the heavy German raids that were taking place nightly over London, the atmosphere between them had been cool for several days.

If ever there was going to be a time when Rose might need to turn to someone, it was then, Kathleen realised, when there was so much for Rose to be anxious about, both in England and in Jersey.

Tension had increased in Jersey since September when every Jewish person had been ordered to register with the authorities. Any businesses owned by Jewish people had to be clearly marked as such. As there were rumours of the hostility directed against the Jews in Germany, singling them out in such a way was causing a great deal of disquiet.

And with the nights full of the sound of aircraft in flight and of anti-aircraft fire, and with planes passing low above them in the day, often at a frightening speed, everyone was consciously afraid for their safety and that of their family and friends.

The weather, too, had become the enemy of people attempting to minimise the disruption to their lives, as for the past month or so Jersey had been battered by gales and heavy rain.

At such a time, the harsh reality of the Occupation was felt, along with the deprivations it was causing, such as a lack of food. Only a month before, a communal kitchen for children had been opened, and there were suggestions that kitchens for adults might also open before too long.

Hunger, and having to obey enemy orders, weighed heavily on everyone, and Rose was likely to be feeling in need of a warm, friendly shoulder. But with a degree of strain between her and Tom, that shoulder might not be Tom's.

So had she turned to Joshua? Kathleen's desire to find out had been the reason behind the visit to Joshua at a time when Rose was scraping potatoes in one of the farmhouse barns.

Reaching the front door of the ivy-covered house, she propped her bicycle against the wall, took off her scarf, shook her hair and did the best she could with her fingers to push the strands of blonde hair back from her face and into the knot she'd wound at the nape of her neck.

Then she knocked on the door, stood back and waited.

No one answered, so after a minute or two, she went to the side gate, pushed it open and walked round to the back of the house, as she used to do whenever she visited Emily.

When she got to the yard, a movement in front of the

barns that lay on the far side of the yard caught her attention. She saw that Joshua had emerged from one of the barns, and was heading toward the fields.

'Josh!' she called, raising her hand to wave.

Hearing her, he turned and saw her, and promptly changed direction.

'Well, this is a surprise,' he said, coming up to her, grinning. 'To what do I owe the honour?'

'Does there need to be a reason for one friend to call on another?' she asked playfully.

'Oh, we're still friends, are we? I thought that now you were moving in more illustrious circles, you might have forgotten your old friends.'

She glanced very obviously at the tanned chest visible beneath the white shirt that hung open. 'No one could forget you, and you know it,' she said, injecting a coquettish note into her voice.

'I could almost think you were flirting with me, but I must be wrong. I can't give you chocolate or nylons, or take you gallivanting across the island in a monster of a car,' he said with a laugh.

She laughed too.

'You're right that you're mistaken about me flirting,' she said. 'I'm just being friendly. I'll leave the flirting to Rose. I imagine she excels at it.'

He frowned slightly. 'Rose? She doesn't flirt,' he said. 'And she's married.'

Kathleen gave a tinkling laugh. 'Now was it you, or another Joshua, who was almost caught with his pants down by a banker who'd come home unexpectedly early one day? I bet that particular Joshua still has a scar on his rear from climbing out of the window with unseemly haste.'

They both laughed.

'Don't worry,' she added. 'I don't want to inspect the area to establish who you are. I'll leave that for Rose to do.'

He shook his head, looking bemused. 'What's all this about Rose?'

Kathleen rearranged her features to convey concern. 'I'm really sorry—I shouldn't have said anything. What you and she do is no one's business. Forget I spoke.'

He gestured helplessness. 'I don't understand why you thought Rose and I would be flirting with each other, and all that. What made you think that?'

'I suppose it's because she talks about you a lot. She's said more than once that she thinks you're handsome, and she comes here as often as she can. She managed to get Mum to agree to her spending more time here than she used to do. And when I arrived this morning, I saw that the grass in front needed cutting, so I assumed that you were too busy doing something else. I'm sorry if I got it wrong.'

'I'm afraid you did.'

Kathleen raised an eyebrow. 'Really?'

'Yes, really.' She heard a trace of annoyance in his voice. 'She's an attractive woman, and you know me for attractive women, but she's not my sort. Admittedly, that might not stop me from obliging if it was offered on a plate, if you see what I mean, but she's never done anything to make me think she wants more than a friendship.'

'I see.'

'And I'm not the sort of person who'd push himself on anyone,' he went on. 'No need. There're plenty of fish in the sea. Even if fishermen need a licence these days to go after them, and the beaches are mined,' he added with a laugh.

She forced a laugh in response.

'But you, Kathleen,' he said, his voice filling with warmth. 'Now that's something different. You look stunning.

And if you were to come here instead of Rose, I'd find it hard to keep my hands off you.'

She laughed. 'You managed all right a few years ago.'

'True. But I was young. I didn't then know what a golden prize I had within my grasp. Your German's a lucky man.'

She cleared her throat in sudden embarrassment. 'Okay. I can see that I was wrong about you and Rose,' she said. 'But that wasn't the reason I came here. I didn't know if you'd heard that the Germans have ordered all young men between eighteen and thirty-five to register.'

'I did know. Paul told me. Some soldiers went to our family's farm to see the heifers, and also to find out if they'd any chickens, and if so, how many. And to remind them that if they had pigs, they had to be notified every time there was a litter. They'd count the number of piglets, Paul told me, and keep an eye on them till they were slaughtered.'

Kathleen nodded. "I know—we've got pigs.' She gave him a sly grin. 'There're ways around this, you know. Dad says that when one of his pigs dies a natural death, he'll have it examined and given a certificate. Then he'll pass the dead pig to another farmer, who'll also get a certificate for it. To the Germans, a pig's a pig. It can be passed around until it smells, and each of the farmers who gets a certificate will be able to keep a pig for his own use.'

'Hey, that's clever,' Joshua said in admiration. 'I wish the Gorins still had pigs. I'm partial to a bit of pork.'

'Me, too,' Kathleen said. 'To any meat for that matter. With meat being rationed, we're eating so many vegetables, and they take forever to prepare.'

'But *you* get meat in restaurants, don't you? I bet your German takes you out for slap-up meals.'

Kathleen blushed. 'Sometimes he does. But I'm not just going out with him to be fed, you know. He's really good company. And so are his friends,' she added with a touch of defiance.

He held up his hands. 'I'm not getting at you. I agree about the soldiers. Paul said that the ones who went there about the heifers were very friendly. They had a chat, and then they warned Paul about that order you mentioned. He need not worry, they told him, as he's more use to them as a farmer. When Paul told me that, I was relieved, I can tell you. My rear end has already been defaced, as you seem to know, and I want to protect it from further damage.'

They giggled. Then Kathleen asked about Paul's heifers that the Germans had inspected.

'They didn't find them good enough and went off to plague another farmer.'

'I'll do the same, then,' she said. 'Go off, I mean. Not plague another farmer.'

'Come on over again,' he said with a grin. 'If your German will allow you. You're always good company. And you're good to look at, Kathleen. Really you are.'

'I will,' she said.

So there wasn't anything between Rose and Joshua, she thought, as she set off along the track to her house. Nor was there likely to be.

Despite the hints she'd dropped to suggest otherwise, Joshua was certain that Rose had no interest in him, and he clearly had none in her. To her surprise, she felt quite pleased about the lack of anything untoward between them.

So much for having Tom come upon Josh and Rose in the act of betraying him, she thought ruefully as she pedalled along. Of course, it didn't mean that she couldn't make it *look* as if there was something going on between them, even if there wasn't. It would take a bit more effort on her part, but it could be done.

But did she still want to do that?

No, she didn't, she realised, puzzled. She didn't want to think of Rose with Joshua, whether it was the truth or a lie.

She'd enjoyed that chat with Joshua just now—he was easy to talk to, fun to be with, and actually very attractive with his lean build, tanned skin and with light brown hair that was bleached by the sun.

So much so that if she hadn't been in love with Klaus, she might have gone in hot pursuit of him. And she had a feeling that he might have let himself be caught.

But she loved Klaus and that wasn't going to happen.

As for Rose. In the absence of any other obvious candidate for the role of guilty party with Rose, and with people increasingly focused solely on getting through the difficulties that faced them daily, it was unlikely that there'd be anyone else to fill that role.

A gust of wind blew her headscarf across her face.

Furthermore, the wintery weather wasn't conducive to romantic frolics, and with the days drawing in, she was bound to be wasting her time if she tried to make it look as if something was taking place when it wasn't.

Also, having a curfew was limiting. Rose wasn't the sort of person to agree to a late-night post-curfew assignation, so planning something along those lines was out of the question until the days had lengthened.

All things considered, she would have to drop the idea until at least the following spring, when the weather was better. Inhibitions melted, or could be made to appear as if they'd melted, beneath the rays of a warming sun.

But even though she would have to wait a few months, she could still take advantage of anything that came her way that could be used to prepare the ground for a future exposé, she realised as she reached the farmhouse.

For example, it wouldn't hurt to present Rose in a bad light whenever possible. There was always the hope that Rose's marriage would collapse in the increasing tension of their situation, and highlighting Rose's faults might speed that up.

'HOW WAS JOSH?' Annie asked as Kathleen came into the kitchen where William, Tom and Rose were sitting.

'Fine,' Kathleen said, sitting down. 'He knew about having to register, though it won't affect him. But I thought the farm looked a bit tired, and wondered whether to give him a hand. Just to get it ready for the winter months.'

'Does he need you as well as Rose?' Tom asked in surprise.

Kathleen shrugged. 'It seems a lot of work for two people, especially when neither is particularly experienced. He got help in, but help costs money and he's had to let them go now that the harvest's over.'

'What's wrong with the farm?' William asked.

'I got a general impression, that's all. The debris from the trees needs to be raked off the front lawn, and the grass cut. I didn't go far round the back, but I noticed that the vegetable garden needs someone with green fingers to sort it out. If the war ended tomorrow and the Gorins came home, they'd have a fit.'

'The Gorins chose to leave the farm,' Rose snapped. 'They're lucky to have the help they've got. Other farms have been shut down. If you think I'm doing such a bad job, Kathleen, why don't you go each day, armed with a spade, and do better?'

'Now, you two,' Annie said. 'I think we'll leave things as they are, Kathleen. As Rose said, it was the Gorins' decision to go to England. They're reasonable people and I'm sure they won't be expecting their farm to have been run in the same way as if they'd stayed.'

William nodded. 'Your mother's right, Kathleen.'

'And we're in danger of getting behind with the work that has to be done here,' Annie continued. 'Meals are taking longer to prepare as we're eating so many vegetables, and we're having to find substitutes for things like tea, sugar and coffee, unless we want to buy them from black marketeers and pay their extremely high prices.'

'How high is high?' William asked. 'A bit of real tea would be a treat.'

'To give you some idea, they're asking for the equivalent of fifteen shillings for a pound of sugar, and twenty-five pounds for a pound of tea. I know they're not as nice, but at least bramble leaves for tea and ground acorns for coffee are free.'

'That *does* sound a lot,' William said.

'And I won't pay it,' Annie said firmly. 'I'm not buying on the blackmarket. So we've now less time in the day to do the things we used to. If you go over to the barn, for example, you'll see a pile of potatoes waiting to be scrubbed.'

Kathleen groaned aloud.

'That's all very well Kathleen,' Annie said briskly, 'but in the absence of cornflour, we're going to need more potato flour than we've been making. I bought two sieves today, so we'll be able to sieve the flour ourselves. And we must get in the apples. We need to peel some of them if I'm going to make black butter as I usually do. We can't give any more time to the Gorins' farm than we're doing now. They won't expect us to run their farm at the expense of ours.'

'I hope you heard that, Kathleen,' William said firmly. 'I don't want to hear any more criticism of Rose, veiled or not.'

She glared at her father.

'And now,' he went on, 'Mrs Le Feu's son came over today. Tony apologised for not being able to bring any mussels and crabs this time, but the beaches aren't safe. Instead, he gave us two rabbits, and Annie's made us a rabbit stew and broccoli. So let's put any nastiness aside, and enjoy it in peace.'

25

Jersey, February 1941

With a loud clunking at every turn of the wheel as the metal pieces holding the makeshift tyres in the rims hit the snow-dusted ground, Rose and Tom pushed their bicycles down the hill from Royal Square, past intermittent heaps of snow and ice lodged at the base of shop walls and in recessed doorways.

Ahead of them, the cold morning light glinted on the steel-grey sea.

'The trees on the esplanade looked almost ghostly, didn't you think?' Rose asked, her breath a column of white mist. 'I'm so surprised we've had more snow. When it snowed in January, I thought that was it for this year. Thank goodness I planted the sweet peas and love-in-a-mist last week. The ground would be much too hard to do it now. I want our front garden to look really pretty this year.'

'It will do, I'm sure.' He smiled at her, then glanced at the empty shop window they were passing. 'I shouldn't have left it till my trousers were so full of holes that they resembled black lace. I don't know what I'll do—there's nothing left in the shops.'

'I doubt your mother will be able to help. She's struggling to get supplies. The shop's totally out of wool. And so's the Summerland factory, which was a shock. You saw how worried she was when she got back yesterday. All our shops and factories are empty because the Germans are all over the island, buying up absolutely everything.'

'You can't really blame them,' Tom said. 'If you remember, in one of the clothes shops we went in, we heard that German saying that there was virtually no clothing to be had in Germany.'

'I suppose so. And at least we still have food. But that's because we live on a farm,' she added. 'Not everyone does. There's a real shortage of milk and butter. I know that Annie's finding it hard to keep up with making food parcels for the people she knows who need help, and for anybody else she hears is hungry.'

He nodded. 'Knowing my parents, they'll find something to give for as long as people are starving.'

'Look, Tom!' she exclaimed. 'There's another clothes shop. Perhaps you'll be lucky this time. I hope so. It's a little chilly to have to wear swimming trunks all day. Not that I'd mind if you did,' she added with a giggle. 'Though I'm not sure how much work I'd get done.'

He grinned at her. 'We could test that when we get home,' he said, and he leaned across and hugged her.

They reached the draper's shop, and stopped abruptly.

Crudely painted across the window, in bright yellow, was the Star of David.

As they stood there, shocked, the shop door opened and

the manager appeared. 'I saw you hesitating,' he said. 'Is there anything I can help you with?'

'If I didn't want anything, I'd be tempted to buy something, anyway,' Tom said, 'just to spite the Germans. But I do want trousers. I don't suppose you've got any?'

The manager shook his head. 'I'm sorry, I haven't. I've got a couple of shirts, though.'

'You must be about the only place in Jersey that has, then,' Rose said. 'I imagine people are nervous about going into your shop because of the artwork.' She indicated the Star of David.

'It won't be there for much longer,' the manager said. 'I'm buying the shop from the owner for a modest price. I'm not Jewish, but he gave me a job when I needed one, and I'm glad to have a way of showing him how grateful I am. When the war's over, he's going to buy it back from me for the same amount.'

Tom smiled. 'That's a great thing to do.'

The manager shrugged. 'Several of us are buying shops for the duration of the war, with the intention of selling them back to the owners for what we paid. There aren't many Jewish people in Jersey these days as most left with the evacuation—I think there're only about thirty now. But the least we can do is look after the ones who're still here. They're Jersey people, too.'

'Regrettably, I don't need a shirt,' Tom said. 'I'll be back, though.'

The manager hesitated. 'Perhaps I shouldn't have said what I did about buying the shop. I hope I was wise to trust you. You hear of people reporting on their neighbours, even on people who'd been their friends.'

'We'd never do that,' Tom said. 'And we'll see you in the future at some point.'

They set off again. 'That's such a kind thing for that man to do,' Rose said warmly.

Tom smiled. 'It is, isn't it? And it's nice to see you looking so cheerful this morning.'

She laughed. 'I feel cheerful. Hearing that everyone back home is well has really lifted my spirits. I'd been so worried, what with all the bombing in London. And it didn't help when we were forced to hand over our radio for three months at the end of last year. When you don't know what's going on, you fear the worst. We shouldn't have been punished because of so-called espionage in Guernsey. It was so unfair.'

'But it underlines the fact that there's no point in attempting any organised resistance—the Germans have proved more than once that they're prepared to punish innocent people if there's any act of resistance. Darn!' he exclaimed. He stood still and stared down at his bicycle tyre.

'Has it punctured again?' she asked in despair.

'No, it's the hose unwinding. The bit of metal that's been holding it in place has fallen off. And I thought I'd done such a good job of replacing the tyre, having ditched my glue and patches system in favour of Dad's advice and used the garden hose. He helped me measure it, cut it to the right length and wrap it around the rim of the wheel, so I know that part of the process was well done. I can't have fixed the metal bits at each end properly or one wouldn't have slipped off.'

'We've time for you to put it back now, even if you have to redo it when we get home. We could sit over there by the weighbridge while you do it.'

Tom nodded. 'Let's do that, then.'

He picked up the metal grip and with his tyre unwinding

a little more at every turn of the wheel, they headed for the wooden bench closest to them.

Rose sat down and watched Tom turn the bicycle upside down, balance it on the handlebars, and remove the rest of the hose from the wheel. Then he carefully rewound the hose around the rim.

'Hold the hose in place, would you, please?' he asked Rose. As she leaned forward to do so, they heard a wave of laughter and loud cheering, and raised German voices.

Both turned towards the sound. A number of German officers were coming out of the Pomme d'Or Hotel with the flamboyance of those who had just enjoyed a good meal washed down with plenty of wine. Among them, several Jersey girls were chattering and laughing as they clung on to the soldiers.

At the heart of them was Kathleen.

Tom promptly sat down, his back to the group, his expression furious.

'Don't let them see you looking at them, Rose,' he hissed. 'With luck they'll go up Mulcaster Street and not come towards the harbour.'

To their relief, the group turned away and headed towards the north of the town, taking their noise and exuberance with them.

'I'm pretty sure one of those officers was Kathleen's Klaus,' Rose said. 'So, she's still seeing him, then. Did you know that?'

'Of course not. You told me you'd spoken to her and pointed out the danger she was putting us in. She's obviously ignored what you said, and this is how she's used the Saturday that Mum and Dad have given us off.'

'I did the best I could,' Rose countered. 'I really hoped she'd listen.'

'Didn't you try to see if she had?'

'And how could I do that?' she asked, getting angry. 'I didn't dare watch her from the window again. She'd have been furious if she'd seen me, and who knows what she would've done.'

'I still think you should've realised that she might not have taken your advice,' he said.

'And so should you!' she retorted, her eyes blazing. 'She's *your* sister, after all, and if anyone knows what she's like, it's you. No one was stopping you from checking that she was in her room.'

He reached out and took her hand. 'I know, and I'm sorry, Rose. I was out of line just now. It's just that I'm so disappointed. And I'm frustrated because I can't see what we can do about it. *I'll* have a word with her this time, but I doubt I'll have any more success than you.'

'I hope you do. I may not be close to Kathleen, but I don't like to think of people calling her a Jerrybag, which they will, and looking on her with contempt because she's with a German. It's a shame that she doesn't feel anything for Joshua Mauger. At least, I assume she doesn't or she wouldn't be with Klaus.'

'Josh!' Tom exclaimed. 'Is he interested in her, do you think?'

'I don't know for sure. But you told me they used to go out together, and lately when I've been at the Gorins', Joshua's mentioned Kathleen a few times, especially after her last visit there. It was seemingly casual, but I've once or twice wondered if he wasn't regretting that they weren't together anymore.'

'Well I never,' he said.

'If she ignores your warning about her friendship with Klaus, maybe Josh could be encouraged to show an interest, if I'm right about him having some. At the very least it could distract her, or it could rekindle her interest in him.'

Tom nodded. 'It'd be worth a try. But now, if we're going to get back home today, I'd better finish the tyre.'

STANDING at the window on the upstairs landing, Tom saw Kathleen emerge from the barn where she had been milking the cows, and come towards the farmhouse.

He got ready to move.

His parents were standing outside the *pressoir*, talking to each other, and he knew that Rose was in the cottage, and was going to allow him time to speak to Kathleen before she came across to help with the preparations for dinner.

By timing it carefully, he was coming down the stairs at the moment that Kathleen was about to start climbing up to her bedroom. Seeing him on the staircase, she stood back to let him finish coming down before she went up.

'What a pleasant surprise, Kathleen!' he said, stepping off the bottom stair. 'You're back. Presumably to have a meal before you go out again. But surely not. You can't be hungry again so soon.'

'If you've something to say, Tom, why don't you just say it?' she said acidly.

'Rose and I saw you in town today, and I should think a lot of other people did, too. People who know us. You were with a raucous bunch of Germans coming out of the Pomme d'Or. And with other women, too, who, like you, are willingly collaborating with the Germans.'

'We aren't collaborating. That's when you help the other side to win the war. We're not doing that—we're fraternising. And that's not wrong, even though you might not like it. Listening to you, Tom,' she went on, 'anyone would think you were jealous of my life. But why wouldn't you be? It's clearly more fun than yours.'

'When the Germans lose the war, you and they will be lucky to have any life at all.'

Kathleen laughed. 'You will have your little jokes, won't you? The Germans aren't going to lose anything.'

'But you are,' he said bluntly. 'If you haven't done so already, you're going to lose your reputation as a nice girl from a good family, a family that's been part of the backbone of Jersey for many years. You're going to be known as a Jerrybag, a woman who willingly gets into bed with a German. Once you lose a good reputation, it's very hard to get it back again. Is that really how you want to be seen?'

She scowled at him. 'Your trouble is, you've become sanctimonious and dull. I expect you caught that from your sanctimonious and dull wife. There's nothing wrong with wanting to have a good time, and if prim maiden aunts across the island don't like it, it's tough luck to them, I say.'

'And what about the danger you're putting us in?'

She raised an eyebrow. 'What danger? I've never invited Klaus into the house, and he's shown no interest in coming in.'

'The danger you'll be in, and so shall we, when he wants to get rid of you.'

'You think Rose will love you forever, don't you?' she said aggressively, her face hard. 'You think that you're so lovable that once someone loves you, they'll never stop. So, if *you* can be loved for ever, why d'you think it's impossible for someone to love *me* forever? Am I so unlovable that even if someone starts to love me, they'll soon stop? That's what you think of me, is it?'

Flushing, Tom shifted his weight to his other foot. 'No, it's not, Kathleen. Of course it isn't.' He leaned back against the newel post, and looked at her. 'So you genuinely think that Klaus loves you, and isn't just out for a good time? I'm not trying to be nasty, I just want to know.'

Her expression softened. 'To be honest, I don't know. I hope he does. I'm really fond of him. He isn't married, if that's what you're thinking. Things he's said, and things his friends have said, prove that. I know he's a few years older than I am, and you'd expect him to have a wife at home, but before the war he focused on building his career.'

'He wouldn't be the first person to do that,' Tom said.

Kathleen smiled. 'Exactly! He's quite possessive and if he didn't have strong feelings for me, he wouldn't be bothered about what I did, would he? At least, I hope I'm right.'

'For your sake, I hope you are. Well, we'll leave it at that, then. I need to check the cider situation. I'll see you at dinner.' And he went out through the back door and across the yard.

'THERE'S nothing else to be said,' Tom told Rose that night as they lay in bed. 'She genuinely seems to like him, and she thinks it's reciprocated. I only hope she's right.

'I wonder,' Rose murmured.

Tom glanced down at her. 'What're you thinking?'

'We know he sometimes brings her back at night as I've heard the car. And we know they meet in St Helier in the day, and maybe in other places, too. So the chances are that he collects her from somewhere near here at least some of the times they go out in the day. But he doesn't come up to the house, and according to Kathleen, he's never shown any desire to come into the house.'

'What of it?' Tom asked.

'It means that he isn't interested in meeting her family.

Even though he must know that he wouldn't be welcome, I would've thought that after the time they've been going out together, if he were really keen on her, he'd have wanted to meet her parents by now.'

Tom bit his lip. 'You're right,' he said. 'So it could be that this isn't something he sees as lasting. And if he met someone who took his fancy, who was a fresh face compared with Kathleen, he might drop Kathleen without a second thought.'

'That's my worry. I don't think Kathleen's being realistic. And I can't see her going quietly, can you?'

'No, I can't. And that could rebound on the farm,' he said slowly.

Rose shivered.

Lying facing each other, their eyes were wide open.

26

Jersey, October 1941

Dejected, they retrieved their bicycles from outside their local all-purpose shop, a two-storeyed farmhouse with a sloping roof and a front extension which had served as a shop for as long as anyone could remember, and wheeled them across to the opposite side of the road, which was lined with mauve Michaelmas daisies.

They propped their bicycles up and for a few moments, leaned back against the saddles, unwinding a little in the warmth from the late autumn sun.

'So that's it, then,' Rose said flatly. 'No more tinned goods left, and as we can only shop where our ration cards are registered, we can't try anywhere else. It means an extra helping of turnips every night. What a truly depressing thought.'

'It is, but we'll get through this.'

'Maybe. But how much longer will we have to put up

with this?' she said, her voice heavy with weariness. She stared towards the wooded slope that rose up behind the shop.

'You look lovely, Rose,' Tom said quietly, studying her profile as she gazed up the hill.

She smiled at him ruefully. 'It's nice of you to say so, but I've lost too much weight. There's a limit to how many turnips, potatoes and swedes one can stomach. I've had to take all my dresses in. I look too thin.'

'You look perfect. And that colour's just right for you.'

She blushed with pleasure. 'I love this shade of blue. It's actually the colour of your eyes.'

'I don't know what I can say to that,' he said with a grin. 'Perhaps I'll *do* something, rather than say anything.' He took her hand in his, raised it to his mouth, and kissed each of her fingers in turn.

She giggled and pulled her hand away.

He took it again, and held it tightly with both hands. 'I've a suggestion to make. I've been thinking about this for a while.' There was a hint of awkwardness in his voice. 'I know we said we'd wait before having a baby, and I know there's a shortage of food and none of us is well-nourished these days, but I think we should try for one now. Don't say it's a daft idea,' he added quickly. 'I don't know how much longer the war will last or what further hardships there'll be, but I do know you'd be a wonderful mother, and I want you to have the chance to be one.'

She went red. 'Oh Tom, I'd love one, too. But it's the wrong time. If we hadn't decided to give ourselves a couple of years to get to know each other first, we've might have had a child before the Germans came. But we didn't. And now we're in a sort of prison. I'd rather wait till we're free, and able to eat good food again. I refuse to believe the Germans will be here for ever.'

'Well, if you change your mind, just say the word and I'll stop digging into the supplies I bought in the days when the French sailors were able to get to Jersey and sell them, and we'll let nature take its course.'

She put her hand to his cheek. 'I love you, Tom, and I'd love a miniature version of you. It's very tempting to say to hell with it, and try for that baby. And if the war goes on for much longer, maybe we will.'

'It's a shame the day's still so young as I feel ready for bed,' he said. 'Perhaps an afternoon nap would be in order.'

She giggled. 'Alas, we've promised to go with your parents to the Royal Square this afternoon to hear the army band.'

Tom groaned. 'Must we? I can think of much better ways of spending a Saturday afternoon.'

'Yes, we must,' she said with mock severity. 'We don't get out enough, and it'll be fun. They're playing bits of opera, which I love. Your parents have been to the Saturday after-noon concerts before, and they said the band's really good. And as they ask the crowd for suggestions, they play a good selection. I shall ask them to play the Londonderry Air.'

'I suppose it's better than the cinema,' Tom said. 'The last time we went to the Gaumont, there was so much blatant German propaganda that it's no wonder it was just German soldiers in the audience, the Jerrybags and us. Everyone else must've known what to expect. Never again.'

'And going out in the afternoon is better than going to a dance at Sion Hall. With all the gunfire, and bright flashes in the sky, I don't feel safe being out at night. And you have to watch the clock all the time because of the curfew, or risk having to dodge the German patrols all the way home. And there're a lot of them.'

Tom nodded. 'It was different when we could use the car, but it's quite a distance to cycle, and it's harder now that we have to ride on the right-hand side of the road.'

'I can't get used to the change. I hate it,' she said. 'And another thing, we'd miss the nine o'clock news if we went out at night. With nothing much coming through from my family, the wireless news is almost our only lifeline to what's happening in London.'

Tom nodded. 'You're right,' he said. 'I'm suddenly feeling enthusiastic about hearing the band this afternoon.'

They smiled at each other

'I hate to say it as it's so lovely here, and the scent of the flowers is glorious,' Rose said after a few minutes, 'but I think we ought to get going. You were going to clean out the pigsties before lunch, and I've promised to collect the last of the apples and help Annie with the butter. And there are—'

'—potatoes to scrub,' they both said at the same time.

Laughing, they got back on their bicycles and started pedalling towards St Aubin.

'WELL, that's the last of the people gone,' Tom said, walking into the kitchen.

'When I took the apples to the *pressoir*, I saw them in the wheat field. I recognised some from round here, but not all. What were they doing?' Rose asked, looking up from the potatoes she was scraping.

'They're people without a farm. It's even harder for them than it is for us, especially as it's been a poor potato harvest this year, and the Germans have taken most of what there was. I imagine there'll have been a lot of them at the Gorins' farm, too.'

'But we don't grow much wheat, and you've cut what there was, so what were they doing?' Rose asked, bewildered.

'Gleaning what was left in the field. They do it with their bare hands. It's really hard work—the stalks cut into them as they pull them up.'

'That sounds painful,' she said.

'They'd say it's worth a few cuts. They'd rather have sore fingers than an empty stomach. If they get enough, they'll grind it in their coffee mills and make a sort of bread. With bread rationed, everything like that helps. They're interesting people to talk to. They tend to travel around, so they pick up things before they're made official, and they told me some pretty alarming things.'

The back door slammed shut.

They turned to see Kathleen coming in from the yard, carrying a basket of washing.

'Aha!' said Tom. 'Here's someone who'd know if what I've been hearing is right.'

Kathleen put the basket down on the floor in front of the range and poured herself a cup of the coffee that had been warming on the hot plate. She took one sip of it, pulled a face and poured it down the sink. 'That's undrinkable. Mum's used ground dandelion root again. I'd rather have water.'

'Is it true what people have been saying, Kathleen?' Tom asked.

'I've not been talking to them so how would I know? I've been to the shop with Mother, and then I helped with the washing.'

Tom shrugged. 'I thought your Klaus might have said something.'

She gave him a sly look. 'Suppose you tell me what you've heard.'

'That the Germans aren't satisfied with having look-out posts every half mile or so, and with having gun emplacements and ammunition and fuel dumps across the island, and just about everything else you can imagine. So they're bringing in workers to build walls, towers and more gun emplacements, and so on. Is that right?'

'Yes, it is, but it's Hitler's idea. He's ordered the islands to be much better fortified than they are now. Don't blame people like Klaus. They have to do as they're told. And because the fortifications will be too much for the army to manage, they're bringing in Organisation Todt. They're military construction workers, not soldiers. The man who founded the organisation, Dr Todt, is coming next month to see what has to be done.'

Tom frowned. 'What's behind this, Kathleen? Did Klaus tell you?'

'He said that Hitler wants to make sure that this little bit of the Reich is never lost. He said that we have strategic value. After the war, the islands will stay German and will be a base for U-boats. Hitler thinks it will help with relations between Germany and Britain as it's a lovely place for Nazi families to take their holidays.'

Tom smiled at her. 'Thanks for telling us that. You didn't have to.'

'As you're being so pleasant for a change, I'll tell you also that not all the Todt workers will be Germans. The Germans in the group will wear a military-style uniform, and will be armed, but the foreign workers will wear their own clothes, and must take orders from the Germans. According to

Klaus, the Todt workers are a scruffy lot, and some are quite a bit older than proper soldiers.'

'Then I take it the Jersey ladies won't be flocking after them,' Tom said drily. 'That won't be easy for them.'

'It won't bother them,' Kathleen said airily. 'They're opening a brothel for the Todt workers in the Abergeldie Hotel in St Clement's Road. And that's all I know. In return for my telling you, you can do the ironing, Rose.'

Laughing, she ran out of the kitchen, and a moment later, they heard her footsteps on the corridor above them.

'So Jersey will be like an armed fortress,' Rose said. 'Even now, we don't feel safe, and despite all those fortifications we'll have, or because of them, we're going to feel even less safe in a few months' time.'

27

Jersey, December 1941

T he clock in the farmhouse sitting room ticked loudly.

Tom and Rose sat close together on the mahogany-framed sofa opposite William and Annie, whose floral-covered armchairs were on either side of the fireplace. Their Bakelite wireless stood on a table against the wall behind William's chair.

'I won't be sorry when this year comes to an end,' Annie said. 'I don't recognise our lovely island any longer, with so many concrete structures everywhere. As for those workers the Germans have brought in! Goodness knows where they've come from—they look half-starved and half-clothed. And they could have any number of diseases.'

'It's everything else they're doing, too,' Tom said. 'Like even more rationing. And the thing you said, Dad, about them wanting a list of Jersey residents, stating which ones were born in the United Kingdom. That's seems very strange. I wonder what they're up to.'

'I'm trying not to think about it, just as I'm trying not to think about what Kathleen's doing. She's not pulled her weight on the farm for some time now since she's out so much in the day, and I know she's ignoring my requests and is going out in the evenings,' William said in a weary tone. 'She makes it hard to love her. I do, though. But at present I don't like her very much.'

'D'you think it's worth trying again to get through to her?' Tom asked.

William shook his head. 'I'm afraid I don't. If we say any more to her about him, she might walk out for good. Disappointed though I am with her behaviour, I wouldn't want that.'

'I only hope this thing she's got going with the German doesn't end up badly for her. Or for us, for that matter,' Annie said.

William nodded. 'Me, too. We killed a pig this morning, and I'd hate to be found out. But I don't think she'd ever tell on us.'

'She's being so stupid,' Tom said angrily, 'and so shortsighted. What happens when the Germans lose the war? Since the Pearl Harbour attack and America coming in, it's looking distinctly possible. We're all getting our hopes up. If it turns out that way, where will that leave Kathleen?'

'Possibly still with Klaus,' Rose volunteered. 'She thinks he's serious about her. They might marry, I suppose.'

'I can't see that myself,' Annie said, shaking her head. 'He's not made any attempt to meet us. Night after night, it's just the four of us sitting here. Kathleen must know that she and Klaus would be welcome to join us. Well, maybe 'welcome' is the wrong word, but if they're serious, we should get to know him.'

Rose coloured slightly. 'I hope you don't mind us sitting in here with you every evening,' she said to William and Annie. She gave an awkward laugh and picked up her glass of cider. 'I feel guilty that we're over here more than we're in our own home. You see us in the day, so you must feel there's no escaping us.'

Annie smiled warmly at her. 'Not at all. Both houses are your home, Rose, and it makes us so happy to know that you want to spend time with us. Doesn't it, William?'

'Of course it does,' he said, smiling broadly at them both.

'That makes me feel better. Thank you for saying so.'

'Also, as it gets colder, all of us being in one house will help with the fuel,' Annie added. 'We'll need less wood, which is just as well as there's already hardly any. Most of the trees have been chopped down now, frequently by the Germans, but equally often by locals who'd rather risk being caught than freeze to death. Soon, the only wood we'll have is any twigs we find by the wayside.'

'You could do as the Le Feus have done—chop up the furniture and shelves. I hate that chest of drawers in my old bedroom,' Tom said cheerfully.

'This is serious, Tom,' Annie said. 'If the Jersey government hadn't set up communal kitchens and ovens, people would now be dying of starvation caused by lack of food and fuel.'

William glanced at his watch and made a sharp exclamation. Turning to the table behind him, he switched on the wireless. 'It's time for the news,' he said. 'I can't tell you how glad I am we threw out that old Pye wireless. Recharging that enormous battery every week would have been difficult. This is so much easier—as long as we've got electricity to run it off, that is. Right, let's hear what's happening in London. And just maybe they'll remember the Channel Islands, too, and say something about us.'

As William switched off the news, he shared an anxious look with Annie.

'Well, it's not really a surprise, is it?' Annie said sympathetically. 'They were bound to extend the call-up, given how long the war's been dragging on and how many lives have been lost.'

'I know, and I was sort of expecting it. But at the same time, I was hoping like mad it wouldn't happen,' Rose said. 'At least Father won't have to fight as he's over fifty-one, and he's got a bad leg, anyway. But what about Violet and Iris now that they've called up unmarried women between twenty and thirty? And they're dropping the schedule of reserved occupations. That's frightening.' She bit her thumbnail.

Tom moved closer to her, and gently took her hand from her mouth.

'I think you went into an instant panic and stopped listening too soon,' he told her. 'Students are exempt. Although Violet's helping with schoolchildren, she's registered at a teacher training college, so she's a student. She won't be going anywhere.'

'You're right!' she exclaimed. 'Phew! You don't know what a relief that is.' She paused. 'But what about Iris? She's not a student.'

'How old is she?' William asked.

She thought for a moment. 'She'll have turned nineteen in August.'

'There you are, then,' he said, in triumph. 'She's still below the age, so she's exempt, too. Provided the war doesn't last much longer, she won't have to do military service any more than Violet will. What about another glass of cider to celebrate that? And then we'll talk about what we're doing for Christmas.'

LEANING BACK against the stone wall of the farmhouse, Kathleen smiled seductively up at Klaus. 'You could come into the farmhouse next time you collect me, and say hello to my parents,' she said. "In all the months we've been together, you've never come in and you've never met my parents.'

'And I'm happy to leave it like that, *mein Liebling*,' he said lightly. 'I think your parents prefer that, too. Conversation between us would not be easy.'

'You and I manage well enough, don't we? You speak excellent English. I just thought you might like to meet them, and if you felt comfortable with them, perhaps you'd like to come for Christmas. Obviously, we won't be having the usual huge meal, but my parents will try to make it special.'

He looked regretful. 'It is tradition that we German officers spend *besondere Feiertage*—special holidays—together. It would not please my superior officers if I would not be with them. And I think,' he gave her a wry smile, 'that your family would rather hear the Channel Islands' Christmas Day broadcast, than listen to me.'

She pouted. 'I think they'd rather meet you. They've heard the King before, so they don't need to hear him again.' She rubbed her hand up and down his arm. 'Even if you don't want to meet them beforehand, why don't you come on Christmas Day, even if it's only for a short time? I'll be so bored if you're not there.'

She ran a finger across the metal breast eagle above his pocket, and then slid her hands up the front of his dark green gaberdine wool tunic to his stiffened collar. She played with his collar tabs, and feathered her fingers towards the back of his neck.

He gently withdrew her hands and let them fall to her sides.

'Then I'm afraid you will have to be bored, *mein Schatz*,' he said firmly. 'Just as you have traditions to follow, I do, too. Now I must go.' He turned to go back to his car, but stopped and looked at her. 'As you say, one of your traditions is that you have a big meal on Christmas Day,' he said. 'You must remember that most of your animals belong to us. None should be killed by you. There will be an inspection of farms, including yours, tomorrow, to count the pigs and cattle. Your parent might wish to know this,' he added, a touch of amusement in his voice.

He grinned at her, and with a salute, continued to his car.

KATHLEEN SAT and stared at her reflection in her dressing table mirror.

She didn't know what to think.

For the past couple of weeks, she'd begun to wonder if Klaus wasn't losing interest in her. It was nothing she could put her finger on, but things weren't quite as they'd been in the early days of their friendship.

What fun it had been in those first heady days!

Whenever she'd been able to get away from the farm and the shop, he'd dispense with a chauffeur and drive her himself, and together they'd explored every inch of the island. And if she hadn't been able to see him for several days, he'd pick her up on the esplanade in the evenings, and they'd drive somewhere out of the town.

Their goal had invariably been to find the most secluded coves, or hidden glades deep within the woods, and when they'd found a place where no one would ever see them, they'd lie down together and she'd snuggle up to him.

In the beginning, he had seemed satisfied with kissing, but after a few times, he'd become so keen on her, he'd told her, that he wanted more. He had assured her that he'd prevent any risk of a child, so her family would never have to know what they were doing.

She'd been reluctant to go as far as he'd asked, and to do something that would appal her parents if they knew. And she'd felt highly embarrassed at the thought of him seeing her when she wasn't fully clothed.

But her instinct told her that if she didn't show him how strongly she felt about him, he'd find someone else. And as she did find him very attractive indeed, and as he obviously felt the same about her, making it the most natural thing to do, on their fourth outing she'd agreed to let him remove her clothes, and teach her what to do to please him.

And after the first few times, she'd found herself increasingly looking forward to being alone with him.

He was a beautiful man, gleaming and golden and without an ounce of fat. Any girl would be over the moon to know that such a man loved her, and she was only too happy to be doing what any other girl would have been thrilled to do with such a man.

Also, as everyone knew she was the girlfriend of an officer, the Germans treated her with respect.

Not so the Jersey residents, it was true.

Jersey people regularly turned from her, and hissed 'Jerrybag' at her as she walked by. She just tossed her head and ignored them. She didn't care what they thought. She was the girlfriend of someone on the winning side, someone with whom she was sure she had a future, and they were jealous.

And when the day came that the Germans had won the war, the people who'd insulted her would pay for their rudeness, she used to think gleefully, while she would be enjoying life with a handsome man who loved her.

She frowned at the mirror.

But *did* he love her?

Had he actually said that he did, or had she assumed it because of the things they did together?

Thinking back, she realised that he had never actually said those words. He'd whispered words of endearment in German, and she'd assumed that he was telling her that he loved her, but he hadn't used the actual word 'love'. At least, not in English.

And if she were being honest with herself, things had changed since those early days.

Recently, he'd started showing more enthusiasm for hanging around St Helier than for exploring the island, and they seemed to be spending more time with his friends than they did by themselves, whether she met him in the day or in the evening.

Also, they used the car a lot less. He had started encouraging her to cycle all the way to St Helier, rather than go down to the St Aubin end of the esplanade, as she used to, and wait for him to pick her up in his car.

He had cited the increasing shortage of fuel and had said that it was common sense to avoid using the car unless you really had to. He'd added that it would be harder to find concealed places in the way that they used to, with so many workers on the island, building the fortifications.

But she'd seen some of his officer friends going around in their cars, their girlfriends at their side. They clearly weren't bothered by the lack of fuel and the influx of workers.

And much as she'd been trying to push it out of her mind, there'd been an upsetting occasion the week before when she'd been helping in the haberdashery shop.

She had been just inside the front window, rearranging the few items they had for sale, when she'd seen him coming down the road. She'd straightened up and waved excitedly, indicating that he should come into the shop.

But he'd walked straight past as if he hadn't seen her.

She'd told herself afterwards that he hadn't, but really it would have been hard for him to have missed her, standing as she was by the window, wildly waving her hands. She had tried to reassure herself that he would have seen her mother and Rose behind the counter, and he hadn't wanted to meet them in so casual a way.

But it had been hard to convince herself of that being the explanation for his hurtful behaviour.

Although, after what he'd told her that evening, that might have been the truth, she now thought. After all, if he didn't have strong feelings for her, why would he have warned her about the inspection and told her to pass it on to her father?

He must have known that at this time of year, farmers would be killing animals they'd hidden so that they could make a special occasion of Christmas and the New Year, and he would have assumed that her father would do likewise. But because of his feelings for her, he didn't want her family to be caught breaking the rules.

Most people on the island agreed that the Germans were treating them with courtesy and consideration, but only as long as they obeyed the rules. The punishment meted out to those who broke them was harsh—they could be thrown into prison or beaten, or sent to camps in Germany. Klaus had wanted to spare her family such a fate, so he had warned her of what was going to happen.

So he must genuinely care for her.

But if so, why wouldn't he join them for Christmas? He must have realised that whatever they'd thought of him before, they'd be grateful that he'd helped them, and would have been welcoming.

She stared into the mirror, looking for an answer.

Her face stared back at her, pale and anxious, no answer visible.

28

Jersey, June 1942

Willuam thumped the table, pushed the *Jersey Evening Post* away from him, and called to Tom to bring the women in from outside. Tom ran to do so without hesitation, his heart thumping fast, fearful of what his father must have read.

He found them cleaning fish in the barn that had a large sink, as he'd expected he would. His mother had been given three dogfish from a supply secreted under one of the empty fish counters in the fish-market. It was a thank-you, the fishmonger had indicated, for the eggs and butter that the Benests had been quietly distributing among the townspeople.

And then they'd been given four spider crabs by Joshua Mauger, when he had dropped by earlier that day. A fisherman friend of his had caught them, he told William as they sat over a coffee. Although fishermen had to give ninety percent of their catch to the Germans, the Germans didn't much like shellfish, so a number of spider crabs were left over, and the fisherman had shared them out among his friends. Joshua had thought that the Benests might enjoy them.

'We stink of fish,' Kathleen complained as she followed Tom into the kitchen, closely followed by Annie and Rose. 'I was about to wash it off before it seeped into my skin. What's so important that it couldn't wait, Tom?'

'This,' William said, pulling the newspaper back in front of him and spreading it out.

They clustered around him and read the main article: all wireless sets had to be handed in at once. They were to be taken to a collection point and must be clearly labelled so that they could be reclaimed at a later date.

'The Bailiff will be able to prevent this,' Annie said with confidence. 'Having a wireless is essential. It's our only way of keeping in touch with the outside world.'

'I don't know that he will,' Tom said slowly. 'This doesn't have the feeling of being a punishment, like the last time they confiscated our wirelesses. It's more as if they want to stop us from finding out how the war's progressing. And that'll be because things have been going better for us this past month. They'll realise we know that and they'll be aware that Churchill's last speech was one of the most encouraging he's made, which has boosted our morale. They won't like that. This will be about keeping us in the dark.'

Rose nodded. 'That makes sense, Tom. With no one allowed to visit the other islands, and people unable to go to France anymore, we'd be completely isolated without a wireless. I know we're getting Red Cross messages now, but they're slow, very short and infrequent.'

'Well, what else d'you expect the Germans to do?' Kathleen asked sharply. 'The BBC keeps saying there'll soon be an allied invasion of the Continent, and that everyone should help the invaders when they land. It's not surprising that the Germans are silencing them.'

'We've a right to know what's going on,' Rose said angrily.

'Then people shouldn't antagonise the Germans, should they?' Kathleen rounded on her. 'Klaus and I went to the Opera House a few days ago to see *The Merchant of Venice*. Every time Shylock came on, he was loudly applauded, just because Shylock was Jewish. Can you blame the Germans for being angry?'

'Yes,' Tom said bluntly.

Rose's eyes narrowed and she stared at Kathleen. 'Just where do you stand on the wireless order, Kathleen? Are you going to run to your German friends and snitch on anyone who disobeys the command?'

Kathleen went red. 'Of course not!'

'Kathleen would never do anything to put us in danger, Rose, nor any of our neighbours,' Annie cut in. 'Would you, darling?'

'Of course I wouldn't. Not that I expect any of you to believe me,' she stormed, and stalked out of the room.

Tom stared hard after her, then turned away. 'At least, the BBC's given instructions for how to make a crystal receiver,' he said. 'I suppose we'll have to make one. I'll miss our wireless, though.'

'Cheer up, Tom,' Annie said. 'You look like a wet Monday.'

'What's there to be cheerful about?' he asked morosely.

'Just that I've been known to disobey instructions at

times,' she said airily, and she broke into a broad smile. 'You remember that old Pye set?'

'You mean that cumbersome one I told you to throw away when we got the new one?' William asked.

She nodded. 'That's the one. Only I didn't throw it away, did I?' she said triumphantly. 'It was too good to throw away, even if it was really awkward to use. I thought it might come in handy some day, so I put it in the loft.'

'How on earth did you get it up through the narrow gap into the loft?' Tom asked in amazement.

'It's surprising what you can do when you're determined,' Annie said with a satisfied smile. 'Go upstairs and push the trapdoor up. Feel around on the right, and you'll find it. That's the one we'll hand over to the Germans.'

'Come on, Tom,' William said, jumping to his feet. 'Thanks, Annie. It was an inspired thing to do.' He gave her a huge hug, then he and Tom half-ran up the stairs to the landing.

'Where will we hide the Bakelite set?' Rose asked as she and Annie went into the sitting room to pick up the wireless. 'It needs to be somewhere easy to get at, but where it wouldn't be found if the Germans did a search.'

'What about the chimney breast?' Annie suggested, facing the fireplace.

'You'd have to take out some of the front stones, wouldn't you? Then you'd have to make a shelf for it inside the flue. And what about the leads? It needs electricity, doesn't it? And then you'd have to make the stone wall look as if it'd never been touched, which would be very difficult to do. Also, we need to be able to hide it at a moment's notice.'

'Rose is right,' William said, coming into the room with Tom after leaving the Pye wireless on the floor in the corner of the kitchen. 'If others are doing what we're doing, and I'm certain a lot of them are, they're sure to think of the chimney breast, too. It'll be like false walls: if the Germans find sets in a couple of chimney breasts, those will be the first places they search.'

'Well then, what about somewhere they'd think unlikely because it would be staring them right in the face?' Annie suggested.

'What d'you mean, Mum?' Tom asked.

'I think it'd fit into the bread oven. When you open the oven door, you see the heating stones. Behind them, there's a wall of loose bricks. And there's another wall at the very back of the oven. Between the two walls, there's quite a gap. We could remove the loose bricks, put the wireless in the gap, and replace the bricks. If we scattered some crumbs on the heating stones, it would seem as if the oven had been recently used.'

They went into the kitchen and stood around the oven.

William opened the metal door, removed the wall of bricks, inspected the gap and put the bricks back in place. 'I think you've hit on it, Annie,' he said. 'It just means that we'll listen to the news in here, not in the sitting room.' He paused. 'We must be very careful, though. Anyone with a set will be in serious trouble if they're caught.'

'You don't need to worry. William. None of us would be silly enough to tell anyone we had a wireless,' Annie said. 'Sit down, everyone. I'll get what passes for coffee these days.'

'It's not just that,' William said sitting down, followed by Tom and Rose. 'We must never mention anything we've heard on the news, as that would give us away. The Germans have eyes and ears everywhere, and I know some instances where neighbours have told on each other out of malice.

Keeping the set a secret could genuinely be a matter of life or death.'

'I see what you mean,' Annie said, coming across with a tray of cups and a jug. 'We'll all be extra careful about what we say.' She poured the coffees.

William took a cup, sipped it and pulled a face. 'There's one other thing we ought to do as a precaution.' He turned to Tom. 'That crystal receiver you mentioned. I think we ought to make one, just in case there comes a day when we don't have any electricity.'

'Good point,' Tom said. 'It should be straightforward enough.' He hesitated. 'I suppose we'll have to tell Kathleen what we're doing.'

'Yes, but not until we absolutely have to. She seldom listens to the news with us, even if she's at home, so it could be a while before she realises that we've kept the wireless.'

'She wouldn't tell anyone,' Annie said firmly.

'I hope you're right,' William said. 'Better not to put it to the test, though.' He took a breath. 'Josh told me something this morning, and I've been waiting for the right moment to pass it on. It's better that Kathleen doesn't hear it. Apparently, when he was in St Helier yesterday, he stopped at the Caesarea, and he saw Kathleen's German there. He's seen him a couple of times, and he was sure it was Klaus. He told me that Klaus seemed to be having a very good time with a woman who certainly wasn't Kathleen.'

'So you think it may be over,' Annie said, sitting back. 'If it is, it would explain why she's seemed out of sorts these past few weeks. I'll be so relieved if that's true. I've heard some of the things our neighbours have been saying about her, and the sooner they've got no reason to say them, the better.'

'It means she's less likely to tell the Germans about the wireless, then, doesn't it?' Rose asked.

'You would think so,' William said. 'Unless she thought that by telling Klaus something he could act upon, which would earn him praise from his superiors, she'd get back into his good books. No, I think we'll keep quiet about it for as long as we can.'

A WEEK LATER, the whole family sat round the kitchen table on which the *Jersey Evening Post* lay open. Rose was doing some sewing while she and the others listened to William read out an order from the German Kommandant posted in the paper.

The Kommandant had arrested ten people in Jersey, he told them, and they were being held as hostages. A group had been printing leaflets denouncing the confiscation of wirelesses and distributing them all over the island, and there'd been some sabotage in connection with the telephone. If the perpetrators didn't give themselves up, the ten hostages would be sent to internment camps on the Continent.

'I'm beginning to dread seeing the *Jersey Evening Post*,' Tom said when William had finished. 'Every day, the Germans seem to make another announcement.'

'I saw one of those leaflets,' Annie said. 'I couldn't help thinking it would've been better not to complain about the confiscation. We all know that the Germans punish innocent people to make the guilty confess. But as it happens, when I saw Madeleine Le Feu earlier today, she told me that the brothers who did it owned up before anyone got hurt. It was a pointless thing to do, though. Such actions irritate the Germans, but that's all they do.'

Tom looked at his mother in surprise. 'That's a bit defeatist, don't you think?'

'No, I don't. Take that painting of V signs last year. Everyone started painting a V on walls, doors, gateposts, trees—anywhere you could put a sign. It was meant to be a silent protest against the Germans. The result? Our wireless sets were confiscated for a while, and anyone caught painting a V was arrested and put into prison.'

'People had made a protest, though,' Tom said, 'and the Germans will have noted it.'

'Indeed, they did. They started daubing V signs everywhere themselves, and the whole thing fizzled out. We'd all suffered to no purpose'

'I still wonder if we shouldn't be doing something active against the Germans,' Tom said, frowning. 'Something subtle.'

'We're already doing our bit, Tom, and it's a practical bit,' William said. 'We're feeding people. Despite all the restrictions, and all the German orders telling us what to grow, and despite having to hand over so much of what we produce, we're growing as much as possible behind their backs, and passing on what we can to people in need of help.'

'I agree with Mum,' Kathleen said. 'The something active you're talking about, Tom, would be asking for trouble, and it would get you nowhere. But I'll leave you to it. I've got better things to do than sit here, listening to you criticise my friends.' She stood up and flounced out of the room.

William watched her go. 'The brothers were well-meaning, but foolhardy,' he said when the door closed behind her. 'They should have taken a leaf out of the editor's book. The Germans need the *Evening Post* to pass on their news to the general population—by news, I mean their notices and propaganda. So when they give Arthur Harrison a news story to insert, which he can see is really propaganda, he makes sure it appears in a poor translation. That way we know what we're reading. But it's done in a way that won't rebound on anyone.'

'What a clever idea,' Rose said. She returned to lining up the two halves of the old sheet she'd cut down the middle and arranging them so that the less worn bits were in the centre. Stretching the fabric between the thumb and fore-finger of her left hand, she started making tiny stitches.

'Watching you takes me back some years, Rose,' Annie said, looking admiringly at Rose's work. 'We always extended the life of a sheet that way. And you've got a partic-ularly neat hand.'

'Mum used to do this,' Rose told her, 'and she taught the three of us how to do it. Iris is the best out of us. She can make anything. She doesn't even need a pattern.'

'You're clearly skilled girls,' Annie said with a smile.

'And lucky ones,' Rose said. 'At least, *I* am. Doing the occasional bit of sewing and helping you in the shop as much as I do, gives me a welcome break from washing potato pulp. It quite perks up my weekly routine.'

'Talking of routine.' William checked the clock on the wall. 'It's almost seven,' he said. 'Time for the six o'clock news from England.' He shook his head. 'When will this madness end? Come on, Tom. Let's get the wireless out, and perhaps we'll get an answer to my question tonight.'

'Well, at least one of my parents is an optimist,' Tom said, going to the bread oven with his father.

29

Jersey, September 1942

On her own in the cottage, Rose stared hopelessly at the piece of writing paper on her lap. How on earth could she condense the events of the past month into the twenty-five characters she was allowed to send her family? She leaned back against the sofa and sighed.

August had been particularly difficult, she mused, as she gazed through her sitting room window at a seascape framed in wood.

The tide was out, and together the late afternoon sun and the briny sea had leached every suggestion of yellow from the wide expanse of wet sand, transforming it into a carpet of silver.

Kathleen had been irritable all month, snapping at anyone who spoke to her. She was still seeing Klaus, they were sure, but not so often. And Rose was certain that once, when she'd been hunting for shoes in St Helier, she'd seen Klaus walking up the hill in front of her, his arm around the shoulders of another woman.

She'd seen only his back, not his face, as she'd swiftly slipped into the nearest open doorway, clutching the wooden-soled sandals she'd bought, keen not to be spotted. But she'd glimpsed him often enough over the past months to have recognised the way he moved and held his head.

Kathleen must realise that Klaus had started striking up other friendships, and that would explain her mood.

Not only had Kathleen's frame of mind affected life in the farmhouse, but there had been increased tension throughout the island during the past month.

The atmosphere had altered quite dramatically with the arrival of large numbers of Russian men and boys sent to the island by the Germans, and housed in the huge camps that the Germans had begun to erect.

The first batch of prisoners had been brought in to do hard labouring, and then hundreds more had arrived, including women.

She had been in St Helier, working in the shop one day, when she'd heard footsteps suggesting a crowd of people coming down the street. The sounds of movement were accompanied by loud German voices issuing orders. Like many others, she'd gone out into the street to see what was happening, and had seen a straggling column of prisoners filing past.

She had gazed at them in mounting horror.

When she'd heard that Russian slave workers were going to be working on the fortifications, she hadn't expected to see a line of bedraggled wretches, who were quite obviously starving.

Dressed in filthy rags, they looked like walking skeletons, with pallid faces and emaciated bodies. Some were even shoeless. The feet of one of the prisoners walking down her side of the road were wrapped in bloodstained rags, she noticed, and the man was walking as if every step was acutely painful. And there were others, too, who were similarly shod.

Flanking the line of prisoners were several Germans in slightly different uniforms from those the Jersey people were used to seeing the soldiers wear.

They were members of Organisation Todt, her neighbour had told her. Equipped with whips, the men were using them brutally on anyone who was too slow, thereby keeping the column moving.

Some of the Russians looked so young, so in need of warmth and kindness, that her heart had gone out to them. She had longed to help them, but had no idea how she could. The people standing on the pavement alongside her were shocked, too. Many were crying.

When she went back into the shop, she realised that her face like theirs, was wet with tears.

NEXT THING, the Germans took over the Telephone Exchange, so no calls could be received or placed for a day. All construction work was stopped, and the Russians remained locked up.

For a whole day, no Germans were to be seen, and everyone wondered why. And then the news filtered through. The British had landed in France, and had made a big raid on Dieppe.

It was said to be the biggest raid that the British had ever made and the Germans had taken fright, thinking the British had landed in France for good.

German officers were said to be practising their proce-
dure for evacuation, just in case the English got a permanent foothold in France. The ordinary German soldiers, it
was rumoured, would be left in Jersey to man the guns.

Kathleen's mood had been vile.

But the Germans didn't stay hidden for long. Two days
later, there was a new order saying that the curfew was to be
ten o'clock, not eleven o'clock, and there was a long article
in the *Jersey Evening Post*, talking about a frustrated British
landing. The poor translation of the report underlined that
it had originated with the Germans.

AT THE BEGINNING OF SEPTEMBER, the farmers in the Coin
Varin district were ordered to evacuate their farms within
ten days, taking all their cattle, but leaving their furniture.
The reason for this, everyone seemed to think, was that the
Germans expected the British to land in St Ouen's Bay, go
straight to the nearby airport, and from there march down
into St Helier.

The Germans, at that time in Coin Varin where they had
heavy guns, would then shoot at the British.

In the few days they'd been allocated before they had to
leave their farms, the Coin Varin farmers had struggled to
find alternative land for their cattle. Since then, all farmers,
including William and Tom, had been on edge that the
same might happen to them.

And as if that wasn't bad enough for the farming
community, the Germans had then taken a keen interest in
their wheat.

On the Saturday evening of the day before the churches
held their Harvest Festival services, the Germans issued an
order that all the wheat must be gathered in by the Sunday

night. As a result, all the farmers had worked hard throughout the Sunday, bringing in the wheat.

With only a small amount of wheat at the Benest farm, William had stayed to deal with it while Tom had gone to the Gorins' farm to help Joshua.

As had happened the last time the farms had been ordered to speed up the harvesting of the wheat, both farms were visited at regular intervals throughout the day by teams of inspectors, one of whom told William that both the inspectors and the farmers would be in trouble if the harvesting didn't go more quickly.

Fortunately, the weather was hot, which helped the harvesters. It was, in fact, one of the loveliest days they'd had for a long time, but all the farmers and workers were too busy to enjoy it. No one was able to breathe easily until the vans were loaded.

People were saying among themselves that the reason for this haste was that the Germans feared that the British were about to invade the Channel Islands.

Just the very suggestion of a possible British invasion had left everyone feeling unsettled. They were afraid to be hopeful, lest their hopes be dashed, as the pain of that would have been greater than if they had never allowed themselves to hope at all.

THEN THERE HAD BEEN another unsettling incident a couple of Sunday evenings after the harvest.

They had just returned the wireless to the bread oven, when they heard footsteps in the yard.

There was a collective intake of breath.

No one moved.

Then Tom went out to find three Russian prisoners in

the yard. They had clearly escaped. One of them was a young man who wasn't much more than a lad. They must have accessed the yard through the narrow door in the front wall, which one of the family must have inadvertently failed to lock, Tom realised.

The three Russians, dressed in rags, looked frighteningly thin and exhausted. Through the holes in their clothes, Tom could see red welts, signs of the brutality of their treatment.

They gestured their need for food, and ignoring the rancid smell from their bodies, he took them into the kitchen and gave each of them a crust of bread, some boiled potatoes, a couple of apples and some cold coffee. Then they went on their way.

The family wished that they could have given the prisoners more, but even though they had a farm, much of their produce was taken by the Germans, and what remained they were sharing with their non-farming friends and neighbours, so there was little left.

They had even wondered whether, if a lone prisoner came to their farm, they should hide him in the place that they'd built for Tom, which hadn't yet been needed. But they were nervous, the future being unknown, at losing the only place they could hide Tom, and at the real risk they would be taking, given Kathleen's friendship with the German. And they decided against it.

But they were determined to keep on giving something to any prisoner who came, even if it wasn't much.

How to condense all of that into twenty-five words, Rose wondered in despair.

Well she couldn't, she realised.

Instead, she'd write everything in a long letter and

before she visited her family again, which she was confident she'd be able to do one day, she'd send them the letter.

They would then understand how life had been for everyone on the island, so they wouldn't need to talk about it when they met. Their life in occupied Jersey was going to be something that was best left in the past, and when freedom came. it would be better to talk only about their relief they felt, and the future.

After she had written the letter, she'd write a twenty-five word message for her family, saying they were all coping well, and that no one should worry about them. She glanced at the clock. It was later than she'd realised: she'd have to leave her letter-writing until after she'd listened to the news.

As she got up to go across to the farmhouse, she heard the back door slam shut. Footsteps pounded up the stairs. In alarm, she put her hand to the throat as the sitting room door swung open.

Tom stood in the doorway, gripping the handle, his face white.

She grabbed the back of the sofa. 'What is it, Tom?' she whispered.

'It's an official announcement in the evening paper,' he said, drawing his breath in ragged gasps. 'Any British subjects who don't have Jersey as their permanent residence, are going to be deported to a German internment camp. And all males between sixteen and seventy who weren't born on the islands, together with their families. That's us,' he said.

'It can't be,' she said, her voice a whisper.

'It is. I was born in London. It's why they drew up a list of the islands' residents a while ago, including where they were born. They're now acting on it. It means we'll all be sent to Germany in the next two or three days. Twelve hundred of us have got to leave for Germany as early as tomorrow.'

The paper and pen that Rose had been holding fell to the floor as she stood there, the blood draining from her face.

30

L *ater*

THE FAMILY, including Kathleen, sat in William and Annie's sitting room, all of them white-faced, waiting for William to return from making a telephone call.

'How can families be expected to tie up their affairs, give away their possessions, deposit their monies in banks, say goodbye to their friends, and get to the harbour in just a few hours?' Annie asked at some point, of no one in particular.

William came back into the room, and they sat bolt upright.

'Well?' Annie asked, gripping the arm of her chair.

'The order's from Hitler himself,' William said, sitting heavily down. 'Apparently, he issued the order a year ago, at the time they drew up the registers of residents, and he's pretty mad that the order wasn't carried out. It means that the Kommandant and officers don't dare ignore it this time, and everyone must assemble at the weighbridge, taking with them only what they can carry.'

'Where will they send us?' Annie asked fearfully. 'If we don't know, how can we be expected to know what to take and what to leave?' She burst into tears.

'And what about the farm?' Tom asked, his arm tightly around Rose.

William went across to Annie, bent down and put his arms around her. 'I'm sure they'll exempt us, Annie,' he said, hugging her. 'That's what I've asked for. We all work on the farm, and heaven knows, they need food. They won't want to lose the next potato yields, nor any of our animals and produce. I doubt that any of us will be going anywhere,' he added reassuringly, looking around as he straightened up.

Annie jumped up and flung her arms around his neck. 'Oh, thank you, William,' she said, her voice muffled by his shirt.

'I wasn't on the list, was I?' Kathleen asked.

'You're part of Tom's family, aren't you? So, yes. But I've told them you're essential to the efficient running of the farm. As is Rose.'

'What happens next?' Annie asked, wiping her eyes.

William took a breath. 'I think each of us should make a pile of what we would take if we had to leave, but not go as far as packing anything. Even though I'm sure we'll be staying put, it's as well to be ready in case something unforeseen occurs. I'm going to make a start now.' He turned towards the door.

'What will happen to the farm if we have to leave?' Tom asked in concern. 'What about the animals?'

William paused. 'As the Le Feu family is French in ancestry, rather than British, they won't be deported. I'll pay them a quick visit now and have a word with them. If the worst comes to the worst, we'll know there's someone keeping an eye on the animals we've got left.' He went across to the door.

'I'm ringing Klaus first thing in the morning,' Kathleen called after her father's retreating back. 'He won't realise I'm on the list, and when I tell him, he'll take me off it.'

William looked back at her. 'Pack a bag, Kathleen, just in case.'

She glared at him and opened her mouth to speak.

'Don't argue, ' he said, and he went out.

LESS THAN AN HOUR LATER, William returned. Rose, Tom and Annie were back in the sitting room, waiting for him.

'The Le Feus will watch the farm, if needs be,' he told them, his voice tired. 'And they'll take us in their wagon to St Helier tomorrow if my request fails.'

'What shall we do now?' Annie asked.

'If you've sorted out what to take if we have to go,' he told her, 'get some sleep. If I haven't had an answer about an exemption by the time we've had breakfast tomorrow, I'll telephone the Bailiff's office to find out where we stand.'

Tom stood up, followed by Rose. 'We'll get back home now,' he said. 'You'll let us know, won't you, as soon as you've got any news, no matter the time?'

William nodded. 'Of course.'

Just as Tom and Rose reached the front door, the telephone rang. Their hearts stopped. They all drew in a deep breath and held it.

William ran to answer the telephone.

Annie stood in the hall, her hand to her mouth, her shoulders hunched.

Kathleen emerged from her bedroom and came to the edge of the landing at the top of the stairs.

A couple of moments later, William returned, his face pale. 'Tom, Annie and I can stay—we're exempt, being farmers. But Kathleen and Rose must leave.' He gestured his frustration and helplessness. 'I tried as hard as I could. I asked who'd deal with the potatoes, make the potato flour, and everything else. It's too much for my wife alone, I told them. But they wouldn't listen.'

They heard movement on the landing and saw Kathleen disappear towards her room.

William went to the foot of the stairs. 'When you plead for yourself tomorrow, Kathleen,' he shouted after her, 'you must plead for Rose, too. And don't forget to pack!'

Her bedroom door shut with a bang.

'I don't want to be exempt, Father,' Tom said bluntly, putting his arm around Rose and holding her tightly. 'If Rose is leaving, I'm leaving with her. She's not going anywhere without me.' He turned to Rose. 'Whatever's ahead, we'll face it together.'

'Oh, Tom!' She hugged him hard. 'I love you for saying that, but you've got to stay here. You're needed on the farm. And there's also the Gorins' farm to look after. Kathleen and I won't be here to prod Josh. There's little enough food in Jersey. To make the most of what there is, as many farmers as possible must stay.'

'I hate to say it, but Rose is right, Tom,' William said quietly. 'We need you here. It's too much for just Annie and me.' He looked at Rose. 'You'd better pack your bag, Rose, but hopefully, you won't need it. I'm not giving up. I'm going to telephone the States' office again in the morning, and remind them that we're effectively looking after two farms.

By hook or by crook, I'll find someone there who can strike your names off the list.'

Rose nodded, her face deathly pale. 'Thank you, William.'

He went up to her. Tom dropped his arm and stepped back.

'I'm so sorry, dear Rose,' William said, his voice trembling. And he put his arms around her and hugged her. 'I hope you know how much we've grown to love you.'

STANDING in the darkness outside their house, Rose and Tom stood side by side, holding hands as they stared ahead of them.

The steely black water was lightly tipped with silver from a luminous moon that hung low in the sky. Fragile wisps of white cloud drifted across the face of the moon, casting a mystical aura over the scene.

'I'm imprinting this image in my mind,' Rose said quietly. 'Wherever I end up, I want to be able to close my eyes and see this view and imagine that you're standing next to me, just as you are now.' She looked at Tom. 'I love you so much, and I always will.'

He raised her hand to his lips and kissed the back of it. As he lowered her arm, the cool night air brushed across the patch on her hand that was wet with his tears.

She rested her head lightly against his shoulder, and they stood together, their hearts full, not saying another word more for fear of losing control and giving way to a grief that would overwhelm them.

High up above, a solitary plane flew across the moon, a black silhouette that cut the moon in two.

T hey were all up early the following morning. Kathleen kept to herself, but the rest of the family attempted to bring an aura of normality to the day.

As soon as he'd finished his breakfast, William took himself into the front room, where they could hear him speaking on the telephone. Tom went to deal with the cows, and Annie cooked sausages and potatoes, food that could be packed for a journey.

Rose folded the two thick jumpers given her by Annie, who had seen how few substantial clothes Rose had left, and had put them on the table with the rest of Rose's things.

'I'll take a tin mug, if I may,' Rose said. 'If we stop anywhere with water, I'll need something to drink from, and it could be useful when I get to the camp.'

Wherever in the house they were, all of them bar Kathleen, whose hope was in Klaus, desperately prayed that William would be successful.

But what if he wasn't, they wondered. What would happen next? Would there be a telephone call issuing instructions, or would someone come to the house to tell them where to go and when? None of them had any idea, and not knowing increased their ill-suppressed fear.

Only Kathleen showed any sign of being relaxed as she leant against the windowsill, her back to the glass, sewing a button on one of her dresses. She had spoken to Klaus, she told them at breakfast. He would be at the assembly point and would extract her from the group of deportees.

'And Rose, too,' Tom had said sharply. 'If not, no one here will ever forgive you.'

'I'll do my best,' Kathleen had said airily. 'Not that I want her back. It was better before she got here.'

'Kathleen!' Tom's voice had been threatening.

'All right, all right. I'll get her removed from the list, too.'

Tom had glanced at Rose and shaken his head in mystification.

When she had made food for a lunch that could be packed up and eaten outside the house, Annie busied herself in the kitchen, pouring boiling water on a handful of bramble leaves that she'd dropped in the bottom of the teapot.

She put the teapot in the centre of the table, so there would be tea for anyone who wanted a cup, and returned to her work area where she began to cut up turnips, swede and potatoes to make a vegetable stew.

A few moments later, William came back into the room, his steps heavy. They turned hopefully to him. But his face spoke of his failure.

'I'm so sorry, Rose,' he said. 'I've spoken to everyone I can in authority. But the German officers disobeyed Hitler a year ago, and basically, they're frightened to do so again. I've been told that they don't agree with the deportation idea, but are obliged to go along with it. It seems that this is

Hitler's retaliation to the British internment of five hundred men in Iran last August.'

'What's that to do with Jersey?' Tom cried out in despair.

William shook his head. 'Don't ask me. It doesn't make any sense. But the German officials have been given the numbers to be deported, and they're sticking to them. There would have to be a very strong reason for someone to be taken off the list. Because Rose and Kathleen's work is unskilled, they don't see that as a reason to exempt them.'

Rose burst into tears.

'I'm so sorry, Rose,' William repeated. 'And this must be desperate for you, too, Tom.' He poured himself a cup of bramble-leaf tea. 'More bad news is that everyone left behind is going to have to carry an identity card. It'll have our photo, occupation, date and place of birth on it. It's in case there's a second wave of deportations.'

Rose dried her eyes. 'I think I'll take my things, go back to the house and pack them. It's hard to decide what to take as my brain won't let me think clearly.'

'I'll come with you,' Tom said quickly. 'I'm not wasting a moment that I could be with you.' He picked up her pile of clothes and her mug.

'As we don't know what's happening, we'll have an early lunch,' Annie said.

There was a knock on the door.

Fear weighted the air.

Annie took off her pinafore apron, hung it on its hook and her face deathly white, went out into the hall to open the front door.

An officer from the Jersey Honorary Police and a German soldier were standing outside.

'William,' she called.

He went and stood behind her, putting a hand on each

of her shoulders. Tom and Rose moved across to the doorway and leaned against the doorposts.

The Jersey police officer cleared his throat. 'We're here to let you know that Rose Benest and Kathleen Benest must be on the four o'clock boat today,' he said. 'I'm sorry, Annie.'

'You should know better,' Annie snapped at him. 'Fancy helping them do such a hideously cruel thing.'

'Don't blame me,' he said in obvious discomfort. 'We didn't have any say in the matter. And anyway,' he added defensively, 'isn't it better to have someone come to you who's sympathetic and who's trying to make everything as painless as possible? Or would you have preferred to see two faceless German soldiers when you opened the door just now?'

'I'd have preferred not to see anyone and not to know that my family's about to be torn apart.' Her voice caught in her throat.

'For what it's worth, we think this an appalling thing to do,' the Jersey officer said. 'And so do many of the Germans.' The German soldier indicated his agreement. 'You'd be surprised at how many soldiers have apologised to the residents for having to move them out. They think it's all wrong. But they have to obey their orders.'

She nodded, not trusting herself to speak.

'Four o'clock at the weighbridge, then,' he said gently. 'Each person can take one suitcase only. Tell them to take warm clothes and wear strong boots, and to bring provisions for two days. Also, they should bring couple of dishes for meals, and a drinking bowl.'

He inclined his head to her, then he and the German soldier returned to their car.

.   .   .

BY EARLY AFTERNOON, Rose had packed her small suitcase.

In addition to her clothes, a bowl and a cup, she tucked in a bottle of Jeyes fluid, which Annie had given her, saying she might need it if the place she was sent to was dirty, and a sewing kit that she had made for herself containing some needles, cotton reels, a thimble and scissors. She had also slipped in a couple of photos—one of Tom, and one of her family at her wedding—and a pack of cards.

Like everyone she knew, she had been steadily losing weight owing to the lack of nutritious food, so she was easily able to wear two layers of clothing. She chose to wear her warmest clothes as the Jersey officer's words had made her suspect that the German winters could be bitterly cold, and her thick jumpers alone would have filled the whole of her suitcase.

She tried to suggest to Kathleen that she do the same, but Kathleen laughed in her face and said that as she wasn't going anywhere, there wouldn't be anything more in her suitcase than a couple of dresses, a cardigan, a mug and a plate.

The only reason she was even taking a suitcase, she'd added, was because she was certain her father wouldn't let her go without one, just in case something went wrong.

THE WHOLE FAMILY sat down to lunch together, eating in silence, each lost in fears about what the future held.

After lunch, Annie insisted that Rose take the last of the bread they had, the sausages, cold boiled potatoes, four tins of sardines and a large bag of her grape nuts, which she'd made from mangel-wurzel with a drop of milk.

'There's enough for Kathleen, too, if needs be,' Annie told her. Distraught, she caught hold of Rose's arm. 'Oh,

Rose, I can't believe this is happening,' she cried out in anguish.

She drew back and held Rose at arm's length. 'In case I don't get a chance to say it later,' she said, her voice trembling. 'I feel as if I'm losing two daughters today. For that's how you've come to feel to me, dear Rose. Just like a real daughter.'

'Oh, Annie.' Rose's voice caught in her throat. And they hugged each other tightly.

Then Annie turned away lest her tears be seen.

Since all the Jersey people's cars had been confiscated, William brought one of their farm carts to the front of the house. Annie climbed into the back, followed by Rose and Kathleen. Tom handed them their suitcases, and then climbed up next to William.

William tugged the reins and the horses began to move.

When they neared the weighbridge, they saw that the roads were blocked. They knew they would have to walk the rest of the way, so William tethered the cart in a side street, and they continued on foot.

As they approached the weighbridge, they saw that Germans were posted around the area, their fixed bayonets poised, preventing anyone who wasn't a deportee from approaching the piers. Only Kathleen and Rose were going to be able to go any further.

The noise from the crowd was deafening. But above the screaming and shouting that they had expected, they could also hear laughter.

They stopped walking and looked at each other in surprise.

Annie stared ahead of her. 'I thought I must have imagined the sound of laughter,' she said in a tone of wonder, 'but I didn't. I thought people would be hysterical, and crying and wailing. But they're not. Look at them! They're chatting and laughing with each other. Not all, but a lot of them.'

'It reminds me of Queen's Park Crescent on a market day,' Rose said, forcing a smile. 'I'm glad we're showing the Germans that they haven't broken our spirits, and they never will.' She turned to the others, her lower lip trembling. 'How I'm going to miss you!'

William and Tom held out their arms, and she stepped into them.

'Come here too, Kathleen,' William said, his voice a croak. 'Let's have a hug.'

She shook her head, and continued to scan the crowd. 'No need. I'll be back home before too long. Then you can have all the hugs you want.'

A moment later, a couple of soldiers shouted at Rose and Kathleen to join the people queuing to get to the pier. Rose took a step forward. Tom caught her, pulled her to him and kissed her hard on the lips.

'You're in my heart, Rose, I love you so much.'

A Jersey official came up and pulled Rose away from Tom. 'You've got to go now,' he said. 'And you, too, Miss,' he told Kathleen, who was standing on tiptoe, looking towards the Pomme d'Or Hotel, and he pushed Kathleen on to the weighbridge.

Rose turned to say goodbye to Tom. A surge of love overwhelmed her, dragging her breath from her lungs, and she couldn't speak.

'We'll wait here and see if you do return, Rose,' William said hastily. 'With luck, you'll be with us again in a matter of minutes. But if the worst happens and you don't come back, we'll go to the top of Mount Bingham, and watch you leave. We'll be there till the boat is completely out of sight.'

She nodded.

'Oh Tom,' she breathed.

Then with a slight wave, she turned and hurried after Kathleen, her suitcase bumping her knees.

'Rose, Rose!' she heard Tom shout after her, his voice desperate.

'I'll love you forever, Tom,' she shouted up into the air.

Her words reached him above the clamour of the crowd, and he broke down.

'WHERE'S KLAUS, THEN?' Rose asked as she and Kathleen were swept towards Victoria Pier by the movement of the crowd.

'He'll be somewhere here,' Kathleen said confidently. 'He could've already removed my name from the list.'

'So why're you here with the rest of us, then?' Rose asked.

'Klaus said I have to turn up, give my name to the man, and I'll be told that I'm exempt.'

Rose looked at her in surprise. 'But why did you need to come at all?'

'I asked Klaus that,' Kathleen said irritably. 'He said the lists had already been given to the people checking them, so it was impossible for him to alter them. But he knows we're down for the four o'clock boat and he's coming to the harbour to tell the official to strike me off.'

'Can he do that?'

'Of course,' Kathleen said scornfully. 'The officials can exempt someone if they're ill, for example, or if they've got a newborn baby. Klaus is going to tell them to write that I'm ill and mustn't be deported.'

'Jerrybag,' she heard someone mutter as they pushed past her.

And then a hard shove from behind sent her crashing to the ground.

As she picked herself up, she said loudly and defiantly, 'They'll wish they hadn't been so stuck up about the Germans when they find themselves doing hard labour in the arms' factories in the Ruhr, or working backbreaking hours on the land to feed the German people. Klaus isn't going to remove *your* name, Rose, so you'll have to get used to it,' she sneered. 'I'm sure you eventually will.'

'And you're happy enough for that to be my fate, are you?' Rose said icily. 'How can you have the same parents as Tom? You're nothing but a self-seeking, cold-hearted bitch.'

Kathleen raised her hand to strike Rose. Then she stopped, her hand mid-air. 'There he is!' she cried in excitement. 'I told you he'd be here.'

She lowered her arm and pushed through the crowd to the quay, anxious to get to Klaus. Rose followed her.

Klaus appeared to have gone to the pier with a fellow officer. They saw him say a few words to the official holding the list. And he and the official then seemed to look down at the register.

'He's looking for my name,' Kathleen said happily.

Klaus said something to the official, who nodded. Then he and his officer friend walked away.

'Benest!' the official shouted above the heads of the crowd. 'Benest,' he called again.

Grabbing her suitcase to her chest, Kathleen forced her way forward, with Rose at her heels.

When she reached the front of the crowd, Kathleen identified herself.

'That way,' the official said. He pushed her towards the boat.

'What d'you mean?' she exclaimed, knocking his hand off her shoulder. 'I don't have to go. The German officer you spoke to just now told you to strike me off. You've got to say I'm ill.'

'He told me that you and your sister were suspected of distributing anti-German leaflets and that you must be on the first boat to leave. You need to go on board now. The boat will soon be full and those who don't get on will have to return tomorrow. But I was told to make sure that you left today.'

'There must be a mistake,' Kathleen told the official haughtily. But he'd turned to the next person and was looking for their name on the list.

One of the German soldiers standing on the pier stepped forward and hit her hard with the side of his gun, sending her sprawling on the ground.

'Serves you right,' hissed the man behind her. As he went to step over her, he paused, wiped his dirty feet on her dress, and continued to the boat.

An unexpected wave of sympathy swept through Rose, and she moved quickly to stand protectively between Kathleen and the next person while Kathleen struggled to her feet.

'You've a tear in your dress where the soldier hit you,' Rose said, putting her arm around Kathleen's shoulder. 'We can mend it when we get where we're going.'

'I'm sure that's pleased you no end,' Kathleen said.

She shrugged off Rose's arm, brushed the grit from the skirt of her dress, picked up her suitcase and walked to the boat, silent tears rolling down her cheeks.

Rose stayed at her side.

. . .

ROSE STOOD on the top deck of the boat, leaning against the railings, watching Jersey slowly recede as the vessel moved away from the pier.

Somewhere at the top of Mount Bingham, with a clear view over the harbour, would be Tom, William and Annie, she was sure. She could almost feel the warmth of their gazes.

She scanned the dense mass of people who were cheering them from the hill, and tried to make out their faces, but she couldn't. Everyone was getting much smaller the further they went from the shore.

But she knew that their faces would be somewhere among the handkerchiefs that people were frantically waving, and that was enough for her.

Had they managed to spot her among the jumble of faces staring back at them from the boat, she wondered. She liked to think they had. And in case they had, as she wouldn't want them to see her looking sad, she waved her hand as hard as she could, smiling all the time through her tears.

At her side, Kathleen stared down at the sea, her face bleak.

And then all of a sudden, above the screaming of gulls and the sound of the waves, the strains of *The White Cliffs of Dover* reached them, having been carried to them on the back of the wind.

For a moment, an astonished silence fell on the deportees.

Then they realised that their families and friends were giving them the best send-off they could, and in doing so, were shouting out their defiance and their contempt for the cruelty being inflicted on innocent families.

And all around Rose, the people on the decks started singing along with those on the shore, singing as loudly as they could. And she did, too. The deportees and those on Mount Bingham together sang *There'll always be an England*, followed by *God Save the King*.

Gradually, the voices from the shore were so faint that they were drowned by the roar of the waves and the sound of the engine, until, at last, they could no longer be heard at all.

The singing on the boat dried up and people started to look for somewhere on the deck to settle until they reached St Malo, which rumour said would be their initial destination.

Whatever lay ahead, Rose thought in grim determination as she picked up her suitcase, she was going to get through it. Her certainty that one day she and Tom would be together again, would be all she needed to keep her going.

32

Germany, September 1942

L ying on the bunk in the camp that was to be their home, her meagre meal eaten, the heavy darkness around her punctured by the noises of the night, by women and children, over-tired, tearful and lonely, crying for their husbands and fathers, by screams that rose from the depths of nightmares fuelled by uncertainty, by the drone of distant planes, Rose waited for the oblivion of sleep.

The journey to Germany had been long, slow and gruelling, and the next few months promised to be equally difficult.

Three days ago, they had stayed on the top deck on the boat, and so were among the first to disembark when they reached St Malo at seven o'clock in the morning, and almost the first to board the train that was to take them through France, Belgium and Luxembourg to their final destination, an internment camp in Biberach in southern Germany.

On the boat, people had expressed a fear that when they reached St Malo, they would be herded into cattle trucks and left for hours without any food or water. But they weren't. To the relief of all, they were put into second-class carriages.

The carriage that she and Kathleen had managed to get had room for eight passengers, the seats being in groups of four, two seats facing two seats. She and Kathleen had sat next to each other, and a husband and wife sat opposite them, each with a fretful child on their lap.

Numb at so many distressing things happening so quickly, they had sat back as the train trundled slowly across the countryside, passing war-ravaged towns and villages.

Shunted into sidings at night because of the bombing, and being forced to sleep in an upright position, apart from the children who slept in the luggage racks, they had managed to sleep only fitfully. They were cold, and hearing the roar of planes carrying bombs above them, followed by the sickening high-pitched squeal of each bomb as it fell, they were terrified that their train would be targeted by pilots who thought them the enemy.

Throughout the long journey, hunger had gnawed at them. As they had been given the same meagre rations of bread and sausage as their guards had been given, the food that Annie had packed was very welcome. But as they didn't know how long it would be before they reached the end of their journey, Rose had rationed it out.

The family opposite them, Rose was relieved to see, had also brought food with them. Had they not, she would have felt obliged to share Annie's food.

Their only water came from the fire bucket.

They had reached Rennes, the first stop on their journey, early the next morning, where they'd been given soup, sausage and bread. And they had been given the same at Luxembourg, where they had briefly stopped after Rennes, and at Ulm, which they reached late in the evening. At Ulm they were told that they would reach their destination the following morning.

That had been the first time that they had heard the name of Biberach.

Throughout the journey, Kathleen had remained silent, except for one occasion.

At some point on the journey through France, she had lost her temper with the man opposite her, ordering him to shut up and stop telling the children for the millionth time that they would be safe. They weren't just going on an exciting holiday, and hearing that they were every hour since they'd got on the train was more than enough for anyone to bear, she'd snapped.

The wife had glanced across at her husband and raised her eyebrows. 'What do you expect from a whore like her,' she'd said, loudly enough for everyone in the carriage to hear.

Kathleen had gone red.

A little later, when the father had repeated those same words of comfort to his children, Kathleen had thrown him a look of contempt, but had refrained from making a comment.

They had all been greatly relieved when they finally reached the station at Biberach, which they had learnt was about thirty minutes' walk from their internment camp. As they'd stepped down on to the platform and stretched their aching limbs, they had drawn deep breaths of fresh air.

In getting down from their carriage, the wife had accidentally brushed against Kathleen. The wife had jumped back fast.

'Slut' and 'contamination,' they had heard her say to her husband, and she and her husband, grappling with their luggage and children, had managed to distance themselves from Rose and Kathleen and get into one of the furthest lines of five into which the Germans were putting them.

Exhausted after too little sleep, and carrying a suitcase that felt heavier by the minute, Rose had struggled up the steep hill in the heat of the day, weighed down by her two layers of thick clothes. For Kathleen, wearing one layer only of light clothes, and having little in her suitcase, the walking was easier.

As they came within sight of the camp, Rose fell back from her line of five, and paused for a moment to gather her breath and look around her.

They were walking through open fields surrounded by dark-green forest-clad hills, she saw. Behind her to the south, a range of snow-peaked mountains soared to the sky. They were the Bavarian Alps, she heard one of the soldiers tell a nearby deportee.

If she weren't so tired, and so anxious about what lay ahead, she might have found the surroundings quite attractive. But she was too exhausted, and this wasn't where she wanted to be.

She wanted to be within sight of the wide beaches of Jersey and the glittering blue sea; to be standing atop the tiered slope, watching the small boats coming into St Aubin's harbour, their white sails furled.

She wanted to turn and see the welcoming amber glow of the granite farm houses, the fertile fields, some of them lush with dark green potato plants, others gleaming gold beneath a mantle of wheat. She wanted to stride across windswept heathlands that were alive with the brilliance of yellow gorse.

She wanted to be free, and at home with Tom, and to feel his arms around her!

A shove from behind from a rifle butt forced her to start walking again, and she hurried to catch up with her line of five. Kathleen was at the end of the line, she noticed, and there was a sizeable gap between her and the other three.

Once again, unbidden, a wave of sympathy for Kathleen washed through her.

Apart the wrench of having to leave her family and the only home she had ever known, and the misery of being trapped among people who despised her, and who felt a contempt for her that they demonstrated whenever they could, Kathleen bore the additional burden of knowing that Klaus had lied to her, and had publicly rejected her in the cruellest way imaginable.

She hurried up to Kathleen, slipped into the gap next to her, and stayed at her side until they reached the camp.

A tangible feeling of despair ran through the deportees as they approached the camp and saw its military style, with barbed wire running around its perimeters and tall watch-towers looking down at them.

Unsmiling guards led them into the central compound, on three sides of which stood severe-looking barracks built of wood and concrete.

Rose's heart sank. It was going to be like being in a prison, she thought, as they stood on the parade ground in their lines of five, waiting for a roll call.

After the roll call, each was given a ticket with a number which was to be their camp number. Their fingerprints were taken, and a photograph. They were weighed and their height measured, and the details recorded on a camp registration document.

After another roll call, their suitcases were searched. They were then told that when it was time for food, they would be sent for. They would collect their food from the cookhouse and take it back to their barracks to eat.

Finally, exhausted from the journey and the process they'd gone through on their arrival, they were taken to the barracks where they would sleep, the women and children in different ones from the men. Boys older than fourteen had to go with the men.

She and Kathleen were in the same barracks, in an open dormitory lined with wooden beds in tiers, with a black pot-bellied stove at each end of the room. When they counted the beds, they found that there were eighty-three, crammed into a space that was clearly intended for a fraction of that number.

On each bunk there was a grey army blanket and a straw-filled mattress covered in blue and white gingham. A locker next to each bed contained a food bowl and a mug, and there was a small space for shoes and clothes.

Rose sat heavily on the upper bunk, waiting for the moment they could go for food. Kathleen sat on the bunk below.

'You look as shattered as I feel,' Rose remarked, glancing down at her.

Kathleen ignored her.

The woman who had the bed on the other side of Kathleen, Marjorie de Gruchy, a sour-faced woman who had been at school with Kathleen, sat with her back to her. Like all the women in the beds near theirs, who were either sitting on their bunks or unpacking their suitcases and trying to fit their few possessions into the small lockers, Marjorie was pointedly ignoring Kathleen.

At a sudden movement at the door end of the barracks, everyone stood up and stared in that direction, then started moving towards the exit. Soon people were streaming along the central aisle, holding the bowls and mugs that had been in their lockers. Rose quickly climbed down from her bed and picked up the bowl and mug given to her.

'Come on, Kathleen,' she said. 'Let's go and get whatever there is. And then we'll clean the area around our beds.'

IT WAS long after midnight before Rose closed her eyes and sank into a shallow sleep, her last thoughts being that it would be breakfast at five thirty the next morning, and every morning after that for who knew how long.

33

T *he following day*

THEIR FIRST BREAKFAST in their barracks over, the women and children were ordered to stand by their beds to be counted by the guards, who then inspected the area around each bed. They would be counted and inspected every day, they were told.

After the inspection, Kathleen chose to remain sitting on her bed, but Rose decided to join the other women, who had crowded in front of the window and were watching the men file out to the parade ground where they were being made to stand in lines to be counted.

To the audible relief of those with husbands and fathers in the men's barracks, a guard who spoke good English had told them that the men would be able to join them during the day. He had also described the daily routine in Biberach.

In the same way as they had collected their soup and

crust of bread the evening before and brought it back to the barracks, and their breakfast that morning, they would have to take their bowl and cup to the cookhouse to collect every meal and bring it back to their barracks. Lunch would be at two o'clock, and dinner at half past five.

They were to be in the barracks every night by half past seven, where they would again be counted, and then they would be locked inside until the morning.

The men would be allowed to join them for the day after being counted on the parade ground, to which they would be summoned by bugle each morning, whatever the weather.

To the intense frustration of the waiting women, the men's count that morning took two hours to complete. 'They're doing this on purpose,' was the muttered refrain.

Finally, a guard came to their barracks and told them they could go outside.

In a buzz of anticipation, the women rushed for the door, eager to escape the stale air in the overcrowded room and anxious to be reunited with their menfolk. When all but Rose and Kathleen had left, Kathleen stood up and briskly made her way out of the barracks.

Rose hurried after her and joined her on the central compound. But Kathleen turned her back and wandered off on her own.

With a slight shrug, Rose went in the opposite direction. Skirting the noisy and excited groups as families and friends reunited, and the children who were running wildly, shrieking with delight at seeing their fathers again, she strolled across the compound.

When she reached the centre, she stood still and stared in the direction from which they'd come, hoping for a glimpse of the world beyond their concrete and wire prison.

But watchtowers and barbed wire hid from sight all but the tips of the Alps.

Turning round to look to the north, she saw that the barracks, outbuildings and watchtowers were blocking that view, too, and she couldn't see the open fields and forested hills she knew to be there.

Her gaze dropped, and she saw Kathleen standing by herself on the far side of the compound, dejectedly kicking the loose gravel on the ground.

She started to walk across to her, but the guards shouted that they should all get into their lines of five again, so both she and Kathleen hurried to the place where they'd stood on their arrival the day before.

They should know the functions of the buildings that formed three sides of the central compound, the guard informed them.

He pointed out the hospital, the storerooms for Red Cross parcels and clothing, the schoolroom, canteen and cookhouse. There was also a table tennis room, he told them, and a concert hall that could be used for dances. Also shower baths, a drying room for washing, a camp police station and a prison.

He indicated a partially visible two-storey block behind a line of barracks, and told them that it housed German officers, the Captain's quarters, a new cookhouse and senior schoolrooms.

Then he reminded them that they should take their bowls and cups and get their lunch from the cookhouse at two o'clock; until then they could have recreation. He clicked his heels, turned and joined one of the small groups of guards standing around the perimeter of the ground.

The lines broke up.

Rose looked ruefully at Kathleen. 'It's not a pretty place,' she said, 'and we're being made to feel like prisoners. It's so unfair as we're free people from an occupied island. But it could have been much worse. Yes, the food's awful, if last night's meal was anything to go by, but at least we'll have something to eat three times a day, which is more than a lot of people in Jersey are getting.'

'It's going to be so boring here,' Kathleen said moodily. 'There'll be nothing to do all day.'

'I suppose we might be able to send letters. If so, we could write to Tom and your parents. And I could write to my family in London. I'm sure they're worrying about us. That's an idea, isn't it?'

'But it's hardly going to take any time at all, is it?' Kathleen snapped.

'What about drawing some pictures of the place?' Rose suggested. 'When we leave here, we could take them home to show the others. I'm sure we'd be given paper and crayons, if we asked.'

'You do it, if you want. I'm not. Once I leave this dump, I'll never again want to see anything that reminds me of it.'

Rose heaved an inward sigh. 'What about table tennis, then? It'd be a way of getting exercise,' she added. 'The people might organise a sort of tournament.'

'They'd let you play in it, but not me,' Kathleen said bluntly. 'But that's fine by me. I don't want anything to do with them.' And she headed off towards their barracks.

Rose kept pace with her. 'You don't know that they won't let you play. Their antagonism might well wear off now that they see you're in the same boat as they are. And there are Guernsey people here, too. They won't know anything about what you did in Jersey.'

'You can bet they will if I try to join in with anything. That whey-faced cow will be sure to tell them, for a start.'

She indicated Marjorie de Gruchy, who was standing in the doorway to their barracks.

As they reached the barracks, they were forced to stand aside to let Marjorie sweep out ahead of a small group of women.

Seeing Rose and Kathleen waiting for them to pass, the women looked at each other and giggled. Then they closed in on each other to keep as far away from Rose and Kathleen as possible.

Rose went into the barracks first, followed by Kathleen. As she neared Kathleen's bed, her heart sank and she stopped.

Kathleen pushed past her and stared at her bunk. The grey blanket, which she had left neatly folded on top of the mattress, was scrunched up on the floor, and looked as if it had been rolled in the dirt outside the barracks. The blue and white striped gingham mattress cover had a long tear in it, out of which a large clump of straw filling was hanging.

Neither spoke for a moment.

'What were you saying about antagonism wearing off?' Kathleen asked at last.

'I brought some needles and thread with me,' Rose said with forced brightness. 'We'll mend it. It won't take us long.' She bent down and took the sewing kit from her locker.

Kathleen sat down heavily on the bunk bed and gazed miserably around her.

Rose held out a needle and a reel of white cotton. 'Here, let's get sewing. And cheer up—it can only get better.'

BUT IT DIDN'T.

Every time they approached a group of people, the people made a point of moving to a different area.

'It's pretty obvious that Marjorie and her ghastly cronies have been telling everyone about me,' Kathleen said a few days later, after the morning roll calls had been done and they were sitting on the ground, leaning against the outside wall of their barracks. 'And it's not just the people from Jersey, either. I've been getting filthy looks from the Guernsey lot, too.'

'It'll wear off in time,' Rose said. She put her face up to the sun. 'What lovely weather. If we were in Jersey now—a Jersey without a single German—we could toss the vegetable knives out of the window, run down the path to the esplanade, cross the road to the beach, take off our shoes and feel the sand between our toes. And then we could walk along the edge of the water and let the waves lap over our feet. How lovely that would be,' she added with a sigh.

'Anywhere would be lovely if we were miles away from the self-righteous citizens here.'

'They won't always be as bad as they are now,' Rose assured her.

'They will,' Kathleen said dejectedly. 'It's clear they're not going to change, no matter how long we're here. They're going to do whatever they can to make my life miserable. And now they're being nasty to you, too, I noticed. They're ignoring you, and calling you names, and doing the opposite of what you ask.'

'You know what they say, sticks and stones will break my bones, and so on. Laugh at them. Show them their nastiness can't get to you.'

Kathleen turned to look at Rose. 'Why are you standing by me, Rose? And lending me your clothes? After all, it's my fault that I didn't bring the clothing I should've done. And you're helping me with things like mending my mattress cover. I don't understand it. If I were in your shoes, I'd be ignoring me. So why're you being so nice to me?'

Rose thought for a moment. 'I don't really know,' she said slowly. 'It's not because I like you, because I don't. Since I got to Jersey, you've gone out of your way to be as nasty to me as you can, and to make it very obvious that you're sorry Tom married me.'

'That's what I mean. So why aren't you shunning me like everyone else is?'

Rose gestured a degree of bewilderment. 'I suppose it's because you're Tom's sister, and he loves you. And I love Tom. And you're William and Annie's daughter. They've been kind to me and I've grown to love them. Tom and your parents would want you to have a friend here, and they'd hate to think of you being badly treated. As no one around here seems to be volunteering to be that friend, I suppose I realised it would have to be me.'

'That's very noble of you,' Kathleen said with the trace of a sneer.

'If you want to see it like that, it's up to you. But I know how much I miss my sisters, and I'd want someone to be kind to them if they were in your position.'

Both fell silent.

'There's something I've wanted to ask you for some time,' Rose said after a while, breaking the mood, 'and this is as good a time as any. You were determined to dislike me even before you met me, and nothing I did was going to change that. Was this only because of Emily?'

'What else would it be?'

'That you thought I might replace you in your mother's shop, for example?'

Kathleen shrugged. 'There might have been a little of

that in it. I wouldn't have been pleased if I'd been ousted from the shop in favour of you.'

'And there's no other reason?'

'Not that I can think of,' Kathleen said.

'Look at those whores,' two women shouted in passing, and a lump of spittle landed on the ground next to Rose.

She and Kathleen stood up, moved further along the wall, slid down and again sat with their legs stretched out in front of them.

'I suppose there might be something else,' Kathleen volunteered.

Rose looked at her in surprise

'I didn't think you really loved Tom,' Kathleen said. 'I thought you just wanted to escape London and go somewhere different, and marrying Tom was your way of doing it. So I thought that for a really shallow reason, you'd scuppered Emily's hopes. I was certain you'd hate being a farmer's wife, which is something Emily would've loved to be, and that you'd get bored with Tom and find someone else. I suppose I was angry on his behalf.'

'D'you still think I don't love Tom?' Rose asked.

Kathleen turned to look at her. 'I'm sure you didn't at first. But in trying to prove me wrong about what you felt for the farm and Tom, I think that maybe you've come to do so now.'

'You're right, I do love Tom very much.' She paused. 'And I did love him when I married him. But what I felt for him then is nothing compared with the way I feel about him now. But you've been engaged, too, I think Tom said. So you'll know that you can love someone, and then, as you spend more time with them and get to know them better, you love them even more, and so on. That happened with my feelings for Tom.'

'So he told you about Arthur, did he? It was ages ago.'

'I'm sorry about what happened,' Rose said sympathetically.

'Don't be. I'd rather not be married than marry someone who didn't truly want to be with me.' She paused. 'It must be that I'm not the sort of person people want to be with. After all, everyone's left me. First of all, Joshua. I really liked Josh, but he made it clear he didn't want to be tied down. Being tied down was how he saw a life with me. It's hardly flattering. You knew I went out with him for a while, didn't you?'

Rose nodded. 'Tom did tell me.'

'And then Arthur, and then Emily—I'm certain her parents would have let her stay with us if she'd begged them, but she didn't—and now Klaus. There can't have been a more dramatic way of getting rid of someone you no longer wanted to have around,' she said, her voice breaking.

'There's a flaw in your reasoning,' Rose said.

Kathleen looked at her in surprise, her eyes full of tears. 'There is?'

'Of course there is. I'm still here at your side, aren't I? And I'm not going anywhere.'

34

London, October 1942

'I don't mind telling you, I'd been getting quite worried,' John said as he pulled down the blackout blind, blocking out the amber-red halo that arched over the city, silhouetting the uneven line of roof tops, and the sight of the night sky fracturing at every explosion.

Having ensured that no light could escape the sides of the blind, he went and sat in the armchair opposite Mabel. 'Yes, it's been so long since we heard from Rose, and even then, it wasn't much.'

'Well, it couldn't be much, could it?' Mabel reminded him. 'But fortunately, some of the restrictions seem to be ending, as our lovely long letter proves. Yes, it was very welcome, indeed, even if what she had to say was alarming.'

'It's very unfair that we hear so little about what's happening in the Channel Islands,' Violet said. 'None of the papers I've read in the library have said anything about the deportations. Rose won't have been able to say too much in her letter as she'd expect it to be censured, but it must be terrifying to be imprisoned in the heart of enemy territory.'

'Tom should've gone with her,' Iris said.

'There'll have been a good reason why he didn't,' Mabel said sagely.

'And what happens if Germany loses the war?' Iris asked. 'What then? What will the Germans do with everyone in the camps?'

Violet frowned. 'Iris has got a point.'

Iris giggled. 'Can I have that in writing? Such praise is not something I often hear.'

'Very funny, I don't think,' Violet said loftily. She shifted her position to look at her father. 'Perhaps a better question is what happens if they *win*. They could, you know. Look at Stalingrad: it's reduced to rubble, and the Germans are pushing the Russians back. The way it's going, the Germans look like taking control of the city. If they do, they could block the traffic on the River Volga and take over the Caucasus oil fields. If they had that oil, they could win the war.'

'You've been reading too many newspapers,' John said firmly. 'The Russians aren't making it easy for them and we don't know what hidden reserves they have. It wouldn't be the first time Germany has tried to make headway into Russia and failed. We mustn't be defeatist, as a lot of the papers are. And certainly not when we write to Rose. We don't want her to worry about us.'

'I can't imagine why she'd have cause to worry about us,' Iris said airily. 'After all, we're only in the heart of London, being showered daily by bombs. Our streets are full of rubble, there are sandbags everywhere and our feet crunch on shattered glass whenever we walk along the pavement.

We're in a city where fires light the sky at night, not street lamps. What's there to worry about?'

John smiled at her. 'You know what I mean, Iris. And it's also possible that she doesn't know what's going on over here, any more than we know much about what's happening in Jersey or Germany. I'm sure that newspapers and broadcasts are censored.'

'She might have heard about unmarried women being conscripted,' Violet said. 'In case she has, I'll remind her when I write that Iris is too young and that I'm exempt as a student.'

'And you can tell her what I've been doing,' Iris said.

'Why don't you write to her yourself?' Violet asked.

'I will, but not at the moment. It's more important that I sort out the sewing equipment. Having three Make Do and Mend classes every week means I'm getting through tons of needles and cotton, and I need as much material as I can get my hands on. But I think she'd be interested in knowing what we're doing.'

Mabel nodded. 'Iris is right, Violet. I doubt Rose even knows we've had clothes rationing for a year.'

'Don't worry, I'll tell her,' Violet said.

'And you could tell Rose that Iris, too, is a teacher, Violet,' Mabel added, beaming at Iris.

'A mending circle's hardly the same as a school class,' Violet said tetchily.

'I don't see the difference,' Iris retorted. 'I teach the women how to make an old felt hat into slippers, a coat they've outgrown into a smart waistcoat, and blankets into dresses and coats. And I teach them how to lengthen a coat with a new hem, or alter the appearance of something with a stylish collar. Or how to make pretty decorative patches to cover worn areas. Or simply how to darn socks. The Government's 'Make Do and Mend' booklet doesn't tell women how to make the things they suggest. I do that. Not everyone's born knowing how to sew, you know?'

'Obviously,' Violet said impatiently.

'And what's more,' Iris continued, 'when they come to my classes, they have fun. That's important, too. They're not sitting at home, worrying about the bombs. They like having a regular place to go, where they can meet other people—somewhere that isn't a damp air-raid shelter. I can't think of a better use for Mid Hams than being home to a mending circle.'

'All right, I'll tell her you're a teacher, too, Mrs Sew-and-Sew,' Violet said with exaggerated weariness.

Iris made a strangled exclamation. 'Agh, not that name again! Ever since the government brought out that leaflet with that ghastly grinning wide-eyed doll, people have been calling me that for fun. So, not you, too, please.'

'I meant to ask you, Iris,' John said. 'Do any men go to your sewing groups?'

'Occasionally,' she said. 'They might come if they've a button to sew on their uniform, for example. They ask to be shown how to do it, and then vanish as soon as we've shown them, as we've done the job for them!' She laughed. 'Why? D'you want to join us?'

'Good heavens, no! It's only that someone saw you walking down Queen's Crescent with a man,' John said.

Iris shrugged. 'I don't know who they mean. It's true I sometimes bump into people I've met at a dance and if so, we might walk along the road together. But that's all.'

John and Mabel exchanged glances.

Iris frowned at them. 'I hope you're not going to tell me to stop going to the dances, are you? There's no better way to escape the pressure of constant bombing and being surrounded by death. Other parents don't mind—Hammersmith Palais is doing better business than ever before. And Violet might be easier to live with if she went to a dance every week instead of going to the library.'

'Of course your father isn't, love,' her mother said quickly. 'Just be careful about who you're seen with on the street, is all he means. You don't want to get a bad name.'

'You can't expect me to ignore someone I've met at a dance just because he's in the street, not on the dance floor, can you?'

Her mother hesitated. 'There's saying hello in passing, and there's walking along the road with a man. I'm sure I don't have to say more, Iris. Or do I?'

Iris glared at her parents.

35

Germany, October, 1942

Rose lay back on her bed, waiting for it to be time for the women to go outside. She wouldn't go as far as to say she was happy, but she had come to feel settled, and she had lost the sense of dread she'd felt when she'd first seen the barbed wire and watchtowers.

There were things that still irked her, such as the length of time it took to count the men on the parade ground each morning, which still had to be finished before the women were allowed outside.

Although temperatures were dropping, it was still mild and fairly dry, and they were all keen to be in the fresh air for as long as possible before November rolled in, which the guards had said would be much colder, with some likelihood of snow. But the lengthy roll call kept them indoors for much of the crisp autumn mornings, and that was a constant source of irritation.

On the whole, though, they were better treated than they'd expected, and although the food wasn't plentiful and was frequently tasteless slop, they were possibly getting more to eat than most of the people back on the islands.

There was a sudden movement among the women as with their long wait over, they start to head for the door. She was just thinking of getting up and going outside, when at the far end of the long room, close to the entrance to the dormitory, she heard a loud commotion.

Sitting up, she swung her legs round and turned in that direction. Two women, clearly flustered, had rushed into the barracks and were bent over, drawing their breaths with difficulty.

Kathleen had risen to her feet, and she, too, was staring towards them.

'Get up!' one of the women shouted as she straightened up and was able to speak again. 'We're moving!'

'Get your things packed!' the other yelled.

With an urgency of movement, and a sense of rising panic, the women rushed to their beds and pulled out their suitcases from beneath them.

But before they could pack anything, one of the guards appeared in the open doorway.

'Stop!' he shouted, raising his hand.

Everyone stood where they were, mid-action, and looked at him.

'The Jersey people are moving,' he said, when there was silence. 'Not the Guernsey people. The Guernsey people will stay in Biberach. Jersey men have been told to return to their barracks and pack.'

'Where are the Jersey people going?' asked a woman standing close to the guard.

'All men who are not married and who are above the age

of sixteen will go to the man's camp at Laufen. The rest of the Jersey men and women will go to the camp at Wurzach. They leave for Wurzach tomorrow.'

'Can't we stay here?' one of the women asked.

The guard shook his head. 'It is not possible. Families are coming here from Dorsten, and they need beds. So you must leave. I am sorry.'

And he walked out.

Amid a general air of helplessness, and with revived fear, the Jersey families started to pack the few clothes and possessions they had brought with them.

THE FOLLOWING MORNING, their breakfast over, Rose, Kathleen and all those in their barracks who were being transferred that day, sat on their beds, their packed suitcases at their sides.

When the guard arrived, everyone stood up. He ordered them to go out to the parade ground at quarter past ten, and to take their suitcases with them.

They did so, and after standing in lines of five in the fresh October air for almost an hour, they were told to start walking down the hill to the station, each of them having first been given a ration of bread and sausage meat.

Too anxious about the future to see the beauty of the forests, its trees tinged with burnished gold, and of the hazy blue Alpen peaks that rose above them, they put one foot in front of another, their heads bowed, until they reached the station. There they boarded a train and sat staring out of the windows, too numb to take note of the rolling countryside and dense green forests through which they were passing.

At half past three in the afternoon, they reached the camp at Wurzach. It stood at the edge of a small village comprising a cluster of houses with red roofs. Being a very large, three-storey stone building, the camp looked like a grand house surrounded by barbed wire.

Filing past the open front door, they glimpsed an ornate entrance hall, from the centre of which rose a curved marble staircase. But they were taken round to the back of the building that the guards referred to as the *Schloss*, and told to wait there to be allocated their rooms.

As they stared up at the forbidding stone exterior, an air of extreme dejection settled on the group. And as they entered the chill interior of the Schloss and followed the guard up steep flights of stone stairs and along stone corridors, that sense of dejection grew.

The first of the corridors led to the dormitories, each of which would house thirty or forty women of all ages, plus children. Boys over the age of twelve were to go with the men, whose dormitories would be on the floor above.

When they were halfway along the corridor, the guard in front of them paused and indicated that this was their dormitory. Those at the front of their group led the way in, and stopped abruptly.

Rose, Kathleen, and the rest of their number crowded in after them, bunching around them, and together they stood there, staring in shocked horror at the long room in front of them.

Plaster was falling from the ceiling. There were high windows down one side of the room, covered in dirt. The bare wooden floorboards were carpeted with grime.

Despite a large black iron stove in the centre of the dormitory, they could feel the damp in the air.

Crammed close to each other along the filthy walls were wooden bunk beds with straw mattresses, each bed with a small table and bench next to it.

Slowly, the women drifted towards the beds. Each found one and hovered there, looking around her in despair.

Kathleen put her suitcase on one of the beds and Rose put hers on the bed next to it.

As the women saw the wretched condition of the latrines and the state of the showers at the end of the dormitory, and that the mattresses they would have to sleep on were damp and infested with fleas, a number of them started to cry.

The guard who had led them to their dormitory told them, by way of apology for the widespread dirt, that the Schloss had previously housed French prisoners of war. A modern wing had been built just before the war, he added, but it remained incomplete. He finished by saying that they'd eat most of their meals in the dormitory.

He turned to leave, but Marjorie de Gruchy stopped him.

'We'll need buckets,' she told him firmly. 'We can't live like this.' She gesticulated around her. 'We must have some way of cleaning the place.'

Cries of 'It's filthy' and 'It's too bad' were heard all along the room as the women found their voices.

There was a shortage of buckets, brooms and other cleaning equipment, the guard told them brusquely. There would be a bucket or two somewhere around and they would have to do their best with what they could find. However, he would send up delousing powder that would kill the fleas in their mattresses, he added, and he left the room.

Rose opened her suitcase and pulled out her Jeyes fluid. 'We can use this,' she told Kathleen. 'I used it a couple of times in Biberach, but we didn't really need it after that so I rather forgot about it.'

Taking it with her, she walked along the dormitory, looking for something in which to put water. Seeing a small bucket near the latrines, she took that and poured a little Jeyes into it.

For the rest of the day, they all of them put their tired-ness aside and got down to cleaning their dormitory. They scrubbed every surface with cold water. With half a brick, they scraped the dirt from the floors, and using pieces of broken glass, they lifted the grime from the tables, benches and beds.

Some of the floorboards were rotten with age, but when they appealed to the guards for wood, they were told there wasn't any, nor was there any glass for repairing broken windows.

As soon as the flea powder arrived, they sprinkled it liberally on their mattresses, each passing it on to the next when she had done her bed.

When it reached Rose, she grabbed it quickly, lest anyone should decide that she and Kathleen shouldn't be allowed to use it. Having shaken a thick layer on to her mattress, she did Kathleen's bed for her before passing the powder to the next person.

Later that day, when they were counted in the dormitory, several of the mothers with children asked the guard if there was a school, and Marie Marrett asked if they'd be able to do any kind of work. They were anxious, she told the guard, about how they would fill the day in such limited, cramped conditions.

There was no work, the guards told them, and no school. There were dungeons, though, and they could teach the children there. But they would have to be the teachers. And there was also a concert hall and ballroom. As for how to fill their time, it would be up to them to organise the camp and to decide how to occupy themselves.

Soon after he'd left, Marie's husband, Arthur, came down from the men's floor, carrying a couple of pieces of paper. They all gathered around him. Rose and Kathleen hovered behind everyone, but made sure they were close enough to hear him.

'I've been going to each dormitory,' Arthur told them, 'telling everyone the same thing. Firstly, we're allowed to eat our meals in your rooms with you and spend the day with you, just as we did in Biberach. But we have to be back upstairs at night in time for the last count.'

'I suppose that's better than nothing,' Marjorie said.

'Secondly,' he went on, 'they made it clear to us, as I'm sure they did to you, that it's up to us to sort out what we do in the day. So, we've organised a camp committee and we've taken responsibility for various aspects of camp life.'

'That's quick!' Marjorie exclaimed. 'Who's doing what?'

'Kenneth will be in charge of the kitchens, and Ian the laundry. We're hoping that you'll do the kitchens with Kenneth, Joan,' he called to a plump woman standing at the back of the group. 'As you're a school cook, there's nothing you don't know about dealing with numbers of hungry people, and about keeping everything clean.'

'I'd be happy to,' Joan said, beaming in pleasure. 'And Susan can do it with me, too.' She smiled at her daughter.

'I'll be responsible for educating the children, if you want,' a wiry woman called Georgina volunteered. 'We'll do a rota of internees who'd be willing to do some teaching. We can ask the Red Cross for materials. The children won't have much to distract them so there's no reason why they shouldn't keep pretty much up with the children back in Jersey.'

'The guard told us there's a concert hall and ballroom, Arthur,' Marie said, 'so we can make our own entertainment. I volunteer to be in charge of that, if no one else wants the job.'

Marjorie smiled at her. 'You'll be excellent at it, Marie.'

'If we could get any materials,' Rose called above the heads in front of her, 'I could organise a sewing group. I doubt we'd get any textiles from the Red Cross, but we might get items of haberdashery, and therefore be able to mend our clothes, or adapt what we've got.'

'I don't think so,' Marjorie said coldly. And she pointedly turned her back on Rose and Kathleen.

'So nothing's really changed,' Kathleen said under her breath. 'Apart from where we are.'

BY THE END of the first four weeks in Wurzach, the lack of good food was becoming a major problem. Their diet was mostly thin cabbage soup and black bread, which they ate with caution after several splinters of wood and glass were found in the bread.

But they knew from Joan that the German guards had better food than they did, and that the Germans liked their potatoes to be peeled before being cooked, so one day a couple of women decided to ask if the deportees could have the peelings. The guards shrugged their shoulders and said they could, so queueing for peelings soon became part of their daily routine, and eating them part of their diet.

Their bread was delivered once a week, and was frequently mouldy when it arrived. As it was kept in a damp store, it rapidly deteriorated further and the mouldy parts had to be cut off. The bread that was thrown away was never replaced, so there was even less bread than there should have been, which was a constant cause for grumbling.

Once they had settled into the camp, they were allowed to write three letters a month. With food, and the lack of it, at the forefront of their minds, all of them wrote to their families in Jersey about the shortages.

They did their best, though, to describe their life in a way that wouldn't cause unnecessary alarm to the families who were helpless to aid them, and who themselves were prisoners of the Germans.

TO ROSE'S AMAZEMENT, and to that of the others, too, their comments about the food must have survived the censorship of their letters, and been relayed by their families to the Red Cross, as several weeks later, a delivery of Red Cross parcels from England arrived at the Schloss.

At the sight of the items they'd been sent, which included small tins of soft cheese, Klim dried milk, butter, tea, cocoa, sugar, tins of Spam and of vegetables, chocolate, jam and packs of the dried beans that Annie used when she made a Jersey Bean-Crock, some of the deportees burst into tears.

'I don't know why you're looking so happy,' Kathleen told Rose bitterly. 'We won't see any of that. Marjorie will tell Joan to give us the minimum.'

Not long after the first of the Red Cross parcels arrived, another incident occurred that further lifted their spirits.

Joan was responsible for an unexpected treat. She and her daughter, Susan, had been in the basement of the Schloss, where the store of potatoes was kept. They had been filling sacks of potatoes for the guards, both of them wearing aprons with deep pockets.

Noticing that the elderly guard supervising them frequently had his back to them, they couldn't resist slipping potatoes into their apron pockets.

When their pockets were as heavy as they dared make them, and the required sacks of potatoes had been filled, they started to leave the basement, with Susan going ahead of Joan. Before Joan could follow Susan out of the room, she felt the weight of the guard's hand on her shoulder.

She was so terrified that she was about to be punished for stealing potatoes, her heart raced in panic. But to her astonishment, the guard, in very poor English, told her to be sure to share the potatoes with the rest of the Jersey people.

There was great excitement when she and Susan returned to the dormitory, brandished the potatoes on high and then thrust them into the ashes in the big stove in the centre of the room, and left them to bake.

No one spoke. They all sat on their beds, staring at the stove, waiting with longing for the moment the baked potatoes were ready. As soon as they were done, each person took one.

So, too, did Rose and Kathleen.

Marjorie and her friends had been so busy putting Red Cross butter on to their potatoes that they'd forgotten to make sure that Rose and Kathleen went without.

'That was wonderful,' Rose said when she finished her potato. 'I hope they didn't notice we had one, too, and I hope Joan gets some more again soon.'

Not long after that, to the relief of the teacher, Georgina, and all the mothers there, a batch of Red Cross parcels arrived. They contained educational and story books for children, each of which had a Geneva Red Cross stamp inside.

Georgina promptly took control of the books. They had

been provided by a Roman Catholic organisation in America, she told the deportees when she'd had a chance to look at the books. She added that in the children's lesson the following morning, the children would write a collective thank-you letter to the organisation and perhaps draw a picture to go with it.

Not long after that, there was another Red Cross delivery of food. When it was handed over to Kenneth and Joan, Kenneth suggested that now that they had tinned goods, it might be possible to swap some of their tinned food for eggs and fresh produce, as that was what the children needed, and everyone else, too.

So it was decided that Arthur and Ian, both of whom spoke reasonable German, should risk climbing over the barbed wire and go into the village that lay just south of the main entrance.

They'd have to take a chance that there was no one in the closest watchtower, and that any villagers they spoke to would feel it was in their interests to keep quiet about them leaving the Schloss.

While everyone watched from the windows, waiting with bated breath, they saw Arthur and Ian get over the wire and disappear from sight. A short time afterwards, to the relief of all, they saw the two men scaling the wire to get back into the Schloss.

Moments later, the men hurried into the women's dormitory, where they were swiftly surrounded.

'We found some friendly villagers,' Arthur told them. 'In fact, everyone we spoke to seemed friendly. When we asked if they'd swap some of their fresh produce for our tinned food, they jumped at the idea.'

'That was lucky!' Joan exclaimed.

'It's lucky for them, too,' Ian said. 'The people in the

village, just like everywhere else in Germany apparently, are suffering badly from wartime deprivations, so it's no wonder they were very ready to trade. We'll need to be really careful whenever we leave the Schloss, though. They warned us that we're almost next door to a Hitler Youth camp.'

After that, each time a Red Cross parcel of food arrived, the two men would take some of the tins to the village inn and barter with them.

On one occasion a few weeks later, they learned on Ian's return that he had bartered for something different—he had traded several tins of Spam for the items needed to build a simple wireless set. He would hide it in his dormitory, he told them with a grin.

Eventually, they started wondering if the guards weren't aware of what was going on.

Although a number of the guards were elderly, or had been wounded and were no longer able to fight at the front, it seemed highly unlikely that they wouldn't have any idea that there was a lively trade going on between the villagers and the deportees.

Most of the guards were kind to them, and used to give sweets to the children. And some of the guards had started accompanying them on walks in the fields outside the Schloss. During the walks, they were allowed to pick dandelion leaves and take them back to share among the internees. Those leaves were their only form of green vegetable.

They decided, therefore, that it was most likely that the guards were deliberately turning a blind eye to what was happening.

Their suspicions were confirmed when Arthur put a map on a wall in the women's dormitory, and every day marked on it in red wool the progress of the Allied armies.

Quite by chance, soon after that, the camp Kommandant happened to go into the dormitory and saw the map. He stopped and stared hard at it, but to their great surprise and relief, he left without saying anything.

After that, the Kommandant frequently went into the dormitory and inspected the movement of the red wool, but he never commented upon it.

The arrival of a Red Cross parcel of pencils and paints encouraged a number of internees to take up drawing and painting. Some planned to illustrate life in the camp and others to make birthday and Christmas cards.

It looked fun, Rose thought, so she decided to join one of the painting groups, thinking to make a card for Tom. But as she sat down in their circle, the paints were swiftly placed out of her reach, and the paper and card they'd been using suddenly disappeared from sight.

She wasn't welcome, she clearly understood, and she got up and returned to the bench beside her bed.

'What did you expect?' Kathleen asked, and continued writing her letter.

BY THE TIME December arrived and snow lay on the ground in a dense carpet of white, the internees had settled into a routine of activities, all of which excluded Rose and Kathleen.

On a number of occasions, Kathleen told Rose to go off and make friends with someone else, saying that she didn't need her and didn't want her company.

On each occasion, Rose ignored her.

36

Jersey, December 1943

'Well, that's the second Christmas dinner we've got through since Rose and Kathleen were sent away,' Annie said, picking up the remainder of the apple pie and carrageen moss blanc-mange. 'I'm sorry that my attempt at a blancmange tasted a bit of salt water. No matter how much you sweeten it, carrageen moss always tastes vaguely of the sea.'

'I washed it thoroughly,' Tom said, 'and got as much sand from it as I could before drying it in what sun there was.'

Annie nodded. 'I know you did. Thanks to you, it wasn't as briny as it might have been. But a touch of the sea will always be inevitable, I suppose, given it's seaweed. I'll leave the sugar-beet cake on the table as you might want a slice of it with my attempt at coffee, which I'll bring in now.'

'It was an excellent meal, Mrs Benest,' Joshua said. 'Hats off to you to have done that during the Occupation.'

'If we'd been limited to the same amount of oatmeal as the people in town, I couldn't have done it. But thanks to your oats, Josh, and to the German at the grain machine letting you keep several sacks of oats for yourself, it was possible. I'm very glad you were able to be here today and to eat some of them with us. Anyway, I'll get that coffee I mentioned.'

She stood up and carrying the remains of the pudding, went across to her working area.

A few minutes later, she returned with a tray holding four cups, a pot of coffee and a jug of milk. She put everything into the middle of the table next to a centrepiece made of holly. 'Pour the coffees, Tom, would you, please?' she asked, and sat down again.

'Did Dad tell you we had a letter from the Department of Public Health, Josh?' Tom asked, handing him a cup of coffee.

'No, he didn't. What was it about?'

'Dirt in the sample of the milk they took. They're so stupid that they don't realise that when the dairyman gets to the depot, he mixes our milk with all the other milk he's collected. So what ends up in our cans is a mixture of milk from different farms. And unfortunately, not all farmers are as careful as we are.'

'What did you do?' Joshua asked.

'Dad wrote and told them they should go to the depot just as we arrive and take a sample from our cans before our milk's been mixed with anyone else's. They've never done that, of course, but we've not heard anything more from them,' Tom said in satisfaction.

Annie glanced at Joshua, who was sitting opposite Tom. 'We're so pleased you decided to spend the day with us, Josh. It would have been a sorry Christmas if it had been just Tom, William and me. But won't your parents have been missing you?'

He grinned at her. 'They won't have had much of a chance to miss me—my three cousins and their families were going to them for lunch. There'll have been five children under six. It's amazing the lure of a farm on a day like Christmas Day,' he added with a laugh. 'I've left Paul to do the honours on my behalf. The only thing my parents will be missing today is a bit of peace. Tom threw me a welcome lifeline when he said I could join you if I wanted.'

William laughed. 'Well, we're glad you feel that way, Josh. As Annie said, we're delighted to have you here.'

Joshua cleared his throat. 'I wondered if you'd had any news of Kathleen?' he asked. 'Have you heard from her at all? Or from Rose, of course?'

'We get a letter from them every so often,' Annie said, cutting four pieces of cake, and indicating they should help themselves. 'I thought we would've had another letter by now, but they're probably delayed because of Christmas. At least we know they're all right. It's kind of you to ask.'

He shrugged. 'Kathleen used to come to the Gorins' farm and pass the time of day. I miss our conversations. Not that we ever said much,' he added quickly.

'We think she's not finding it easy in the camp,' William said. 'Her association with the German's common knowledge, and the women they're with are being quite unpleasant to her.'

Joshua nodded. 'That must be hard on her.' He paused. 'I've seen her German around the town, each time with a different woman.'

'He might have been her German once,' William said, 'or she thought he was, but he certainly won't be now, nor when she returns. But it's Rose I feel sorry for. Kathleen told us that Rose had stuck by her since the day they left and they're shunning Rose, too, because of her loyalty to Kathleen.'

'I didn't realise the two of them were that friendly,' Joshua said.

'They're not,' Tom cut in. 'Kathleen's been quite unpleasant to Rose in the past, but Rose isn't the sort of person to bear a grudge.'

'Personally, I think the women in the camp are taking it too far,' Annie said with indignation. 'Yes, Kathleen befriended the German, and that was extremely unwise. But most of us are fraternising in some way with the Germans, particularly the farmers.'

'We've no choice, though,' Tom said.

'Nevertheless, we're providing the Germans with milk, butter, wheat, oats and potatoes, and a lot of animals, too,' Annie said. 'And over half the islanders are working for Germans one way or another. And black marketeers are taking advantage of the rationing and lining their pockets at the Jersey people's expense. Some of the deportees come from families doing just that. I know it's different from Kathleen's friendship with the German, but it's not so different that it warrants the treatment she's still getting.'

'That German of hers, or not of hers, came to the Gorins' not so long ago,' Joshua said. 'He had a few Todt workers with him.'

'What did he want?' William asked.

'Our apples. They were forcing a huge scooping machine along the narrow lane. The machine was far too wide, and its massive caterpillar wheels were wrecking the hedge. But the Todt workers were laughing their heads off at the damage they were doing—they just didn't care.'

William nodded. 'Those men are worse than the German soldiers,' he said. 'Much worse. Their cruelty to the Russian and Spanish prisoners, and to the other labourers, too, is beyond belief. They're the ones who're really brutal.'

'But the German soldiers can be vindictive,' Tom said, 'if anyone breaks their rules. Like having a wireless set. Look at the people arrested in the past few months and sent to prison or deported, just because they were found to have a wireless set, or to be delivering leaflets, or because they hid and fed an escaped Russian prisoner.'

William nodded. 'That's true. But unless they break the rules, people are mostly left alone. And a lot of the soldiers go out of their way to be pleasant and helpful. Also, just as we're getting hungrier, they are, too. Perhaps not the ones at the top, but the ordinary soldiers are.'

'There's been quite a bit of stealing from the farm lately,' Joshua said. 'I try not to leave it unoccupied more than I have to. Have you found that?'

'We certainly have,' William said. 'For months, we've been losing things. I think it's the German soldiers as well as escaped Russian prisoners who're taking our chickens, rabbits, vegetables, and just about anything else they can carry. We've been keeping the cows and pigs under close watch. And we hardly took our eyes off the wonderful goose we had for dinner.' He smiled broadly at Annie. 'But so far, no one's broken into the house. Unfortunately, a number of our neighbours can't say the same. It's a mess.'

'I doubt this'll go on for much longer,' Tom said. 'The war's bound to end soon. First there was the Allied win in Tunisia in May, and then Mussolini resigning in July—'

'Tom!' Annie exclaimed. And she looked at Joshua in alarm.

He laughed. 'Don't worry, Mrs Benest. I've got a crystal set. There, I've told you. So now you could tell on me, too.'

'You must be more cautious, Tom,' Annie said reprovingly.

'This is Josh you're talking about,' Tom said, and he laughed dismissively. 'To continue then. The heavy bombing we've been hearing on and off in France for the past few months suggests that an Allied invasion of France will happen soon.'

'Let's hope you're right,' Annie said fervently. 'In the meantime, what about a game of cards?'

OUTSIDE THE FARMHOUSE, Tom waited while Joshua put the two packets of leftover cake that Annie had given him into the wicker basket on the front of his bicycle, and unlocked the bicycle.

'You sounded interested in Kathleen, the way you asked about her,' Tom said, leaning back against the wall, watching him. 'Or am I getting it wrong?'

Joshua straightened up and gave an awkward laugh. 'I suppose I do miss her. I've certainly been thinking about her a lot.'

'I know the two of you went out together a few years ago, but then you just stopped. Kathleen never said why. Next thing she was with that drip, Arthur Costain.'

'I was too young to want to settle down, and Kathleen wasn't. That's it in a nutshell.'

'And now?'

'Now that I've been responsible for someone else's farm, at a very difficult time, I've grown up. And I'm finding myself missing her visits.' He shrugged. 'She's probably not even thought about me at all as she was nuts about that German. I'd like to think she has, though, and that she's got over him.' He hesitated. 'When you write to her, you could mention that I was asking about her, if you wanted.'

'Better still, you could write to her yourself.'

In the darkness, Tom saw him smile. 'Maybe I will,' he said. 'But I must get off now. It's almost midnight. It's really good that the Germans decided to extend the curfew for tonight and the next couple of nights without the people at the top knowing, but I don't want to push my luck by being out later than that.'

'Are you going back to your house now or the Gorins'?' Tom asked.

'The Gorins'. I'm there more than I'm not these days, what with all the thefts. Anyway, I'll see you,' he said.

And with a wave of his hand, he cycled off, puncturing the darkness with the rhythmic clunk from the metal clip holding his hosepipe-tyre in place.

Thrusting his hands into his pockets, Tom walked from the farmhouse over to his house. When he reached his front door, he stopped and looked up at the sky.

A black night studded with stars looked back at him.

The last time he'd stood there in such a way he'd been with Rose.

A frisson ran through him.

Coming from somewhere beyond the blackness, he felt her presence.

He caught his breath, and his arms fell to his sides.

Staring up at the sky with longing, he knew with absolute certainty that somewhere in Germany at that very moment, Rose was looking up at the stars, and sending him her love.

'I love you, too, Rose,' he said, gazing up into the cold night. 'And it's breaking my heart that you're so far from me. There's never a minute of the day when I don't think about you and wish we were together. Stay safe, my Rose.'

As he watched, his words floated up to the heavens on a column of mist.

37

Germany, June 1944

Shuddering violently as she saw a line of mice running across the stone step in front of her, Rose stopped climbing up the back spiral staircase that led to the women's floor and stood rooted to the spot.

Then tightening her hold on the basket of washing she'd been sent down to the laundry to collect, she banged her foot hard on the step to frighten the mice, and resumed climbing as quickly as she could.

Joan was forever complaining about the infestation of rats in the kitchen, which stubbornly withstood the most thorough cleaning possible in the circumstances. And the laundry room was just as bad, overrun as it was with mice.

They did the best they could with the few cleaning materials they had, but they hadn't sufficient to get rid of the vermin from all of the parts of the Schloss they needed to use.

Watching where she trod, she continued up the stairs.

Then she heard footsteps above her.

She stopped and listened.

The footsteps were coming towards her. It was one person only, she realised.

Her heart beat fast.

She wouldn't want to be there alone if it was one of the German guards. Not that any of them had ever been accused of forcing a woman against her will, but it would be an uncomfortable situation to be in.

She pressed herself as close as she could against the cold stone wall so that the person could go by without them touching each other.

A moment later, it was Marjorie who rounded the spiral and came into sight, her arms full of mattress covers.

Relief swept through Rose, weakening her with its strength. It was only Marjorie, unpleasant though she was.

She stayed where she was, keeping her eyes down, willing Marjorie to pass her by without comment.

As Marjorie drew level with her, she found that she was holding her breath.

Marjorie stopped, leaned against the wall and stared at Rose, unsmiling. Her eyes narrowed. 'You've got me curious,' she said. 'Back in Jersey, you and Kathleen never got on. When you weren't around, your dear sister-in-law went out of her way to try to turn people against you. Yet here you are, playing the loyal little companion to a woman who's been a bitch to you. A bitch who did a despicable thing, betraying her people by sleeping with the enemy. So why're you supporting her?'

Rose stared hard at Marjorie. 'She's entitled to like whoever she wants. That's up to her. Being over-friendly with a German wasn't the only way of betraying the Jersey people, as you put it, yet I don't see you being hostile towards anyone else. Oh, silly me. You could hardly be hostile towards yourself, could you?'

'I've never been good at riddles,' Marjorie said coldly. 'I haven't a clue what you're talking about.'

'Why, the black market, of course. It was the exorbitant prices that black marketeers got for the food they sold that encouraged them to steal even more from stores and ware-houses—food that should've been available at a reasonable price to everyone. So with shops short of food to sell, if you couldn't afford to line the pockets of profiteers, you starved.'

Marjorie gave an awkward laugh. 'That happens in a war.'

'It doesn't have to. Not if people refuse to buy from the black marketeers. But you and your family regularly bought black market goods, Marjorie, and by doing that, you helped profiteers grow rich on the backs of the needy. Some would say that helping to price food out of the reach of people poorer than yourself was as bad, if not worse, as falling for an attractive German.'

'And some would say that it was thanks to black marke-teers stealing from the Germans that we had any sugar at all on the island! Loads of people bought things on the black market,' Marjorie countered. 'You can't blame us for what they charged.'

'Yes, we can!'

'It was nowhere near as bad as going after nylons and chocolate in the way that Kathleen did,' Marjorie sneered. 'Just lifting her skirt and lying back. There's a word for people like her. Now what was it?' She screwed up her face as if in thought.

'You helped to make it harder for poor people to get enough food, Marjorie,' Rose said steadily. 'That's despicable, and you know it. As for Kathleen, this wasn't about getting nylons or anything else. She was genuinely fond of Klaus.'

Marjorie laughed derisively. 'Genuinely fond of a German, who was keeping us prisoners on our own island?'

'Genuinely fond of a good-looking man,' Rose said. 'Even though you don't like the Germans, you can't deny that many of them are attractive. And most of the time, they're considerate to their women friends. It isn't really surprising, is it, that some of the Jersey girls, like Kathleen, truly fell for them?'

'It's not what they look like; it's what they were doing.'

'Like all soldiers, they had to obey orders,' Rose retorted. 'But there've been many occasions where they were kind to Jersey people. Don't confuse them with the vicious Todt workers.'

'So you're a German lover, too, are you?' Marjorie jeered.

'And look at the soldiers here in Wurzach,' Rose continued. 'They regularly let us go for walks in the fields. They deliberately don't see the men go over the wire, and they ignore Joan taking potatoes on a regular basis. They're doing what they can for us. They probably wanted a war as little as we did.'

'You can't escape the fact that we're held here against our will.'

'That's not the fault of individual German soldiers. And anyway, it's not going to be for much longer,' Rose said. 'You've must've seen the glum faces of the guards this morning. We all know that the Allies landed in France yesterday, though we're trying not to show it. It can't be much longer till the war's over.'

'I know that. I watch the red wool, too,' Marjorie said impatiently.

'You've punished Kathleen every day since we left Jersey, and that's almost two years ago. You saw how she suffered at Klaus's cruel way of ending things. Surely, you can forgive her for what she did, and encourage the others to be nice to her.'

Marjorie shrugged. 'I'm not stopping them.'

'Yes, you are. You're the sort of person people follow. I hope you can show that you are, at heart, a kind person. Enough is enough, Marjorie.'

Not waiting for a reaction, Rose pulled herself away from the wall, and continued up the spiral staircase.

Jersey, June 1944

AS THE LATE afternoon sun sank closer to the horizon, and shadows were lengthening across the fields, William left Tom to finish harvesting the Jersey Royals, and went to lead the cows in for milking.

Annie went off to the potato barn to sort out the new potatoes.

It had come as something of a shock when the Germans had demanded all of their potatoes, saying that they were to be shipped to France the following week to feed the German troops.

But they had to appear as if they were complying with the demand, even though they didn't believe they would have to go through with it.

Not now that the Allies had landed in France.

Two nights before, despite the wind being high and the

sea rough, they'd heard plane after plane cross the sky, and intense anti-aircraft fire from the Germans.

The following morning, they learned that the people on the French coast had been told to leave everything and go twenty-five miles inland, and that the Allies had landed in Normandy.

After the initial excitement about the Allied landing, everything had gone very quiet. It was as if people were afraid to hope, afraid that something that seemed within their grasp might prove to be an illusion. All had gone about their daily business, holding their breaths, in effect, as Tom had remarked in the evening.

As they had been forbidden to use their telephones since the day of the invasion, they couldn't contact anyone to find out what was happening, so Tom cycled to St Helier the following morning.

When he returned, he told William and Annie at lunch that for once, there had been very few Germans in the streets—mostly just dispatch riders. The only Germans he'd seen in passing, he said, had seemed very glum.

But the Royal Square had been crowded with people. The Bailiff hadn't come out to make a proclamation, though, and nor had the Kommandant.

There had been ships in the bay and in the harbour, too, and people were wondering aloud if the Germans were planning to leave in the night.

'I bumped into Paul in town,' he told them. 'He said that last night, a large group of Germans was partying in a meadow near his farm. He couldn't believe it, but they appeared to be celebrating the landing in Normandy. They had a concertina and were dancing and singing till after midnight. He thought it a very strange thing to do.'

'I don't,' Annie said 'They'll have parents and wives and

children they haven't seen for years. I'm sure they're delighted to think they might be able to see them soon.'

William nodded. 'You could be right. But it could also be a way of showing defiance to the Allies. Like us singing from the top of Mount Bingham when Rose and Kathleen left.'

That evening, the *Jersey Evening Post* printed a proclamation from the Kommandant, ordering everyone to refrain from sabotage or hostile acts against the German forces. Such attacks would be punished by death, they were told.

'I think not,' William said with a smile.

When it was time for the news, they took the wireless from the bread oven. Annie produced a small amount of the real tea she had been storing for special occasions, and the three of them sat in the kitchen, savouring their tea as they listened to the King call the nation to prayer.

None of them dared to voice a belief that was still so fragile, that Kathleen and Rose would soon be with them again.

The following night was quieter. They heard planes above them and continual bombardment, but there was no anti-aircraft fire.

Early in the morning, however, they awoke to the sound of machine-gunning. And later they saw that some of the ships in St Aubin's Bay had been damaged, and others sunk. And they knew they had to be patient.

The invasion had been the first step only—the war wasn't yet over.

They were still occupied by the enemy, being given orders by them. They were unable to use the telephone, or to receive or send any more Red Cross messages, and they were forbidden to be out later that ten o'clock. All theatres were closed, and there were no more dances and entertainments.

Worse still, it was becoming clear that with France liberated, food deliveries for the islanders and for the German occupying forces would be at an end. There was already little enough as it was, and not having those extra supplies could mean starvation for many.

When they went to bed the following night, their hope that they might soon see Rose and Kathleen again was fading fast.

London, June 1944

'BUT THE WAR'S ALMOST OVER,' Iris said in irritation when Mabel reminded them it was time to go to the corrugated steel shelter in the garden. 'Everything's much quieter now, so why do we still have to go to the shelter? I'd rather sleep in my bed. Wouldn't you, Violet?'

'I suppose so, if it's safe,' Violet said. 'It's true that there're far fewer night raids these days with the Germans so bogged down in the Russian winter, but the war's not over till Churchill says it is.'

'What d'you think, John?' Mabel asked. 'Shall we stay indoors tonight? Iris is right, it really is much calmer now.'

John looked up from the report he was reading and smiled at the three of them. 'I suppose we'll have to move back to our beds at some point, so it might as well be tonight. Get your things from the shelter, girls, and go on up. You, too, Mabel. I'll just finish these last few pages.'

IRIS OPENED her eyes and stared up at the darkness.

There was a strange sound in the sky, and it was coming closer.

She frowned. It wasn't a plane engine, she was sure—she was used to the noise they made. No, this was different. It was more of a continuous droning, with a rattle to it. And it was getting louder.

She pulled her eiderdown up to her chin. The noise was above her, then silence fell.

Relaxing, she loosened her hold on the eiderdown.

'Under your beds!' she heard her father scream from downstairs.

She threw herself to the floor and scrambled under the bed as a massive explosion blasted the air. The windows shattered and the room filled with dust. Her hands flew to her ears, and she lay there in terror. Above her, the bedframe sagged, and her eiderdown slipped to the floor.

Then all was still.

Coughing, she crawled out from under the bed, shook her slippers and put them on, then tried to stand up. But her legs were shaking so much that they wouldn't support her, and she sat down heavily on her bed.

She felt very cold.

From along the landing, she heard her mother shouting, 'Girls, are you all right? Answer me!'

'I'm fine,' she called. 'Just shaken.'

'Me, too,' came from Violet's room.

She coughed again and made another attempt to stand. Once upright, she steadied herself, and took a few steps towards the door. Her slippers crunched on the floor. Looking down, she saw that she was walking on fragments of plaster and glass.

'Where's Father?' she heard Violet call as she opened her bedroom door.

'I'm down here, unhurt,' John's voice came to them up the stairs.

She took her dressing gown from the back of the door, wrapped it around her, and went out on to the landing. Seeing her mother and sister on their way down the stairs to her father, she went down after them.

'You've got a cut on your face,' Mabel told John in concern when she reached the bottom of the stairs and studied him.

'It's nothing,' he said. 'I heard what I thought was a bomb, shouted to you and dashed for the back door, thinking to get to the shelter in time. When I pulled open the door, it came away from its frame and struck the side of my face. It's only a scratch, though. Indeed, we're lucky that none of us was seriously hurt.'

'I wonder if any other houses in the street have been damaged,' Mabel said, 'apart from having broken windows, that is.' She went to the front door, opened it and took a few steps down the path. Iris and Violet followed her.

A number of their neighbours had come out of their houses and were looking around. An elderly lady from a few doors down the street was kneeling in the road, praying.

Iris went to the end of the path and stared down to the bottom of the road. A group of white-helmeted wardens was hurrying across the end of their road.

'Well, all the houses in Allcroft Road seem to be standing,' she said, turning back to the others.

'It was close, though,' Mabel said, her voice shaky, and she shooed them back into the house.

'You're right,' Iris said, shutting the front door behind them. 'It was too close. I know what I said earlier on, but ignore it. I'm going to use the shelter till we know that the war's definitely over.'

.   .   .

'I DON'T KNOW if you're planning to write to Rose again while we're still unsure if anything's getting through to her, Violet,' Mabel said the following evening as she was draping pastry over the meat and vegetables in the pie dish, 'but if you are, it might be better not to mention last night's doodlebug. We don't want to give poor Rose something else to worry about.'

'I wouldn't dream of telling her,' Violet said indignantly. 'They're far too scary. And she'd find it as hard to believe as we do that there's a type of aircraft that doesn't need a pilot. That silence before it landed was terrifying. Rose doesn't need to know that.'

38

Germany, April 1945

'I was near the side door when a tank rolled up, and I was terrified, I don't mind telling you,' Marjorie said, standing in the middle of the dormitory, her words tumbling over each other in tearful excitement. 'A man got out and asked for someone who spoke French. French, not German,' she went on, tears streaming down her cheeks.

'They were French soldiers,' she said. 'I called to Marie. Her mother was French, you know. And she came down and spoke to them. They wanted to know where the main gates were and she told them.'

Marie rushed into the room and ran across to the nearest window. 'They're coming,' she shouted. 'The French are coming.'

They all ran to the windows, pushing one another aside in their desperation to see outside.

There was a general gasp as they saw the line of tanks

approaching the main gates. Blinking against the midday sun, they stared down at them in stunned silence.

The first tank reached the gates, and stopped.

Two of the French troops climbed from the tank, holding something in their hands. They went up to the gates, smashed the locks and swung them wide. Moments later, the tanks and jeeps rumbled through the open gates.

When the first tank reached the main entrance, the convoy came to a halt. A soldier got out of the front tank. He looked up at the faces of the men and women lining the windows, grinned at them and waved.

Then he shouted up some words in French.

'We're free,' Marie whispered in disbelief. 'He's telling us that it's all right, that we can go down now.'

The room erupted. Shrieking in excitement and crying tears of joy, they rushed from the dormitory, along the corridor and down the central marble staircase.

Keeping pace with them, Rose and Kathleen reached the foot of the staircase, ran through the open doors and flung themselves outside.

Standing side by side in the fresh air, they shouted, 'We're free!' Instinctively, they fell into each other's arms and hugged each other tightly.

Then, suddenly awkward, they drew apart.

Avoiding looking at Rose's face, Kathleen turned and went back into the Schloss.

Rose crossed to the internees who were crowding around the French soldiers, and stood behind the groups who were hugging their friends and crying as they asked the soldiers over and over again, when they could go back to Jersey.

The French hadn't known that they were there, they learnt in amazement as Marie translated their words. Until an hour or so before, the French had thought that the Schloss was the local Nazi headquarters. They'd had no idea that it was an internment camp.

They had gone first to the village and found it abandoned by the German soldiers, so they had turned to go to the Schloss.

It was only when they'd seen the German guards, accompanied by the head of the village, coming towards them carrying a white flag of surrender, that they had discovered that the Schloss was a prisoner of war camp.

The Americans would be arriving in a few days, the internees were told, and everyone should remain in the Schloss until then. No one should go wandering off, the French cautioned. It would be very dangerous to do so as both they and the Americans were hunting people down and might assume that they were the enemy and shoot them.

'We've put up with our incarceration for almost three years,' Marjorie said as they started to go back inside the Schloss. 'I think we can cope with a few days more.'

39

Jersey, 9th May 1945

'That was so special,' Annie said as they stood in the middle of the crowds in the Royal Square. 'Just to hear Churchill say "our dear Channel Islands", and that hostilities would officially end at one minute past midnight, made me feel so emotional.'

'Me, too, Annie,' William said, visibly moved.

'And then to hear the Bailiff tell us that a British Commission was on its way,' she continued, 'and that British naval units were already approaching the island. And to see them take the German flag down from the Pomme d'Or, and put the Union Jack in its place.' She shook her head. 'I'll never forget today.'

His arm around her, William nodded. 'Nor me,' he said.

'I finally feel free,' Annie went on. 'I know the Germans told us this morning that the war was over, but it didn't feel real till now.'

'Not even after the King's speech last night?' William said in surprise. 'And seeing all the cars and motorcycles that have been pulled out of haystacks and barns this morning? Didn't that make it all real?'

'No, not quite,' Annie said. 'It's only now, with all the excitement around us, and Union Jacks everywhere, and hearing bits of the National Anthem every few minutes, that I know, absolutely know, that we've survived this and are free.'

William smiled down at her. 'I felt free a little sooner than you, then. When we didn't have the usual celebration for Hitler's birthday last month, a week or so before the coward took his own life, and when people started buying Union Jacks while the Germans stood by and did nothing, I think it was then that I felt it was over.'

'The moment of truth for me,' Tom said, 'was when all the radios that had been hidden suddenly appeared on windowsills, and music blared out, and people started dancing. And all the bells rang out across the island. That's what freedom sounds like. And to know that I'll soon see Rose— that's what freedom means.'

'It does, son,' William said, putting his free arm round Tom's shoulders, and giving him a brief hug.

Standing back from the crowd, a German soldier watched dejectedly as ecstatic groups of people milled around in front of him.

'You can't help feeling a bit sorry for some of the Germans,' Tom said, indicating the soldier. 'Everything they believed in has been defeated. And the ordinary soldiers have lost so much weight, like we have. Some are as much victims as we were. They were made to leave their families and homes, and they don't even know if the people they love have survived the war.'

'But they're still the enemy,' William said sharply. 'And because of their actions, we've had no electricity since Christmas, and no gas since long before that. And if the war had carried on for much longer, we wouldn't have even had any candles left.'

'I know all that,' Tom countered.

'I, for one, won't forget in a hurry what it's been like,' William continued, 'spending our winter evenings, cold and in semi-darkness, with just the light thrown out by a tin full of diesel oil with a bootlace for a wick. And having cold water, and that only for a few hours a day. Don't be in too much of a hurry to forget that, Tom.'

'Of course I won't,' he said tetchily. 'I'm only pointing out that we aren't the only ones on the island who suffered.'

'And if the Red Cross ship hadn't arrived at the end of December with parcels of food,' Annie reminded him, 'far more of us would have died than did. We were literally starving. Those Red Cross parcels saved our lives. As for the pleasure of having soap again, it's indescribable.'

'And shoes,' William added, 'instead of having to walk on thin worn-out soles that were beyond repair, or hard pieces of wood.'

Tom opened his mouth to say something else, but Annie stopped him.

'The sun's finally coming out' she said firmly. 'I think we've said enough for today about the struggle we've had. This is a day to celebrate, and to focus on the future. Just think, we'll soon see Kathleen and Rose again. It won't feel completely right till they're back with us.'

GERMANY, June 1945

.   .   .

'IT'S BEEN a month now since Jersey was liberated,' Rose said, standing in the compound, staring towards the south. 'I didn't expect to be stuck here for so long after being told we were free. I thought we'd be off home in a day or two. Until we get on the trucks tomorrow, and are driven to the airport by Americans, not Germans, I don't think I'll ever believe we're free.'

'At least we had the use of a ballroom while we waited, and there were some dances,' Kathleen said. 'It's a shame the Americans and French didn't get on, and had to be kept apart, as both lots of troops were fun. The Americans particularly seemed keen on dancing and really appeared to be enjoying themselves.'

Rose glanced at Kathleen in surprise. 'I didn't know you liked the dances. You refused to dance with anyone.'

'Can you imagine what Marjorie and her lot would have said if I'd got up and danced?' Kathleen said with a laugh. 'I didn't dare risk it. In the past few months, they seem to have stopped being quite so nasty to me, and I'd no intention of giving them a reason to start again. Inside my head, though, I was dancing, and loving it. And the rest of me was enjoying the atmosphere.'

Rose smiled broadly. 'Now you sound more like the old you. Except, you were more pleasant to me just now than the old you used to be,' she added with a laugh.

Kathleen glanced at her quickly. 'Do your parents and sisters know I was nasty to you, and did you tell them about Klaus?'

Rose shook her head. 'No to both of those. I might have worried them, and I didn't want to do that.'

'I hope they like me,' Kathleen said after a few minutes.

'I'm sure they will. You've got a lot in common with Iris, and I can't wait for you to meet her. But it's infuriating that they haven't lifted restrictions on travel to the Channel Islands yet, so we're having to go to England and stay there till they do.'

'It'll give me a chance to meet your sisters, though,' Kathleen said.

Rose pulled a face. 'I feel guilty saying what I did as it sounds as if I don't want to see my family again, and as if I don't want you to meet them, and I do. But I so miss Tom, and I miss my life in Jersey. I want it to be just the same as it was before the Germans came.'

Kathleen turned to Rose. Her eyes filled with tears. 'It won't be the same,' she said.

Rose looked at her in concern. 'What d'you mean? Why're you crying?'

'It won't be the same, Rose—it'll be better. I promise it will. Emily wouldn't have stood by me in the way you've done,' Kathleen said, her voice catching. 'I don't think many people would've done. For almost three years, you've shared your clothes, you've looked out for me and you've been the only person to talk to me, even though everyone here shunned you for doing so.'

Tears ran down Kathleen's cheeks.

'And you've never once blamed me for that,' Kathleen went on. 'You've been like a real sister to me—better even than a real sister might've been. And when we get home, I'm going to make it up to you.'

Rose put her arms around Kathleen and hugged her. 'You don't have to make up for anything, Kathleen. You've felt like a true sister for a long time,' she said. 'And you always will.'

40

London, July 1945

'So that's Lower Hams,' Rose said as she and Kathleen left the shop and turned in the direction of Allcroft Road. 'Now you've seen all three shops. There'd have been more if there hadn't been a war. At least Upper and Lower Hams are back to being shops again and aren't being used as depots any longer. But from one or two comments that Father's made, I suspect there're going to be further changes in the future. I haven't a clue what they are, though.'

'I really enjoyed our visit to Mid Hams,' Kathleen said. 'Iris certainly knows what she's doing. I was so impressed with the group she was helping in the back room. She said last night that clothes rationing would probably last a few more years, so people were going to have to keep on adapting their clothes, but in a stylish way. And this morning I saw how brilliant she is at helping them to do that.'

'I'm amazed at how well she's done—I think my parents are, too. She really seems to have grown up. Violet's not changed in the same way—she's always been studious and interested in what's going on in the world, and she still is. I'm sure she's an excellent teacher. She certainly enjoys teaching people. Including us,' she added with a laugh.

Kathleen smiled. 'That doesn't surprise me. When we were talking about clothes, it was Violet who jumped in to say that despite all the advertisements promising new styles, the shops were still fairly empty because although production's increased, most of what's made is exported.'

Rose laughed. 'Yes, that's typical Violet.'

'I seem to recall you saying I had a lot in common with Iris,' Kathleen said, glancing sideways at Rose. 'If you still think so, I'm flattered.'

'I do think you have. Mind you, I don't really know what Iris is like now. I *do* know, though, that Father's worried that Iris is a little too friendly with some of the male customers. But she was always very socially minded,' Rose went on, 'much more so than Violet and me. And Father and Mother were always anxious about her, so that's nothing new.'

They walked along in a companionable silence for a few minutes.

'You didn't use the word "flighty" to describe Iris, but I think that's what you meant. Was that the similarity with me?' Kathleen asked. 'I'm not annoyed if it was—I'm just curious.'

'Maybe there was a bit of that in it,' Rose said with a giggle. 'Both of you are sociable, and that's a good thing. But I think you might have become a little more serious-minded, and Iris has, too. War ends up changing everyone.'

They reached the top of Allcroft Road and turned the corner.

'What about you, Rose?' Kathleen asked, as they started walking down the road. 'Has the war changed your mind about what you want from life? Now that you're back again in what was your home, d'you still want the life you'd have on a farm in Jersey, or would you rather stay here?'

Rose stopped and looked at Kathleen. 'I can't wait to get back to Jersey and Tom,' she said tremulously. 'I miss him so much. We waited so long to be free, and now that we are, we stuck in England. It's so unfair. The war's not altered a thing about the way I feel. Tom and Jersey are home to me, and you, William and Annie will always be part of that home.'

Her voice broke.

'I'm so glad you feel like that, Rose,' Kathleen said quietly. 'I would've hated to lose my sister. And it means I haven't ruined anything for you.'

'You definitely haven't,' she said, wiping her eyes with the back of her hand as they set off again. 'And what about you? You always intended to stay on the farm until you married. Has being deported changed your plans? Or seeing the sort of life you could have here in London? I'm sure you could stay with my family if you wanted.'

Kathleen considered for a moment. 'I haven't really thought that far ahead. I just wanted to be free. I wasn't looking forward to going back to Jersey, to be honest, and to seeing all those people who thought they had the right to judge me. But it's now about two months since Jersey was liberated so people will be getting on with their lives. And with Marjorie and the others being less nasty towards the end of our time in Wurzach, I'm not as concerned about going back as I was.'

'As for men, I expect there'll be some new men on the

island now, and you might very soon meet someone you like.'

Kathleen went red. 'Perhaps. But actually, I've rather missed Josh. Mother mentioned in her last letter that Josh has stopped by the farm on several occasions to have a meal with them, and she said he always asks about me. Maybe he's missed me, too.'

Rose beamed at her. 'That would be perfect. He's really nice.' She hesitated. 'And I expect you're looking forward to seeing Emily, too.'

Kathleen shrugged. 'I suppose I am. But not as much as you might think. After all, I don't need a friend who's so close to me that she's like a sister, as I've got a sister now.' She looked into Rose's face. 'No blood sister could have been a better friend to me than you've been, Rose. I'm so pleased Tom met you, and that you're going to be staying in Jersey.'

'That makes two of us.' They smiled at each other, then started to head slowly down the hill.

As they neared the house, Rose saw a figure sitting on one of the steps leading up to the front door. Her steps faltered. She caught Kathleen's arm.

'It's not, is it? It can't be,' she whispered. Her vision blurred. 'It can't be.'

The figure stood up and faced her.

Kathleen stopped walking, and gently freed her arm from Rose's hand.

Rose took a few more steps towards the figure, and stopped again.

'It *is*. It's Tom,' she breathed, her voice filled with wonder. 'It's my Tom.'

He started to run up the road towards her.

'Tom!' she screamed. Dropping her bag, she ran to him and flung herself into his arms.

'Oh, Tom,' she cried, burying her face in his jacket as he wrapped his arms around her. 'I've missed you so much.'

'And I've missed you, too, Rose, every single minute of every single day.'

'I can't believe you're actually here,' she cried, tears running down her cheeks as she held him close. 'It's such a surprise, such a wonderful surprise. I didn't think you could come over here. They won't give us travel permits till all restrictions are lifted.'

'It's easier for us to get one. I just had to see you,' Tom said. 'Every morning since you've been free, I've knocked on the door of the States' Building. I think they finally gave in just to get rid of me.'

She pulled back, and stared at him, shaking her head in wonder. 'I can't believe it's you.' She put up her hand and felt his face. 'Oh, Tom,' she said, her words a long, heartfelt sigh. 'I can't describe what it felt like, not being with you.'

'You don't need to. I felt it, too,' he said, his voice breaking. 'You're the other half of me, Rose, and I never want to feel so incomplete again. And as Dad's going to cover me on the farm till I can bring you back, I'll never have to.'

'So many words,' she said, a note of amusement lilting her voice. 'But are you ever going to stop talking and let actions take over from words. Just for a moment.' She lightly touched his lips.

He grinned at her. 'How's this for starters?' He cupped her face in his hands. 'But be warned! I'm out of practice, so I'm going to have to try this more than once.'

In an explosion of absolute joy, their lips met, husband and wife once more.

IF YOU ENJOYED 'THE LOOSE THREAD' …

… it would be very kind if you could take a few minutes to leave a review of the book.

Reviews give welcome feedback to the author, and they help to make the novel visible to other readers.

In addition, reviews help authors promote their books as a number of promotional platforms now require a minimum number of reviews.

Your words, therefore, really do matter.

Thank you!

LIZ'S NEWSLETTER

You might like to sign up for Liz's newsletter. Liz sends out a monthly newsletter with updates on her writing life, where she's been travelling, and an interesting fact she's learned. Subscribers also hear of promotions and offers.

Liz would never pass on your email address to anyone else, and if you write to Liz, which you can do through her website, you will always get a reply.

As a thank you for signing up for Liz's newsletter, you'll receive a free novel.

To sign up and get a free book, go to Liz's website:

www.lizharrisauthor.com

INTRODUCING 'THE SILKEN KNOT'

If you enjoyed reading *The Loose Thread* – and I hope you did – you might enjoy *The Silken Knot*, the next in the series.

Although the novels are part of a series titled Three Sisters, each novel is complete in itself, and tells the story of a different Hammond sister. *The Silken Knot* is Iris's story. It will be followed in 2025 by Violet's story.

In the next few pages, you can read the first chapter of *The Silken Knot,* which will be published later in 2024

THE SILKEN KNOT: CHAPTER ONE

April 1947

Jersey

Iris Hammond sat down on the wooden bench outside the farmhouse, and stared at the view in front of her.

Beyond the curve of yellow sand in the distance below her lay St Aubin's Bay, a navy blue expanse of water splintered with gold by the late afternoon sun. High above the wide sweep of the sand and the sea, slender white fragments of fragile cloud drifted slowly across a clear blue sky.

This was almost certainly one of the last times she'd see that scene, she thought flatly.

Hearing the sound of movement behind her, she turned and saw her sister coming out of the cottage next to the farmhouse, carefully holding two glasses of cider.

'Here,' Rose said, handing a glass to Iris, and sitting down next to her. 'Now that Freddie's gone to sleep, and Grace, too, I decided that we deserved a few minutes to ourselves. I thought we could start with a toast.' She indicated her cider. 'After all, you're getting married tomorrow.'

'Don't remind me!' Tears brimmed in Iris's eyes. 'I'm marrying the wrong person.' The tears rolled down her cheeks. 'If only I was marrying my George! If I was, I'd feel happy and excited like a bride is meant to be, not all miserable and depressed.'

Rose leaned across and squeezed Iris's hand with her free hand. 'I know you wouldn't have chosen this, Iris, but what choice did you realistically have? Marrying George would have been somewhat difficult—he's married already.'

Iris gave a loud sob.

Rose straightened up. 'From now on, you must think about what's ahead of you, not what's behind you,' she said firmly. Then she gave Iris a bright smile, and raised her glass. 'I hope you'll be really happy, dear Iris,' she said, and she took a drink of her cider.

Tears continued to trickle down Iris's cheeks as she sat there, her glass untouched.

Rose gave an audible sigh of exasperation. 'Try to be happy, won't you?' she said. 'I don't know Pierre well, but the few times I met him I thought he seemed really pleasant. And Tom said he's loyal, honest and reliable.'

Iris pulled a face. 'Have you any idea how dull that makes him sound?'

'Perhaps a little dullness is no bad thing,' Rose retorted. 'And most people would think his qualities are ones to relish, not disparage.'

'Then I'm not most people. I'm twenty-four, and about to be buried alive in some small medieval town,' Iris cried, wiping her eyes with her hand. 'I'll have a husband who'd feel more at home in the Middle Ages than he does in the world today. There's nothing about that to relish.'

'You're assuming he's old-fashioned, but you don't know if that's true. You've not yet met him,' Rose said gently. 'What you *do* know is that he's prepared to take on someone who's never been married, but has a child. That alone speaks well of him. And given that Grace's real father has long gone, you should be grateful to Pierre for what he's doing, and look for the good in him, rather than hunt for things to criticise.'

'It's easy for you to say that,' Iris sobbed. 'I loved my George.'

'But he was never *your* George, was he?' Rose said bluntly. 'He was married to someone else. He was *her* George. Focus on that.'

Iris stared at her accusingly. 'I suppose you think I deserve to be punished for being stupid enough to believe what George told me, and you think marrying Pierre will be a just punishment.'

'Of course I don't!' Rose exclaimed. 'No one blames you for believing George. It's easy to deceive someone if they want to be deceived, which you did. We know you were genuinely fond of him. If Tom's parents thought badly of you for trusting George and throwing caution to the winds, or if we did, we wouldn't have said you could stay here. Father could've found a place for you in a home for unmarried mothers in Kentish Town.'

'If you don't blame me, why do I have to marry someone I don't know, who doesn't sound at all seem the sort of person I'd choose to be with?'

'We want you to enjoy your life, and we think that with Pierre, you'd have a chance of doing so. And it's the best thing for Grace. She'll have a name, and be brought up by two parents.'

'How d'you know we'll get on? We don't know each other. And thinking of it, what kind of man would marry someone he's never met? He must be so awful-looking that he can't get a wife the normal way.'

'I know it's not usual to marry someone you haven't met till the wedding, but it's not unknown. As for why he's marrying you, I suspect that Tom will try to find that out this evening. You're not the only one who's curious. It's just a shame you couldn't meet each other first. But Tom's been so busy on the farm since the Occupation, and I've had my hands full with little Freddie, so we've not been able to take you to France. And Pierre's been tied up teaching his cousin how to run the warehouse before he hands it over to him, so he's not been able to get here.'

'I shall be spending all day tending to a strange man's needs and those of his twelve year-old daughter. And I bet she'll resent me and be extra difficult. That's not exactly a state of bliss.'

'And nor is being an unmarried mother,' Rose said sharply. 'Such women are frowned upon and bring shame to their family. If you returned to London, Father would insist on you calling yourself by a married name to save face. I'm sure he'd give you a home and a job, but would such a life make you happy? I don't think so.'

'Why can't I just stay here? I could help Annie in her shop?' Iris pleaded. 'I know all about haberdashery.'

'Because it's time you left,' Rose said firmly. 'No sooner had Kathleen got married, and moved out, you moved in. And a few months after that, little Grace was born. You know how demanding new babies are. Now that both Tom and Kathleen have left, William and Annie need to adjust to being on their own. They've not been able to do that yet because of you and Grace.'

Iris opened her mouth to speak.

'And before you ask, you can't move in with Tom and me. There're already three of us in the cottage, and hopefully there'll be a fourth before too long. There just isn't room. And anyway, after the nightmare of the past few years, Tom and I need time on our own.'

'So that's it, then? What I want doesn't matter.'

'I'm not sure you know what you want! If you were being honest with yourself, you'd realise you'd never be happy living here. You'd have to work as you'd have to support yourself and Grace, but you hate farm work.'

Iris started to protest.

Rose put up her hand to stop her. 'Don't deny it. You do as few chores as possible. Our main crop is potatoes, but when you were asked to help with harvesting them, you looked aghast. If you pulled as many as two, I'd be amazed. Whenever there's farm work to be done, you always manage to be visiting the Le Feus under the guise of improving your French.'

'That's because you said Pierre's English is so poor that he and Tom always speak in French,' Iris said, colouring. 'And Tom said Pierre's family don't speak English at all. I have to be able to talk to Pierre, don't I? I asked the Le Feus for help because Tom's always so busy.'

'Some people could have fitted in a few more chores, too. I'm afraid you're another mouth to feed, but one that isn't earning its keep. And before too long, Grace will make it two extra mouths. And it's not fair on me, either. I've been doing some of your work as well as mine. At the same time, I've been looking after little Freddie. It's a bit hard on Tom, too. I always seem to be exhausted these days.'

Iris slumped back in her seat. 'I'm sorry, Rose. You make me feel really bad. I should've done more to help, I admit.

But after Grace was born, and not knowing what was going to happen to me, I suppose I've been thinking only of myself. I'll try harder in the future, I promise.'

'Even if you did, it wouldn't make you enjoy farm work. I think we both know that.'

Iris thought for a moment or two. 'No, it wouldn't. You're right,' she said at last. 'But there *is* an alternative. I should be able to make a living as a dressmaker and doing repairs and alterations. I wouldn't make a fortune, but it'd be enough for Grace and me. I could rent a small house not too far from here.'

'Staying in Jersey is out of the question,' Rose said with finality. 'On a small island like this, you'd struggle to find anyone who'd rent you a house. You'd be seen as a threat to the community.'

Iris glared at her. 'And what's that supposed to mean?'

'That the wives will see a pretty woman, whose child is evidence that her morals are lax. They'd worry that you'd go after their husbands. After all, it's other people's husbands you're most likely to attract. The marriage bureau told you that men looking to get married don't want a woman who's had a child out of wedlock, a child for whom they'd have to provide.'

'So that's it, is it? I'm to be married off to a stranger because none of you want me here.'

'I'm sorry, but you've made your bed, Iris, and you're going to have to lie in it. And as it'll be Pierre who lies in it with you, not George,' she added drily, 'my advice is that you have a smile on your face when you meet Pierre. If you don't, Pierre might decide you're not worth facing the wrath of his Catholic family for bringing a woman with a baby by someone else into a house where there's an impressionable girl, and he might walk away. It's not too late for him to do so. And where would that leave you?'

She held up her glass. 'Let's try again, shall we? To your happiness with Pierre.' Glancing surreptitiously at Iris, she took a sip of her cider.

Iris hesitated, and then, with a slight shrug, raised her glass to her lips.

Pierre put his glass of ale down on the table, and sat back in the seat opposite Tom. He glanced around at the mahogany walls and clusters of tables, and at the glasses and bottles stacked up behind the bar, then looked back at Tom.

'I'm glad you recommended the Aurora,' he said. 'My room's very comfortable, and the price moderate. I know you kindly suggested I stay with you and Rose, but I didn't want to risk seeing Iris before we meet at the Rectory tomorrow.'

'And it's nothing to do with the fact that you heard little Freddie screaming in the background when I phoned you, and I mentioned he was teething, was it?' Tom asked with a grin.

Pierre laughed. 'Maybe a little. But it's an unusual enough situation as it is, so I wanted to observe custom as far as possible.'

Tom nodded. 'That makes sense. And as we've just seen, the food here is excellent so you've not exactly suffered for your decision.'

'True,' Pierre said. He looked around him again. 'I'm quite surprised you suggested coming here. I'd have met you somewhere else, if you'd preferred. I know that during the Occupation, the Germans used to gather here and in the Caesarea. Both places must hold unpleasant memories.'

'Not really,' Tom said. 'This is one of the oldest pubs in

Jersey, and I thought you might like it. I don't come here very often, but that's not because they were German haunts, but because the farming day's a long one—abnormally so at the moment—and I'd rather spend what's left of the evening at home with Rose and Freddie. These pubs are a monument to survival. After coping for five years with the most difficult of conditions imaginable, Jersey people are now free. I'll never tire of being reminded of that.'

'That's understandable,' Pierre said, and he took a sip of his ale.

Tom leaned slightly forward. 'Tell me if I'm out of line, Pierre, but I can't help wondering about you and Iris. To be honest, I was astounded when out of the blue, you volunteered to marry her. I'd only phoned to give you Mother's haberdashery order!'

Pierre laughed. 'I must say, I surprised myself. I don't usually do anything that impulsive. But you had a problem. So did I. And when you told me about Iris, and about her needing to find somewhere to live, I saw that marrying her would solve both of our problems.'

Tom sat back. 'I know you said you don't judge Iris for what she's done, but you *do* know about her past. It seems an extreme way to solve a problem. Wasn't there any other?'

'Not that I could see. It's because I'm moving. And dealing with the move is why I've been unable to get to Jersey.'

Tom shook his head. 'You've lost me.'

'When I was in Granville, my cousin Laurent's wife used to look after our house. She did so even before Monique was killed. Now that Laurent's taking over the warehouse and I'm moving to Dinan, I'll no longer have his wife's help.'

'I was more than surprised when you told me you were

leaving Granville. You and your family have been there for years.'

'I'm going because of Danielle. Ever since Monique was killed, she's wanted to be close to Monique's family. I thought she'd go off the idea, but even though it's been three years, she hasn't. She seems very fond of Monique's parents and brother, Léon. And they want us there, too. I'm sure it's partly that they want me to help with the administration of their shop, but they're genuinely fond of Danielle.'

'And how do you feel about moving?'

He shrugged. 'It's no bad thing to have a change from running the warehouse, which I've done for a long time now. And I want Danielle to be happy. If she is, I'll be fine. But I need someone to keep house for me, and to be there in the evenings if I want to go out. Iris needed a home, so marrying her seemed an answer.'

'Couldn't you have employed a housekeeper who lived in?'

Pierre grinned. 'Only if she was very old and very ugly, and I don't think either Danielle or I would've liked that. In Dinan's Catholic community, if I wanted to have a young woman living in my house, I'd have to be married to her. But also, with Danielle now twelve, I really do need someone there who'd be able to help her with personal things. If the woman was a harridan, Danielle wouldn't go near her.'

'Don't get me wrong,' Tom said, 'I'm delighted you're marrying Iris, but surely there must've been other women who'd fitted the bill, who weren't burdened in the way that Iris is. You're a good-looking man, after all. If there wasn't someone in Granville, what about in Dinan?'

'If I'd moved into Dinan without a wife, Monique's parents would have devoured me. The last thing I wanted was to have to depend on them for help. If I became beholden, I'd never have any life of my own.'

'I can see that,' Tom said slowly. 'It wouldn't be the best position to be in.'

'And also there's Elodie,' Pierre said with a sudden grin.

Tom laughed. 'All right. Who's Elodie?'

'She must be about the same age as Iris. She lives in Lanvallay, just across the river from the port of Dinan, which is where my house is, and where I've bought a small shop. It's the area where Monique's parents live. Elodie's been helping in the Dinan shop for a few years now. It's a bit embarrassing,' he added, colouring slightly, 'but she's always seemed to hero-worship me. Monique used to tease me about it whenever we visited her family. But I'm worried that if I didn't have a wife, it might give Elodie ideas.'

'And I take it you don't see her as wife material?' Tom asked.

'Good gracious, no! Never! I'll always think of her as a child, even though she isn't one any longer. But you don't get over your first impression of someone. So, as you can see, I'll be doing myself a favour by marrying Iris, as well as helping Iris by giving her a home and a name.'

'Except,' Pierre added with a wry smile, 'as I'm sure you know, in France a wife doesn't usually change her name when she marries. She keeps her birth name, and simply acquires the use of her husband's name. Monique remained Monique Pascal.'

Tom smiled. 'I imagine Iris will chose to be called Madame Rousseau.' He hesitated. 'I hope for both your sakes that marrying Iris will become more than just a matter of convenience. She's a pretty woman, and although she can be a little irritating, I'm sure she's got a good heart. She could make you an excellent wife.'

'And I'm sure she will,' Pierre said. He picked up his glass and held it aloft. 'To Iris and our life together,' he said.

'I'll happily drink to that,' Tom said, and he did.

London

The atmosphere in the small sitting room in the house in Allcroft Road, Kentish Town, was bleak.

John Hammond was sitting in one of the two armchairs that flanked the cast-iron fireplace, his expression downcast. The fire in the grate within remained unlit. His glass of sherry on the occasional table next to him was untouched.

In the matching floral armchair on the other side of the fireplace, Mabel Hammond clutched her sherry glass with one hand and wiped the tears from her cheeks with the other.

Curled up on the upholstered sofa facing the fireplace, Violet looked from one parent to the other, bemused.

'Surely, you're pleased that Iris is marrying tomorrow, aren't you?' she asked. 'There couldn't be a better outcome, could there? Pierre's been Tom's supplier for years, so they know each other quite well. From what Rose said, he's very pleasant.'

Mabel looked at Violet with watering eyes. 'That may be so, love, but he and Iris will be living in France. First, Rose married Tom and went to live in Jersey with Tom's family. And now Iris is going to be even further away. All we know about this Pierre is what Tom and Rose have said. We can't judge for ourselves. Our daughter's marrying a man we've never met.'

Her voice caught, and she put her handkerchief to her eyes again.

'He's overlooking the fact that Iris had a baby by

someone else, and is marrying her, isn't he? Surely that speaks well of him?' Violet said in irritation.

'We'll obviously meet him at some point, Mother,' she added, her voice softening. 'People are now able to go to Jersey again so we can visit Tom and Rose whenever we want, and we could go from there to France. We could've gone to Jersey for the wedding and met Pierre ourselves, but you said no.'

Mabel gave a sob. 'It wouldn't have felt like a proper wedding, would it? Iris said we wouldn't be allowed into the Rectory for the service.'

'But we could've been with them for the meal afterwards,' Violet said with a trace of weariness. 'I'm sure Annie and William will give them a lovely send-off. You've known Tom's parents since long before the three of us were born, and you've always said how kind they are. They like Pierre and so does Tom, which are all points in Pierre's favour.'

'It's a bad time to leave the shops, 'John said gruffly. 'We'll go next summer. Going this year would have been the wrong time for Annie and William, too. Iris has been there for several months, and once she's gone, the last thing they'll want is anyone else staying there for a while. And Rose and Tom need time without visitors. Rose said that Iris spent almost as much time in their cottage as she did in the farmhouse. And Iris and Pierre need to get to know each other before they have to worry about guests.'

'But what kind of wedding is it, taking place in a small house next to the church, not in the church itself?' Mabel said, and she wiped her eyes again. 'And none of her family allowed to go. It's as if Pierre's ashamed of Iris, of her having a baby and all.'

'Of course he isn't,' Violet said sharply. 'He's taking her to live near his family, isn't he? They've got to marry in the

Rectory because he's a Catholic and she isn't. That's why they're not allowed any guests, only witnesses. But it's a proper wedding all right. And as Rose and Tom are their witnesses, Iris *will* have some family with her.'

Her father nodded. 'Violet's right, Mabel. This is a good thing for Iris. We both agreed that she couldn't stay here once she started showing—the embarrassment would have been too much for us, a respected family that's traded in Kentish Town for generations. But when we sent Iris to Jersey to stay with Tom and Rose till the baby was born, we weren't thinking any further than that. Now that we are, we can see that as an unmarried mother, poor Iris might not have had much of a future at all. No, it's a blessing that Pierre's a widower, and wants to marry her and will provide for little Grace.'

'I'm not sure that Pierre would consider it a blessing to have lost his wife in the war, and for his daughter to have lost her mother,' Violet said drily.

'You know what I mean, Violet,' John said, waving his hand in impatience.

'You're right, John,' Mabel said, nodding. 'I no longer feel so worried. I can see that Iris has been very lucky. And that Pierre's family are haberdashers, too, just like us, makes it even better. Iris did outstandingly well with her sewing circles during the war, and with luck, she'll be able to put her skills to good use in France. Yes, when you actually think about it, we've got a lot to be thankful for.'

She tucked her handkerchief in the cuff of her cardigan.

'We'll definitely go to Jersey next year,' Violet said firmly. 'I can't wait to see little Freddie. He'll be about two years old by then, and that's long enough to leave it before we see him. And we can go on to France and see Iris. I can't wait to meet Grace, too.'

John nodded. 'That's what we'll do.'

Violet leaned across to her sherry and picked it up. 'Then let's have that toast to Pierre and Iris that we talked about ages ago, before our glasses are covered in dust.' She held up her glass, and waited for her parents to do the same.

'To Iris,' she said, 'and to Pierre, the newest member of our family. May he and Iris be very happy together.'

ACKNOWLEDGEMENTS

Once again, I'm immensely grateful to my brilliant cover designer, Jane Dixon-Smith, for another superb cover, which perfectly captures the tone of *The Loose Thread* and to my excellent editor, Lorna Fergusson.

A huge thank you also to Stella, my Friend in the North, whose eyes are the first to see every completed manuscript, and who invariably gives me the constructive criticism needed at such a stage.

As with all of the years since I was first published, my year has been enhanced by lunches and writing retreats with writer friends. They know who they are. A huge thank you to them all for helping to make the writing of *The Loose Thread* such an enjoyable process.

In writing *The Loose Thread,* I drew upon many resources, not least upon my trip to Jersey to research the novel in situ. The Channel Island Military Museum at St Ouen was a source of much fascinating information, and I also spent a considerable amount of time in the Jersey Museum & Art Gallery in St Helier, and in the Jersey War Tunnels, which was a step back in time.

I drew also upon many books for the information I needed I order to bring alive that period in time. There are too many to name them all, but I should like to highlight *When the Germans Came*, by Duncan Barrett, *The German Occupation of the Channel Islands*, by Charles Cruickshank, *The Model Occupation*, by Madeleine Bunting, *A Doctor's*

Occupation, by Dr. John Lewis, *Jersey Occupation Diary*, by Nan Le Ruez, *Voices from the Occupation*, by Penny Byrne & Liz Wackett, *Growing Up Fast*, by Bob Le Sueur, MBE, *A Cake for the Gestapo*, by Jacqueline King, and *Wartime Britain 1939-1945*, by Juliet Gardiner.

If there are any mistakes, the fault will be mine alone. I should like to stress, also, that all the characters are fictional. If I have chanced upon the name of someone who lived in that location at that time, it was purely accidental.

Finally, once again I'm tremendously grateful to my husband, Richard, for the support he invariably gives me, and for letting me close my study door behind me during the day and live in my fictional world uninterrupted.

ABOUT THE AUTHOR

Born in London, Liz Harris graduated from university with a Law degree, and then moved to California, where she led a varied life, from waitressing on Sunset Strip to working as secretary to the CEO of a large Japanese trading company.

Six years later, she returned to London and completed a degree in English, after which she taught secondary school pupils, first in Berkshire, and then in Cheshire.

In addition to the eighteen novels she's had published, she's had several short stories in anthologies and magazines.

Liz now lives in Windsor, Berkshire. An active member of the Romantic Novelists' Association and the Historical Novel Society, her interests are travel, the theatre, reading and cryptic crosswords. To find out more about Liz, visit her website at:

www.lizharrisauthor.com

ALSO BY LIZ HARRIS

Historical novels

The Colonials

Darjeeling Inheritance

Cochin Fall

Hanoi Spring

Simla Mist

The Linford Series

The Dark Horizon

The Flame Within

The Lengthening Shadow

Distant Places

The Road Back

In a Far Place

The Heart of the West

A Bargain Struck

Golden Tiger (formerly The Lost Girl)

A Western Heart

Three Sisters

The Loose Thread

The Silken Knot (to be published September 2024)

Printed in Great Britain
by Amazon

41582496R00205